Heard It On

The Grapevine

by

Richard Hernaman Allen

ISBN: 978-1-326-59809-9

PublishNation
www.publishnation.co.uk

Publications by Richard Hernaman Allen

1. Customs & Excise stories

(Already published)

The Waterguard

A well-respected man

The Summer of Love

Nothing was delivered

Something in the air

Bankers' Draught

Along the Watchtower

Heard it on the Grapevine

(Completed, awaiting publication)

Brussels Sprouts

Our Friends in the South

Copper Kettle

Magic Clarinet

On a Carousel

Old Ghosts

Medicine Man

Ghosts in the Machine

Market Forces

2. Other "Nick & Rosemary" stories

Murder at the Baltic Coast Hotel (already published)

Death on the Volga

The Body in the Marine Buildings

Empty Lands

Sunrise, Sunset

3. Saga novels

Through Fire (already published)

By Water (in publication)

Out of Sight

4. Other novels

Barton Stacey/Stacey Barton – Missing

Sid Mouse & the Electric Cats of Death

The Disappearing Crows of Jurmala

More details on www.richardhernamanallen.com

INTRODUCTION

Though I enjoy writing about Nick and Rosemary Storey, I realise that there is a limit to what I can cover, to be consistent with what I have already written about them and also to provide a story with sufficient meat on the bones. Though it may require amendments to a few words in a couple of places, I believe I can go back to a time when Nick and Rosemary were on secondment in Brussels, where they might reasonably get themselves involved in uncovering CAP fraud along with other commercial fraud involving goods imported into the EEC, as it was still called then. I might also take them into southern and central Europe for a change. As with most of these stories, I'll set off and see how I get on.....

Quite rapidly I got on to wine – both adulterated and mislabelled – as a fertile area for fraud. I've brought forward the scandal involving the adulteration of certain Austrian wines with diethylene glycol by a few years and I've also suggested wine frauds in other countries. While I haven't used any wine name that I've ever heard of, it's possible readers might believe that these are covers for wines which are commonly known. I have certainly not intended to mention any wine currently or previously sold anywhere and where it's possible to deduce that I'm referring to specific wines or wine regions, I should make absolutely plain that I am not suggesting in any way that those wines or regions have been involved in the practices covered in this book. Though "the authorities" in some countries don't come out of this story in a particularly good light, I also wish to make it plain that I do not suggest in any way that they are or have behaved in the ways depicted herein. Just as "management" or the UK Civil Service elite have been singled out as fall guys in several of my books, I make the same statement here as I have elsewhere. This is a story, set in a historical context and a

1

particular environment. The details are fiction – including names of companies, individuals, etc. I have used a number of locations I know, especially in the chapter set in Rome, and undoubtedly I've played around a bit with history there. But I've wanted to take an opportunity to record places which will live long in my memory – notably for the people I've met there.

And as it reminds me of happy times on holidays in Italy, in particular, I'd like to dedicate this book to my late parents-in-law, Dave and Laurie, who gave us such love, help and enjoyment. And as usual I'd like to thank Vanessa, Jo and Kat for their encouragement and love - and to Josh for allowing me to use my computer chair from time to time.

Richard Hernaman Allen
March 2014

WINE WHICH
COULDN'T FREEZE

In the late spring of 1975, Rosemary and I were into our second year on secondment as "national experts" in the Service Européenne contre la Fraude Fiscale, known as SEFF. In the light of what we'd learnt in the Soviet heroin smuggling case, I was helping to get a directive agreed by the EEC member states that would improve the sharing of information and better co-ordination between them. Rosemary was working with Interpol, among others, to improve the ability of the police and fiscal authorities to trace money in criminals' bank accounts. Despite what the British press used to say about idle EEC bureaucrats, we were extremely busy – as were Emily and Sarah in the local international school, near the Park du Cinquantenaire, which had recently expected them to do certain classes each day speaking entirely in French.

However, it was no surprise to be summoned to the office of Knud Henriksen, our boss, first thing on a Monday morning.

"I realise you are both very busy," he began, in his matter-of-fact way. "But there's something I need you to do for me. Danish Customs were on to me when I was in København over the weekend about adulterated wine from Austria. The Customs chemical analysis unit in Denmark have recently come across several instances of wine adulterated with diethylene glycol, a chemical which you and I might regard as being closely related to anti-freeze."

"Wouldn't that make it poisonous?" I asked.

"Apparently not…and they only use infinitessimal quantities of the stuff. But it is illegal, of course. And they've asked SEFF to look into it."

"Why can't Danish Customs handle it themselves?"

"They believe it's an EEC-wide problem and if the Austrians are doing it, it's almost certain that others are...the Yugoslavs...and the Danish view predictably is that if anyone is fiddling anything, the Italians are bound to be involved. Not that they have any evidence, of course."

"But as you've reminded us from time to time, SEFF is supposed to be advisory, not undertaking our own operations."

"And as you've suggested on several occasions, getting our hands dirty from time to time gives us a better idea of what we need to be doing...and if we do it well, it does a lot for our credibility......Furthermore, to be honest, if we're going to do operations of this kind, I'd rather we did them while the two of you are still here. The Soviet stuff and that bloody Trebzow showed what you were capable of. What we've got now are decent people, but they're bureaucrats...and exactly what Capitano Ruggieri is capable of, I've no idea, as he's done virtually nothing ever since he first came here. I'm well aware that we've only got about another year of you two, so I'd like to get the most out of it."

"But if you've got hold of some bottles of wine which has been adulterated in this way, can't the Danish Customs just follow up through the wine merchants and the shippers back to the exporters and producers in Austria?" asked Rosemary. "What extra are we in SEFF supposed to be providing?"

"Danish Customs believe that the producers involved in this practice are both inside and outside the EEC and that it'd be better if the EEC took a grip on the whole problem. If the Danes and other member states picked on Austrian producers and the Austrian Government protested that the Italians, for instance, were doing exactly the same thing but were being protected because they were in the EEC, it'd be politically very awkward for the EEC, to say the least. So we look at the Danish information and then try to see how far we can follow it up, both inside and outside the EEC."

"And that's what we're going to be doing on top of our day jobs?" I asked.

"No. I'm proposing that most of your day jobs, as you put it, should be passed over to your colleagues. Hans-Georg Meyer can certainly handle most of what you do…and his French is a lot better than yours, so he can butter up the French better than you can. And though Ruggieri won't do anything he doesn't want to do, Marc Dierich is a decent fellow and will certainly do whatever is needed on Rosemary's side….Though I accept that you'll probably need to keep up your Interpol stuff yourself….In any case, I'm expecting this to be a three month job or something like that. What I want is to have an idea of the scale of adulteration of wine that's going both outside and within the EEC. If there are culprits we – or the relevant national authorities – can go after, so much the better. But I don't think I want a full-scale criminal investigation – more an examination of the scale of the problem and an identification of who seem to be the main people involved. Now does that seem reasonable?"

"As you know, we enjoy doing this sort of thing more than drafting directives and encouraging Member States to go along with them…..But Rosemary's work on tracing hidden assets depends a lot on what she's learnt…." I began.

"But, obviously, I'd need to leave it in a form that our successors could use without starting from scratch," added Rosemary. "It's not so much that which is bothering me. Is this going to involve us in much travel to other countries?"

"I guess you'd need to go to København for a day or so. But you could probably manage it in a day. Then you'd need to go to Vienna, I suspect. Beyond that – who knows?"

"It's our children I'm worried about. Though it was kind of you and your wife to look after Emily and Sarah when we were in Rotterdam, they get very worried when we're both away. They've convinced themselves that whenever that happens, we're going to be threatened by gunmen or whatever….And, of course, when we took them with us to Riga, there was some shooting. Though

5

no-one was killed, it looked quite serious and they were both scared. Naturally, that reinforced their view that every time we go to a different place in the course of some sort of investigation, we're going to get shot. So if we're going to do this, we'll need some arrangements that won't mean they're apart from us for several days while we're hundreds of miles away."

"I'm sure we can arrange something. But presumably if you got there and back in a day to meet some Danish Customs people, that wouldn't upset them too much?"

"I doubt that'd need both of us anyway. Nick could do that on his own. It's mainly a Customs matter after all."

So with nothing resolved about how Emily and Sarah might be looked after if both Rosemary and I had to be away together, I took an early flight from Zaventem to Kastrup the following Monday. I expected to get the train into the centre of Copenhagen, but I was met as I went through Customs by a man in uniform, who led me through the back of the Customs controls and into a small suite of offices. One was evidently a small meeting room and in it were a man and a woman. The man was my height, slim, with greying hair and a serious face. The woman was almost as tall, with dark, shoulder-length hair, quite a broad face, and metal-rimmed glasses.

"Good morning, Mr Storey. I am Erling Jensen and this my colleague, Karin Sorensen. I am the Director of Customs Compliance and Mrs Sorensen is Head of our EEC liaison team. Knud Henriksen has explained your background on the phone," began Jensen in perfect, virtually accent-free English.

"I understand you wish to brief me on your seizures of Austrian wine containing diethylene glycol?" I said.

Just as I said that strong, rich coffee and small cakes arrived.

"Yes. We picked them up at Rødbyhavn off the Puttgarden ferry. We've been getting small quantities of heroin coming in from the Balkans by way of Vienna, so the local staff decided to pull this lorry over. There was something about the driver's manner that made the officers suspicious. But they couldn't find

6

any drugs, so they decided that there must be something about the cargo. It consisted of Hungarian, Yugoslav and Austrian wines – eight different wines in all. They took a bottle of each and sent them off for analysis at our Customs laboratory in Frederikssund. We were expecting that heroin might be found dissolved in one or more of the bottles of wine perhaps. But all we got back was that one of the Austrian wines – 'Edel Veltliner' – contained significant quantities of diethylene glycol, which is known to sweeten dry or acidic wines. We traced the consignment through the importer and discovered most of it was in a warehouse in Valby, with a couple of crates already on their way to a local supermarket. We managed to pick it all up before any was sold. Not that it's harmful unless you were to drink the wine in impossibly large quantities – over twenty bottles a day, I believe. Naturally we also seized all the Austrian wines in the Valby warehouse, but only this 'Edel Veltliner' had been adulterated. We're presently checking all stocks of Austrian wines at importation and in warehouses to see how widespread a problem this is – or whether it was just an isolated occurrence. But so far we've found two more wines - 'Franz Josef selekt' and 'Kaiserin der Heurigen' similarly adulterated…But there may well be others. I reckon we're only about half way through so far."

"So what quantity of wine are you talking about?" I asked.

"Getting on for ten thousand litres. Austrian wine has a good reputation here in Denmark. And we like our white wine sweeter than you do in Brussels."

"Is there any pattern to the producers or the shippers?"

"We've got a dossier for you, including all that I've told you plus photocopies of the entries and other documentation…including the various wine standards declarations. The 'Edel Veltliner' has all come through a single shipper and a single producer, as far as we can tell. But the other wines have no clear pattern discernible as yet. They all seem to come from the Weinviertel region, the 'Edel Veltliner' producer being registered in the city of Moedling. The documents in the dossier contain all the details."

"You've suggested that SEFF could look at this because you believe similar wines from Yugoslavia and possibly Hungary may be similarly adulterated? And also Italian wines? Is there any evidence for that?"

"Mainly because the Austrian wines which have been adulterated in this way are ones where in a bad summer, the wine turns out to be too thin and acidic. The diethylene glycol adds both sweetness and body to the wine. Yugoslav and Hungarian wines suffer from the same problem from time to time….as, indeed, do our West German neighbours. But we tend to the view that the Germans regulate such matters with considerable thoroughness. On the other hand, northern Italian white wines are likely to face some years when the wine is thin and acidic – and we have little confidence that the Italian authorities carry out anything like the level of checks which the Germans do. In all cases, the wines produced are for mass consumption….so the wine is cheap and produced in large quantities. A year when the wine cannot be sold would be disastrous. So though we have no direct evidence, we believe that the commercial pressures that have made the Austrians adulterate their wine in this way are the same for the Yugoslavs, Italians and probably the Hungarians too."

"I see. Why are you less sure about the Hungarians?"

"Mainly because though we in Denmark import a fair quantity of Hungarian wines, we don't know how far that extends to the rest of the EEC. So we aren't certain whether their production of the white wines we drink here is on what you might term an industrial scale or not."

"Do you know how they got this adulterated stuff past their standards authorities?"

"Other than the fact that these wines had the appropriate certificates, not really. We surmise that their wine standards authorities were given a different, unadulterated wine to sample.

But, of course, they should be thorough enough to prevent that sort of thing happening. I believe that may be something which SEFF may wish to consider."

"You haven't mentioned the French. They produce white wine in regions that are considerably further north than Austria and must presumably face the same problems."

"It's possible. We don't tend to get cheap French wine here in Denmark. If it's French, it's usually expensive appellation contrôlée wine. But I guess some of the mass market Loire region whites and rosés would face the same problems from time to time."

"Maybe the French wine standards authorities are more diligent. The French pride themselves so much on the quality of their wine that they may be really thorough with their checking....But I suppose I should add them to the list, as the nature of your suspicions about the Italians applies equally to them."

That seemed to be pretty well that. It wasn't entirely clear to me why they couldn't have sent the dossier to SEFF and I could have rung them after I'd read through it. But the lunch was pleasant enough, if a little fishier than I really enjoyed. At this point, I began to realise why a face-to-face meeting had been engineered. Karin Sorensen spent much of the time discreetly pumping me about what was going on in relation to customs and fiscal matters in SEFF and the Commission. Had I been a fiscal attaché from UKREP, I might have been able to be more helpful, but I'd been concentrating on getting my directive properly drafted and then taken through the arcane procedures of the Commission, a Commission working party, an EEC Council working group, with Coreper and an EEC Council of Ministers still to come. So I feared that I had a deep knowledge of the furrow which I was ploughing, but limited knowledge of what was happening in the next furrow, let alone an adjoining field.

But at least I was home in time to eat dinner with my family – and bring back some small gifts for Emily and Sarah… 'the little mermaid' in the form of chocolate-covered marzipan.

I read through the dossier the following morning. It added little to what I'd already been told, apart from the details of the names of the shippers and the producers. But what next? Rosemary and I often had lunch together in the Council restaurant, which was heavily subsidized and therefore provided food acceptable to French and Belgian bureaucrats while remaining cheap. It also had the advantage of a fair number of nooks and crannies with two-seater tables, which I guessed were generally used for international tête-à-têtes of an amorous nature. Even though we'd been married more than ten years and had Emily and Sarah, Rosemary and I certainly weren't beyond that sort of thing, but it always seemed a little desperate. At any rate, we pre-empted some burgeoning international romance and occupied one of these tables.

"It's a good thing you go running as well as swimming occasionally," observed Rosemary. "Otherwise with all this steak and chips, you'll start putting on weight."

"I'm feeling rather hungry. I had smorgasbord mostly with fish for lunch yesterday, so I really only ate enough to be polite. And there's something about even short plane journeys, so I didn't feel all that hungry yesterday evening. But now I could eat a horse!"

"Which may well be what your steak is." Rosemary smirked. It was a standing joke between us.

"But was it flat or national hunt?"

"Probably a Belgian drayhorse, pulling barrels of all those weird beers round Brussels."

"Oh – and there was me thinking you were having gueuze with your salad!"

"That is one of the most disgusting drinks I've ever tasted. Even that stuff with scotch in it was marginally better!"

"Ah, Adelschott. I think I'm rather German about all of this. I really only like beers that meet the Rheinheitsgebot. No adulterations whatsoever......And talking about adulteration, I wanted to have a word about what you think we should do next."

"The only hard evidence comes from Austria. But if we're going to do what Knud Henriksen wants, we've somehow got to

10

find a way of widening our search in a way that the authorities in other countries regard as legitimate. If I was the Yugoslav or Italian authorities and we went to them with the stuff the Danes gave you, I'd tell us to take a running jump."

"I wonder whether it's worth talking to any of the wine policy people in the Commission…..the ones who deal with the wine market, not the tax people. They might have some ideas not just about adulteration, but how we might go about checking….."

"But you'd need to be careful who you spoke to. You can't really require them to keep your conversation confidential and so many people go blabbing back to their home countries, if there was adulteration of wine going on in Italy, for instance, the people doing it would learn that we were carrying out this work, months before we even knew who the Italian wine producers were…"

"And they might reasonably feel we were treading on their toes…..I suppose the best thing I can do is check and see if there's someone over there who could keep his or her mouth shut."

"Have you thought of talking to someone in UKREP? They might've picked something up….and if we ask them to keep it confidential, there's a fair chance they will."

"The trouble is Martin Finlay's time is almost up. I'm due to meet his replacement, Simon Darby, next week. And Martin is spending all his time chatting up people in the Commission or Council Secretariat to try and get a job here, so he doesn't have to go back to London. He's not likely to be any help in keeping his ear to the ground and Darby has only been here about ten days or so."

"I suppose we could invite Martin round for dinner. Even if he isn't going to do anything before he leaves or gets a new job, he might have something useful stored away in his memory."

So the following morning I got in touch with Martin Finlay to arrange dinner. Within ten minutes I got a phone call back from his secretary. Apparently, in his busy schedule, it would have to be that very evening or not for a month or so. I went along the corridor to the room which Rosemary shared with Marc Dierich and, in theory, Capitano Gaetano Ruggieri. But the Italian was absent on important, if unknown, business more often than not. I explained the haste and we agreed to spend the lengthy EEC lunch hour doing some shopping. Getting away early would be no problem and it was exceedingly unlikely that Finlay would reach us before 8pm. In the event, we visited the Commission shop, the one place where we knew we could get British bacon and sausages. Since Martin spent his days and nights eating canapés or all the varieties of food Brussels could offer, we decided to give him a traditional British fry-up, with eggs, bacon, sausages, baked beans and baked potatoes. I would like to have added black pudding, but that was one thing the Commission shop didn't stock and the only mushrooms on offer were too large and not the sort of thing you'd see in a typical British fry-up. In addition, as we'd be eating at about the time Emily and Sarah were normally preparing to go to bed, we'd let them stay up late, give them a snack after their afternoon's activities and let them enjoy one of their favourite meals before going to bed.

Martin arrived at nearly 8.30. We'd just decided to let Emily and Sarah eat or they'd be in bed so late they'd spend the next morning yawning in front of their quite strict teachers. By the time we were able to chat to Martin, it was close to 10 pm.

"That was a pleasant change, I must say," remarked Martin as he sipped the obligatory post-dinner brandy. "That's one thing I will miss, assuming I manage to stay here."

"We wondered how you were getting on," said Rosemary, as I returned from finishing the girls' bedtime story.

"I think I've just about got an offer of a suitable post in GUD (the Customs Union Directorate). There are just a few details to be ironed out here and in London, but I've got another three years here and by the time it's up I'll either have got myself here on a permanent basis or I'll've decided prospects look rosier back in London.....I take it you're still determined to go back to London? You realise after all that stuff with the Dutch and Germans, your stock is remarkably high. There are plenty of permanent jobs you two could probably walk into if you wanted a word placed in the right ear."

"No thanks," replied Rosemary. "We're enjoying our time here…as are Emily and Sarah. But I wouldn't want to live here permanently. It's too much like living in a bubble."

"I can see what you mean. I suppose you either like that or you don't…..And that reminds me. I came across a former C&E colleague at an international shindig in Paris recently….Mervyn Jordan…works for OECD…..He asked to be remembered to both of you…and asked whether your games of squash were as dangerous as those you used to play in the Houndsditch….Being Mervyn, he wasn't going to explain what any of that meant. I take it you do?"

"That's going back ten years. He and I were involved in a case where a member of staff in C&E was leaking information to someone in the City. They used this particular squash club to do it…..If you bump into him again, please pass on our best wishes."

"But I take it you'd like me to sing a little for my supper? But what's the tune?"

I explained about our latest task and how we needed to get some background in relation to how the wine standards regime operated in different countries and ideally, when we were approaching other countries' authorities, which we could trust and which we couldn't.

"It's not an area I've had much to do with," explained Martin. "The amount of wine produced in the UK is so tiny, when it comes to all the standards stuff, we get ignored…and rightly so, in my opinion. Have you actually ever tasted any English wine? And of course the so-called British wine, made from fermented imported grape must, is an abomination! I take it neither of you are devotees of Wincarnis or Sanatogen?"

"I guess it was the sort of stuff our parents and grandparents kept in a cupboard for use as a tonic…like glucose stout or milk stout for nursing mothers," I replied. "But I can't say I've ever tasted any."

"There are worse….believe it or not. Try drinking black beer! I did once…and reckoned I'd be safer painting a wooden fence with it….But thinking as I go along….You'd do well to steer clear of pretty well all the EEC wine standards people. They may not like each other much, but they'll all stand shoulder to shoulder against the non-wine-producing countries like the UK and Denmark. And there are some – most probably all – who would certainly blab to their producers if we expressed any concern about wines being adulterated…..The best person to speak to is probably Ian Webster in RDA back home. Not only is he responsible for the wine duties, he's also a wine snob….Doubtless why he's been angling for a job out here for the last eighteen months. But he'll have all the contacts with the UK people – either in MAFF or the UK Wine Standards Board. They're all likely to be discreet…and you probably should be letting MAFF know what you're up to anyway. I've no idea who's responsibility it is over there, but Ian will know….And if you don't fancy a trip back to London, Ian will be only too happy to come over here. It'll give him another opportunity to show his face in the right places."

"We weren't planning to go home for a while. Our house is rented out, so we haven't got anywhere to stay. So if Ian is keen to come over, that'd probably be simpler."

"I'm sure he'll appreciate that…..he's a very knowledgeable guy…Just don't mention Lambrusco to him. About eighteen months ago, he drew the short straw and had to represent C&E on a tour the Italians put on for Member States to prove that Lambrusco was as sui generis as champagne. I assume you've drunk some?"

"Both Lambrusco and champagne," replied Rosemary. Martin had a tendency to ignore her, unless she was wearing a short skirt – and then his eyes tended to wander downwards.

"I'm sure you'd agree that about the only thing they have in common is that they are effervescent. Lambrusco is generally sweet, if not sickly….and comes in red and pink varieties, as well as white. Imagine a wine snob having to spend two days drinking exclusively Lambrusco of various shades – morning, noon and night – while the Italians tried to sell this stuff as deserving of a special duty rate. Ian said….after he'd recovered…that he'd happily charge it the same rate as spirits, if it stopped people drinking such awful stuff."

"It's good to be forewarned." Whether Martin was too tired to notice or impervious to Rosemary's gentle sarcasm, I couldn't tell. But shortly afterwards, he announced his departure – admitting he had to complete some briefing for Coreper before he went to bed.

"To be honest," observed Rosemary, after we'd closed the door of our flat and heard him drive away, "I didn't find that white Lambrusco we tried a few weeks ago too awful. But then if you're a wine snob, you probably turn your nose up at Prosecco, which I actually prefer to champagne. It tastes lighter and happier. Champagne always seems heavy and formal by comparison."

"I wouldn't mention that to Ian Webster…"

"Always assuming I do meet him. I'm not sure I'm really needed at this stage."

"I wonder if you had to keep sampling any wine – even the poshest – for a couple of days, whether you wouldn't get fed up with it? Spending a couple of days only drinking Prosecco might well put you off it, even though you liked it to begin with."

"If I spent a couple of days only drinking Prosecco, I'd be completely pie-eyed and ill for the next three days!"

"And with all that gas, you'd probably…."

"I doubt the world is quite ready for that thought yet!"

A WINE SNOB

Ian Webster was a large man. Though he was about my height, he'd make two of me. He wasn't exactly fat – more a man with an extensive bone structure which was well-padded. He had greying, curly hair which he grew quite long, with a centre-parting and had a face resembling an owl, an impression to which his metal-framed round spectacles contributed. He affected a plummy, upper-drawer accent, which I was pretty certain was learnt, rather than natural. He also affected dark green and dark brown suits, often with loud checks, and sported white linen suits and a panama hat in the summer. What with a variety of velvet waistcoats and occasionally matching (otherwise clashing) bow-ties, he was by no means the image of a typical Civil Servant, still less a member of HM Customs and Excise. Indeed, I immediately saw in him a kinship with a creature that was a cross between Billy Bunter and Mr Toad. My understanding was that he'd started his career as an AP in the Ministry of Defence, but had arranged a swap with someone from C&E shortly after he was promoted to Principal, because of his deep loathing for the work, the people and the institution, according to what Martin Finlay told me in passing a day or so later, as we queued for lunch in the Council restaurant.

I met him just under a week later. He claimed that he was coming over to Brussels to meet a contact in the Commission for a discussion on the beer harmonisation directive, mainly at the insistence of the Brewers Society. It appeared the only time we could meet was late morning going into lunch….and naturally he knew a nice little place about ten minutes' walk from the Commission building…

I booked a meeting room in the Commission building, as it was more convenient for him. Rosemary had decided not to join us, on the basis that this was probably an occasion when three would be a crowd.

"We've met, haven't we?" suggested Webster, grasping my hand in a blancmange-like handshake.

"I don't remember ever seeing you in London," I replied. "But I attended a meeting of the Council Working Group examining the Excise Harmonisation Directives you attended last summer."

"Where were you before you came here?"

"VM…VAT Machinery."

"That explains it. I've been avoiding VAT like the plague. Since I joined Customs I've done betting and gaming, customs and more recently alcohol and tobacco duties….Didn't someone say you were ex-Outfield?"

"I was there for about three years when I started. I've spent longer in HQ, but I'd quite like to get back to the Outfield at some stage in my career."

"You're not tempted by the fleshpots of Brussels?"

"No. Rosemary and I see our careers being in London…and though the international school here is good for our daughters for a year or two, we'd like them to have an ordinary English education."

"As a divorcé, I'm footloose and fancy-free….and Brussels seems much more simpatico than London to me, at any rate. My meeting earlier on was to dot some "i's" and cross some "t's" for a job in DGXIV. It's excise harmonisation stuff, but it'll do for a year or two…"

I realised that he enjoyed the sound of his own voice, but I needed to get him on to the issue of wine standards and adulterated wine. So I explained my current task.

"This is one of these things that could be quite widespread – or might be extremely localised. The only producers who'd do something like this are those aiming at a mass market. No-one aiming for a quality market in anything above the minimum appellation would dare take the risk…and the standards authorities are generally much hotter on checking the quality stuff. That's what their reputation depends on. But mass-market stuff is either exported or drunk by people who believe they're getting good value if they pay a couple of pounds for a bottle of plonk."

"So are you saying that the national wine standards authorities don't really care if this happens with cheap wines?"

"I'm not sure I'm saying that exactly. It's more that they bother less with the low quality end of the market. What concerns them is the quality of the top end – and that's where they'll put most of their effort. But an adulteration scandal affects the reputation of all their wines…and if you're like Austria, with mainly a relatively low quality product, your export markets could go down the tubes like nobody's business. And there are plenty of countries like Australia and the US trying to get into the market, so once you lost your export markets, you might have a hard job getting them back."

"How do they try to maintain quality? And prevent this sort of thing from happening?"

"Mostly, they'll have some form of inspection and sampling regime. Of course, for the best wines, the sampling is entirely about the quality of the wine…and a lot of that can be predicted from the weather. But typically they'll employ people to check the vines a couple of times during the season….and check acreage…It's not been unknown for the grapes from adjoining vineyards to be added to those of a noble cru. Even a master of wine could find it hard to detect something like that. But since the overall quantity bottled has to be declared and can be subsequently checked against what gets distributed, it's generally possible to estimate how much wine any given acreage will produce given the weather conditions in any particular year. You'd be surprised at how scientifically it can be calculated. So you might get away with adding a few gallons, but you might have to end up drinking the extra wine yourself."

"But presumably that wouldn't be a problem with stuff like this Edel Veltliner?"

"No. To me, that stuff is just rats' piss. So even if you sweeten it a little with diethylene glycol or add some grapes from the next door vineyard, it's still rats' piss. The bigger problem would be if you did that with appellation contrôlée wines, using grapes that were destined for table wines, whether local or imported. But whether any of that goes on, I've really no idea. If you had a French table wine....call it 'Rouge du Grand-père'...whether you added wine from another part of France or from Algeria or Morocco, who's going to grumble at about ten francs a bottle? But if that stuff was getting into a 'Côtes du Rhône' or 'Châteauneuf-du-Pape', then the French wine industry would be in serious trouble."

"Shouldn't the inspection regimes catch that sort of thing?"

"In theory. But if you're really only interested in your top quality wines, you may put less effort in. And, let's face it, some countries do this sort of thing more effectively than others. Think of the famous 'olive belt'. If Don Corleone was importing loads of cheap and nasty Algerian red and sticking it into his Marsala, it'd be a brave wine inspector who was prepared to come out into the open and say it wasn't proper Sicilian Marsala....I'm a bit surprised about the Austrians, though. Generally, you tend to expect them to operate more or less like the Germans."

"But I'd imagine substituting or mixing cheap stuff from outside the EEC would be more prevalent than adulterating the wine?"

"Yes. Though the sources are quite limited. Shipping low quality Antipodean or South American wine wouldn't really be economic. So the most likely substitutes are North African and Iberian wines. You'd tend to think of red rather than white, but not exclusively."

"And if I wanted to find out what was going on, what would you think would be the best way to approach it?"

"It might be worth having a chat with the Wine Standards Board in London. They represent the top-end shippers as well as chains like Wasco and Marks and Spencer. For obvious reasons, they keep their ears close to the ground, so if there is any funny business happening, they may have some idea where it's going on.

19

I wouldn't trust any others....other than the Danes or the Dutch. Once you're in a wine-producing country, they'll protect their own from outsiders....especially the Commission....and if there is something iffy going on, they'll aim to clean it all up on the QT, so there's no damage to the reputation of their wine industry."

"Would MAFF know anything? Or their equivalents in Member States?"

"You could try MAFF.....My oppo there is a bloke called Peter Bone. Of course, MAFF's interest in wine is minimal. The English wine industry is piddlingly small and its output is extremely variable. Otherwise, it's more about protecting the abomination known as British Wine. They're beginning to learn how to deal with the rest of the EEC, but Peter doesn't have much of a toehold, for obvious reasons. You could assume that the MAFF equivalents in wine-producing countries will be as unhelpful as their wine standards authorities, for the same reasons. It's possible there might be someone in the Commission – either in DGXIV on the fiscal side or DGVI on the wine market side.- but you'd have to assume that if your contact was from a wine-producing country, your enquiries would get back to them."

"There don't seem to be many places I can go."

"I'm sorry I can't be more helpful, but as I said, this isn't really my area of expertise and, as you can see, virtually everyone involved has an interest in keeping any funny business hidden and dealt with behind closed doors.

It seemed to be time to go out to lunch. Despite the fact that I'd been in Brussels over a year whereas Webster only came out from time to time, he evidently knew the right places to eat much better than I did. We walked a few streets away from the Commission building and into a small restaurant I never knew existed in the rue le Corrège. It was Belgian-French, very much of that version of gastronomy that believes that all the parts of an animal's anatomy that are generally avoided are, in fact, the most interesting delicacies. Webster was plainly a devotee of this cuisine. Fortunately they included a pâté — I didn't look too closely at its ingredients — and liver, which I hadn't eaten since childhood, but was at the most conservative edge of the menu. Webster appeared to choose brains as his starter and a stew containing, among other things, pieces of tripe, sweetbreads and kidneys. Naturally, all this was washed down with high quality (and highly expensive) wines — a Chablis for the first course, which seemed odd in view of what we were eating, and a Nuits St Georges to accompany the main course. I managed to get away with about a glass and a half of each. Webster happily downed the rest, enthusing all the time about the food and, especially, the wines. He was evidently extremely knowledgeable about Burgundies and, when a student at Cambridge, had spent two vacations working in the vineyards there, living, according to him, in a tent in a field on the outskirts of Beaune and cycling to the vineyard each day. I assumed he must have been a good deal slimmer then — or would have required a particularly robust bicycle.

I could see why he wanted to move to Brussels and pursue a career within the EEC bureaucracy. If you were a gourmet like him, Brussels was certainly well suited to your needs and you could certainly get to places like Burgundy for a long weekend without much difficulty. It seemed to me that he would fit in well with his future EEC colleagues, many of whom regularly took long lunches like this…and presumably did the same for dinner. I was well aware that the top two men in SEFF - Gerry Fitzpatrick and Knud Henriksen frowned on such long lunch hours — and most of their staff, Rosemary and me included, were happy to avoid them. Indeed, Rosemary and I needed no persuasion. But our French and Italian colleagues regarded this as an integral element of working for the EEC and carried on as before.

Fortunately, he was happy to drink more than two thirds of the wine and barely required me to make conversation. I wondered how he'd get on having to negotiate with someone

21

over lunch – one of the common excuses for such long and expensive lunches – when he loved the sound of his own voice so much. But perhaps he had a separate, negotiating mode which he could switch into if required. Certainly, within C&E, he was seen as eccentric, but intelligent and effective. But, of course, having originated from an OGD, he was never going to be regarded as "one of ours".

And at least he'd avoided somewhere where I couldn't avoid escargots, frogs' legs, etc. And I'd been invited to lunch with a couple of officials from the Japanese Embassy and had felt obliged to eat a whole series of foods that turned my stomach – not least raw fish, fleshy shellfish and some form of sea-urchin – just managing to get back to the office before I was sick. So, by comparison, a pâté whose ingredients were probably better left unknown and an almost raw slab of liver, were almost palatable. (I confess I'd been expecting something like the well-, if not over-cooked liver and bacon of my childhood).

I felt that from Webster's point of view, I was a mediocre host. Though I could tell the wine we drank was good – certainly several levels above what we normally had – I had no knowledge of vineyards, grapes, good and bad years, etc and I'd always regarded the descriptions of wine-tasters as pompous and sometimes absurd. So, in keeping with my normal approach, I let him hold forth, but I avoided giving high-falutin' opinions which would've been bogus. It tasted like good wine, but if you asked me why, I hadn't the faintest idea.

Shortly after 3.30 pm – after a couple of tarte tatins, a black coffee and, on his part, a large cognac – we went our separate ways. I returned to work feeling bloated but clear-headed enough to "drive a desk", in the well-worn phrase. And though I'd got such information that I needed before lunch, it was part of the rules of the game that SEFF would pay for a good lunch in return. However, as Rosemary and I had considerable difficulty spending our entertainment allowance, a very expensive lunch like this would cause problems only for my digestion, while creating no financial indigestion whatsoever.

"You look like a bear with a sore head," remarked Rosemary, when I finally got back to our flat in Woluwe St Lambert. Most days she left earlier than me to pick up Emily and Sarah from the international school.

"I feel more like an over-inflated football that's been kicked about a field all afternoon," I replied. "I don't know how anyone could appreciate fine wines while eating food like that. It's so powerful, it suffocates the taste of the wine…I admit I wish I could've been sick when I got back to the office, like I was after lunch at 'Mont Fuji' with those Japanese that time."

"Did you get anything useful from this man Webster?"

"A lot about people we shouldn't contact because they're unreliable. A contact in MAFF and a suggestion we should meet someone from the Wine Standards Board in London. Otherwise, not much. He knows an incredible amount about wine, but mostly as a consumer…and he largely warned me off trying to talk to anyone in the Commission…"

"I suppose anyone from a wine-producing country is unlikely to co-operate."

"Yes…But interestingly, he indicated…or at least, I think he was indicating that the use of cheap foreign wine from outside the EEC – Spain and North Africa – either mixed or under the labels of EEC-produced wine was likely to be a much bigger issue than adulterated wine. I need to have a word with Knud Henriksen about that. Does he want us to stick to adulterated wine or should we cast our net wider?"

"I suppose the question must be does it matter?"

"I guess if wine-growers are getting EEC subsidies for wine which is actually grown outside the EEC it's fraud against the CAP. And I realise cheap wine is cheap wine, and Côtes du Rhône', for instance, may be quite cheap. But surely I'm entitled to drink wine that actually is Côtes du Rhône', not Spanish or Algerian plonk on which someone is making twice the profit. The fact that something is cheap doesn't entitle someone to cheat you. That was a bit of the flavour of Webster's remarks......If you're only prepared to pay a couple of quid for a bottle of wine, it serves you right if you're being cheated...and you probably wouldn't notice the difference anyway."

"I could see that sort of attitude getting up your nose."

"I'm sure it isn't universal. But British wine snobs almost seem to believe that ordinary working people shouldn't be drinking wine at all....Webster didn't actually say 'Chateau Wasco', but I've heard that sort of thing from others like him. As we've joined the EEC, there's no reason why ordinary people shouldn't drink wine, just as their counterparts do over here. They're not required to doff their caps to their betters and only drink beer." I stopped in mid-diatribe. There was too much of my father creeping into what I was saying and I didn't want to let my tongue lead me into an argument with Rosemary.

"So what now?"

"From my side, I'll try and fix up a meeting with this bloke Peter Bone in MAFF. He should be able to give me a contact in the Wine Standards Board. But you'd think if there was any significant fraud going on in the wine industry, Interpol might know something about it. Would it be possible to find out, without tipping anyone off?"

"I've got a couple of reliable contacts in Interpol since I've been doing this drug money tracing work. But I'll need to think how best to approach the subject. They're expert in financial dealings – accountants like me – and they might well be less cautious than I would about asking colleagues from wine-producing areas about fraud involving the wine industry."

"Perhaps your former colleagues in London...?"

"I doubt whether they have anything. Wine fraud scores very low on the Met's radar...unless it's being organised by the Mafia or some organisation like that...and then they'd tell us to keep our noses out..."

"Which would be excellent advice, it seems to me."

24

The man from MAFF, who was in Brussels for a fruit committee the following week, was the total opposite of Ian Webster. We met over lunch in the Council restaurant, where he chose the old British favourite - steak, frites and salad with a Jupiler beer. To be fair, it was commonly chosen by many of those who used the restaurant from different Member States – including me. Peter Bone was short, spare, light-haired, with a thin, sharp face and silver-rimmed spectacles. He was taciturn and struck me as, clever but an observer and commentator, rather than a doer. However, he was knowledgeable about the "wine market" and could've told me considerably more than I needed to know about the various national equivalents of the appellation contrôlée system. As I'd managed to photocopy all I felt I needed from an EEC publication, I was able to divert him from that on to the question of fraud and potential fraud.

"I've heard about this Danish discovery of adulterated wine from Austria. At least...there's a strong rumour going round. There's a wine market committee in a couple of weeks and I expect to learn more about it then from the Danes themselves," he explained.

"The Danes didn't swear me to secrecy, so I can probably tell you what they told me," I replied. And told him.

"And what is the interest of your organisation?" he asked.

"Our interest is in fiscal fraud, smuggling and frauds against the CAP. My main area is indirect tax fraud, but I have a background in customs work. I've been asked to look at this because I've some experience in picking my way at a problem until it can be clarified and hopefully resolved. I'm not a CAP expert...But in a way that's not really the issue here. The areas I'm trying to learn more about are adulteration, like this Austrian case, and more widely, the sale of wine from outside the EEC as EEC wine."

"And what exactly do you want from me?"

"I'd welcome your advice on how I might identify the possible scale of the problem – in both cases, adulteration and misdescription, and who I might talk to, and where I might get relevant information or evidence."

"This tends to be the sort of thing individual countries like to keep behind closed doors. There was a scandal a few years ago, I believe, when some French table wines were found to be of Algerian origin. We only learnt about via one of the supermarket chains. I can't remember whether it was Wasco, Sainsbury or Marks and Spencer. Apparently, whichever one of them it was had to be told because some of the wine had been sold on to them. I reckon the French were concerned that someone in the UK would discover the true origin of the wine and the press there would make a great song and dance about it. And as most of the popular press are anti-EEC, it would've been yet another problem for Ted Heath to resolve when he was selling EEC membership to the electorate….and, of course, it wouldn't help Harold Wilson with his referendum next month."

"Did they really believe that chains like Wasco actually test the wines they sell? I thought that they sold table wine as cheap as they can?"

"There's a fair amount of that. But Wasco, for instance, are careful and sophisticated wine buyers. Lots of British people are starting drinking wine regularly for the first time and while they may not have particularly refined tastes, they know wine from vinegar, if I can put it that way. And they especially don't like being cheated. So if Wasco got caught out selling a French wine, however cheap it might be, when it was really Algerian, it'd harm their reputation considerably. Customers might decide to buy their wine elsewhere…and the more sophisticated customers who are buying wines from Wasco at £5 to £10 a bottle would almost certainly go elsewhere. Wasco and the other British chains are seen as a massive area of growth for EEC wine producers, so they don't want to prejudice that."

"So what sort of checking up do they do on the wines they're buying?"

"I know they employ some professionally-trained tasters, who claim they can pretty well recognise the vineyard a particular wine has come from. How well that holds at the vin de table level, I'm less certain. Not least, because it's perfectly acceptable to blend wines at that level, and it's widely done. Exactly how you'd detect an Algerian wine rather than a cheap vin de pays, I've no idea. It may be worth your while talking to a couple of people in Wasco and Marks and Spencer, for instance....I can provide you with the appropriate contacts."

"I assume it's not capable of chemical analysis?"

"There are strength limitations on vins de table. If the Algerians, say, produced wines with a higher strength, I don't know whether someone mislabelling them would just hope no-one spotted it, or whether they'd water them down or blend them with a much weaker wine. Of course, chemical analysis would detect added chemicals like diethylene glycol, but I'm afraid I don't know whether it could determine whether a wine came from Algeria or southern France, for instance."

"Would firms like Wasco keep their ears to the ground about possible mislabelling or adulteration?"

"I guess so. I haven't spoken to them about it. They and Marks and Spencer seem extremely sharp to me. So I wouldn't be surprised if they do."

"Is there anywhere else where I might get some help in finding out if anything fishy is going on, and if so, where and how much of it there is?"

"It'd be worth your while talking to the Wine Standards Board. Of course, they're really more interested about this sort of matter from the quality end. I reckon they're happy to leave the table wine end to companies like Wasco and Marks and Spencer, who have a direct business need in such matters. I can give you a couple of names....But you should understand that this sort of thing doesn't figure much in MAFF's thinking at the moment. As I'm sure you can imagine, we're under a lot of pressure from Ministers and EEC Renegotiation and Referendum people in the

Cabinet Office to provide what they call 'neutral and unprejudiced' information about the whole EEC agricultural and fisheries sectors. Imagine trying to set out the CAP and the CFP in a way that Joe Public can understand! And when we're back to normal, wine will still be close to the bottom of MAFF's list of EEC priorities."

That was all the useful stuff I got out of him - and to some extent it felt like drawing teeth. I did get the names of various contacts. But I didn't feel I was getting anywhere fast.

"The trouble is that those who know won't tell and those who'd tell don't know," remarked Rosemary, after I'd told what I'd learnt when I got back to the flat in the evening. Inevitably, it was accompanied by a trademark smirk.

"I bet you've been working on that all day," I replied, slightly grumpily.

"Not entirely. I had a useful meeting with a couple of Swiss financial regulation men who were more helpful than I'd expected about tracing drug money through Swiss banks. Despite all their banking secrecy laws, they're not terribly keen for someone like Commissioner Giulizzi or even President Ortoli to criticise them in public for laundering drugs money."

"At least you made some progress….."

"I reckon some of those businessmen might be more helpful. After all, they've got a strong commercial interest in not selling their customers wines that have been misdescribed or adulterated."

"Yes…It'll be interesting to see how they go about it. If it really isn't possible to tell cheap French table wine from Algerian plonk, they can't very well check through sampling. So they've either got to have some sort of gen about the wine or perhaps there might be something fishy about the labels or corks, perhaps?"

"Well, I guess if you're aiming to sell the wine for a couple of pounds, including your own mark-up, you can't go in for fancy labels."

But when I met Billy Madden of Wasco a few days later, I realised I was labouring under a large misapprehension about the nature of the table wine trade. Billy was in Brussels to lobby the Commission about certain proposed food labelling requirements they were intending to propose in a draft Directive. I knew that Wasco were a growing force, but I'd no idea they were so rapidly up to speed with the EEC that they were already lobbying Commission officials before draft Directives had even seen the light of day. Impressive – I thought.

And, indeed, that was what I made of Billy Madden. To look at, he was nothing special. If he reminded me of anyone, it was one of those tough footballers who try to control the middle of the field through determined tackling and sensible passing. He was shorter than me, but well-built in the manner of a well-muscled footballer. He had a face that could easily be mistaken for being quite ordinary, but only if you ignored his very observant, highly intelligent eyes. Besides, a company like Wasco didn't make someone their International Director in his early thirties without him being extremely well thought of. Indeed, it was plain from what he said that this was a three year job, intended to give him some international experience before moving on to bigger and better things. In other words, unlike all these UK Civil Servants swanning over to Brussels for good money and a fairly easy life, he was looking forward to getting into managing all of Wasco's foods or their storage and distribution.

We met for lunch in the Council restaurant. I had thought this was perhaps a little down-market for a senior UK businessman, but he explained it was just what he wanted. I noticed he had a little Manchester City lapel badge.

"One of the things I really don't like about this place," he said in his noticeably Mancunian accent, "is those lengthy lunches, with too much food and wine. It takes up too much of your day and it's difficult not to appear inhospitable if you don't eat and drink your share. I don't really have the time to waste two to three hours over lunch, especially when I know I'm not going to be running at full throttle for a couple of hours afterwards. So a steak and salad and a beer here is preferable."

"I explained on the phone who I work for and what my current piece of work is," I replied, deciding not to say I completely agreed with him (which I did, of course – my father's puritanism being inescapable in such matters) for fear of appearing over-anxious to please. "I've been pretty well warned off going to the appropriate authorities in wine-producing countries because even if anything fishy is going on there, they'll close ranks and I'll get nowhere. So without revealing commercial any secrets, I was hoping you might be able to help me understand how Wasco try to avoid selling adulterated wine or wine that purports to be French table wine, for instance, but is actually Algerian or Moroccan."

"Provided you don't go publishing it in the EEC Journal, I'm happy to tell you how we go about it. Our customers are ordinary people who don't have lots of pennies to spare, so they don't want to feel they've been diddled. And telling someone they've bought a French wine when it was actually Algerian makes them feel that Wasco have diddled them. It doesn't matter if someone diddled us, we're the face they see, so we're the ones they take it out on...by taking their business to our competitors. So we put a lot of effort into ensuring that what we tell our customers we're selling is accurate. I'm not an expert about wine. I rarely drink the stuff myself. But I know we ship it in two ways. At the upper end of our range, the wine comes already bottled and labelled. For table wines, it travels in bulk, not all that different from bulk milk or petrol. We bottle and label it at one of our bottling plants."

"How stupid of me!" I exclaimed. "Why didn't I remember that wine is shipped in bulk! I've even seen it arrive at Tilbury ten years ago or so."

"We rarely use Tilbury. We try to run the business with as few costs as possible and having to factor in delays because of strikes in the London docks means that we go elsewhere."

"Presumably you're vulnerable to wines being misdescribed whether it arrives in bulk or already bottled?"

"Yes. It's virtually impossible to tell one red table wine from another provided the same grapes are used. So a cheap Spanish cabernet sauvignon is indistinguishable from a cheap French cabernet sauvignon to all intents and purposes. Certainly we couldn't afford to undertake the level of detailed chemical analysis that might detect some differences, but probably wouldn't. So we rely on two main things – a tight control over our suppliers and shippers, which means getting to know them thoroughly and making sure their contracts penalise them heavily for messing up. If one of our suppliers sent us misdescribed wine, they'd not only cease working with us immediately, they be subject to some heavy penalties, which we'd enforce through the courts if necessary. The second is an almost obsessive checking of the paperwork. So we expect to see invoices, bills of lading, ship's manifests, delivery notes, and so on and examine every one of them extremely thoroughly to detect anything that doesn't look right. Anything that catches our eyes gets chased up – even if it's only a discrepancy in a couple of dates. We sell quite a lot of Spanish wine – both red and white. And though it's cheap, we know you could get Algerian or Moroccan wine even cheaper. So we require all the documentation from where the wine is bottled or put into bulk containers, the route to the port and the relevant documentation with the transport company, all the port documentation, including Customs declarations, valuations, whether there were any spot checks, the name of the ship, its route, the full manifest…and so on. And we require as much as possible in advance. What we don't want is to find our wine gets loaded at Cadiz on to a ship which previously put in at Ceuta and which has a tank full of Moroccan red wine sitting next to our tank of Spanish red wine. What the documents tell you in cases like that may not represent reality."

"So you'd tell your shippers to await another ship?"

"If necessary."

"Doesn't that increase your costs?"

"It doesn't increase ours. It may increase theirs. We make it plain that bulk wines are not to be shipped with any similar wines. What is going to be loaded on virtually every ship is known well in advance. Certainly, something like wine. You wouldn't just turn up at Ceuta with several tankers full of wine and hope you could get it on board. That gets booked well in advance - and we expect our shippers to be alert to such things. Otherwise, it's their loss not ours. So it pays them to keep alert."

"I guess that's about as tight as you can get it without actually being physically present to check what's going on."

"It's a business imperative for us...Just like not having long queues at check-out tills."

"Do you reckon there's much misdescription of wines going on? Or adulteration?"

"I'd say there's very little adulteration. Of course, I only know the UK market. British tastes tend to be drier than much of the rest of northern Europe, so adding diethylene glycol to a white wine wouldn't really be necessary. And, of course, it's too easy to pick up through chemical analysis. It may be a commercial necessity for certain vineyards, especially in years of bad weather. But I doubt it's a significant problem. On the other hand, we do believe that there's a lot of mislabelling going on. We haven't done an analysis because we keep such a firm grip on our suppliers, but we suspect that in both the table market and quality sectors, there's a fair amount of mislabelling or blending of better wines with inferior ones. Demand for wine is going up all over the developed world. That's why the Australians, New Zealanders and South Africans have started investing in vineyards...and South America will be a growth area too. Where there's strong and growing demand and you can sell your product at a premium, there'll be a strong commercial interest in selling more of your product at those prices. For various reasons, you can't expand the area of your vineyards...not least because the way the appellation contrôlée regimes operate...so your only alternative is to buy in

32

cheaper stuff and blend it. And when it comes to wine tasting, I'm a sceptic. I suspect that a lot of the basis of wine snobs' discrimination is snobbery and the knowledge - which anyone in the know can get hold of – of good, bad and mediocre harvests."

"But that must be checkable, through examining the sort of documentation you use to control your suppliers."

"I would think so. Getting hold of it might be more of a problem. We have commercial contracts which require it to be produced. I guess the wine standards authorities have the right to do so. But who knows whether the documents they get sent in such circumstances equate to what's actually been going on?"

"Exactly. And I guess if no-one is making any waves, what the eye doesn't see, the heart doesn't grieve over."

"So you're going to be making waves?"

"At some stage, possibly. But at the moment, definitely not. I need to get a much better idea about the scale of whatever fishy business might be going on….and I suppose I also need to work out what the EEC interest is. I don't think SEFF are really supposed to be involved in consumer protection work and if it's about the integrity of labels on wine bottles, I'm not sure that's really for us either. But if there's fraud – against the CAP, for instance – then I think we have a legitimate interest."

"But if you come across anything that looks illegal – or just odd – what will you do with that information?"

"It'd depend a bit on what it was, but I guess I'm most likely to tell a suitable person in MAFF."

"That'd certainly be helpful. MAFF are well aware of British companies' concerns over some of the feeble controls operated at some of the EEC frontiers."

I thought that he might've asked me to pass on any information relevant to Wasco's business to him. But either he'd worked me out or he knew that Civil Servants who played things straight wouldn't agree to such a thing. In any case, I felt he was the kind of person who made sure he had the right contacts – and could get any information he legitimately needed from a contact in MAFF. But of one thing I had no doubt – if Wasco's up-and-coming executives were anything like him, they were going places!

As I said to Rosemary that evening, he'd given me a lot to think about – not least a possible way of digging out information that might allow us to get a greater feel for whether there was any funny business going on, and if so, how much.

My final fact-finding meeting was with Mr Grenville Porteous, Secretary of the Wine Standards Board, a scion of an old wine-shipping family, who claimed his forebears had been shipping "claret and canary" since the late seventeenth century. Evidently, the novelty of being part of the EEC hadn't worn off yet, as it seemed everyone and his wife who had a passable excuse to come to Brussels was doing so. Mr Porteous appeared only a couple of days after I'd met Billy Madden. He was not what I expected. He was a small, wiry middle-aged man with an old-fashioned short haircut and a prominent nose which made him look like an undecided anteater.

We met for coffee in a coffee bar about a hundred yards from the Commission building in the rue Stevin.

"I'm sorry I couldn't spare any more time to see you," he explained in one of those voices that sounded it had come from an early BBC recording in the 1930s. "But today is very much a flying visit, with meetings with various people in the Commission and other wine standards organisations....But I understand you have an interest in adulterated wine?"

"Yes," I replied. "The Danes picked up some white wine adulterated with diethyline glycol and asked my Deputy Director to see whether we could assess how far this was a general problem or whether it's specific and sporadic."

"There's been something of a ripple round the trade about the Danish incident. My continental colleagues have been claiming that this sort of occurrence is extremely unusual and that the Austrians have been extraordinarily naughty......"

"But?"

"But my members are less sure. If a bad grape harvest means you'd have to discard a whole year's production, there must be a strong commercial need to do something about it. I'm not saying it happens all the time, but there must be years and vineyards where the temptation is too strong to resist....especially as when you're concerned with table wines, the average consumer is unlikely to notice. With due respect to the customers of some of our larger corporate members, the stuff they drink indicates their palates are scarcely discriminating."

"So far I've only heard it said that white wine is likely to be adulterated. Could you also do it for reds and rosés?"

"In theory....certainly with rosé...but there's no reason why you couldn't do it with red, I suppose. I've never heard of it, however."

"So what should wine producers do if their harvest isn't up to it?"

"Turn it into vinegar. You could send it off for distillation into brandy or industrial alcohol if you denatured the resulting spirits. You wouldn't make so much money, but you'd get something...and you'd still be getting plenty of EEC grants under the Common Agricultural Policy...Not the Austrians or Spanish, of course. But they'll be getting their own subsidies, of course. England is about the only country that doesn't subsidize wine production...But at least entering the EEC has stopped our wine duty actually favouring that revolting British wine...I know some of our members sell the stuff, but calling it 'wine' of whatever sort is utterly repugnant to anyone's idea of what wine is...."

"My impression is that it's a dying industry...especially now it doesn't get any protection from the structure of the excise duty."

"And thank God for that!"

"Would the Wine Standards Board ever get information about wine being adulterated? Or wine being mislabelled?"

"We receive allegations about both, mostly mislabelling. By and large our members would deal directly with any problem themselves, but they would inform us so that we could inform

35

other members. But as I'm sure you understand, many feel they are in competition with each other – so if company A discovered that a particular French wine was actually relabelled Algerian wine, for instance, they might feel it was up to company B and company C to find it out for themselves. They'd certainly inform us, but not necessarily in a timely manner."

"So if we wanted to find out what might be going on – if anything untoward was going on – it might be better to keep in touch with some of your members?"

"I would say so – though we'd welcome being kept in the picture. And there are likely to be two types of this kind of thing – relabelled cheap wine masquerading as relatively cheap table wine from an established wine-producing country and cheaper wines blended into quality wines to increase the amount that can be sold. The latter is riskier, because such wines get tasted by professional masters of wine more frequently, but the profit margins are significantly higher."

"I get the picture, I think."

With that he had to be off. And the cost of two coffees was hardly going to put a large hole in my entertainment allowance, which was a good thing, I reflected, as the coffee was like what they served up at meetings in the Commission – exceedingly strong and eye-wateringly bitter.

I didn't need to wonder what sort of wine Mr Grenville Porteous would be having with his lunch. Definitely nothing that would be classed as a table wine! I wondered whether Ian Webster and he had ever crossed each other's paths. It seemed to me that was a match made in a wine snob's heaven.

ANALYSIS AND ITS LIMITATIONS

I didn't feel there was anyone else I could talk to at this stage, without risking putting a lot of people on the defensive. It was time to do what Billy Madden had indicated might be helpful – working my way through a lot of information about wine shipments, declarations of yields from grape harvests, etc to see whether anything odd stuck out. It would be looking back, by necessity. But until I had some idea as to whether there was a problem that could be identified, there was no point in seeking possible solutions. How one might predict that something untoward was going on and catch those involved red-handed could wait until I was certain that people were up to no good.

Rosemary had freed up time to help.

"So what exactly are we looking for?" she asked, as we made our way from the tram from Woluwe St Lambert to the SEFF offices, having dropped Emily and Sarah off at the international school.

"I'd like to see what the patterns of movement of wine are," I replied. "The Commission library has lots of information about wine imports and exports, including the names of shippers and ports of entry. I want to link that to information about individual shippers. For instance if Leblanc and Lenoir of Bordeaux ship top quality claret to the UK, would they also be importing dirt cheap red wine from Morocco? Suppose they import a hundred gallons of Moroccan plonk – can we work out where it goes? And can we link their imports of cheap wine to whether the harvest in the Bordeaux region was good, mediocre or bad? I'm hoping that might give us some idea whether the higher quality wines are being blended with cheaper ones."

"It seems a bit by and large. What will you do if nothing odd emerges?"

"We need to get hold of the figures which are held in the Commission about the acreage of individual vineyards and then look at how much wine each vineyard claimed it had produced. Apparently the Commission library will hold that sort of information on a historic basis...and we can also find out whether the harvest was good, bad or mediocre. Plainly we can't cover every vineyard in every country, but we could test out whether it's possible to use a rule of thumb that in a good year an acre of vines yields X bottles of wine, in a mediocre year Y bottles and in a bad year Z bottles. The question is whether you can use a rule of thumb like that generally, or whether you could only apply it to individual regions. Of course, if each vineyard is significantly different, it won't be much use."

"That could get us there on the top quality stuff — but what about the cheap wines that are either adulterated or misdescribed?"

"I think we still start from whether the local grape harvest is seen as good, bad or mediocre. If it was a bad harvest, you'd expect less wine to be shipped. But do the figures bear that out? If you're buying in some more cheap wine from elsewhere or sticking diethylene glycol into the wine, your production might look remarkably similar whatever the harvest. With any luck, it gives us somewhere to look more closely."

"And I suppose you must know by late summer or early autumn what sort of harvest it's going to be. So you could look out for additional shipments of the sort of wine that might be misdescribed. But you'd need to know where you could lay your hands on diethylene glycol and somehow monitor shipments from there that were going to vineyards or wine-producers....But you realise that what gets declared may not equate to actually happens...."

"You won't be surprised that it was bothering me too. What we really need is to get our hands on the actual documents covering the movement of cheap wine from Algeria or Morocco into France, for instance, so we could see where individual shipments went. If several container loads went to a huge Carrefour depot…."

"Even a giant Géant one!"

"….it ought to be possible to check whether they're selling cheap Moroccan wine on the shelves of their supermarkets. If they aren't, it'd seem likely that something fishy was going on. Similarly, if Proust & Camus, wine shippers of great antiquity and distinction, are getting a container load of Algerian plonk when they only ever ship posh wines, what's going on? Or if Chateau Sartre which sells only the choicest existentialist clarets is getting consignments of this Algerian stuff, there's definitely a very fishy smell about it."

"But it'd be difficult to get hold of the relevant documents without alerting the French authorities….and their loyalties might well be more with their French wine producers and their international reputations than with us truth-seeking puritans from SEFF…..and the idea of fishy-smelling wine is quite disgusting!"

"Undoubtedly. But we can cross that bridge when we come to it. We probably won't get that far. And if we're going to have to lay our hands on the documents, I reckon Knud Henriksen and Gerry Fitzpatrick will have to take some awkward decisions……I've booked a meeting with Knud tomorrow afternoon to tell him where we've got to and what we're proposing to do. I was assuming you'd want to come along as well?"

"Of course. These two years are likely to be the only time we get a chance to work together, so we should do as much as we can together."

We found the Commission's archives in the rue van Maerlant, in a smaller Belgian version of the Prudential Assurance building in High Holborn, just east of Grays Inn Road – a Gothic red brick building. Our Commission passes were sufficient to get us inside and we spent a useful ten minutes with one of the archivists enabling us to track down the information we were seeking.

While Rosemary checked through the information to see which years had produced bad and good harvests for red wines in Burgundy, Bordeaux, Chianti and Valdicocce and for white wines in the Loire, the Rhine, the Moselle and Italian Soave, I searched for information about wine imports into France, Italy and West Germany. At this stage, I was trying to see whether there was any correlation between poor harvests and increased imports of similar wines.

Rosemary handed me a short list:

WINE REGION	GOOD YEAR	BAD YEAR
Burgundy	1971	1973
Bordeaux	1974	1970
Chianti	1972	1971
Valdicocce	1972	1969
Loire	1974	1970
Rhine	1968	1972
Moselle	1968	1972
Soave	1973	1969

"The book explains that these definitions are quite by and large," said Rosemary. "Within each area, there may well be vineyards that differ. It's even possible that due to accidents of nature, one vineyard could have a good year when the region as a whole was having a bad one – and vice versa."

"We're going to have to assume quite a lot at this stage," I replied. "Ideally we should look at half a dozen years to see whether any figures we get are typical. But let's see what comes out."

"As these regions don't cover the whole of a country's production, I don't quite see how you'd know that if the wine harvest in Burgundy was bad, but somewhere else...Bordeaux even…was good, the import of foreign red wine might remain roughly the same."

"If it does, it'll show that these figures are too general and I'll have to think of a way to get more detailed ones somehow. I'm suggesting we look at imports through Marseilles for France, Genoa and Livorno for Italy and Rotterdam, Bremen and Hamburg for West Germany."

We spent a couple of hours looking through the import figures through the ports I'd identified. The results were mixed and I wasn't sure what they told us.

WINE REGION	GOOD YEAR	BAD YEAR (change in imports)
Burgundy	1971	1973 (+)
Bordeaux	1974	1970 (+)
Chianti	1972	1971 (- Genoa, + Livorno)
Valdicocce	1972	1969 (+ Genoa, - Livorno)
Loire	1974	1970 (level)
Rhine	1968	1972 (+ Rotterdam, Hamburg & Bremen level)
Moselle	1968	1972 (all level)
Soave	1973	1969 (+ Genoa, Livorno level)

We went off for a salad in a nearby café. In any case, we needed to rest our eyes and let the information sink in.

"So what has it told us?" asked Rosemary.

"Less than I'd hoped….We need to get information on the imports at the level of the individual shippers, with some idea of who the end users are. As far as I can tell, they don't keep figures at that level of detail here. But I'm pretty sure Member States share that information with the Commission…The Stat used to send lots of stuff on microfiches every month.......When we get back to the office I'll try and check where they send it...I guess some sort of EEC statistical office."

"And what are we looking for from those figures?"

"We keep the good and bad years' list. But then we try a big shipper of Burgundies and see whether they import more in a bad year than a good one...and where the wine comes from. We might be able to get some advice from the Wine Standards Board on whether there are shippers that deal only with posh wines and others who handle the ordinary stuff....If someone seems to import wine that might look as though it could be blended with a posh wine or re-labelled as an ordinary table wine, we may have something worth looking at."

"But remember we were asked to look at this adulteration with diethylene glycol. Knud Henriksen didn't actually suggest we should be going after this sort of fraud."

"We're due to see him later, so we can see what his reaction is. From the people I've been talking to, adulteration seems to be regarded as a fairly small and containable problem, whereas substituting cheap imported wine, in whole or in part, for the real thing is a much bigger problem."

"You realise there is a question about how far we could take this?"

"Go on..."

"Let's assume that people import cheap foreign wine to replace shortages in years when the grape harvest hasn't been good. If we were really going to nail someone, we've only got this year....and there must be a fair chance that there isn't a bad harvest this year. So we may not get anywhere at all."

"I see what you mean.......But I suppose if we got together evidence of what seems to have happened in the past, whoever replaces us in SEFF could take it over."

There didn't seem much point in digging around further in the archives, so we headed back to the SEFF offices in the rue de la

Loi. At 4pm, I put my head round the door of Rosemary's office and we went along to Knud Henriksen's room.

"We've been doing some preliminary research on this adulterated wine matter...." I began.

"Nick has been doing the lion's share of it," added Rosemary.

"As far as adulteration is concerned, it's not thought to be a widespread problem. It's only likely to be done in years when the grape harvest has been poor, so the wine is acidic and weedy..."

"Weedy?" asked Knud.

"Thin, weak......And it's unlikely to be done to quality wines, because the product is more likely to be sampled. So it mostly goes into cheap table wines – like the Austrian wines which the Danes discovered. Quite a lot of that is sold by supermarkets or what we call 'off-licences' in the UK, who are increasingly part of a commercial chain. Much of it gets imported in bulk – and is likely to be sampled, certainly by some British supermarkets, before it gets bottled."

"So, you are saying it's not a large problem?"

"I think if it gets discovered, it's a very big problem for the country concerned, as I guess people will stop buying their wine. And it seems to me that you could provide a fairly straightforward way of catching it – and deterring it. As it's possible to know whether a grape harvest has been poor or not in particular wine-growing regions, it should be possible to set up sampling checks when wines enter the EEC or cross the boundaries between Member States.....I realise the Commission is trying to abolish Customs and other checks at internal EEC frontiers, but I guess there are always going to have to be a few. And if you knew that certain wine-producing regions in Austria had suffered a poor harvest in 1975, you could set up checks to cover the period when this wine would be shipped into the EEC. I reckon that it'd only take a couple of cases where adulteration was identified and no one would touch the wine from that region."

"And if you ask me, if we let it be known informally that this was what SEFF was going to set up, I reckon the wine standards people in these regions would step in before any adulterated wine left the country," added Rosemary.

"So you reckon the local wine standards people know what's been going on?" asked Henriksen.

"If they aren't keeping their ears to the ground to pick up that sort of thing, what use are they?"

"So that's problem mostly solved is it?"

"Not really," I replied.

"Now why doesn't that surprise me?"

"We think there's a much bigger problem with the use of cheap imported wine, which either gets re-labelled as an EEC wine – generally at the cheaper end of the market – or is blended with higher quality wines, to maintain or even increase the volume of expensive wine which they can sell. It's possible that the re-labelling only happens in years when the local grape harvest has been poor, but I guess it's conceivable that it happens all the time. However, I'm guessing that the blending is more likely to happen only in years when the harvests are bad."

"I'll need to speak to Gerry about that. There are plenty of toes you are likely to be treading on if you get very far....But how do you intend to proceed?"

"We need to be able to look at some of the detailed import information. We should be looking at imports made by individual shippers in a few sample wine-growing regions, to see what wine they import and whether it changes between years when there are good or bad harvests..."

"And there may also be figures for the volume of wine each vineyard produces," added Rosemary. "If could get our hands on them, we could see whether the quantities produced varies according to the harvests or not. If it doesn't and everything else has remained the same, there must be something worth looking at in greater depth."

"But we're not sure where we'd be able to lay our hands on these figures," I continued. "We went to the Commission library this morning, but there was less there than we hoped. And I know that the UK Statistical Offices sends details of imports and exports to somewhere in the EEC....some equivalent I suppose...but I haven't time to find out what it is or where it's located yet."

"It's called Eurostat," explained Henriksen. "They've just finished the process of moving staff from Brussels to Luxembourg...and from what I know, they're located in several buildings over there, while they await the completion of the new EEC building. You should look through the staff directory to see whether there are any British over there...or Danes...and make contact with them. It's not an organisation I know much about, but you should probably steer clear of anyone from the wine-producing countries. But before you go shooting off to Luxembourg, we'd better confirm that Gerry is OK with this."

In fact, Rosemary and I had to shoot off anyway, as there was a parents' evening at the international school. We were almost late, arriving panting, having run from the tram stop. Mrs Unsworth-Thomas, the headmistress of the junior department, glared at us, more noticeably at Rosemary than me. Was that because mothers were expected to be on time while fathers weren't? Or because Rosemary worked, whereas most "Brussels mothers" didn't? Or just because, working in a more relaxed, cosmopolitan office where only Gerry Fitzpatrick wore a suit and the women wore mini-skirts whether it suited their legs or not, Rosemary was showing an unsuitable amount of thigh?

Perhaps it was our children? But that didn't seem to be the case. Emily was too quiet, as usual. Sarah was too noisy and excitable – as usual. Both seemed to work hard, though Sarah evidently could get bored more easily – especially with arithmetic and learning French. However, she was apparently the best player on the recorder in the whole school already and Emily was particularly praised for her painting and drawing....and both continued to progress at tennis, with "a fierce will to win", acquired from one of their parents...not me! Emily and Sarah weren't present while all these things were being said about them by their teachers. Along with all the other pupils, they were in a separate room, reading. But just before we left, we were entertained by a small concert – a choir, in which all the children sang....inevitably a selection of children's songs from France, Belgium, Holland, Italy, Ireland, Denmark, West Germany and the UK. (Presumably Luxembourg children sang only songs from another Member State!) Sarah and a couple of other recorder players accompanied several of the songs.

We decided that we wouldn't go straight home, but eat out, so we could tell Emily and Sarah how pleased we were with how they were getting on. Fortunately there were no "yellow arches" in the vicinity, so we took the tram nearer to our flat and ate in a local restaurant, where the grown-ups could eat sausages and stoemp and the children burgers.....and Rosemary and I refrained from our usual joke about whether if you tapped the burger with a fork, it would moo or neigh!

"If we're going to have to spend a day or two looking at figures in Luxembourg, we're going to have to stay overnight," remarked Rosemary, as she lay with her head on my shoulder just before we went to sleep that night. "What are we going to do about Emily and Sarah? I know Knud Henriksen will offer to have them again, but they hated it when they were there...and I think they also associate it with that worrying day in Riga when your friend Modris got shot."

"I doubt we could get my mother over for a couple of days – especially not at short notice. She's got friends and a couple of ladies' clubs she goes to.....Perhaps we could take them with us? If they'd got something to do and Eurostat have some sort of creche...or a room where they could keep out of people's way....? And I realise that Sarah, at least, believes that every time we go off on our own, we're likely to be shot at....even by EEC statisticians!"

"It'd probably be good if they could come somewhere with us where nothing out of the ordinary happens. It'd be the best way of putting some distance between that day in Riga and whatever is at the top of their minds."

The following afternoon, Knud Henriksen told me that Gerry Fitzpatrick had no problem with us widening the scope of our "remit", as he called it.

"But at this stage, we won't be saying anything to Commissioner Giulizzi or the toad Paolitti," he added. "They know you're looking into the adulteration matter, but as Italians, their first interest is in protecting their home country. And if there is any funny business going on with re-labelling wine, you can bet your bottom dollar the Italians will be at it. Even though you're in their good books because of that drugs stuff….and identifying Trebzow as the spy and getting Paolitti off the hook, that wouldn't stop them spiking your guns if they thought Italian interests were being threatened…or even if there was the remotest possibility they might be threatened."

"I'm surprised they weren't upset that I discovered a spy in part of their organisation?"

"Oh no. SEFF is seen as Gerry's baby…..So they see it as his failure, even though Paolitti sat on the appointment panel that selected Trebzow and neither Gerry nor I did….But the success with the drugs investigation – especially as it also involved the West Germans and Dutch – along with the information-sharing Directive, has made SEFF look effective, though perhaps not in the way that was originally intended. And so we've made Giulizzi look a lot more effective than he is."

"We'll try to make sure we keep out of their way…But we really are only at the information gathering stage and whether that will allow us to pinpoint where there might be something fishy going on, I've no idea."

"In any case, please make sure you record how you've gone about this. It's a methodology which our successors may need to use for different purposes and there's no point in them starting from scratch if we've already trodden the same path."

Rosemary had been checking through Commission directories and making a few phone calls. When we had lunch together, she told me where she'd got to.

"I found a man called Derek Widdowson, who's both British and working on trade statistics," she explained. "I told him who we were and where we work. Naturally, he wondered why we were interested in his detailed trade statistics. I explained that SEFF was a new organisation and we were trying to see what use we might be able to make of the figures collected and analysed by Eurostat to see whether we could identify possible frauds or other possibly illegal practices which EEC Member States might not be able to detect from their own information. That seemed to satisfy him. He suggested that if we wanted to look at the figures ourselves, we'd need to have a suitable letter of introduction from our organisation and that it'd probably be best to arrange to meet him and he'd make sure we got through the formalities as smoothly as possible....At least the office is in the middle of Luxembourg...so he said.....He gave me an address which I've written down in my notebook."

"Had you thought when we might go there?"

"I thought we might go at the beginning of next week. It'll give us time to sort out Emily and Sarah's school and give Mr Widdowson time to organise things."

"Did you tell him what we were interested in?"

"I said we were interested in the excise duties and we'd decided to take wine and beer as examples and see what we could learn from the import and production figures....I explained we'd need to get to the greatest detail possible......"

"He didn't have any problems with that?"

"Not that he said."

For all that there was an air of formality about it that I hadn't found in English schools - at least since my children had started school – the international school appeared to see no difficulty in allowing Emily and Sarah to be away for up to three days the following week. Naturally, they were delighted to be having a short holiday and it seemed that Rosemary had satisfied them that we weren't going to be roaming the streets of Luxembourg at the mercy of passing gunmen, but that would all be spending our days in an office building, with she and I grinding our way through page after page of detailed information. We arranged with the school for them to have some schoolwork they could be doing while our noses were to the grindstone...and Derek Widdowson promised that he'd find a room for them somewhere reasonably close to us where they would be out of harm's and other people's way.

Normally we would've travelled directly by train from Brussels to Luxembourg on the Monday morning. But it seemed a pity not to do some exploring during the weekend. So on the Friday evening, we took a train to Namur and stayed in a cheap hotel near the station and enjoyed a wander around the town the following morning. Apart from the splendid town hall with a rather fine military tower next to it, there was less to see than I'd imagined...but, in any case, our children weren't expecting a weekend of dragging round historic sights, interesting architecture, cathedrals and churches. So we had lunch and got a train to Liege - or Luik, as the Flemish called it. The station seemed rather a long way from the centre of the city, but fortunately there were buses. And though the river Meuse there was pleasant, it seemed rather more of an industrial town than I'd expected, with nothing of the historic beauty of Ghent, Bruges or Brussels itself. So we got a bus back to the station and found a hotel nearby, having a fairly mediocre dinner there.

On the Sunday, I fancied going to Trier, which I was confident would be more historic. But as the trains seemed to go via Luxembourg, it seemed sensible to put that off for another day and just head to Luxembourg and explore there. It was an unexpectedly hilly city, but more important than historic buildings for the children, there was a pleasant park with a large playground. So we had an enjoyable, if not very cultural day. The hotel was a couple of levels above where we'd been staying the previous nights, mainly because SEFF were paying for our room. Indeed, we'd had "family rooms" in Namur and Liege, with children's bunk beds alongside the parents' double bed. In Luxembourg, Emil and Sarah had a separate room, next to ours, with an internal, lockable door. They preferred this arrangement, feeling very grown up. Rosemary and I concurred – free to make use of the large shower and crisp white sheets for activities you don't do in front of your children.

The following day we set off for the centre of the city, where we were due to meet Derek Widdowson at the Centre Louvigny, near the main post office. Derek Widdowson met us at the entrance.

"There's been a bit of a problem ever since most of the staff were transferred from Brussels…before my time, of course…I've only been here since the middle of '74….we're in four different buildings and the rooms here aren't really big enough. Fortunately, you've chosen a week when there's a series of workshops with the policy people in Brussels, so while you've been travelling south from there, a dozen or more of my colleagues have been heading in the opposite direction."

There didn't seem to be too many formalities – our passports and Rosemary's and my Commission passes seemed to do the trick. Widdowson led us to the lifts and then along a corridor to a couple of rooms which looked out over the street. They were two-person rooms, with desks which faced each other, with little barriers of metal, containing an in-box, out-box and several "pending" or storage trays full to the brim with files. Each room had a bookcase containing dozens of statistical publications, as well as the inevitable collected EEC treaties. Apart from locked wooden cupboards, that was it. No pictures on the walls and no signs of any individuality. Possibly items of personal interest had been locked away in a desk drawer, but other than the initials on the outside of the doors, there was no indication of who worked here – and even less about what they were like.

"I thought your daughters might use this one," he suggested. "And I've laid out the material you requested on the phone on the table in the next door room....There's a restaurant of sorts on the top floor and a coffee machine in the lobby by the toilets, just by the lifts. There's also a drinking water fountain there too."

We thanked him and settled Emily and Sarah into their room, with their schoolwork, some stuff for drawing and several books. With luck, that'd keep them quiet for an hour, possibly longer. Rosemary and I then settled down to look at the information which we'd asked for. We'd divided the work up so that I would examine import figures for shippers in certain wine-growing regions in a good and bad year, while Rosemary would look at the production figures for vineyards in the same regions at the same times.

Inevitably, there were a fair number of interruptions when one or other of us went next door to keep an eye on Emily and Sarah. Neither of them was used to keeping their concentration without a teacher to apply their noses to the grindstone. So it meant that we didn't get as far or as fast as we would've liked.

I looked at the French wine shippers who appeared to have addresses in Burgundy or the Bordeaux region. Quite quickly I was able to narrow them down to three or four in each. But as lunch time approached, I couldn't really spot any significant differences in the amounts they imported between and "good year" and a "bad year". I noticed that the red wine they imported came mostly from Algeria and Morocco. The amounts they declared for export were largely Burgundies, with one – Clarence Grandin et Cie – exporting a similar quantity that they'd imported. But, of course, there was nothing to say that the wines they'd imported hadn't been entirely legitimately sold in France, described accurately.

We decided to go out for lunch, to get a breath of fresh air. We found a small café that did children's lunches – which turned

51

out almost inevitably to be burgers or chicken "goujons" – and spent our time amusing Emily and Sarah. As I should've guessed, Emily had largely completed all the schoolwork she'd been given, whereas Sarah had spent her time drawing and reading…or doing not very much. I could already foresee problems ahead – if not that day, certainly the next one.

Rosemary and I continued to plough ahead during the afternoon – with the occasional break - until we reckoned we'd tried our daughter's patience to its limits and finished for the day. We found a park with a playground and let the children work off as much of their surplus energy as they could. We felt we owed it them to keep them amused, so we weren't able to discuss what we'd found until after we'd put them to bed, after dinner in our hotel.

"How far did you get?" I asked.

"I picked vineyards in Burgundy and then Bordeaux, as we agreed and compared what they declared they'd produced in a good year and a bad year. In most cases, there was a drop in the quantity produced of between 5% and 20%. But sometimes there was no or virtually reduction. In no case did anyone produce any more in a bad year than a good. You might say that those that had produced virtually the same quantity were suspect, but as I was thinking about it, I realised that we've no idea whether a bad year should mean a drop of, say, a third in production and therefore if they declared a drop of only 20%, that might be equally suspicious…..I didn't start on the Italian ones this afternoon."

"Nor did I. I can't say I found much of a pattern. The difference between what the shippers I looked at imported in a good year and a bad year was generally around 5%. But, of course, the quantities are quite large, so I guess that if some imported wine was being diverted to top up one of these posh vineyards in a bad year, it might not be detectable from these figures. In any case, if these are reputable shippers, they might not want to get involved in that sort of funny business. And the wine-growers mightn't trust them not to report them either. So it's entirely possible that any wine that might be used in this way comes through different shippers and quite possibly misdescribed."

"This doesn't seem to be getting anywhere fast."

"I suppose it's showing the limitations of what can be achieved by SEFF carrying out this sort of central analysis. But let's see if the Italian stuff tells us any more."

It would've been unusual if the different surroundings of a hotel bedroom and shower hadn't encouraged us to make love, with the interconnecting door locked, to ensure no inconvenient interruptions. And a day spent mostly poring through detailed figures had left us with plenty of energy. But it was only as we lay in bed afterwards that an unwelcome thought sprang into my head.

"I've a nasty feeling that as far as the French wines are concerned, I've been barking up the completely wrong tree," I said. "If I owned a posh French vineyard, but the grape harvest hadn't been very good, I wouldn't top up my production by adding cheap wine from Algeria, I'd get it from lower quality French vineyards perhaps twenty or fifty miles away....and I might even just get their grapes...though I suppose that might leave them with a noticeable gap in their production figures. That way, I save on transport costs and I guess the cheaper wine is less likely to be detected than imported stuff."

"So the work you've been doing looking at imported wine might've been a waste of time?"

"I reckon so. What you've been looking at isn't....and whether the Italians would be doing the same, I don't know......I guess that at the cheaper end of the market, re-labelling of foreign wines might be a way of making up for a drop in production....But I don't think we'll uncover a scandal in the posh wines market this way."

"But if the amount they produce doesn't seem to be affected by a poor grape harvest., that does suggest something fishy might

53

be going on......But I guess the problem is how you can prove it. If it can't be done through chemical analysis, I doubt whether the opinion of some wine snob would constitute reliable evidence."

"You'd need documentary evidence of wine going from another vineyard to the posh one or physical observation of the cheap wine being blended with the posh stuff. Not an easy thing to do while remaining unobserved, I guess."

"So what are you going to do tomorrow?"

"If you look at the Italian production figures for the Soave and Valdicocce vineyards, I'll see what level of imports the shippers made. As these are table wines rather than posh ones, it's possible that they may be more likely to re-label foreign wines."

The next day was like the previous one – though we had to spend a bit more time with our rather bored children. However, as Rosemary reminded them, they wouldn't have been doing much different at school. By early afternoon, we realised we'd got as far as we could and decided to go back to our hotel to collect our luggage and then get the train back to Brussels. Keeping Emily and Sarah from racing up and down the train meant that we couldn't talk about what we'd discovered until later.

"I do believe they're looking forward to going into school tomorrow," remarked Rosemary, after we'd put them both to bed. "But I don't think a couple of days having to keep themselves amused will do them any harm....and Emily did say she was glad they'd come with us, rather than having to stay with the Henriksens."

"If a bit of boredom is the worst they have to put up with in their lives, they'll be fortunate......What did you find out about the Italian production?"

"There didn't seem to be a lot of difference for either Soave or Valdicocce between a good year and a bad year. Generally, the quantities the wine-producers claimed to have produced was marginally lower, but what that means I don't know."

"I suspect we need to talk to one of our wine experts about what we've found. The shippers seem to have imported more foreign wines in a bad year rather than a good one. But, of course, if you had a shortage of cheap red wine, you might just get some Algerian or Spanish plonk to stick in the supermarkets if people couldn't get their usual Valdicocce or Camarolo. You'd need to look in an Italian supermarket or wine shop to know whether the imported wine was actually being re-labelled or not."

"That seems sensible...Otherwise I'm not really sure we can go much further in this direction."

"I agree....We might need to talk it through with Knud Henriksen again and see what he thinks."

"I meant to ask....Did you thank that man who arranged everything for us in Luxembourg?"

"I'll ring him tomorrow....After he met us yesterday, he seemed to make himself scarce. But I'm told that statisticians are a funny bunch......I must say it's nice to be back in our own bed....I know it's not ours strictly speaking...but I've got used to it and I generally sleep well in it."

"Just as long as sleep wasn't the first thing you had on your mind."

VIENNA

Rosemary and I reported back to Knud Henriksen the following morning.

"I guess this may be something which needs to be carried out in the field," he remarked. "But who does that we should consider...Meanwhile, the wine adulteration matter has moved on. My Danish colleagues have been in contact with the Austrian authorities, who were naturally concerned....and extremely embarrassed. They weren't very happy when Erling Jensen told them he'd passed the information on to SEFF and that we were looking at the matter from a wider perspective. But when I spoke to Michael Reznik of the Austrian Zollamt, I explained that we weren't looking to have a public hanging, but we did want to get a fuller idea of what was going on generally in wine market fraud. A couple of hours later he phoned me back and suggested I should go to Vienna and discuss the matter with himself and other interested parties....You understand I know him from the past when we attended CCC meetings."

"CCC?" asked Rosemary.

"Customs Co-operation Council. It can be a bit of a talking shop, but it has done some good work in some areas. I assume you must've had something to do with it, Nick?"

"No," I replied. "There's an international division in C&E that does all that stuff....Don't forget I've been dealing almost entirely with VAT since 1967."

"A pleasure in store for you, no doubt....But I told Michael Reznik, I can't just go swanning off to Vienna for a day or two....I explained that you two were dealing with this matter, so if he and his colleagues wanted to speak to someone, it'd have to be the Storey family."

"And?" said Rosemary.

"And you're invited to meet Reznik and his colleagues in Vienna, ideally in the next fortnight."

"That could be difficult for both of us. We can hardly expect Emily and Sarah to sit around all day long again while we have meetings with these people."

"I would suggest that perhaps just one of you should go, but I believe there are both customs and police aspects to this, so ideally I'd like both of you to go…..Your children could stay with us, of course….But Merete felt they were uncomfortable. They were feeling they had to be on their best behaviour all the time, perhaps…And our Sophie is a little quiet, whereas I guess your two are more…boisterous…..Let me think about this…and I'll come back to you."

"Unfortunately, I think they associate it with the shooting in Riga….It seems as though they fear that every time we go off on our own into some strange city we're going to get shot at."

Rosemary and I decided not to mention the possibility of a visit to Vienna until something had been sorted out.

"I can't see how it'd be less than a couple of nights away," I suggested, as we were travelling into work the following morning, having dropped Emily and Sarah off at their school. "I don't like the idea of a flight at the crack of dawn when you need your wits about you in a meeting with people when you don't know what they're up to. And I never like feeling a meeting is being constrained by having to catch a flight back."

"Knud didn't say whether these Austrians were going to speak to us in English or German. If it's German, there's no point in me going….."

"I guess they were expecting to do it in English, if Henriksen was proposing both of us…..and presumably he has some reason for wanting us both to go."

Henriksen summoned us later the following morning.

"Perhaps I might explain a little more," he began. "It seems to me that the Austrians will want to minimise the impact of this. So I guess Reznik has been put up to reassure me. I reckon they believe that because we've met each other several times and shared a few beers and schnapps on occasions, he can smooth it all away with me. But whatever is said, they'll pick their words carefully. If I just suggested Nick went to Vienna, they'd undoubtedly wish to speak in German and we could hardly refuse. If Rosemary goes, they'll have to speak English and you might find it easier to spot things that don't quite sound right. But Reznik is a Customs guy. He'll be more comfortable dealing with another Customs person...and there'll be the Customs jargon, as well. That's why I was keen for you both to go."

"But...?" interrupted Rosemary.

"But... your children.........Michael Reznik said that though they have a crèche in their offices, your girls were plainly too old...They can't allocate someone to keep them amused while you are meeting Austrian officials, but they could attend the international school in the morning and either have lunch there or meet you for lunch. Your meetings would be in the morning – and you'd be free to do some sightseeing, or take your girls to the Prater, or whatever in the afternoon....He's suggested that if you flew out next Wednesday evening, you could meet them on Thursday and Friday mornings, with the afternoons free with your girls. Then you could stay on for the weekend, if you wished.....Though from previous experience I should tell you that if you were planning to do any shopping, Viennese shops close at noon on Saturday. How does that seem?"

"We need to talk to Emily and Sarah about it. They've only just got back into their routine from our trip to Luxembourg....We'll certainly encourage them, but I don't want to force them to come...They've already had to make new friends since they came here...and though that's probably not a bad thing, I don't want to keep disrupting them."

To my surprise – and Rosemary's too – Emily and Sarah both said they were happy to spend a couple of days in the international school in Vienna. I guess it probably seemed better than days stuck in an office trying to amuse themselves.....and from something I overheard Sarah saying to Emily about koala bears, it was possible that they thought they were going to visit Australia. At least, unlike the notorious "raddle", no-one could say we'd put the idea into their heads!

So it was arranged. We had a quiet weekend and Rosemary and I spent the first days of the following week getting as much detail about adulteration of wine, the Danish case, Austrian vineyards, the Austrian bureaucracy, etc. Though I wanted to do some follow-up work on our visit to Luxembourg, I decided to leave it until after we returned from Vienna. Henriksen's secretary booked our flights and hotels - though we paid for Emily and Sarah's room and all the rooms for the Saturday night. Though SEFF would certainly have paid, I was a puritan about such things.....doubtless some residual effect of my father's view about the corrupt nature of bureaucracies!

The flight took less than two hours and a bus took us into the city centre quite quickly, passing what looked like an immense chemical factory on our way. The Hotel Austria was along an alley off the Fleischmarkt, not far from the Danube and (in the opposite direction) the Stefansdom. It was quiet and conservative, efficient rather than friendly. Fortunately, Emily and Sarah had a small children's annexe next to Rosemary's and my room. And while the receptionist spoke little to the children, he didn't give them the distrustful look I'd seem from time to time in hotels further north. We had sufficient time to do a bit of sight-seeing before dinner. So we walked up the Rotenturmstrasse as far as the Stefansdom and had a wander around inside, without lingering too long. Then we discovered an open area – I'm not sure I'd really call it a square – with a wonderfully ornate baroque memorial to the plague and, more to the children's taste, a café offering ice cream, as well as Viennese coffee and cakes for the grown-ups.

There was a little while before it'd be time to eat so we walked back towards the hotel, as Emily and Sarah wanted to see the Danube. So we walked to Franz-Josefs-Kai and across the

Marienbrucke, along Obere Donaustrasse and back to Schwedenplatz. That was more than enough walking for Sarah, who spent a third of the journey sightseeing from my shoulders. But it gave us all a healthy appetite. We found a local restaurant near the hotel and all of us enjoyed soup with dumplings in it and while the girls had sausages and chips, Rosemary and I had goulash, washed down with a glass of beer. In normal circumstances, I might've tried the local wine – but that seemed inappropriate somehow.

We all went to bed early – though for differing reasons – but woke up refreshed and in plenty of time to enjoy a continental breakfast with excellent coffee. Michael Reznik had arranged for us to be met at the hotel and at 8.30 we were waiting in the lobby, when a large, solid-looking middle-aged man, with light brown spiky hair and a matching moustache appeared, evidently looking for someone. Immediately he spotted us, he came over, moving quite fast for a bulky man.

"You are the Storey family?" he asked in heavily-accented English.

"Yes," I replied. "This is Rosemary, my wife, Emily and Sarah, our daughters, and I'm Nick."

"Good morning to you. I am Michael Reznik. We shall now drive to the Holy Trinity school and then on to the Customs offices, if that is satisfactory to you?"

"Certainly."

As we went outside and got into a beige Mercedes, I realised that, whereas the international school in Brussels was non-denominational, the one here in Vienna was almost certainly Roman Catholic. Though I didn't believe that a couple of days' exposure to popery would have any lasting effect on my daughters, I could almost feel the wave of anger that would've come over my father if he'd heard about this. And the rather undistinguished seventeenth century building which they entered, ushered in by some species of nun, would undoubtedly have appeared secretive and probably 'jesuitical' to him. On the other hand, Emily and Sarah seemed to find it rather exciting – and it was certainly a contrast to the modern building of the international school in Brussels.

We drove on through narrow streets lined with buildings which I guessed were mostly pre-nineteenth century. But as we were still in the "old city", that wasn't perhaps surprising. We drove up an alley into a building which was probably nineteenth century. We parked in a courtyard and entered through a large door in a sort of cloisters running all round the courtyard. It seemed that we didn't need passes and Reznik took us to an old-fashioned lift, with gates as well as the usual doors. We went up two floors, along a corridor which felt more ecclesiastical than bureaucratic, and into a large room, overlooking the courtyard. A table in a brown, heavily-veined wood, in a baroque style, took up about half the space, along with eight chairs made from similar wood, with plush crimson seats. By the door there was a small, marble-topped table, with a jug of coffee, a matching jug of milk and a container of multi-coloured sugar crystals....and a large plate containing a variety of cakes and dried fruit – mostly figs and dates. Standing by them was an elderly, wizened man with a shock of grey hair and only one arm, wearing a white jacket. Evidently, he served the coffee. Just as we entered the room, another man appeared. He was no taller than Rosemary, with a thin, cunning face and dark brown hair, thick on top, but completely shaved from an inch above the top of his ears.

"May I introduce my colleague, Dr Karl Schmiedler," said Reznik. "Dr Schmiedler works for the Austrian Government's Analytical Laboratory Service."

We introduced ourselves and, according to the European customs, all shook hands. We took our coffee and sat down round one corner of the table. A young woman with shoulder-length mid-brown hair and black-rimmed glasses slipped in beside Reznik and took out a notebook. She was not introduced.

"As you have probably been informed by Knud Henriksen, my colleagues and I were concerned to ensure that the EEC

61

Commission were aware of the extent, ramifications and possible implications of the discovery by Danish Customs of diethylene glycol in certain Austrian wines," Reznik began. "We are grateful to you for coming here to meet us. This morning Dr Schmiedler and I will explain the Customs aspects and the testing programme which is undertaken on all Austrian wines, whether exported or consumed within this country. Tomorrow morning, Friedrich Molnar of the Agriculture and Forests Ministry and Stefan Karnegg of the Austrian Wine Growers Union will explain our procedures for dealing with the possible adulteration, misdescription or mislabelling of wines."

"You won't mind if we take notes?" I asked.

"We have no objection to that….But might I first ask why the Service Européenne contre la Fraude Fiscale is interested in this matter? And specifically why it is seen as a matter of interest to the police service?"

"I understand that our Commissioner – Commissioner Giulizzi – agreed to extend the scope of SEFF not long after it started, mainly because it would be difficult to deal with purely fiscal fraud, when the cross-border nature of such fraud would be difficult to disentangle from customs frauds and fraud against the CAP." I was glad I'd heard Gerry Fitzpatrick and Knud Henriksen give this explanation, apparently persuasively, several times in the past.

"The adulteration of wine is linked to CAP fraud," I added.

"And the police interest?"

"In many EEC countries, the police services are involved far more in customs matters than happens in the UK," replied Rosemary. "Our main interest, however, is in the possible involvement of criminals and criminal organisations in cross-border fraud…and in money laundering." She had been required to explain this so often to different people in Interpol that she was word perfect.

"In this case, my interest is whether criminals or criminal organisations have been involved or whether the profits might have been laundered through EEC banks," she continued.

"Well, as far as we are aware, no serious criminals have been involved in the cases of adulterated wine in Austria," replied Reznik. "But perhaps I should explain what has been happening here. Unfortunately we knew nothing about the adulterated wines until our colleagues in Denmark contacted us. As you would expect, we then started a lot of work to find out what the size of the problem was, to prevent further exports of this wine and to determine where any adulterated wine had gone. So far nine wine producers have been identified who have been doing this adulteration. We have prevented over three hectolitres of this wine being exported and identified eight hundred litres which has already been exported – mostly to West Germany and Scandinavia. The process of getting this wine returned and destroyed has been commenced. Because we thought we could trust our wine producers, we've rarely tested exported wine recently. But now we are testing every commercial consignment....As you will understand, the reputation of Austrian wines is fragile. One lapse we might get away with, but if it occurs again, no-one will buy any Austrian wine....even most Austrians."

"So your additional checks have identified some of the nine wine producers who've been adulterating their wine?" I asked.

"We have found six. All from the same region. There are twelve wines concerned – all table wines. About half was destined for export. My colleagues tomorrow will explain what they have done to rectify the position and try to prevent this occurring again."

I wondered where the other three errant wine producers had suddenly vanished to? But perhaps this would be explained later?

"If I may add something," said Schmiedling. "A sample per hundred litres of wine has been required from all those wine producers involved in this matter. A sample per two hundred and fifty litres has been required from all other vineyards throughout Austria. We shall test all of them…and we have also requested that the field staff should undertake random sampling. We are determined that the reputation of Austrian wines should not be put further at risk." His English accent was good, although with a curious Brummie twang.

"What do you propose to do with this information?" asked Reznik.

"You seem to be carrying out what is necessary to identify the adulterated wines that've been exported," I replied. "Our interest is more in making sure that EEC Member States are aware that adulteration with diethylene glycol has occurred and that they may wish to increase the level of sample and what they analyse when they take samples…..I reckon at the moment, they're mainly checking for alcoholic strength rather than what may have been added to the wine….From what I've been told, this type of adulteration would normally be expected only with white wines. Is that your view?"

"I doubt whether there's any reason not to put it in red wine, but I've only ever heard of it in white wines," said Reznik.

"We've been told that the reason for this adulteration was because the grape harvest wasn't good last year and it was necessary to add sweetness and body to the wine. Is that what you've been told?" asked Rosemary.

"Essentially yes. It's a risky thing to do and in a normal year, they would make a profit. But if the wine was so sour and weak, so that customers might not buy it, they could face a tough time. One year they might survive. But two years of poor harvests and some wine-growers would undoubtedly go bankrupt."

"And there's no reason to suppose that there are any serious criminals involved?"

"No. We believe that to be unlikely."

"Where would these wine-growers get this diethylene glycol from? Presumably it might raise eyebrows if they bought it too openly?"

"It's widely used in the production of all manner of things, including polyester resins, polyurethanes, brake fluid, lubricants, wallpaper strippers and products such as skin creams and lotions and deodorants," explained Schmiedling. "Provided it wasn't ordered in the wine-grower's name and was delivered to a warehouse rather than the vineyard, the chemical manufacturer would be none the wiser. And plenty of chemical companies will have stocks of this chemical. AMV, which you will have passed on your way from Schwechat airport, will undoubtedly produce it. It's a hazardous and highly poisonous chemical, of course, so it must be transported in the correct vehicles. So the containers used by the wine producers must've been the proper sort."

"How much of it would be in a litre of wine?"

"A tiny amount. Otherwise people drinking the wine would be affected by it."

"So presumably it would've been purchased in quite small quantities?"

"I guess so."

"Wouldn't that be unusual? When it's used to make industrial or consumer products, presumably quite large quantities may be used. But the wine-growers must've needed no more than a litre or so, if that. Wouldn't a purchase so small seem rather odd to the manufacturer?"

"I...I don't know.....I'm not sure anyone has asked...."

"Would it be expensive?"

"Not especially......I have no idea how much it costs, but there's no reason to suppose it's expensive."

"Are you suggesting that there was something untoward about the purchase of the diethylene glycol by the wine-growers?" demanded Reznik.

"I'm just following a line of questioning," replied Rosemary. "It seems odd that a chemical that would normally be bought in large quantities, presumably by manufacturers, was sold in what seems likely to have been quite a small quantity. Shouldn't the manufacturer have been suspicious? What sort of container would they have used? Would you really have the right sort of container for such a small amount of this highly poisonous stuff? Did the manufacturer ask what the stuff was being used for? And if not, why not?"

There followed a rather stunned silence. While it was reasonable to expect Austrian Customs to be concentrating on preventing the export of adulterated wine and their colleagues in the Agriculture Ministry to be identifying the culprits & getting their hands on all the wine, surely someone should've been looking at where the diethylene glycol had come from?

"We don't know about that," replied Reznik, staring at Rosemary from under half-closed eyelids. "Is it of great importance?"

"It seems to me that your problem in dealing with wine getting adulterated," Rosemary replied, "is that you have to deal with it after it's already happened….And you can never be sure whether some of the wine hasn't slipped past your controls. For instance, if I put this adulterated wine in a large chemical container and called it diethylene glycol, with all the chemical hazard notices and the export documents looked all right, would you check it and sample the contents?"

"Probably not."

"So it might be safer to catch people at it before they've put the diethylene glycol into the wine. If you could identify how it was getting to the wine-growers and whether it was possible to pick it up at that stage of the operation, it should make your life a lot easier.….I doubt whether the manufacturers want to be seen to be supplying a chemical which is used to adulterate Austrian wines and damage their reputation internationally."

Silence was resumed.

"Would you mind it greatly, if we adjourned for half an hour or so, while we consult some colleagues," said Reznik, not looking at us in the friendliest of ways. "You've given us matters to think about and we would do well to address them……I will arrange for fresh coffee to be brought to you."

With that they departed.

"You did that extraordinarily well," I said to Rosemary, giving her a hug and a long kiss.

"I was just doing what you always do – follow where the path seems to lead....I don't think they liked it very much."

"I'm not sure how often they get put under pressure by a woman at least ten years younger than them." (And I didn't need to add that when wearing a short skirt, she tended to look ten years younger than she was).

"I'm not sure how important it is for our side of things – but it seems sensible to me to try and cut off the chemical at source, rather than once it's got to the vineyards or wherever they make the wine."

The one-armed man re-appeared with a fresh pot of coffee, followed by a middle-aged, scrawny woman in a dark uniform, with a tray of cups, saucers, a jug of milk, etc. He poured out our coffee adeptly and silently, leaving us to add cream and/or sugar. We sipped at the coffee and talked about whether what we'd seen of Vienna so far matched our expectations. We realised that our only knowledge of the city came from "The Third Man", made in the immediate post-war period and shot in black and white. We were just discussing whether we'd hear any zither music, when Reznik and Schmiedling reappeared with a man of about fifty, with stiff, grey hair and matching moustache in what I guessed was police uniform.

"May I present Colonel-Inspector Kravelitz," began Reznik. "He commands the group of our state police which deals with commercial and financial fraud. In view of the way our meeting has developed, it seemed sensible to invite him to join us....Unfortunately, he has only limited English, so Frau Dremmler will translate."

Frau Dremmler was evidently the name of the note-taker. Colonel-Inspector Kravelitz glared at us with barely-concealed annoyance. I guess his schedule had just been messed around with and he evidently wasn't best pleased.

"Director Reznik has informed me of the nature of your questions," said Kravelitz, in the Austrian version of German which sounded rather odd to my ears. Frau Dremmler translated for our benefit. I decided there was no reason to tell them I could understand what he was saying – not only because that might tempt them to cut Rosemary out of the conversation, but also so I could tell how accurately the translation reflected the original. "I believe you should understand that our primary concern has been to ensure that this unfortunate occurrence should receive as little unwelcome publicity as possible. The potential damage to the reputation of Austrian wine – and therefore to an important element of the Austrian economy – is considerable. It has therefore been considered in the public interest that as few as possible should be aware of what has occurred. So examining staff and records in several chemical manufacturers has not been considered advisable." He stared hard at Rosemary, who wouldn't have been the Rosemary I knew, if she hadn't continued to return his stare.

"What you do here in Austria is entirely up to you," she replied. "We're not trying to tell you how to go about your business. What I have been trying to do is to see whether the problem could be repeated and whether there were ways of preventing it from happening, by getting advance warning of the purchase of diethylene glycol by wine producers."

"It would surely be possible to obtain the necessary information without revealing the nature of the problem," I added. "There must be a number of legitimate reasons why the Austrian authorities might wish to examine the sales of diethylene glycol by companies that manufacture it. From what we've been told, the small purchase that would've been required by these wine producers should stick out like a sore thumb...."

"And suppose it doesn't? What then?" demanded Reznik.

"You have a problem. It's possible that the manufacturer whose books you're examining wasn't the source of the diethylene glycol used by the wine producers. But it may be it was sold off the books. If I was looking at the matter, I'd want to know whether it'd be possible to do that and whether it'd be possible to pick it up."

"You are experienced in police procedures?" demanded Kravelitz, glaring at me for a change.

"No. But I've been heavily involved in devising procedures for collecting value-added tax from businesses of all shapes and sizes. Working out how to detect and deal with tax evasion has been an important part of that."

"Perhaps you do not realise that the wine growers have significant political importance in Austria," observed Reznik, while Kravelitz rumbled, like a shortly-to-explode volcano. "There is no political congruence between them and our large chemical manufacturers.

"I understand that the public interest often coincides with political convenience," I replied, sounding like an undiplomatic echo of my father. "But if we look at this from the point of view of the EEC countries, who I suppose I represent, they might well be nervous that though you have closed off many avenues for those who might wish to continue to export adulterated wine, some remain open."

"So what will you suggest, young man? The EEC will ban our wines unless we carry out procedures which you require?" Kravelitz exploded.

"I think that SEFF would wish to assess the risks of not keeping tabs on the chemical manufacturers against the work you have already undertaken to tighten up your controls," said Rosemary, who, I guessed, feared that I was getting into an argument with Kravelitz that would generate more heat than light.

"What in God's name is SEFF?"

Rosemary explained.

"I can understand why the EEC would wish to take this stance," said Reznik. "But from where we sit, it feels like a pistol pointed at our heads."

"We should remember what started this off," Rosemary reminded him. "Adulterated wine from Austria."

As this was translated, Kravelitz gave a snort like an angry rhinocerous. If he'd been summoned to overawe Rosemary, it wasn't working – apart from being based on a complete misconception.

"An error is made – and the EEC intends to humiliate Austria!" exclaimed Kravelitz.

"I don't believe either of us has said that," I replied. "But the EEC necessarily has to consider its consumers.....and you will recall, you invited us here. All we have done is indicate that there may be a loophole in the controls you've instituted. You could hardly expect us to ignore that in our report back to Knud Henriksen and our Commissioner."

"The point I wish to make is the one about the speck in another's eye and the beam in one's own!" continued Kravelitz, almost shouting. "Haven't the bloody EEC not realised that the West Germans get up to this sort of thing....and the bloody Italians. Where do you think our wine-growers got the idea from? And all that's nothing compared to the vast quantities of Italian wines that aren't what they say on the labels. You buy Camarolo or Valdicocce. You think it's from northern Italy. It could've come from anywhere...Italy or north Africa...or the Balkans....At least half our wine industry isn't in the hands of criminal organisations!"

"That's an extremely interesting statement," replied Rosemary. "But what evidence do you have to back it up?"

"Plenty," retorted Kravelitz. "I don't have it with me. I wasn't expecting to attend this meeting this morning. Evidence can be made available – but not this instant."

"We would be happy to see it. We're not trying to single out Austria. If there are frauds going on elsewhere, particularly in EEC countries, we are just as keen to identify them and tackle them."

"Very well. How long are you staying here?"

"We have meetings tomorrow morning and fly back on Sunday afternoon."

"I will see whether something can be arranged for tomorrow."

"It'll have to be fitted in during the morning. As Mr Reznik can explain, our children have come with us and we will have them with us in the afternoons."

Kravelitz gave her a look of disbelief mixed with what looked like contempt. I felt like reminding him that we could make life a lot more difficult for him than he could for us, if he continued with his unpleasant attitude, but I didn't want to let SEFF...or, more accurately, Knud Henriksen and Gerry Fitzpatrick...down. So I did what I usually did in such circumstances and held my tongue.

"Very well then..." Kravelitz stood up, as if to depart.

"You do understand, I hope," Rosemary said, "that this must be the sort of evidence which could hold water in a court of law. Allegations based on hearsay or inadmissible evidence won't be worth much...and you've made very serious allegation, Colonel-Inspector Kravelitz."

He looked as though he was about to retort, but instead just turned on his heels and left the room. Reznik and Schmiedling looked at each other and almost shrugged their shoulders. Certainly the temperature in the room returned to tepid.

But that was pretty much all we had to discuss with them. Just after midday, Frau Dremmler led us down to an awaiting car, which took us to the international school. As we pulled up, Emily and Sarah emerged from inside the building. Armed with a street map which our hotel had given us, we headed for the centre of the city and somewhere to have lunch.

"How did you get on this morning?" Rosemary asked Emily and Sarah.

"It was different," replied Emily. "The nuns did a lot of praying...sometimes in Latin, I think....and in my class we spent the morning doing arithmetic and then the rest of my class learnt German, while the nuns let me do some drawing...so I drew the classroom and then the view from the window. I hope they'll let me bring them home tomorrow....But they said they wanted to look at them this afternoon."

"It was quite strict compared to our school," added Sarah. "We all had to do writing practice for hours. I was copying lots of words I didn't understand...Some had two dots over some of the letters....But playtime was nice...and then I got to play a wooden recorder...It sounded really nice...I'd like to get one like that for my birthday...."

"But you're happy to go there again tomorrow?" asked Rosemary.

"Yes," replied Emily. "It was interesting for a change."

"Yes," said Sarah more doubtfully. "But I hope they'll let me play the recorder again."

Apparently the nuns had told Emily that while we were in Vienna, we shouldn't miss Schoenbrunn palace and the Belvedere. We could get there by tram and bus. So first we made our way on to the Ring and took a tram and then a bus out to Schoenbrunn, which was huge and impressive – even to the children. But they preferred going up to the Gloriette, Sarah travelling part of the way on my shoulders. They were also fascinated by the large naked statues in the Neptunenbrunnen. But on the whole, they said they preferred the Belvedere, with its less formal architecture and the statues which contained parts of women, eagles and lions. We didn't go inside any of the buildings, but walked from the Lower Belvedere to a park near the Karlskirche, where there was a café which provided large ice creams mixing several flavours for the children and coffee and cake for their parents. Afterwards, we dragged Emily and Sarah into the Karlskirche – for our benefit rather than theirs, it has to be said. Then we found a tram that would take us back along the Ring, getting glimpses of various large formal buildings on our way, as well as a building which from a distance looked like some sort of modernist orthodox church, but the street map informed us was the Sezession building. We got off the tram near a huge,

72

Gothic cathedral, which the map told us was the Votivkirche. It looked interesting, but Emily and especially Sarah were tiring rapidly. I realised we were still a long walk from our hotel and we got on another tram in the right direction, but I misread the map and we ended up getting off and heading for the wrong end of Fleischmarkt. As far as Rosemary and I were concerned, this particular cloud had a silver lining when we came upon the beautiful church of St Maria im Gestade at the top of a steep flight of steps, a deceptively simple church with an amazingly decorated rounded tower and a restrained Gothic interior. Why was it, Rosemary and I wondered, that in so many cities we'd visited, it wasn't the big, famous cathedrals that we liked best, but the smaller, more intimate churches like St Maria im Gestade here in Vienna and Sainte-Chapelle in Paris?

By the time we got back to the hotel, we were all tired. Even Emily had succumbed to fatigue and was on my shoulders, while Rosemary was carrying Sarah. We slumped in the bar of the hotel and the girls had fizzy lemonade and Rosemary and I had tea, having decided that if we had any more coffee we wouldn't need the stairs to get back to our room. After a rest in our room, we ate dinner in the hotel, as it provided straightforward food for children and, inevitably, Schnitzel for Rosemary and me. But it had felt like a long day and we went to bed early.

Tiredness didn't stop Rosemary remarking, shortly before she went to sleep, with her head on my shoulder as usual,

"If Colonel-Inspector Kravelitz has good evidence about wine fraud, as he said, why hasn't he done anything about it?"

I thought briefly about it and then slept.

We felt refreshed enough in the morning to shower together and were almost dressed by the time Emily and Sarah appeared in our room. It was about 7.15.

"We're starving!" exclaimed Sarah. "Aren't you ready for breakfast yet?"

"Don't you think you should knock before you come into someone else's room?" suggested Rosemary.

"Sorry," replied Emily. "We forgot….But we woke up feeling ravenous."

We finished dressing and went downstairs to have breakfast. Fortunately, chambermaids always knock, I reminded myself. Though whether I'd be more embarrassed by an unknown chambermaid or my children finding Rosemary and me naked on the bed or in the shower, I wasn't at all sure. Perhaps a reminder to keep doors locked!

The car arrived again at 8.30, with a young man in it. He looked about seventeen, blond, thin, thin-faced and evidently half-asleep. He didn't tell us his name, just checked who we were and led us to the car. At first we followed the first part of the previous morning's journey to the international school. But then we drove out of the old city and along the Ring past the Karlskirche and the Stadtpark, and back into the old city by the Stubentor. Close by we drove into the courtyard of what I thought was probably another nineteenth century building. We got out of the car and the young man led us to the inevitable entrance lobby, where we were given day passes and then were led up a flight of stairs that felt like the servants' staircase, to an elegant room furnished in eighteenth century style, with suitable portraits and rural scenes along the walls, a large table that could take well over twenty people round it and at least two dozen chairs. As we entered the room from one end, two men appeared from a door at the other end.

"Good morning," said the first, a plump, bald man with a merry face and a dark beard. "I am called Friedrich Molnar. I am the Director responsible for viniculture in the Agriculture and Forests Ministry. May I introduce my colleague, Stefan Karnegg, General Secretary of the Austrian Wine Growers Union." He spoke English with only a faint accent.

Karnegg was about my height, a spare man in his late fifties, with a military bearing and the face and eyes of an extremely cold fish. He nodded by way of introduction. I wouldn't have been surprised if he hadn't clicked his heels together as well.

Rosemary and I introduced ourselves. I wondered whether Kravelitz was. But perhaps the pleasure of meeting him was being deferred until later, while he gathered his evidence together? However, at this stage, we were asked to explain our interest in the wine adulteration "matter", which we did.

"I understand that the Austrian Government invited representatives from SEFF to come to Vienna," I continued. "So it'd be helpful if you could tell us what you wished to say to us."

Molnar then held forth at some length about the hitherto unblemished reputation of Austrian wines, how they were an important part of the Austrian economy and how the adulteration of a few wines was a regrettable and unique lapse from grace. Karnegg nodded occasionally in support, but said nothing. Molnar went on to explain how widespread publicity about the adulteration would be highly damaging to the reputation of Austrian wines and therefore to a significant sector of the Austrian economy. I replied that we understood and that SEFF's interest was more in identifying and tackling frauds affecting EEC countries as a whole than making an example of the Austrian wine industry, but that plainly we were interested to see what the Austrians were doing to prevent it happening again. Molnar repeated much of what Reznik had said the previous day about Customs controls and internal inspections.

"Who inspects wine production?" I asked.

"The Ministry has a number of inspectors," Molnar replied.

"Do they take samples of wine regularly so that it can be analysed?"

"Up to now, it hasn't been routine. But in order to protect the reputation of Austrian wines, samples will regularly be obtained and sent to the Analytical Laboratory Service."

"Are you doing anything to check whether potential additives to wine are being sent to wine producers – or perhaps by checking their records and premises for such things?"

"I understand you have an interest in such matters. At present, all I can tell you is that we are working on plans. We are uncertain

75

whether our inspectors have the legal authority to search premises for such products where there are no grounds for suspicion. Legislation may be required."

"Is the EEC intending to ban Austrian wines?" asked Karnegg.

"Not as far as I'm aware. When we were asked to meet you and your colleagues here in Vienna, there was no suggestion that a ban was being considered."

"But depending on the nature of what you report back, one might be considered?"

"You and your colleague have told us about what you are doing, both to track down the wines which were adulterated and also to prevent it happening again. We shall report that back to our Director and Deputy Director. I can't speak for them, of course, but I'd be surprised if they recommended banning imports of Austrian wine...Of course, individual EEC countries may have a different view. I would think it's more likely that certain EEC Member States may decide to do their own sampling of imported Austrian wines. It seems likely that at present they're more interested in the alcoholic strength of the wines than whether the wine contains any additives. I'd expect them to undertake a wider chemical analysis....But I guess they might wish to do that on wine imports generally, rather than specifically Austrian wines."

"That's not an entirely helpful response."

"I'm sorry about that. But we can only report back accurately what we've been told. It'll be for others to take any decisions....But I can assure you that we've no axe to grind and that we shall report accurately what you and your colleagues have told us."

"Axe to grind?"

"I'm sorry....We have no interest or position in regard to the wine market or Austrian wines. We are neutral about the position of Austrian wines compared to wines from other countries. Being British, there is no significant wine production to support. And we have no links with any EEC or other wine producers and we've spoken to no-one from any of them."

"I gained the impression from reports of your meeting yesterday that you were somewhat hostile."

"I believe that relates to a point which we raised about controlling the diethylene glycol which was used to adulterate these wines. It seemed to us that there was a possible loophole in your controls. Assuming you carry out frequent checks of wine exports, if I was a wine producer who had adulterated my wine, I'd describe it as something else in the export documentation and, unless Austrian export controls are a lot more intensive than British ones, I could reasonably expect not to get my shipments examined. But if you could control sales of diethylene glycol to non-industrial users, that would do a lot to cut off the possibilities of adulteration at source....or so it seemed to us. I didn't see that making this point was hostile. Indeed, it was intended to be helpful."

Karnegg snorted.

"I can see where you are going....I suppose we have tended to regard our wine producers as being as careful of the reputation of Austrian wines as we are here in this Ministry....But I suppose when you fear bankruptcy, you do whatever is necessary," commented Molnar. "But I believe my colleague may wish to add something."

"I believe that Colonel-Inspector Kravelitz mentioned the fact that not only do other wine-producing countries adulterate their wines, but they also mislabel them, often claiming wines from other countries as their own...and that includes several EEC countries," declared Karnegg, in his clipped accent that suggested even more to me a military background. "If unfair publicity were to appear about Austrian wines, we might feel obliged to counter with information about illegal practices regarding EEC wines."

"That would be your decision," I replied. "But I believe you'd have to be extremely careful in what you said. Making any sort of allegation without strong evidence could backfire on you – especially if anyone decided to sue you."

"And I'm not sure that if the EEC decided to make public the fact that some Austrian wines had been adulterated that it'd be unfair, as you put it," added Rosemary. "Surely, they would merely be reporting facts which you can hardly deny."

"I believe that Colonel-Inspector Kravelitz will be providing you with evidence..." retorted Karnegg. "But where do you think the Austrian wine producers got the idea to use diethylene glycol from? Our wine producers are extremely conservative. They've been using the same grapes and the same blends for generations. They wouldn't have thought of something like this in decades. They got it from the West Germans. Both Rhenish and Mosel wines have been adulterated in this way in previous years. If you can get hold of a table wine called "Weissenrosen der Mosel" from 1966, there's a good chance that chemical analysis will show it has diethylene glycol in it."

"I guess there might still be some bottles lying around somewhere, but I believe I'm right in thinking that table wines like that are intended to be drunk within two or three years," I replied. "That doesn't mean that I deny what you're saying is true, but unless there is actual evidence, your allegations remain just allegations," I replied.

"Do you know why the West Germans did that? Or why other EEC countries mislabel wines, as you suggested earlier?" asked Rosemary.

"In the case of Rhenish and Mosel wines, it'd be a poor harvest – the same excuse used by our wine producers," replied Karnegg. "As for the mislabelling, it's a matter of quantity. If demand for, say, the Italian wine Camarolo, increases, it may be impossible to meet it with grapes from that region. It's not a wine of such quality that you could double the price and people would still buy it. No Italian would touch the stuff at that price and it'd lose out to competitors in external markets. So in order to get the extra profits, more wine has to be provided. If you look at the ownership of Italian wine production, you'd quickly find some very shady people involved. These things may look like cooperatives, but who owns the land and who owns the production? Not the names of the producers you see on the labels, but who is the real owner? Get to the bottom of that and you'll understand why we feel so aggrieved that the EEC are singling Austrian wines out for this treatment."

"As I said, the EEC has done nothing so far. Indeed, instead of just setting up additional border controls on Austrian wines, we were asked to come here to meet you and your colleagues to see what you had to say. We've already started to take a broader look at the whole wine market, but as I must keep reminding you, even though claims about what goes in the wine market may be entirely justified, but we can't do anything without sufficient evidence," I replied.

"We have felt that you were unnecessarily hostile."

"As I've already said, we identified what seemed to us to be a loophole in how you were proposing to deal with this problem. We could've kept silent and reported that back to the EEC. Instead, we've been open with you, so you have the opportunity to do something about it. It has certainly not been our intention to be hostile."

I felt like saying that when the Austrian wine industry had been caught with its pants down, it was a little rich to call us hostile for trying to help them pull them back up again. But it appeared that Karnegg had shot his bolt and returned to his former disgruntled silence. I felt I could've made a good case that if anyone had been displaying hostility, it was him.

Fortunately, at this point an attendant with more coffee and cakes appeared and Molnar, evidently trying to lower the temperature, asked us about what we'd seen of Vienna while we'd been here and what we thought of it. Just as we were finishing Colonel-Inspector Kravelitz came in, carrying a large leather briefcase. I hoped it had some definite evidence in it. If what he said was at the level of Karnegg's intervention, it wouldn't get us very far......and we would probably be criticised for being obdurate.

I wondered whether Karnegg and he would make common cause, but as Kravelitz refused a cup of coffee, Karnegg downed his and made his excuses and left. I wondered whether Molnar might not follow suit, but I realised he was technically our host - and what Kravelitz was going to raise was as relevant to him as it was to us.

"You wished to see some evidence of EEC countries labelling wines as coming under a particular description or country of origin when in fact they come from somewhere else," he began. "I have brought some documents with me that show three instances. The first concerns two wine producers in the region of Camarolo in Northern Italy – Ceresini and Greffon. In 1972, their vineyards in the denominated Camarolo region produced 2,200 or so litres of wine between them. Yet the wines sold in Italy or exported amounted to nearly three thousand litres. The difference came from mostly Spanish wine imported through Genoa and about a fifth from vineyards which they own in Southern Italy. I have here the documents signed by various functionaries which show the production of Ceresini and Greffon within the Camarolo DOC region and records of sales within Italy and exports – mostly to the United Kingdom. I have set out the calculations on a separate sheet....Please examine them."

We did so and could certainly confirm that his calculations were correct. The documents seemed genuine enough, although they were photocopies.

"Then I have a separate set of documents involving Falcoberti and Ceresini in relation to Valdicocce. This region is next to Camarolo. You will see that the same thing occurred here, also in 1972."

We examined the documents, which told the same story. It seemed that around a thousand litres of wine that wasn't Valdicocce had been sold as such.

"Finally, a different EEC country – France. In 1970, the Burgundy wine of Lastier-Couvrou, one of the major vineyards of the famed Cote d'Or, there was an incident of contamination of wine at the fermentation stage, causing them to lose about a third of their wine. They replenished their stock with a table wine from southern France, blending it with the rest of the wine. You will see the relevant documents here."

Rosemary and I looked at them. Again, they were photocopies of various records, but it seemed clear from copies of the vineyard records and various invoices that what Kravelitz had said had indeed occurred."

"Are you satisfied that Austria is by no means the only country to have broken the rules?" demanded Kravelitz triumphantly.

"That certainly seems like good evidence of fraud," I replied. "But why hasn't the Austrian Government done anything about it?"

"Politics, I imagine," replied Molnar. "You shouldn't forget that Austria may become interested in joining the EEC and we wouldn't want the Italians as our implacable enemies who might veto our entry. If something like this got out, it could have a damaging effect on Italian wine exports....and perhaps on the reputation of European wines as a whole. You are aware, I'm sure, that there is increasing competition from the USA, Australia and South Africa. So you will understand that to an extent, European wine-producing countries have something of a common interest. Indeed, I suspect that if your organisation wasn't headed by an Irishman and a Dane, but by a Frenchman and an Italian, your enquiries wouldn't even have been started."

"I can understand that. But as our enquiry has started, would it be possible for us to have copies of these documents? "

"I am afraid not," replied Kravelitz. "These documents were acquired in what I might term an unorthodox manner...and for that reason, we could not allow them to be disclosed further."

"And presumably for that reason they could not be brought before a court," observed Rosemary.

"Indeed."

It seemed that was all the evidence which he prepared to offer us. So the meeting broke up at about half past eleven. We weren't due to collect Emily and Sarah from the international school for another hour. On foot, it was no more than twenty minutes away, I realised. So we explained that we'd make our own way there and were escorted out of the building and walked towards the centre of the city until we found a congenial place to have some coffee, true Viennese coffee, close to the Palffy palace, the café - inevitably - being called the Café Palffy.

"At least they didn't seem to feel the need to follow us," observed Rosemary, trying to sip the coffee through the thick cream.

"Is that why you're trying to disguise yourself with a moustache?" I said. "Why would they want to follow us anyway?"

"Where do you think those documents came from?" she asked, wiping the cream off her upper lip.

"I hadn't really thought too much about that...I suppose from some smugglers or criminals who gave them that stuff in return for leniency?"

"That might be the source. But my bet is it was their secret service. I reckon any country that wants to join the EEC would like to have a few aces up their sleeves. Think how complicated the negotiations were for Britain to enter. There were all sorts of things we wanted – special deals, special protection and that sort of thing. Some of those things mattered to all the EEC countries, but some only to some of them. And it all ended up in a great compromise which probably nobody liked very much. Supposing the Austrians expect the Italians to be difficult about something. If they need to, they've got this stuff which they can show the Italians – in private, of course – to ensure that they don't put up too many obstacles. And they don't want it out in the open at this stage, because once it's out in the open, it's no use as a bargaining lever."

"That's very clever of you! It certainly sounds right. And, of course, if we don't have any documents, we can't say anything publicly for fear of being sued."

"Exactly."

"But why should they follow us?"

"They'd obviously done their homework on us and on SEFF. But when Molnar mentioned 'the Irishman and the Dane', I wondered why they didn't mention that our Commissioner is Italian. I wondered whether they might think that Giulizzi had put Fitzgerald and Henriksen up to find out whether it was possible to identify Italian wine frauds – and particularly whether the Austrians had anything on them."

"They plainly don't know Gerry or Knud very well then. Or their relationship with Giulizzi and Paolitti."

"And if they are following us, they're going to have a rather dull time."

"I hope not. I hope Emily and Sarah have been told some other places we should visit."

"But perhaps some that involve rather less walking! Emily and Sarah were exhausted yesterday evening…and my feet were quite sore…I didn't really bring shoes for walking all over the place."

"Would you like a piggyback over to the international school?"

"And you say I smirk!"

We got to the international school a couple of minutes late, not least because we hadn't given ourselves enough time to get across town when we needed to consult the street-map several times. The moment we arrived, Emily and Sarah rushed out of the door.

"Did you have a nice morning?" asked Rosemary.

"Yes," both replied.

"But I prefer our school at home," added Emily. "It's more fun. The nuns seem very serious here…and they forgot to give me the pictures I drew yesterday."

"I got to play the recorder again," said Sarah. "I really want one like that for my birthday."

As they were hungry, we fund a nearby café and had pizzas and ice cream.

"Where did they suggest you should go this afternoon?" I asked Emily and Sarah.

"They said we should go to the Prater. There's a giant big wheel there," replied Sarah.

"They told me that we should look at the Hofburg and look in a museum with a funny name nearby," added Emily. "It was a long name and began with a K."

I looked in the street-map.

"The Kunst-Historisches Museum? Was that it?"

"That sounds like it. It's got loads and loads of interesting things there, lots belonging to the kings who used to be here called the Hapsburgs."

"From the stuff on the back of the map, it looks as though the museum is open on Saturday and Sunday......and the Prater is too......But the shops close at midday tomorrow. So if we wanted to do any shopping, we should probably do it this afternoon and do this sightseeing tomorrow and Sunday morning," suggested Rosemary.

"I hope we can find a music shop," said Sarah.

"Oh, I thought you might be interested in getting a dirndl and the other clothes that Austrian children wear?" I remarked.

"What are those?" asked Emily.

"We walked past a shop with children's clothes in on our way here. I'll show you."

Unsurprisingly, they were horrified at the idea of wearing traditional Austrian girls' clothing. But we found the streets where the shops were and bought a few items for them and an unusual dress for Rosemary. I traded her suggestion of lederhosen for a leather belt. And as we walked back from the tram which dropped us near the Stefansdom, we spotted a large music shop which sold not only sheet music and LPs, but also a variety of instruments, including nice wooden recorders - ranging from Moeck at over a thousand Schillings to ones we could afford. So while Rosemary distracted Sarah, I bought one.

The rest of our time in Vienna was pleasant and uneventful. We had an enjoyable time at the Prater for much of Saturday, the highlight of which was a family trip on the giant wheel. On Sunday morning we spent just over an hour in the Kunst-Historisches Museum. It was enough time to sample the amazing riches there without getting sated. Then it was back to the airport and home to Brussels, in time for dinner and an early night....or in Rosemary's and my case, early to bed.

THE POSSIBILITIES OF CAP AUDIT

"So what did you think of Vienna?" asked Knud Henriksen, when he met Rosemary and me the following lunch time.

"It wasn't really what we expected," I replied. "I was expected something out of *'The Third Man'*, but plainly the city has rebuilt and prospered since then."

"And it's in colour," added Rosemary with the faintest of smirks. "But for a city which seemed quite relaxed, the people we met were far from that.....generally unfriendly, defensive – even quite aggressive on occasions."

"I suppose they have the reputation of an important sector of their economy to protect," observed Henriksen. "But I'm surprised they were discourteous."

"They may have misread the purpose of our visit," I replied. "But they also seem to believe they have several aces up their sleeves – evidence of wines being relabelled in Italy and France – and they also claimed that the Austrian wine-producers got the idea of using diethylene glycol to improve poor wine from the West Germans."

"It's easy to make accusations. Did they provide any evidence to back up their claims?"

"Yes. In the form of photocopies of various documents. They appeared to be genuine, but they wouldn't let us take copies away with us."

"Assuming the documents are genuine, we reckon the Austrians are holding them as a bargaining counter if the EEC make a big thing about the adulterated Austrian wine...They claimed that they'd come by the documents in – and I quote – 'an unorthodox manner'...." Rosemary continued.

"So it's more in the nature of political than judicial evidence," Henriksen concluded.

"But I did note down as much detail as I could," said Rosemary. "But Nick and I aren't sure where we should go with it. We certainly don't think it's worthwhile bringing to the attention of the Italian or French authorities. While what the French wine-producers did might have slipped past the French authorities, we can't see how the Italians didn't know and go along with it."

"And getting any evidence requires operating in an 'unorthodox manner', which presumably means illegal..."

"And probably undertaken by the Austrian security service."

"I was going to say that you two are known for using unorthodox methods – but self-evidently, you don't act illegally...and neither you nor SEFF have the ability secret service people have to get your hands on material others wish to keep secret."

"But if that sort of thing is going on, it goes against the whole idea of the EEC," I remarked. "It creates unfair competition and lets down all those who want laws and regulations applied the same in every EEC country."

"Well, you know what they say about the olive belt..." said Henriksen. "And we have to remember SEFF's remit...."

"But that's an excuse.....It seems to me the EEC is in exactly the same position as the Austrians...only the EEC scandal hasn't happened yet. But if we make waves about the Austrian's adulterating their wine, you can bet they'll retaliate – and then what'll happen to the reputation of EEC wines?" observed Rosemary.

"There's another aspect," I added. "I don't really understand the CAP properly, but I'll bet there are a series of subsidies and export refunds that are presumably being abused by this sort of cheating.....and isn't that part of SEFF's remit?"

"Oh hell! You're probably right!" exclaimed Henriksen. "You'd better speak to Conor O'Leary. He isn't technically our

CAP expert, but he knows how it all works – and our CAP expert is Henri Kervran. He's a good man, and a Breton – but he's still French and his first instinct will be to protect the interests of France....and as seconded National Experts, none of you have any institutional loyalty to the Commission anyway."

"I hope he may be able to help us work out what we can do," said Rosemary. "I can see that we ought to be doing something. It's just I'm not at all certain what we can do."

We'd been discussing what we'd learnt from our visit to Vienna earlier and had reached the same conclusion. Though there was probably a fair amount of fraud going on in the wine market, we couldn't see how we – or anyone from SEFF for that matter – could get hold of any evidence without some sort of cooperation from the relevant national authorities. And given that the Italians had almost certainly connived at the Camarolo and Valdicocce frauds, why would they wish to cooperate with us? And whatever our views about crooks getting away with things and a preparedness to bend the rules sometimes, illegal entry to buildings and stealing or copying documents were several steps beyond where we were willing to go.

My knowledge of the Common Agricultural Policy - known almost universally as the CAP - was intermittent, Rosemary's virtually non-existent. When it was explained to me, I remembered how it worked for perhaps a week, then my understanding faded away. If I had been required to deal with it on a daily basis, it would undoubtedly have stuck, but I had avoided it so far in my career and lived in hope of continuing to do so.

Conor O'Leary shared a room with Giuliano Gozzoli's successor, a Customs expert from Livorno, called Andrea di Pietro. Plainly we couldn't hold a conversation about how CAP worked in regard to the wine market in front of him. It was already possible that our interest in wine fraud had got to his and Kervan's ears – but this was still in the context of adulterated wines, rather than mislabelling or wine frauds more generally. But we'd got into the habit of having lunch in the Commission restaurant either together or with a colleague or two. So inviting O'Leary to join us for lunch the following day wouldn't appear unusual.

"Essentially the CAP was a bargain between the West Germans and the French, so they say," O'Leary explained in his soft Irish accent. "The Germans got free trade for their industry while the French retained protection for their farmers. It's a simple system that can get very complicated in the details. Basically, farmers get a subsidy for growing food, keeping beasts and producing milk for instance. Mostly production is subject to quotas. So, we Irish and you Brits have quotas for the total amount of milk we're able to produce. Any surplus gets poured away, though if it's turned into milk powder and can be stored, the Commission may arrange for it to be stored and sold on the world market at the right price. In some cases, farmers are paid subsidies not to grow produce. Where there's over-production, there are incentives to let the land grow fallow. For example, in certain parts of the EEC, vines are supposed to be grubbed up and production stopped – and farmers are paid to do it. But for many goods, if prices drop too far, the Commission buy up produce at a guaranteed price, so that farmers don't suffer serious losses. There are also subsidies for produce being exported outside the EEC....And, of course, to prevent currency fluctuations distorting the market, each day exchange rates for CAP goods are announced by the Commission for all the currencies of the Member States. And when you qualified for a subsidy or some form of export rebate will be affected by what CAP exchange rates were in force at that time. This can determine when produce gets exported."

"So if I make wine, I get a subsidy for growing it – or possibly for pulling up some or all of my vines and not growing it. Who's supposed to check that I don't just claim both subsidies and never get rid of the vines?" I asked.

"The local tax authorities or whoever on behalf of FEOGA…."

"FEOGA?" asked Rosemary.

"It's short for Fonds Européen d'Orientation et de Garantie Agricole. They're the part of the Commission that run all the subsidies, export rebates, exchange rates and so on for the CAP."

"Do they have any people on the ground themselves?" I asked.

"I believe they might have the odd inspector around. I can't say I've ever come across them at home. But I guess they rely on the authorities in the Member State and whatever checks the EEC Auditors undertake…..And those guys are pretty thorough…."

"But, as auditors, presumably they're looking exclusively at paper records. They wouldn't go out and check whether a vineyard that was supposed to have pulled up its vines actually had done so?"

"I wouldn't think they'd do that."

"And what'd happen if the EEC over-produced wine?"

"I guess it might be poured away. I suppose it could be converted into vinegar or even used in the production of denatured alcohol…But there'd probably be difficulties with the firms that produce denatured industrial alcohol. In theory it could be stored….a wine lake next to the butter mountain!"

"Do these FEOGA people keep track on how much of these products are produced? If there are quotas, presumably they must have a system of knowing when a quota has been filled. How do they know that?" asked Rosemary.

"I guess they rely on what the relevant authorities in Member States tell them. Producers have to make declarations of what they've produced….and, of course, exports can be monitored by the Customs authorities, as the goods will be accompanied by CAP forms which will need to be signed off if the goods are leaving the EEC or will fall under the CT regime….."

"CT?"

"Community Transit. Goods transiting between Member States need to use the CT system – a series of forms – which should provide a paper trail of where they started from and where they ended up."

"So if a wine producer produced ten per cent more than his quota, what would happen?"

"I think it'd be down to the relevant authorities. The quotas are national. So if one wine producer produced more than the quantity agreed, it'd depend whether it could be offset elsewhere within the country. But as with much of agriculture, you can't predict in the spring what's going to happen by the summer or autumn. So you end up with - at least in theory – the right amount of land in production, but a surplus in a good year....and FEOGA will, in effect, buy the surplus and arrange for storage or disposal in whatever way seems best....In theory, stored products like grain could be released if the following year had a bad harvest in order to stabilise prices....Don't forget, the origin of the CAP was a worry in the post-War era about EEC countries not being able to feed themselves....so over-production wasn't seen as a problem and price stability for farmers to ensure they kept production going was more important than prices for consumers. For much of the time you could get much agricultural produce cheaper on world markets. But if we allowed EEC prices to drop to that level, EEC farmers would go out of business – and then we'd no longer be self-sufficient. There's a logic to it – even though it may be increasingly outdated....But there are plenty of Irish farmers that love the CAP, I can tell you."

"If a wine producer brought in wine from another region or even another country to boost his production, and claimed subsidies on all of it, would that be a fraud against the CAP?" I asked.

"Yes. You can only claim for what you produce yourself. In theory, wine from another region would also be eligible for subsidy...and you could say it'd all even out. But subsidies are paid to individual farmers – not to the Member State – so robbing Peter to pay Paul is illegal......And am I to assume that this work you're doing on adulterated wine has broadened itself out somewhat?"

"Yes. Not least because wine market fraud seems potentially a lot bigger....But Gerry and Knud are keen that we don't make it too obvious."

"Well, I can see that.....And why you spoke to me about the CAP rather than Henri Kervran....That may not be entirely fair on Henri. From what I've seen of him, he's a public servant first and a Frenchman second....the type of fellow who believes it's better to address scandals rather than sweep them under the carpet.....and as a Breton, he has no sympathy for the wine industry...Indeed, whenever I've had a drink with him, he's gone for cider first and then beer, rather than wine."

"From what we've learnt so far, anything with the French is likely to involve a small amount of wine but a large scandal, whereas with the Italians it'd be a lot of wine and almost certainly official connivance."

"Of course, Andrea di Pietro isn't Gozzoli, thank heavens. And he strikes me as an honourable man. But I think he'd feel obliged to report stuff like that back to Rome – and I don't believe you'd get much help from there....But, as far as I can tell, he isn't a snitch for Paolitti."

"So you reckon we could safely have a word with Henri Kervran?" asked Rosemary.

"I should say so."

We decided that we probably should consult Knud Henriksen about that, but he appeared to agree with O'Leary's assessment. But if we now invited Henri Kervran to lunch, it was going to look suspicious to some of our colleagues, who might start putting two and two together and getting who knows what number. So I managed "accidentally" to leave the office at the same time as him and we agreed to have a quick drink in a neighbouring bar. It was one of those places that served about eighty to a hundred different Belgian beers, some extremely strong, some dark, some thick with yeast, some with added cherry or even whisky flavour, many unpalatable. Kervran chose a cider from Normandy. I followed suit.

"This isn't as good as Breton cider," observed Kervran. "But it's the best I can do. Is this social? Or is it connected to the work you and your wife are engaged on?"

"I wanted to seek your advice."

I explained the nature of our task and the allegations made by the Austrians.

"It doesn't entirely surprise me," remarked Kervran, in his remarkably good English. "Demand for good wine is so strong that no label wants to lose out because of a poor harvest. And naturally some vineyards will be more careful of their reputation than others. I doubt whether Gevrey-Chambertin or Clos Vougeot would stoop to blending inferior wines into their wine. They would just produce less – and recoup it through higher prices. But Lastier-Couvrou are, I guess, a tier below and might well feel they couldn't recoup the loss in quantity through higher prices."

"Do you have any ideas how one might go about getting the evidence to bring this sort of fraud before a court?"

"It would be difficult. Though a fraud is committed in such cases, prosecution is in the hands of the French authorities, rather than the Commission. We would step in only if the French authorities were manifestly failing to prosecute this sort of offence…..But how would you go about it? Difficult. In such cases, I doubt there would be much paperwork. You would make a few phone calls and the wine would arrive at the vineyard in some sort of disguise – and probably not during the working day. Few people would know about it – and the supplier would be well rewarded for keeping silent……You would need to know that the vineyard was suffering a poor harvest. Something they would be at pains to disguise, unless it was more widespread in the region. But you couldn't hope to observe the vineyard for several weeks probably without being noticed by the locals. And post facto, money would change hands and there would be some scraps of paper. Ideally, if you knew where the wine was coming from, there might be discrepancies in how their wines or grapes were disposed and what normally happens. But you would need to know who they were, of course. And quantities. Anyone can lose a few gallons of wine. But if you're talking about twenty gallons or more, it would be difficult to finesse that amount being sent somewhere secret. But I guess there would be a real recipient in the books. But you would only know whether they had received it by checking up. And that would be for the French authorities. I would not put it past French vineyards and shippers to refuse to tell anyone from the EEC Commission anything, especially if they have been up to something."

"And the French authorities?"

"It would depend on the individual. But even if they were prepared to cooperate, you might very well find that they would not wish to prosecute anyone you caught adding inferior wine to a noble one. The offender would be dealt with – but not in public. They would need to feel that they were in charge and that the EEC's role was purely advisory.......But if you had information about something that had occurred in the past, they might be interested....and I guess the vineyard would probably get their wine from the same place as before."

"I don't suppose you have any contacts in Burgundy?"

"I've spent all my working life in Paris and Rennes......I might have a former colleague working in Dijon, but I would need to check. I had a feeling he had moved on."

"And the Italians?"

"I couldn't help you there, I'm afraid. About the only EEC representatives they allow to do any checking are the auditors, and I'll bet they're not keen for them to see for themselves what things look like out in the fields and vineyards."

We turned to other matters – not least his continuing struggles to get the right job on his return. He was currently being threatened with a posting to the French Customs training centre near Bordeaux, whereas he wanted a regional command in the north, ideally in Brittany, closer to his home in St Brieuc. As I told Rosemary when I got home, the cider from Normandy tasted better and was lighter than any English cider I'd drunk....and presumably the Breton cider was even better.

"But was your conversation helpful?" she asked.

"I'm not sure on the French side of things. It depends on whether his contact is still based in Dijon and that he might be prepared to help.....But when he mentioned that the EEC auditors examine the records of everyone receiving CAP subsidies or refunds, including Italian wine-growers, I wondered what information they might have that we might be able to use."

"Will they let us get a look at it?"

"We can see what Knud knows. Otherwise one of us will just have to find out where they are and have a chat."

But Knud knew little about the EEC auditors and suggested Gerry Fitzpatrick might well know rather more. Rosemary and I booked a meeting with him after lunch.

"I've been meaning to have a word about how your present task is progressing," Gerry began, sitting us down at his coffee table, pouring out strong, dark tea. "I got a bit of muttering on the phone from a fellow from the Austrian Government who I used to meet at EFTA gatherings...about why I'd sent officials who evidently didn't understand the delicate nuances of international commerce and international relations. I asked him whether you'd done anything other than try to find out what had been going on and how, and what they were doing to prevent it happening again. He said he supposed not. I guess you were probably a bit too young, junior and not deferential enough. We northern Europeans prefer straight questions. Further south and east, they prefer them wrapped up in layers of honey and marzipan, if I may put it that way....I take it you weren't wholly convinced?"

I explained what we'd spotted and suggested in relation to the supply of diethylene glycol, which had struck us as a loophole in their controls.

"Did Knud Henriksen mention the evidence which they showed us about wine frauds in Italy and France?" I continued.

"Yes. He said you were intending to sniff around and see whether there was any way of getting some sort of evidence."

"It doesn't seem to be very straightforward. Not least because the national authorities either connive at the frauds or certainly don't want them to become an EEC matter. But I was chatting with Henri Kervran about it the other day and he mentioned that the EEC Auditors have some sort of right to examine records and documents relating to CAP subsidies and refunds. But we know nothing about them, other than the bumf in the EEC handouts...and that they're based in Luxembourg."

"They're in the process of being beefed up. Heinrich Aigner, the chairman of the European Parliament's Committee on Budgetary Control, has been pushing for a bigger and stronger audit body to operate more effective controls over EEC spending. There's a treaty being discussed right now to set up something called the EEC Court of Auditors, which will take over the role – and presumably the staff – of the existing EEC auditors."

"I confess I wasn't aware of any of that."

"You're seconded National Experts not Commission lifers, so there's no particular reason why you should keep tabs on this sort of thing.....and I gather you've no intention of trying to stay on here after your two years are up?"

"No," replied Rosemary and I in unison.

"So there's no reason to take an interest.....But, as that suggests, the auditors aren't presently a particularly powerful group. Their methods are desk-based, examining row upon row, column after column of figures, adding them up and noting down any disparities. They have no power to do anything with any apparent discrepancies. They report them back to the relevant

96

area of the Commission responsible for that area of expenditure to do with the information what they want. The auditors also produce summary material for the Parliament, which is what has got Herr Aigner so hot and bothered....mostly because he believes it's inadequate...So don't expect too much from them."

"Would we be allowed to look at the information they've collected and analysed?" asked Rosemary.

"I can't see why not. You'd better see if there's a Brit among them. I don't have any contacts at my level....and it might be easier to go in at working level anyway."

After Rosemary set off to collect Emily and Sarah from the international school, I went to the Commission library and tried to track down the EEC Auditors and who worked for them. After not getting very far, I got hold of a phone and rang the C&E number in Southend, where I knew the Internal Audit team worked. The lady on the switchboard gave me a name – Doug Deacon – which meant nothing to me. But after I'd explained who I was and that I needed to get in touch with a Brit in the EEC Auditors, he gave me a couple of names – both former C&E auditors.....Steve Bacon and Dave Neville. After a further half an hour of rooting around in various Commission directories, I finally came across them. Exactly what area of EEC spending they covered was utterly unclear from the directory, as their organisational chart seemed to be related to what were called "budget lines", which were pretty well unknown territory as far as I was concerned. But there were phone numbers against their names and I debated with myself calling them. I decided not to – mainly because I wanted to think about exactly what I wanted to say to them and whether it wouldn't be better to say as little as possible over the phone and go to Luxembourg and meet them face to face.

Rosemary suggested that it'd be sensible if I went to Luxembourg on my own to make initial contact, reminding me to check whether I was being followed. Though it seemed unlikely, once there was a suspicion that some country's secret service might be involved in this, we felt it prudent to be on our guard.

The following morning I rang both Bacon and Neville which a brief and vague description of why I would be grateful for a meeting. Being former C&E blokes, they suggested lunch time on Friday, as the earliest time they could make. Apparently they usually went out "for a few beers and a choucroute" with a couple of Brits from Eurostat. Though it'd mean an early start, I reckoned I could get there and back in the day by train and agreed to meet them at the "Flèche d'Or" in the Rue des Capucins at one o'clock.

As I sat on the train from Brussels on the Friday morning, I hoped these blokes weren't the sort who drank the equivalent of half a dozen pints on a Friday lunchtime, maintaining an old - and, to my mind, not particularly welcome – C&E tradition. I was already thinking up a few excuses for moderation, as the idea of travelling back to Brussels while in a half-drunk stupor appealed not at all. But at least I had an appetite for the choucroute, as the walk from the station to the centre of town was further than I'd remembered. The Rue des Capucins was just beyond the Place d'Armes, which unsurprisingly I recognised from my recent visit. The "Flèche d'Or" seemed to be quite an old tavern on several floors, with the usual extravagance of dark wood, which either was genuinely sixteenth century or intended to appear so.

I arrived there about ten minutes early, so I shocked the waiter and asked for a litre of tap water which I promptly drank as fast as I could. Apart from feeling quite hot after the walk from the station, it should dilute the beer a bit. Of course, I had no idea what Bacon and Neville looked like. Fortunately, they were rather more plainly British than I'd expected, with very English haircuts, sports jackets and ties. Though both were well into their forties, they looked like slightly aged OCXs. They evidently decided that I looked like a typical Brit too, as they came straight over to where I was sitting.

"Nick Storey?" asked the taller of the two, a square-built Mancunian with curly hair and beard. "I'm Steve Bacon."

"Dave Neville at your service," added the other. He was shorter, but if anything rather wider, with a receding ginger hair and a cheerful face – a deceptive face for an internal auditor, it seemed to me. His accent resembled mine – London gently merging with BBC English.

Naturally I bought the first round and we spent the first half hour or so explaining our background in C&E - all of us being former OCXs – and discovering various friends and colleagues in common. They'd both been auditors in C&E until about eighteen months previously, when the chance of better pay and much lower taxes had encouraged them to move with their families to Luxembourg. They appeared to be enjoying a fairly easy life.

"My main area of work is auditing CAP import levies and export refunds," explained Neville. "It's all paper-based, of course, so I never get a sniff of a port or airport, more's the pity. The one thing about audit in C&E, you were able to go and have a butchers at what happened on the ground, just to see whether there was any resemblance between the paperwork and what was actually going on."

"I cover CAP subsidy payments to fruit growers.....at least all fruit growers apart from those that grow grapes...or, as they put it, cultivate vines," added Bacon. "I'm the orchard man, me."

"Do any of the EEC auditors ever go out into the field to check whether the world is really like the paperwork?" I asked. "Presumably someone might be claiming a CAP subsidy on an orchard which doesn't exist?"

"I don't believe it's verboten, as my German head of department would say. But it ain't part of the traditions....and we're quite big on traditions, even if we're less than thirty years old and about to be transformed into something bigger and better...and certainly much grander....an 'institution of the EEC' no less."

"So how do you check that an orchard actually exists?"

"From time to time we do a map reference check, both to see whether an orchard isn't slap bang in the middle of Düsseldorf for instance, nor that it's also being claimed as a field of wheat or grassland for sheep...or, technically speaking, not sheep, but sheepmeat...presumably with legs attached."

"So how do you go about checking that CAP subsidy payments were correct?"

"Generally, we examine the records provided by the EEC country. For most regions we've got a scale of parameters, as they call it round here, which gives a range of how much grain is produced per hectare, for instance. So we can assess whether the payments look reasonable....and we can check on local maps whether the acreage claimed is accurate...and that it looks in the right place. You start up to pick up stuff that looks fishy remarkably quickly. I reckon I could spot a phoney orchard on a map within a couple of minutes."

"Suppose I'm a wheat farmer and I have a poor harvest. What's to stop me smuggling in wheat from outside the EEC and claiming it as my own?"

"I suspect you haven't understood how the CAP works. It's based on the area of land in production of a particular crop, not the quantity produced."

It was at that point a large penny dropped and I realised that perhaps Conor O'Leary's grasp of the intricacies of the CAP was not quite as much greater than mine than I'd thought....and when I'd spoken to Henri Kervran, both of us had been making the assumption that I had a firm grasp of how the CAP worked.

"So why would a wine producer buy wine from another region or abroad in order to boost production of wine under their particular label?"

"Not to get a CAP subsidy...Just to increase profits. I suppose if Chateau Bacon sells at a higher price than the wine you're selling under its label, you've got a nice little earner...."

"But someone ought to pick that sort of thing up," added Neville. "If Chateau Bacon covers five hectares and you'd expect that to produce, I don't know – five hundred litres of wine, but records covering national sales and exports amounting to say, a thousand litres, something fishy must be going on – and it'd be bloody obvious!"

"But it's not something you'd necessarily pick up?" I asked.

"In theory we could do, but, of course, we're looking at CAP payments not wider fraud."

"Hmmmm," said Bacon. "I'm not so sure there wouldn't be a CAP fraud involved. Wine which was exported from the EEC would get an export subsidy. So if any of this wine went outside the EEC and the shipper claimed an export subsidy, it'd be a fraud."

"Even if the wine was genuine Chateau Bacon?" I asked.

"Yes. If the other stuff sold as Chateau Bacon wasn't."

"So there's a genuine EEC interest?"

"Yes. I reckon so."

"Would you be able to detect this sort of fraud from the information you use to audit the claims of wine producers like that?"

"Not entirely. We'll have information on the acreage of the vineyards involved and what they claim they've produced. I guess someone must have figures somewhere about their exports. Of course, if it's only the Italian Government, you might find it hard to get your hands on it."

"I think Eurostat may have information down to that level of detail. It'd certainly be worth looking."

"If you have any names, I could certainly make sure one or other of us has a butchers at the CAP figures and lets you know what we've got."

"That'd be very kind of you.....The main problem is that you'll be looking at last year's figures and so will I. If we found any discrepancies, it'd be too easy to claim that there'd been some cock-up in the accounting systems – and we wouldn't have much chance of disproving that."

"To get up-to-date stuff, you'd need to be in and around the premises of the people you suspect. Not an easy task!"

"Unless you were with an EEC Audit team," suggested Neville. "I know we don't normally visit traders, but now we're going to be this high-falutin' Court of Auditors, perhaps we might. If we came across something suspicious, there's nothing to stop us…and I wouldn't mind a visit to an Italian or French vineyard or three."

"I'm due to go to Rome next month as part of an EEC audit team," explained Bacon. "If you really wanted to get into the murky details, perhaps you should get yourself invited along?"

"That's an interesting idea….But I guess there'd be quite a lot of people to square….."

"We were all OCXs at one time of our lives. If we can't sort out something like this, nobody can."

That led us nicely into different areas of conversation and then an attack on a mountainous plate of choucroute, along with another couple of beers. I realise that they probably continued well into the evening, but as I was about to make my prepared excuse to depart, three other blokes of about our age and also evidently Brits appeared. It gave me the opportunity I needed. I thanked them and agreed we'd stay in touch. Then I walked back to the station and enjoyed a fairly somnolent and largely thought-free journey back to Brussels. An espresso in both stations meant that I was sufficiently alert to carry out my usual Friday evening activities with my family….and I could be certain that Rosemary would quiz me about what I'd learnt in the morning.

"Was your trip worthwhile?" she asked, as I sipped a cup of milky coffee somewhat gingerly the following morning.

"I think so. If nothing else, I think I finally understand how the CAP system works….and it's not straightforward…It's not the amount of grain or wine produced, but related to the acreage of the wheat-fields or vineyards. But if you brought in a lot of extra grapes or wine and claimed it as your own, apparently there'd still be a CAP fraud."

"Is there anything these audit people can do about it?"

"Not a lot, I suspect. They are essentially office-based, but the two I met – Steve Bacon and Dave Neville – are both ex-OCXs, so they're willing to do some work on the ground, if they identify anything fishy from their analysis of the figures. Bacon is due to go to Rome next month to carry out an audit, which will include wine in the Valdicocce and Camarolo regions. They invited me along, if we could swing it with our different organisations."

"Rome in June. Won't it be rather hot?"

"I guess so. I need to think over whether it'd be worth it. Knud or Gerry might veto it anyway....And I don't really want to swan off somewhere like that without you....and they didn't appear to envisage a family group joining them."

"I don't think Emily and Sarah would like the heat....and if you were spending a week or more in an office poring over figures, boredom would soon set in....They're a bit young to appreciate the Colisseum or the Vatican....And if you found something fishy about the wine in the Valdicocce and Camarolo regions, presumably the auditors wouldn't just steam up there and go poking around."

"I don't know what they'd do. I'm not even sure they know what they'd do."

When I spoke to Knud Henriksen about the idea, he was in favour. He felt that it was part of SEFF's role to identify all areas where we could discover possible fiscal, customs or CAP frauds, using resources available to the Commission. And since the EEC auditors had no powers to do anything with anything illegal or just untoward they came across, it seemed to him that SEFF would be the logical place for them to bring any evidence of possible frauds in "our" areas. So he was keen that I – or Rosemary and I – should accompany the auditors on their visit to Rome. And though SEFF wasn't awash with money, the cost of one or both of us going was easily manageable. The one fly in the ointment might be that the auditors mightn't want someone from SEFF tagging along. But both Gerry Fitzpatrick and he were experienced in the ways of the EEC, who to contact, who to soft-soap, who owed who favours, etc. Whether that meant they had any pull over the EEC auditors I'd no idea — but they had 100% more than I had.

ROME

I wasn't entirely surprised when Knud Henriksen told me about ten days later that my attachment to the EEC Audit team visiting Rome in early June had been agreed. Apparently, the newly-established "EEC Court of Auditors" wished to start by giving an impression that it wasn't just a change of name, but that they intended to be more assertive and to test more of the results of their analyses through some "physical examinations". So I would be described as an "advisor" on the visit to Rome, assisting them with planning what "physical examinations" should take place and how.

Rosemary had already made it clear that including her on the visit would be impracticable, because of the need to look after Emily and Sarah. We felt they'd had enough of being dumped during the day and resisted the suggestion that places for them might be sought in one of the international school in Rome.

Little else happened on my "wine job" meanwhile. Instead, I had to play my part in a Commission working party specifically set up to discuss SEFF's Directive on information sharing and, where we had got to now, sort out the detailed arrangements for how information would be shared and how the authorities in each EEC country would ensure the necessary degree of contact.

I'd just about got used to the way the working party worked. Chaired by Knud Henriksen, I and on this occasion Rosemary and Henri Kervran sat opposite, flanked by representatives from the EEC countries, with the British team led by Simon Darby from UKREP, with Roderick Ogden from C&E's International Division and Richard Sawyer from the IB, representing the UK. The meeting was about what sorts of information-sharing there should be – for instance, urgent or routine – and what the contact points would be in each EEC country. Most countries were reasonably helpful, though it rapidly became clear that definitions of what was considered "urgent" and what "routine" differed considerably. Also which authorities should be contacted would vary according to the status of the information and the time of day/day of the week. The only exception was, yet again, the Italians who sent one of the men from their Permanent Representation to the EEC, who studiously read "*La Stampa*" and the "*Corriere delle Sera*" during the contributions by other delegations. When he spoke, the Germans, Dutch and French not only picked up their newspapers, but ostentatiously removed their headphones. The Italian read out a prepared statement. Immediately after he'd finished, Knud Henriksen called a halt to the proceedings for half an hour. Naturally everyone drifted out into the corridor outside the meeting. I saw Henriksen pounce on the Italian and exchange five minutes of angry words with him. Afterwards the Italian sped off, looking shaken.

"I asked him whether the Italian Government really wanted a report from this working party to go to the next Ecofin complaining about the failure of the Italian Government to cooperate in setting in hand arrangements to ensure the proper working of a Directive which Ecofin has so recently signed up to," he explained to Rosemary, Henri Kervran and me. "The Italians have never liked the Directive and fear that once we start using it, some of their less savoury practices may risk being uncovered. In practice, I know that the Danes wouldn't tell them about anything involving drug smuggling as, rightly or wrongly, our people believe that anything they get told gets leaked back to the Mafia. For my part, I think that's rather too strong. But when you're in Rome, Nick, you'll need to remember that whether or not they know what they are, the Italians you meet will all believe there have been things going on which they don't want the EEC to know about.....And if you start to come across anything untoward, any initial courtesy will evaporate and you'll find that the temperature in your meetings at least equals that outside."

So, with a new lightweight jacket and trousers, I flew to Rome in early June, having agreed to meet my colleagues at the Hotel

Piramide in the Viale Giotto. I took the train from Fiumicino airport to the Roma Ostiense station and discovered from a map of the area displayed in the station that the Viale Giotto was close by. The Ostiense station seemed to have been built in the style favoured by Mussolini, as I'd seen from the windows of the train as we passed EUR. I walked down the hill from the station, already feeling the searing heat heavy on my head and shoulders and reached a large square with a somewhat incongruous pyramid facing me, with what looked like the Roman or possibly medieval city gates, massive in red brick. From my guide book, these were the Pyramid of Caius Cestius and the Porta San Paolo. The Viale Giotto was away to their right, apparently running along the inside of the ancient Roman wall, which was a lot higher than I'd imagined it might be. Having followed the example of the locals and braved the traffic which appeared to ignore the pedestrian crossing markings, I found the Viale Giotto was lined with trees which reduced the discomfort of the heat considerably. The hotel was an elegant brick building, looking remarkably like the surrounding apartment blocks, a couple of hundred yards up the hill. I booked in and found I was the first to arrive, so I dumped my stuff and walked back down the Viale Giotto. As I stepped out of the shade of the trees, the heat smacked me over the head again, but I found a patch of shade to take a longer look at the Pyramid and the Porta San Paolo. I decided needed a cool drink and walked past a pleasant looking restaurant, named "Di Pietro", the same as my Italian colleague in SEFF, and found a small, reasonably friendly bar, appropriately called the "Bar Piramide", with a small seating area at the side, shaded by several trees. I bought a beer and sat outside on my own. Customers came and went – mostly downing tiny espressos in one, chatting to the owner of the bar and a small mongrel dog, which appeared to inhabit the place too.

After about half an hour, I left the bar and carried on along the Viale della Piramide Cestia, past several restaurants with canvas canopies for people to dine outside. I was tempted to explore further, but felt I should get back to the hotel and see whether my colleagues had arrived. Despite the shade, but the time I got back up the hill to the hotel, I was clammy with sweat. Fortunately, my colleagues hadn't turned up yet, so I was able to cool down and change my shirt. I went downstairs and sipped a glass of mineral water until they arrived – looking hot, tired and somewhat bedraggled. As Steve Bacon explained, when he joined me in the bar after checking in and dumping his stuff in his room, cheap flights from Luxembourg which meant that you used Ciampino airport, also required you to get a coach from the airport to the main Rome railway station (Termini) and then Rome's only stretch of underground – from Termini to Piramide. The metro was crowded, largely with commuters changing at Piramide for the suburban railway line that ran from the next door station called Porta San Paolo. So they were all baking even before they got outside. He was sinking his second beer by the time he finished his explanation.

We were soon joined by his colleagues – Geert van Zyl, the Dutch leader of the audit team, Jean-Marc Duvergne from France and an Italian auditor, Luigi Capriano, who was also acting as liaison and translator, as required. Van Zyl looked like a sailor, who preferred navigating northern waters in rain and fog. Duvergne also seemed to be a northerner, with a sharp, pallid face, silver-rimmed spectacles and a bit of a beak. Capriano was in his early twenties, tanned, dapper, with a rather bland face and carefully-trimmed beard. All of them followed Bacon's example, except for Capriano, who drank a hasty espresso followed up by a grappa and a glass of tap water.

After the inevitable description of the horrors of their journey, the auditors got down to business. It had been agreed that we'd meet officials from the Italian Agriculture and EEC Ministries at 8 am the following morning. This would be entirely formal – and then we'd be handed over to our Italian equivalents, who would provide us with the information required, as well as office accommodations and so on. Though no-one had been involved in any previous audit of the Italian figures, van Zyl had been told that it was likely we'd be put in spare offices in the FAO building close to the Circo Massimo. The FAO - the Food and Agriculture Organisation, a UN agency – had its headquarters in Rome in a large building which even "the laziest and most inefficient of all UN organisations", according to Van Zyl, was unable to fill up. So there were always rooms there for the use of visitors who the Italian Government didn't want wandering around their own Government offices. How accurate any of this was, I'd no idea – but I supposed auditors were sceptical by nature.

And it explained why this hotel had been chosen. It was within walking distance of the FAO building, pleasant but sufficiently far from the centre of the city to be reasonably priced. It was also generally agreed that the restaurant prices would be "reasonable". I mentioned that I'd seen several on my brief excursion and we agreed to meet at 7.30 in the bar and I'd lead them to the restaurants "round the corner". The first restaurant we came to, "Di Pietro", seemed to be closed, but the second one, "Taverna Cestia", although crowded, managed to squeeze us into a table inside. We asked Capriano to translate the menu and tell whether there was anything he'd recommend. He suggested "fiori di zucchina", followed by a "taglialino cacio e pepe" pasta and either "Tagliata di Manzo al Rosmarino" or "Abbacchio alla Scottadito" for the main course and a "Greco di Tufo" white wine to start with, followed by a "Sagrantino" from Umbria, as the red wine to accompany our meat. I must confess that the "fiori di zucchina" – courgette flowers cooked in batter with a tiny piece of anchovy – were much tastier than their description, the pasta was neither too bland nor too spicy and the "tagliata" of beef, extremely well cooked and enhanced by the flavour of rosemary, of course! I had a glass of each of the wines and began to realise that perhaps the Valdicocce and Camarolo wines that were so prevalent in Britain were by no means representative of the best Italian wines, which perhaps they preferred to keep to themselves. I was too full up for a dessert, but apparently we were expected to follow the traditional Roman tradition of finishing with a coffee and a "digestivo". Capriano recommended either Limoncello or an "amaro". On his advice, I had a small glass of an "amaro" called "Lucano", which wasn't too bitter and actually seemed to be doing what a "digestivo" should be doing. Certainly an enjoyable meal – and a lot less expensive than I'd expected. Perhaps Rosemary and I might visit at some stage – ideally on our own and at a cooler time of year!

By the time we'd finished, it was a lot cooler and while my colleagues decided they needed to go back to the hotel, I felt I needed some exercise. So I continued along the Viale della Piramide Cestia, past a metro station and ended up by a vast open area, which looked a bit like a running track, but with two sides much longer than the other two. Fortunately, the name of the metro station told me what this probably was – Circo Massimo. I took a different route back, walking up the Via di San Saba and then getting lost in a warren of different roads until I finally emerged on to the Viale Giotto and found my hotel. I made a short phone call to Rosemary and then lay back on my pillow thinking that so far, Rome had been much more impressive than I'd expected. Indeed, that was why I wrote down that first meal in my notebook. I'd tended to think of Italian food as being minestrone, pizzas and pastas. But an ordinary restaurant half a dozen stops on the metro from the centre of the city had shown me the error of my ways.

The following morning, we gathered over breakfast – the usual continental one – and set off shortly after 7.30 to walk to the FAO building on the corner of the Viale Aventino close to the Circo Massimo. We walked up the Viale Giotto, past some large Roman remains, which I thought I recalled from my guidebook were the Baths of Caracalla, and a running track, turned downhill and reached a main road, with the FAO building on our left and more Roman remains on a hill in front of us to our right. It was already beginning to feel quite warm and the bureaucratic formalities of the FAO weren't guaranteed to help us cool down.

Eventually, with photographic passes and additional paper forms, we were allowed through and escorted to a room which I guessed must look out on the Viale Aventino – a busy, noisy thoroughfare. The room had half a dozen tables and chairs and was, I supposed, the room where we would be expected to carry out our work.

After about half an hour, Capriano was despatched to find the whereabouts of our hosts. He returned about ten minutes later, along with a very smooth young man who led us to a conference room on the floor above. There, waiting for us, were Marcello Urrioni from the Agriculture Ministry, Giorgio Roscovano from the Guardia di Finanza and Giuliano Gozzoli from the EEC Ministry. We greeted each other, Gozzoli and I at a temperature which was several degrees below that of the air-condition room we were in. I wondered whether it was always intended that he would attend, or whether my presence had been the cause of his?

After a good twenty minutes of pleasantries conducted in English, Urrioni asked van Zyl to explain the nature of the EEC audit. Van Zyl replied, explaining also how the change of title of the EEC audit organisation was also intended to sharpen up the audits and widen their scope as necessary.

"Is that why you have a fiscal expert from the Service Européenne contre la Fraude Fiscale as a member of your team?" demanded Roscovano, a bulky man with a shaven head and the features of what I would describe as a Southern Italian peasant.

"Yes," replied van Zyl. "This is in the nature of an experiment. We are examining expenditure of EEC funds in the agricultural sector as part of the Common Agricultural Policy. Mr Storey is here to help us, but primarily to see what information his organisation might be able to provide us to help us with our work and conversely what information which we uncover which might be of use to his organisation. It's quite possible that we shall find little, if anything. But our Directors believe that an experiment or two should be tried."

Gozzoli whispered something in Roscovano's ear.

"I understand that Mr Storey is not an expert in the Common Agricultural Policy."

"That is correct. As I have explained, we are trying to see whether the information which we analyse could be of use for fiscal purposes – or whether a fiscal analysis of the information might help our analyses of CAP expenditure."

"I'm sure that from his own secondment to the Service Européenne contre la Fraude Fiscale, Signor Gozzoli will be aware that both the interests of the organisation and my responsibilities within it remain flexible while it settles into its position in the Commission," I added. "Signor Gozzoli will undoubtedly recall the flexibility of his own position while he was there."

I glanced at Gozzoli, who promptly looked away. I wasn't going to let someone who'd been stupid enough to be blackmailed by a Soviet agent to try and set up one of his fellow-countrymen, to intrigue against me so openly.

"We have provided the records which you have asked for," continued Urrioni, a spare, small, deeply-tanned man, who looked like one of those worrying fit, middle-aged marathon runners. "Gozzoli here and Federico Castagnoli from my Ministry will be your day-to-day contacts. However, if any salient matters arise, I trust you will inform me and we can discuss them as they arise."

"In other words," remarked van Zyl, once we'd returned to our room, "he doesn't want any unpleasant surprises emerging just as we're leaving. If something untoward emerges, he'd like to head us off at the pass, if I may put it that way." He gave a grim smile. "But that's not how it works."

He began to dole out the papers which the Italians had left for us. He had asked for import, export and sales records for Italian wines, which should available in some form or other – but not necessarily involving all those activities – on my behalf. I began by trying to work out which vineyards in the Valdicocce and Camarolo regions supplied Ceresini, Greffon and Falcoberti. By lunch time, I'd identified only one largeish vineyard in the

112

Camarolo region and a cooperative in the Valdicocce region, both supplying Ceresini.

"We take two hours for lunch," explained van Zyl. "This is painstaking, detailed work and we need to give our minds time to relax. Though I'm told there is a staff restaurant which we may use here, whether you decide to use it or not, I advise most strongly that you spend some time out of this building. I realise it's infernally hot outside, but there are parks with plenty of shade and the restaurants will be air-conditioned in some cases, I'm told. We shall see enough of each other over the next week or two and I'd normally like us to congregate for our dinner. So at lunch time, I encourage you to do your own thing....My only request is – no more than one glass of wine or beer, please."

"That's the usual form for these visits – at least where van Zyl is in the lead- or so I'm told," explained Bacon to me. "I suggest we ask Capriano where we can eat lunch in the neighbourhood without being cooked ourselves."

Evidently, he intended that we should lunch together. But for that lunch time, his wishes were thwarted, as Giuliano Gozzoli appeared the moment we left our room and asked if I was prepared to be his guest for lunch. I could scarcely refuse, as it was possible he might have something useful to tell me. But I made clear that I expected to go Dutch – an expression which, inevitably, I had to explain.

"If you don't mind, I'd like to take you to a small place in Testaccio, just off the via Marmorata," said Gozzoli. "It's almost certainly not what you'd expect an Italian restaurant to be like, but it's one of the best places – if not the best place – for lunch in this part of town."

We walked in silence down the viale Aventino, if for no other reason than at least one of us felt that the sun was beating his head into the pavement. We walked as far as the Porta San Paolo and round the side of the pyramid of Caius Cestius, which gave some all too brief shade. Trams rattled past us – both on the viale Aventino and the via Marmorata. About two hundred yards along

113

the via Marmorata we passed a delicatessen called Volpetti, from where wonderful aromas of cheese, fresh pasta and salami emerged. By the shop doorway, we turned off the main road into a side street and a few yards further on, Gozzoli led me into what looked like a small canteen. The place was crowded, with a serving area on the right hand side, with a vast array of different food. Gozzoli handed me a tray, a paper envelope containing cutlery and a small glass.

"This is Volpetti Piu," he explained. "We queue up for our food at the counter and then do our best to grab a couple of seats."

We joined the queue and I took a couple of artichokes as a starter, with a pizza covered in potato and rosemary for my main course, with a panna cotta covered in fresh berries for my dessert, along with a large bottle of mineral water. Though the Enabrea beer looked tempting, I feared it'd both give me a headache and make me dozy in the heat. We managed to get two seats together and said nothing while we ate. The food was delicious and the atmosphere was relatively quiet, ordinary people having ordinary conversations.

"That was extremely good," I said, as we finished, expecting Gozzoli to start talking. But he explained that it wasn't done to linger after one had eaten here, because of the shortage of seats and the large number of customers. Indeed, as we left, I noticed the queue was longer than when we came in – and that all of them looked like Italians, rather than tourists.

Gozzoli walked further along the via Marmorata, almost as far as what looked like a bridge over the Tiber. Then he ducked into a rather trendy-looking bar.

"We can get a tram back to Circo Massimo from just outside," he observed. We ordered coffees, which he accompanied with a grappa and a glass of water. I decided to try a drink called "chinotto", which sounded Italian, while being non-alcoholic. It tasted rather like a fruity, non-alcoholic Campari….and just what was needed in this heat. The bar was about a quarter full. Doubtless it filled up in the evenings.

Now Gozzoli felt able to say what was on his mind.

"Why have you come with this EEC audit team?" he demanded.

"The reason was explained in our meeting earlier. You and I both know that SEFF has only been recently created and we are keen to see what information we can lay our hands on that will help us carry out our responsibilities better. I knew a couple of the auditors from our time in Customs and Excise, so I got in touch with them. As I was the person in SEFF who had done so, I got the invitation to join them on this visit. As you know, I've never felt myself tied down to my detailed job description."

"From what I recall, you were generally more interested in pursuing an investigation rather than just carrying out an experiment, as you say is what you are doing here."

"It's entirely up to you what you believe – and I doubt whether there's anything I might say that'd change your mind anyway…..But you should be aware that when someone adopts this sort of approach with me, I begin to wonder whether they haven't got guilty consciences, something to hide, perhaps."

"The reason I was asked to attend as a member of the Italian Government delegation was because of my EEC experience. Knowing that you had come from SEFF, my superiors decided that I was the appropriate person to keep an eye on you."

"Are they aware of what has passed between us?"

"Some do. But you must understand that the bureaucracy here is not like it is in Brussels – or London from what I have heard. Giulizzi and his acolyte Paolitti are members of a political faction. The fact that I caused problems for Paolitti may make me persona non grata in SEFF and with several politicians and their acolytes in the Ministries here, but to others I am…how do you say it, I am a justified sinner…..Do you intend to use what occurred in Brussels against me?"

"Not unless I felt it appropriate."

"If you did, you might well find it...what is the word?......backfired."

"I would need to reflect on such a possibility."

I was pretty sure he was bluffing. His admission that having got himself into a position where he could be blackmailed by Soviet agents (and possibly still could be) so that he betrayed his colleagues, had actually gained him supporters within the Italian bureaucracy revealed more about the nature of that bureaucracy than about his instinct for survival. It was a salutary reminder why so many bureaucrats from northern European countries put so little trust in their Italian counterparts. I reckoned that this attitude rested on an immense generalisation. Many Italians I'd come across seemed as full of integrity as any Brit, Dane, West German or Dutchman. But men like Gozzoli reinforced the stereotype.

Our conversation moved on to other matters. Indeed, though I realised we'd have little time to explore Rome...and I was due to fly back to Brussels on the Friday evening anyway, while the rest of the auditors would decide how long they needed to extend their visit on Thursday evening.....I thought it'd be helpful to get some idea from him on what sites we might explore in the vicinity of where we were staying and also whether he could recommend anywhere not too expensive that we might eat locally. He turned out to be both knowledgeable and helpful. So we returned to the FAO building on somewhat better terms than when we'd left it.

I spent the afternoon writing down information without trying to think too much about it. It'd be too easy to start jumping to conclusions. In any case, I was dependent on information which the auditors were examining to provide a full picture of the activities of Ceresini, Greffon and Falcoberti. I was looking at wine exports from the Camarolo and Valdicocce regions – particularly those exports outside the EEC on which export subsidies were being claimed. Though individual vineyards or cooperatives made the claims, they had to provide supporting evidence of export, which in many cases showed the shippers to be Ceresini, Greffon or Falcoberti. The stated destination of virtually all the wine was the USA and Canada, exported through the port of Genoa, shipped in bulk in containers. The only things I noticed otherwise were that the quantities seemed large and there seemed to be no record of what ships the wine had actually sailed on. But until I'd got some idea of the quantity of wine produced in the vineyards supplying Ceresini, Greffon and Falcoberti, I couldn't tell whether the Austrians had been correct or not.

We finished at 6pm and made our way slowly back to the hotel, calling in a bar on the way for a cool beer. By dinner time, everyone seemed too exhausted to do more than wander down the viale Giotto and eat in the Di Pietro restaurant, which felt like a friendly family restaurant, greeting us with a glass of Prosecco and providing tasty food at reasonable prices, including a lemon sorbet which contained considerably more Limoncello than sorbet. They, too, offered a "digestivo" with the after-dinner espresso, so I had another "Lucano", which seemed to have helped my food settle down well the previous evening – and ensured that a late night strong coffee didn't prevent me sleeping.

The following day was less eventful as we continued to work our way through the mass of information provided. We were getting a little more accustomed to the heat and after work, climbed the Aventine hill to see a view of St Peter's through a keyhole in a doorway in the piazza of the Knights of Malta and then a more general view of the city from the edge of the hill overlooking the Tiber in the Parco degli Aranci (Orange Park). With the early evening sun low in the West, the sight was tremendous – and I wished more than anything else in the world that Rosemary could be by my side, along with Emily and Sarah. It was bad enough being away from them for nearly a week, but seeing sights like these when they weren't made me feel sad.

This piece of sightseeing, as well as the restaurant we ate at that evening, had all been recommended to me by Gozzoli. The restaurant, "Tutti Frutti" in the via della Robbia in Testaccio, seemed unpretentious from both outside and inside, but the owner called Michele was so friendly and enthusiastic about the food he provided that it felt more like a family homecoming. The food was good, without being fancy, with a choice of mostly local wines, none of which I'd ever heard of. I resolved that when Emily and Sarah were old enough to appreciate such things, we should come back to Rome, so that they could experience the food, the wine and the tremendous hospitality which I had during this week.

By Thursday lunch time, Steve Bacon handed me several pages of figures for the quantity of wine produced by the vineyards in the Camarolo and Valdicocce regions, along with the amount of CAP subsidy claimed and the "destination" of the wine. In some cases it appeared that the wine was bottled - usually by the cooperative rather than an individual vineyard – for local consumption. But a significant quantity was sent to firms which either bottled the wine or shipped it on in bulk. Slightly more than half was despatched to Ceresini, Greffon or Falcoberti.

During an afternoon when there was the most tremendous thunderstorm, with lightning dancing around the sky and rain shooting through the sky like thousands of arrows, bouncing across the road into instantly forming streams, I worked out that wines actually produced in the Camarolo and Valdicocce regions amounted to little more than half of wine exports which Ceresini, Greffon and Falcoberti claimed to have emanated from there. Since I didn't rule out that the room we were working in might be bugged, I said nothing to anyone at the time. Nor did I mention it over dinner in "Da Bucatina", further along the via della Robbia from "Tutti Frutti", which provided excellent "typically Roman" food – though for my part, the portions were rather too large – on the principle that you never know whose ears may be flapping.

On Friday morning, I went to the FAO building with the rest of the team, having told van Zyl as we went along what I'd uncovered. He asked me to send him a memorandum for when he returned to Luxembourg.

"There's another thing which I'm going to try to look at," I added. "You'll see that export subsidies are claimed apparently on all exports. There are no records of any Camarolo or Valdicocce wines being exported to anywhere else in the EEC – certainly not by Ceresini, Greffon or Falcoberti. But I'm certain I've seen wines from both regions on sale in the UK – and Ceresini and Falcoberti seem familiar names to me. And I've seen no documents detailing which ships these wines have been exported on. So I'm wondering whether they haven't been claiming export subsidies on wines that are actually heading to somewhere else in the EEC, not to third countries."

"We'll see whether we can dig anything up from what they've given us. I assume you don't want us to make a great fuss about getting more information?" van Zyl asked.

"No. I don't think we want to tip anyone off at this stage."

"OK. Of course, some of it may be quite natural to ask about. But from Monday we'll be on to white wines from the Friuli and Piemonte regions and then a quite look at some of the local wines from Lazio....But from what I can see of them, they're largely consumed close to home....I'd like to do Chianti as well, but we've only got a fortnight and I'd rather go for depth than breadth."

That seemed to me to be the way of all auditors – and none the worse for that.

At any rate, I spent the morning checking my information and writing it up. At noon, I thanked van Zyl and his colleagues for their help and company and made my way back to the hotel to pick up my case and then struggling further through the heat, which hadn't been affected at all by the previous day's thunderstorm, to Roma Ostiense station and thence to Fiumicino airport. An uneventful flight saw me arriving in late afternoon in a shower of rain in Brussels. It was cool and as the rain ran through my hair and down my face, I felt refreshed. It felt good.

But nothing like as good as when I opened the door of our flat in Woluwe St Lambert to be greeted by my family.

"Emily and Sarah were terribly pleased with their presents," said Rosemary, after we'd put them to bed and were relaxing on the sofa. "And I like all Armani perfumes...But what on earth is in that bottle you brought back?"

"It's called Lucano....It's what they call a 'digestivo' in Rome. You have it after your after-dinner coffee. I rather liked it and thought it might be worth seeing whether it travels or whether it's the sort of thing you do when in Rome."

"You sound as though you enjoyed yourself."

"I'd've enjoyed it a lot more with you and Emily and Sarah...But you wouldn't want to go in the summer months. Even in June it was absolutely baking hot. Every time I went out, I felt as though the sun was beating me down into the pavement. And I reckon Emily and Sarah will enjoy it more when they're a bit older....Not that we had any time for sightseeing. I saw the Rome skyline from a place called Orange Park on the Aventine hill and the Circus Maximus and a few bits of Roman ruins from the outside. At lunch time it was too hot to do anything and by the evening we were too tired."

"Did you find out anything useful about these Italian wine frauds?"

"Yes, I believe so. But there's still a problem about what we can do with the information."

I explained to her briefly what I'd discovered. But it was Friday evening and we'd been away from each other since Monday morning, so there were better things to do for the rest of the evening than talk about work.

1 + 1 = ?

"It seems plain that Ceresini, Greffon and Falcoberti are committing fraud by exporting wine that isn't from Camarolo or Valdicocce, but claiming that it is," I explained to Knud Henriksen and Rosemary on the following Monday morning. "They're claiming export subsidies illegally and I doubt whether you can actually claim that wine comes from a certain region if it doesn't....Though I'm not sure whether that's a fraud against the EEC or just a possible cross-border fraud which would be the responsibility of national administrations. I've got plenty of figures which show what they've been up to....and I hope the audit blokes may be able to show that quite a lot of the wine which they claim is being exported to the USA and Canada is actually being sent to other EEC countries....not least the UK."

"And we should be able to check that," added Rosemary.

"But because we're looking at two years ago because of the audit timetables, all we've got are some paper trails. I suppose there might be some 1973 vintage wine from Valdicocce or Camarolo on British supermarket shelves, with Ceresini, Greffon or Falcoberti labels – but whether there's a documentary chain tying them back to production in Valdicocce or Camarolo or somewhere completely different, I don't know. I don't believe we'd get much cooperation from the Italian authorities and without some hard evidence, I feel that a paper trail won't be enough."

"So what do you intend to do?" asked Henriksen.

"Rosemary and I have been talking it over during the weekend. We think we need to have a couple of days in the UK. I'd like to check UK import information. If I can get the names of the ships the Valdicocce and Camarolo wines were exported in, that'll narrow down the field of search a lot. And I'd also like to have a word with Billy Madden of Wasco again. First, we may be able to check whether he'd got any of these wines still on the shelves of his supermarkets. But more important, we may be able to set something up for later this year or early next – whenever these wines are shipped to the UK."

"And there's still a gap in that we don't know where the additional wine comes from, how it is stored, whether it's blended with the local wines or whether it's just substituted for it," continued Rosemary. "The Eurostat may have some information on imports by Ceresini, Greffon and Falcoberti, though it's possible they use a third party. We really want to get into one or more of these companies to see what information we can unearth….and we think that Wasco might be one way in."

"So you aren't going to follow up the Burgundies?"

"I reckon it'd be much more difficult to spot anything fishy going on from any documentary records and unless Henri Kervran can raise a contact who's reliable and could get our feet on the ground there without alerting anyone's suspicions, I think we might have to leave that to the wine snobs who claim to be able to tell a genuine Lastier-Couvrou from one which has been blended with some plonk from another vineyard," I replied.

"Your Roman experiences haven't turned you into a wine connoisseur then?"

"I had some very decent wine at reasonable prices. But I think it was just the local stuff that the Romans drink. On the very rare occasions when I've had a posh wine, I can't say I've ever noticed the difference – certainly not why you'd pay four or five times as much for it."

"You can take the boy out of Woolwich, but you can't take Woolwich out of the boy," remarked Rosemary with a huge smirk.

"She's been saving that up for several years," I commented.

"So what next?" asked Henriksen.

"We're due to take a long weekend in London later this month to see my mother," I explained. "If we extend it by a day or two, we should be able to meet whoever we need to meet and at least set in hand getting the information we need."

Later that week, I sent a confidential copy of my analysis of the Valdicocce and Camarolo figures to van Zyl in the newly-titled EEC Court of Auditors, along with the conclusions which I had drawn from them. On the Tuesday of the following week I received a note of thanks from him along with a note stating that the ships which had exported Ceresini, Greffon and Falcoberti wines from Genoa were the *"Antonio Pigafetta"*, the *"Giovanni de Verrazzano"* and the *"Manfredo Camperio"*. I realised I could do some homework before we left on Friday afternoon to travel back to London, by searching *Lloyd's List* for whether any of these ships had docked in the UK and when. Since Valdicocce and Camarolo were hardly Beaujolais Nouveau, they were shipped early in the new year, so I went to the Commission library and looked over copies of *Lloyds List* from January 1974. Sure enough, the *"Antonio Pigafetta"* docked in Felixstowe on 26 January; the *"Giovanni de Verrazzano"* in Portsmouth on 23 February and the *"Antonio Pigafetta"* again in Felixstowe on 23 March. As none of these were Dock Labour Scheme ports, I wondered whether any of this wine might've been imported by Wasco. But it'd been a long afternoon ploughing my way through innumerable copies of *Lloyds List* and it seemed pointless to speculate, when I could check directly when I was back in Britain.

We travelled back to London by train and boat, which though longer was cheaper; and Emily and Sarah preferred the crossing from Ostende to flying. We were staying in a B&B in Beckenham, which would give us a chance to check that our tenants weren't damaging our house, while allowing Emily and Sarah to see some of their friends. On Sunday, we went over to my mother's house in Woolwich and took her out for lunch in a local café. As her health continued to decline, she was talking about moving into somewhere smaller and easier to run. It was also plain that she continued to mourn my father's death. For all his intolerant and sometimes bullying ways, it was evident that there had been a deep bond of love between them and that she was finding it hard to cope with such a large gap in her life. Though she welcomed the freedom of being able to meet us and my sister and her family openly and do things he would have vetoed – like buying South African produce on the local market – it was impossible to move on from a lifetime that had been so dominated by her husband. I realised that it was unfortunate that we were living half a day's travel away, but even if we'd been back in Beckenham, I doubted whether we would have seen a lot more of her. For one thing, she was determined to be independent and to build a life for herself locally. My sister had suggested that she might like to get a flat closer to her in Sutton, but she'd almost been rude in declining the offer.

I'd already phoned C&E and Billy Madden at Wasco, so I had meetings arranged for Monday morning and afternoon. It felt very strange walking into King's Beam House, especially as I had to get a day pass. First I met Terry Ellis from the Stat to see if he could dig out any information for me on imports of wine by Ceresini, Greffon and Falcoberti on the *"Antonio Pigafetta"* and the *"Giovanni de Verrazzano"* on or around 26 January, 23 February or 23 March 1974. That appeared to present few problems, as I could be so specific about the dates. Then I met Richard Sawyer from the IB to let him know what we were up to, in case any of those who appeared to be involved had crossed the IB's radar. He was evidently in a bit of a hurry, so whether he really took in what I'd said to him or would do anything about it seemed a toss-up to me.

As Rosemary was taking Emily and Sarah round the Tower in the morning, we met up for lunch. Then I went on to meet Billy Madden at the Wasco London offices, their main headquarters being in Welwyn Garden City. The offices weren't in a smart part of town, and they were unpretentious in the extreme.

"Swanky offices in expensive areas are just an overhead which the productive part of the business has to bear," observed

Madden, as he took me past a reception area dedicated to pictures of Wasco products and sales figures to a small meeting room.

"I understand you had some information for me?" he continued.

"Yes," I replied. "We've been looking at wine frauds, as I mentioned when we met in Brussels. Allegations were made about some Italian wines, so we've been digging around to see what evidence backs up the allegations. We've found that from two regions – Camarolo and Valdicocce – it seems as though around half their production doesn't come from those regions but from outside. We're not sure yet where the wine comes from. But it looks as though quite a lot is exported to the UK. The firms involved are called Ceresini, Greffon and Falcoberti and they shipped wine to the UK through Felixstowe and Portsmouth last winter on the *"Antonio Pigafetta"* and the *"Giovanni de Verrazzano"* sailing from Genoa. It's quite possible that with your tight controls over your wine shipments, Wasco haven't received any of this wine, but I thought you might be able to give me some idea about which of your competitors might've been the importers."

"We use Ceresini,....I'm certain of that. The other two names aren't familiar to me. But that doesn't mean we haven't used them....It's all Camarolo and Valdicocce wine sold under our own labels. It comes in bulk tanks and we bottle it......We don't use Portsmouth, but we definitely use Felixstowe...and the *"Antonio Pigafetta"* sounds familiar too...one of those foreign words that sound faintly ludicrous...Do you know whether the wine we received was genuine or not?"

"No. Because we're operating from information which the Italians have been prepared to give us and purely what is needed for CAP subsidy checks, we only get part of the story. We have documentary proof that Ceresini, Greffon and Falcoberti have been falsely claiming CAP export subsidies and that they've been palming off wine that isn't Camarolo and Valdicocce as the real thing. But it's possible that the substitute wine has been kept for

Italian consumption. But we don't know where it comes from, where it's stored, whether it's blended or just substituted. In theory all your wine could've been genuine Valdicocce or Camarolo…"

"But they're more likely to reckon that the Brits wouldn't know the difference, rather than their own consumers."

"I guess so."

"We might have a few bottles left, but we try not to keep cheap wine on the shelves for too long. So it's likely we would've sold off any remaining few in a special offer. In any case, I doubt whether chemical analysis would tell us much…and evidently no-one seems to have noticed any difference."

"I expect that's what they were banking on."

"But it's irrelevant. If we tell our customers our wine is Camarolo or Valdicocce, it bloody well has to be. Even if it's a genuine error, it's our reputation that ends up in the gutter…and people will buy their wines from our competitors.….Knowing our former reputation, you'll understand that moving upmarket into products like wine is an important part of our general strategy going forward. So we can't afford to get caught like this.….What are you doing about it? Will it become public?"

"I doubt it. The EEC auditors have to find someone in the Commission willing to undertake a prosecution for CAP subsidy fraud. I reckon the wine lobby is so strong politically that they'll do a deal with the Italians to stop doing it in future and show what they're doing to prevent it….though that'll probably be a bit of subterfuge. It's likely that the French and even the West Germans may prefer not to poke under too many stones."

"So you're intending to do nothing?"

"No. But I need to get some concrete evidence rather than bits of paper. Though the paperwork is essential, it isn't enough. I need names and I need to know where the extra wine comes from, where it's kept and what wine goes where. And I can't use the Italian authorities, for obvious reasons. I don't see how I could carry out effective surveillance. And I don't think

126

Rosemary and I could hang around while we were on holiday in the area in the hope we might spot something….."

"You're holidaying there? Is that wise?"

"We won't be very near. We're booked to stay for three weeks on Lake Como in August. Rather too far to the west for a day trip to do some surveillance……"

So? You seem to have given only reasons why you can't do anything so far."

"That's because I'm hoping I can work with you. When we met in Brussels, you mentioned your control over your suppliers included getting to know them. Presumably someone from Wasco has visited Ceresini as part of getting to know them?"

"I'd certainly expect so."

"Well, suppose you'd had complaints from some of your customers telling you that the Valdicocce wine they had earlier this year didn't taste like last year's, what would you do?"

"If we had more than a couple, we'd sent someone – possibly a team to visit Ceresini and get to the bottom of what'd been going on, if anything…..Hmmm…..I see where you're going with this. You want to be a member of a Wasco team that noses around in Ceresini's business…"

"Exactly…..I was thinking that it'd serve our mutual interest."

"I'd need to think about it….But first I need to establish some facts. A lot depends on how big a supplier Ceresini is. If we only get a small quantity from them, any sort of visit would look very odd. If there was any trouble, they'd just expect us to drop them…..And if we're going to do some sort of cloak and dagger thing with a Government official, I need to be clear about our legal position….and whether there'd be any reputational damage……Not that you or your organisation have a bad reputation, but if we look as though we go along with officials spying on our suppliers, we may have problems keeping some suppliers."

"If you've got suppliers who are bothered by an official looking into their business, are they the sort of suppliers you really want?"

"I suppose you've got a point there. It wouldn't do our reputation any good to be using crooks as our suppliers. It's one reason why we've steered clear of Sicilian wines."

"One of the things we don't know about Ceresini or the other firms is exactly who owns them. It's one of a number of problems you face when you don't feel you can involve the relevant national authorities."

"Evidently you don't trust the Italian authorities."

"I can't say I've any direct experience. When I was in Rome, they weren't particularly helpful. But I'm not sure that the UK authorities would bend over backwards to help a team of EEC auditors – especially if you feared there might be things they'd find which you knew nothing about....But my reluctance to use the Italian authorities is based largely on the advice of others who have more experience than me....and I suppose a natural caution on my part. If there's a risk that involving them would destroy any chance of catching these fraudsters, I'd rather not take it....Of course it's possible that we may only get sufficient evidence to make a case to the Italian authorities, but not enough to do anything about the frauds ourselves....I doubt I'd be happy about that. But I'm realistic enough to know that there are limits on what can and can't be done in a semi-official capacity."

"Well, you must allow me to gather some information and think this through. I'm assuming you're not intending to dash over there in the next few days?"

"No. I'm not even sure what'd be the best time. If you or I can find out when Ceresini and the others imported the other wine last year, that might be the appropriate time for you to carry out an inspection, if you decide to do that."

"So that's likely to be much later in the year."

"I guess so. I aiming to get some more information by then – not least on where the wine comes from, who imports it and how they are tied in with Ceresini, Greffon and Falcoberti."

"Whether or not we decide on an examination of Ceresini or whether we can invite you to join our team, we'll certainly be looking into Ceresini and any of these other companies and we'll let you have any information that looks likely to interest you....I'm sorry I can't be more positive at this stage, but there are a quite a few details we need to ponder here before we decide what's best for Wasco."

I hadn't really expected anything else. As I rejoined Rosemary, Emily and Sarah at Charing Cross, fresh from their visit to the Planetarium, I felt more positive about being able to take this work at least another stage further.

"You don't think Ceresini mightn't be tipped off if Wasco start taking a greater interest based on complaints they've supposedly received about the wine they'd shipped?" asked Rosemary, as we sat on a bench watching Emily and Sarah playing in the children's playground in Kelsey Park.

"It's possible, of course. But I can't really see how anyone is going to get any nearer to what is going on if it isn't them. The EEC auditors can inspect them, but they can't prevent the Italian authorities from accompanying them.....And the process is necessarily so formal that I'd expect anything untoward to have brushed away under several carpets well in advance.........I doubt very much whether Ceresini or the others import wine or even ship it around Italy under their own names. It'd be far too risky. But they – or some other company – must have to store this wine somewhere....and somewhere either in or close to the Valdicocce and Camarolo regions so that when it gets shipped out – or bottled – it appears credibly to come from those regions."

"It seems to me it'd help to know whether the wine is imported or comes from elsewhere in Italy. Would one of your wine snobs or the wine standards people not be able to give us some idea? For instance, if you knew the wine was coming from Algeria, presumably you could check from your *Lloyds List* what ships had sailed to a suitable Italian port at the right sort of time and then you could get the importers' names from Eurostat?"

"I suppose so......I think I'd also like to find out why this is happening. Has there always been a greater demand for Camarolo and Valdicocce wines than the vineyards in those regions could supply? Or has it started happening only more recently? For instance, since Britain and Ireland joined the EEC?"

We were due to travel back to Brussels early the following afternoon, but a hasty phone call first thing got me a very brief meeting with Grenville Porteous, who met me in a small, but quite grand, meeting room in a building next to Vintry House close to the northern end of Southwark Bridge. He smoked a fairly powerful cigar and sipped away at some rather rank coffee, which I decided after the first sip that my taste buds and digestive system would prefer the remainder to be left untouched.

"You said you had some more questions for me?" he began. "Am I to take it you've been making some progress in the matter we discussed a few weeks ago?"

"Yes. A certain amount. I was in Rome recently with a team of EEC auditors and it seems that there's a possibility that some Italian companies have been shipping wines as if they came from certain regions when they didn't. The evidence is purely documentary and goes back a couple of years, so it may well not be possible to prove much. The specific areas I'm interested in are Validicocce and Camarolo....table wines, of course. They seem to be quite popular in Britain. Do you know whether there's been any noticeable increase in wines from that region that've been shipped here?"

"When we were in the process of joining the EEC, a number of the supermarket and off-licence chains woke up to the fact that duties on EEC wines would be coming down and, as more and more British people took their holidays abroad, they would become increasingly familiar with wine, and expect to be able to buy it quite cheaply at home. Of course, many of their customers go on holiday to the Costa del Sol and so on, but Spanish plonk still bears import duties, as they aren't members of the EEC, of course. So they hit on Italian wines as the next best thing – cheaper than French and evidently available in considerable quantities. Valdicocce and Camarolo are two of the most popular red wines and I guess you'd barely have found more than a few bottles in the odd off-licence ten years ago. I confess it's not an area the Wine Standards Board takes vast interest in, mainly because the big supermarkets and off-licences aren't keen to share information and their interest in standards differs substantially from that of our more traditional members. Of course, at the upper end of the market, they've become increasingly knowledgeable...But that's a small area of business for most of them. The only real exception is Oddbins, which sniffs around for bargains, mainly among bin-ends or unsold wine...or wine that's regarded as being sub-standard after a really poor harvest. But you can pick up some noble wines from them....even though they knock it about a bit....and if you're lucky, you can land yourself some really decent stuff. But equally you can get wine that's not even fit to be turned into vinegar."

"So there's been a fairly big increase in wine from Valdicocce and Camarolo coming to this country in the last few years?"

"Yes. Whether they produce enough to meet all their markets, who can tell? I guess they could legitimately expand production within their regions."

"But if they couldn't expand sufficiently to meet demand, where would they get their extra wine from? Would they get it from somewhere else in Italy or from another country altogether?"

"Hmmm...It's table wine with unsophisticated customers....and being sent to a country which they'd assume didn't know much about wine.....But the people who actually buy the stuff are knowledgeable. I doubt a Wasco wine-buyer could tell which part of Valdicocce a particular wine came from, but if

131

he'd got a genuine one and an Algerian or Moroccan wine next to each other, he could certainly tell them apart......So unless they're blending a cheap foreign wine with their own produce, I'd tend to favour them getting it from somewhere else in Italy. There are plenty of pretty ropey Chiantis which aren't worth putting in one of those absurd straw baskets which they could get more profit from shipping here than selling locally."

"But presumably the locals would spot Algerian wine relabelled as their local Chianti?"

"I imagine so. On balance, I think it's most likely they'd import some foreign wine – probably from Algeria – and blend it with local grapes and those brought from elsewhere in Italy. You could assume that any area which is mainly dedicated to table wines rather than appellation contrôlée wines could provide some of the extra......so a fair amount of central and southern Italy. It'd tend to be co-operatives or larger producers and the same grapes that are used in Valdicocce and Camarolo - Corvina , Rondinella, and Molinara.....Though if they're blending it, they could probably get away with different grapes – especially if it's table wine and our Italian equivalents were looking the other way."

"But I should probably reckon on imports being Algerian?"

"I wouldn't exclude Spanish or even Portuguese. They certainly produce some distinctly average wine at extremely low cost."

"Enough to ship in bulk?"

"Certainly."

"How would you blend these wines? In a bottling plant or in the tanks for bulk exports?"

"I imagine you'd want to do it somewhere reasonably secure. Plainly you wouldn't want people asking questions. So, assuming they have premises where the wine is poured into tanks for export, I guess they'd do it there. It'll almost certainly be the same place where they store their genuine wine, especially if they're going to be blending it with their own wine."

"Would you expect the Italians to be suspicious of wine being imported from other countries? I've tended to assume that they produce enough for their own needs and if they imported anything, it'd be expensive French or German wine, rather than bulk table wine."

"I guess you're probably right there......So I suppose it might be described as something else or imported through somewhere where people would be less curious."

"Though this is a line I've needed to follow, I'm not sure it's getting me anywhere particularly helpful."

But it was a useful conversation nevertheless, if only for firming thoughts that had been stirring around in my mind. But I let them remain bubbling away while we travelled back to Brussels. Though Emily and Sarah enjoyed the ship part of the journey, they found the train journeys boring – and reading, drawing and playing "I-spy" only lasted a certain time. Fortunately, my resourceful wife had brought with us some games like "happy families" which required only cards. These weren't their favourites – but "pit" was far too noisy to play in a confined space and "contraband" and "cluedo" involved too many extras, like money and revolvers, daggers and lead piping, etc. But it was still quite tiring. So rather than cooking dinner, we ate out not far from our flat in Woluwe St Lambert on burgers, sausages, chips and stoemp – at least one of us eating some of those things, but none consuming all.

But, as we realised once we'd talked through where we'd got to, it seemed unlikely we were going to get a lot more from examining paperwork. Over the next few weeks, we got confirmation that Ceresini, Greffon and Falcoberti had exported wine described as Valdicocce and Camarolo to Britain, by the hectolitre early in 1974. Virtually all had been for large supermarket or off-licence chains – including Wasco. Whether the wine was genuine was impossible to tell. I passed on the information to Steve Bacon at the EEC Court of Auditors, knowing full well that there was nothing they could do about it, other than report to the appropriate part of the Commission that it appeared that these firms appeared to be guilty of falsely claiming CAP export subsidies and that judging from the overall quantities of these wines which had been produced and sold, there had to have been a substantial amount of misdescription of wines given the Valdicocce and Camarolo DOC. But so far, no report had been finalised. Bacon thought that the Italians were querying some of the figures which they'd given us. Presumably someone had been doing his sums and trying to work out what the audit team had been up to and was now trying to ensure that the whole matter was fudged or kicked into the long grass.

I confess I'd expected to hear from Billy Madden sooner, but it was only a couple of days before we set off for our holiday that I heard back from him, by phone.

"It seems that the Italian shipper you mentioned when we met in London does send us a considerable quantity of wine – both from the regions you mentioned, but also red and white wines from other parts of Italy," he said, speaking with evident caution. "We've been unable to establish whether we received anything which we shouldn't, but the quantities involved mean that we shall undertake a visit to their premises. We propose to do so either towards the end of this year or early in 1976, depending on when they propose shipping to us. Our team will consist of one of our accountants, a stock controller and one of our qualified wine experts. I've decided that I shall lead this team and I'm prepared to invite you or someone from your team along, under the description of an 'EEC fiscal expert'. I hope that'll be acceptable to you."

"That's very good of you. I'll need to confirm with my boss, but I'm sure that we'll be sending someone along – quite probably me."

Knud Henriksen was already on leave, so I knew I couldn't confirm anything until the end of August. The EEC - indeed, Brussels generally – seemed to empty out from the first of August for virtually the whole month. We were taking our longest holiday in years – three weeks – staying in Bellagio on Lake Como. We'd decided to travel by train and hire a car as necessary while we were there. Boring as trains were for Emily and Sarah, they were regarded as considerably better than travelling in a car for long distances. And we'd heard tales of immense traffic jams on roads heading south towards the Alps and into warmer countries.

In the event, we found we didn't need to hire a car. The local buses were reasonably plentiful and the quickest means of transport was by boat across the lake. Though the weather was mostly good, none of us had any great desire to learn how to sail a boat and lazing around in the sun was OK for a few days, but then we all wanted to do things. So we ended up finding some tennis courts where Emily and Sarah could play seriously and Rosemary and I could try to avoid mishitting balls into the lake. We found a few nice walks and took several trips to Lecco, which wasn't particularly distinguished – certainly compared to Bellagio – but had rather more ordinary shops and places to eat where British children might escape from Italian food.

Bellagio was pretty, with its hilly, picturesque streets and handsome palaces and hotels….unlike the more modern hotel which we could afford on the outskirts…and, of course, the magnificent views across the lake to the mountains. Several of the small towns along both sides of the lake were pretty, but it was very much the mountains rising behind the gleaming water of the lake that are my main memory. That and sipping a 'digestivo' after my evening meal, watching a tremendous thunderstorm over the mountains and lake to the north and seeing the rain pouring down "like stair-rods", as my mother used to say, grateful that the restaurant wouldn't dream of turning us out into the streets while the weather was so torrential.

Rosemary and I regularly had a glass of wine with our dinner, but - even though we paid a bit more - we resisted the charms of the Valdicocce and Camarolo wines on every wine list….and the Lambrusco, for that matter…but found plenty of red and white wines that seemed perfectly OK to us.

Apart from one rather odd encounter, it was a completely uneventful holiday. The exception was when we were having dinner in a small restaurant overlooking the western side of the lake, a place which seemed to welcome children and didn't expect them to remain seated throughout the meal or to speak only in hushed tones as if they were in church. As a result, they had a fair number of young families dining there....and at a time when we would normally have expected Emily and Sarah to have been preparing to go to bed.

At the next table was a family of Italians, a couple in their mid-to-late forties with a couple of teenage boys, who, unlike many Italian teenagers we'd seen, appeared quiet and undemonstrative. I probably would barely have noticed them if the husband hadn't decided to strike up a conversation with us.

"You are English? Where are you from?"

"London," I replied. "Do you come from this part of Italy?"

"No. We are from Verona. But my mother lives here in Bellagio. So we visit her for a few days."

"We've been talking about going to Verona on holiday next year perhaps. Would we be able to see Venice also if we were staying there?"

"If you wished to do justice to the city of Venice, you would probably need to stay at least a night or two.....We often come here....I don't think we've seen an English family with young children staying in Bellagio before. Most seem to head for the beaches." His accent was quite pronounced, but his command of English was good.

"While we can travel around quite easily by train, we thought we should see places we might well not be able to get to again."

"By train...from London? That is a long journey. Would it not have been easier to fly to Milano?"

"We work in Brussels at the moment. So the train journey was rather shorter."

"Brussels? You work for the EEC? Or Nato?"

"We are both working for the EEC Commission for two years."

"I work for the Guardia di Finanza. You may have heard of it?"

"Yes. In London I work for HM Customs and Excise and Rosemary for the Metropolitan Police."

"Not quite the sort of people I would expect to be working in Brussels."

"We thought some advisory work in Brussels would be an interesting experience and it'd be best to do something like that while our daughters were still small.....It must be pleasant working in somewhere like Verona. I'm told that it can get unbearably hot further south during the summer months."

"It can get hot enough in the Po valley during the summer. Here we are closer to the mountains, so generally it doesn't get too hot....and if it does, you get a thunderstorm like the one we had two days ago. But even though we are quite close to Lake Garda, the mountains are a little too far away from Verona. So it can feel very hot from time to time."

"I've never been completely certain what areas of work the Guardia di Finanza cover. Do you cover all taxes, both direct and indirect, and also financial frauds? Or are your responsibilities purely fiscal?"

"Any crimes involving the finances of the state are our responsibilities....and that has been extended to include organisations that are the equivalent of the state. Not local authorities, you understand, but the EEC. So if someone is defrauding the EEC in my district, it is part of my job to detect it and deal with it."

I confess that I was finding this conversation rather odd – even slightly surreal. From memory of what I knew about the Guardia di Finanza and the location of the city of Verona, I'd say that he was responsible, among other things, for tackling the CAP fraud among wine producers in the Valdicocce and Camarolo regions. Was it really stretching the bounds of

137

coincidence a bit too far to find him sitting at the next table to us, questioning me about our jobs?

"What sort of frauds against the EEC would take place in Verona?" I asked.

"There are many wine-growers who will be claiming subsidies under the Common Agricultural policy. We also grow wheat, some rice and fruit. All of these may qualify for subsidies. Where there is a subsidy, there is invariably a temptation. I am sure you will have come across the same in your and your wife's line of work."

"Indeed. It's a common saying in Customs & Excise that everyone has been involved in smuggling something, is smuggling something or will smuggle something in future.....Apart from Customs officers, of course."

He turned away at that point, without giving me his name and resumed his conversation with his family. Very curious! I wondered what he was up to? And who might've put him up to it? Rosemary and I discussed my curious conversation with him later, but didn't reach any satisfactory conclusions. But we were on holiday and we let it drop for now. We didn't see the man again, nor any of his family.

We travelled back to a still largely deserted Brussels and spent the last week or so of August in a campsite – in a large hired tent – close to the beach at Middelkerke, a resort not far from Ostend. The area was flat and dull – and fairly crowded – but there were plenty of amusements and tennis courts for Emily and Sarah and the weather remained pleasantly warm. It was more of a holiday for our children than for us – but we'd almost certainly enjoyed being in Bellagio more....and in a place where burgers, sausages and chips seemed to be virtually all there was on offer, there was no grumbling about the food. And the occasional glass of Jupiler didn't give us any uncomfortable reminders that we'd soon be back in harness.

SOME PUBLIC SECTOR SNOOPING

"I believe you'll need to encourage Wasco to get this inspection in before Christmas," said Knud Henriksen. "You won't yet know, but I've been appointed to head the Danish Customs Service with effect from 1 January. My successor, whoever that may be, may well have different views about your wine investigation. Indeed, it's more than possible that Giulizzi and Paolitti will try to ensure that I'm replaced by someone who doesn't encourage SEFF to be as active as it's been...or at least as the two of you, Conor O'Leary and Henri Kervran have been."

"Congratulations!" Rosemary and I echoed each other. It was the first week in September and our first day back in the office.

"So your successor might just pull the plug?" asked Rosemary.

"Yes. Or they might just decide to carry out some form of assessment of the work of SEFF and just put your work on ice until you both return to the UK. I doubt whether Gerry would be able to stop something like that...whereas he might be able to prevent anyone just halting your work for no good reason."

"I'll contact Billy Madden and see what I can do," I said. "But if they don't intend to do their inspection until after Christmas and aren't prepared to do change it, there's not much we can do about it. I'm not sure there's really an alternative – other than trying to nobble your successor before Giulizzi and Paolitti get at them..."

"But if they're from a wine-producing country, it may not be worth the effort," remarked Henriksen. "I don't know what notice Wasco are planning to give these firms in Italy, but if they give them too much, you can bet that anything untoward will have been tidied up and hidden in a cupboard before they get there."

"It's a pity we don't know where Ceresini stores their wine. If that's the most likely place where they blend the foreign wine, you might be able to arrange for an eye to be kept on it to spot when any tankers arrived there. I assume that the wine from local vineyards doesn't get transported in tankers?"

"Even if we could find that out, I'm not sure how easily anyone could keep a watch on a storage or bottling facility. They might well bring the foreign wine in during the night. So you'd need round-the-clock surveillance which could be difficult to arrange," said Rosemary. "In any case, if the Wasco team pick up documents that show they've got orders for X amount of wine, but with the grape harvest in, all they've got is Y gallons, it's a perfectly reasonably question to ask where Z which equals X minus Y is coming from. Once the foreign wine is there, it may be more difficult to distinguish the foreign from the local wine."

"If X equals Z, there's no asking Y," I remarked, realising that I was certainly smirking as widely as Rosemary had ever done.

"I'm sure you've been waiting years to get an opportunity to say that," she retorted, smiling almost as broadly as I was.

"I can see why the Brits decided you two were better off in separate organisations," observed Henriksen, also grinning.

I managed to contact Billy Madden later that week. He told me that the Wasco team would visit Ceresini in the first week of December. It'd be helpful if we could confirm who the "EEC fiscal expert" would be at least a fortnight before. I spoke to Knud Henriksen about this and he suggested we should wait until a little closer to the time, as other matters might intervene and might affect the choice of who went.

As it happened, both Rosemary and I were heavily involved in these "other matters" (which I have describe in more detail elsewhere - *'Brussels Sprouts'*) and mostly forgot about the continuing wine investigation. So it was with a bit of a jolt that Henriksen summoned us and reminded us that one or other of us needed to become a member of the Wasco team visiting Ceresini in little more than a fortnight.

"If I might make an initial suggestion," he said, "I consider that Rosemary should do this. It's difficult to know how Ceresini will react to a visit by Wasco. If I remember rightly, Nick, you said they weren't going to be given much notice. So they're likely to be extremely defensive – and my brief impression of Wasco's representatives in Brussels is that they exude toughness, rather than charm. If you were a company with some unfortunate secrets you wished to hide, how would you react to the sight of Mr Madden and his team?"

"With considerable caution. I guess they'd find him typically English, in a way. Direct rather than effusive. To the point, rather than charming. Courteous, certainly. Indeed, I doubt whether Billy Madden ever loses his temper – though I wouldn't mind betting he can pretend to if the need arises."

"And I guess you'd place yourself closer to him than to your typical Italian?"

"Yes...."

"But on the other hand, Rosemary is a woman...a highly attractive woman, who wears short skirts. Of course, she's as tough as you are and doesn't use the simpering charm that some of my female colleagues in Denmark believe is the way to get ahead. But as far as the Italians are concerned....at least, my impression of Italians....is that they are going to be a lot less suspicious and cautious in front of an attractive young woman in a short skirt."

"That is remarkably sexist," observed Rosemary, "but probably accurate....But there is the small matter of my knowledge of the details of the fiscal side of things, let alone the CAP."

"I'm not sure how much you'd need to know about that. This inspection is more about pinning down what quantities of wine are where and how that relates to the documentary evidence, as I see it," I added, not feeling entirely happy about what I was saying, as it was plain from Rosemary's voice that she wasn't convinced that she was the right person for this.

"And I'm sure we could be flexible with Nick's time while you were away, so he could look after your daughters," added Henriksen.

From what I knew of Rosemary, that wasn't what was troubling her. But as she said nothing, I didn't feel it was right to press her – certainly not in front of Henriksen.

Indeed, it was only after we'd put Emily and Sarah to bed and were relaxing with a mug of tea with some anodyne continental pop music playing on the radio that she told me what was on her mind.

"I know I should be looking forward to going to Italy and trying to nail Ceresini, but I'm afraid I'm not as tough as Knud Henriksen appears to think. I'm not like you. You seem to be able to cope in unfamiliar circumstances, even when the ground is shifting under you. I'm not like that. I like to work in familiar territory and move into strange areas slowly and cautiously. This inspection of Ceresini just feels like a complete jump into the dark to me. And how much Italian do I know? Twenty words? You did most of the talking when we were in Bellagio after about a week of reading that Italian text book...."

"I don't think my Italian was much good...."

"But people seemed to understand it. And you seemed to understand what you read and quite a bit of what people were saying....I know we'll be talking in English...But the documents we're looking at will be all or almost all in Italian. I just feel as though I'll be completely useless...."

"But that's not all is it?"

I put my arm round her shoulders. Tears were streaming down her face.

"You know me too well, Nick Storey," she said and buried her head on my shoulder. I stroked her short, dark hair and kissed her head.

"If I have to do something like this, I need to feel I'm on firm foundations," she continued, drying her eyes on a paper handkerchief. "I've never met Billy Madden or any of his team.

142

They may be perfectly nice people, but they're strangers. I know that I'll feel desperately lonely without you – and Emily and Sarah. Even if you were in the same town, I'd feel much happier. I'd know I could talk things over with you and if I felt bad, you'd be there to comfort me....I know you think I'm brave...But I'm not...."

"I don't think anyone is brave about everything. I've seen how brave you are....If you asked me to seize a load of snakes which were being imported without a licence, I can assure you I'd be heading down the road in the opposite direction as fast as my legs could carry me."

She gave a watery smile.

"Fortunately, no-one is asking you to do that."

"And most of what you'll be doing won't involve Italian. You'll be speaking in English and the important part of the documents will be the figures....And we must be able to find out what the Italian for invoice, consignee, delivery and so on are. You could learn them – or have them written down – so you'd know what the figures referred to..."

"But...."

"But that's not all. If you're going to Verona or whether Ceresini are based, I need to go with you - with or without Emily and Sarah. I know they were bothered about us going off, in case we never came back, after their experience in Riga....But checking some accounts in North Italy is not at all like extracting a senior KGB officer from the Soviet Union."

"I guess we'll be there for at least two days. It'll be tough keeping them amused. You might find a historic city like Verona interesting, but I'll bet they won't."

"I was actually thinking of seeing if my mother could come over and look after them. She'll spoil them dreadfully, but with their school and them showing her around the place to all their favourite playgrounds and burger cafes, they won't have much time to worry about us.....and we can't let our lives be completely dominated by our children's fears – especially when they're rather exaggerated."

"I feel so pathetic wanting this….and probably upsetting them when if I was braver, there wouldn't be a problem."

"You don't think they wouldn't worry if it was just you who was away? I'd be far more worried than if it was me going to inspect Ceresini……And they aren't so young they wouldn't spot I was worrying."

"But what if your mother can't come? And what are we going to say to Knud Henriksen?"

"If it comes down to it, we'll take them with us to Verona. But let's see what my mother says when I ring her in the morning…..But hang on! We're an hour ahead, so it isn't too late to ring her now."

I spoke to my mother, without telling a direct lie but indicating that both Rosemary and I needed to be in Italy for two of three days at the beginning of December. She said she'd happily come over – but her only condition was that we should be around with her for a couple of days so she could do some Christmas shopping in Brussels. That was easy to agree to.

I explained to Knud Henriksen that Rosemary was content to be the "EEC fiscal expert", but genuinely didn't like skating on thin ice….unlike her husband. So she would be much happier if I could go along – so that in between her visits to Ceresini, she could ensure that she got all the fiscal stuff right. And if it came to looking at documents, my Italian was – if rudimentary – at least better than hers. And I suspect, without saying anything, we both knew that Rosemary was probably still a little spooked at recent violent events.

"I suspect you work better as a team anyway," he remarked. "I assume you've got your daughters sorted out?"

"Yes. My mother is quite keen to come over to do her Christmas shopping."

So that was agreed. Rosemary and I spent much of the intervening fortnight swotting up on our Italian technical terms

144

relating to wine and business transactions. Emily and Sarah appeared to accept the prospect of their grandmother looking after them for a couple of days with equanimity. Perhaps being told that we were going to be looking at a company's accounts in Italy not very far from where we'd been on holiday made them less worried about what risks we might be running with men with guns. Or perhaps they were just relieved they wouldn't have to stay with the Henriksens for three or four nights.

They were a little tearful – or at least Sarah was – when we left them at their school on the morning we left, but there were no scenes. Rosemary and I took the train out to Zaventem airport and caught a flight to Milan, where we would meet up with the Wasco team.

We were sitting in a coffee bar overlooking the "arrivals" point when I saw Billy Madden approaching with a couple of other people – both men. They joined us and introduced themselves. Harry Whelan was a manager with "logistics" knowledge, whatever that was. He was about my age, stocky, with dark ginger hair and a Northern Irish accent. Keith Stephens was taller and thinner, with a receding hairline and receding chin. His glasses and BBC accent made him look like the typical product of England's grammar school system. He was an accountant who had also trained as a "master of Wine". It rapidly became apparent that both looked up to Billy Madden with something approaching god-like awe.

I'd already explained to Madden about the fact that I'd be accompanying Rosemary and the reasons why, which were a simplification of what I'd already told Knud Henriksen. We downed some less than exciting ciabattas or paninis and a drink – of coke, bottled water or, in Rosemary's and my case, chinotto. Then it was a hired minibus from the airport to Milan central railway station and from there a train to Verona. Evidently Wasco had been sorting out all the details in advance, for in a very crowded train, we had a booked compartment to ourselves. I wondered whether this was because they wanted to discuss how they would be going about the inspection, but it seemed not. Indeed, as we could hear the voices of Italians in the neighbouring compartments and along the crowded corridor, perhaps Madden had decided there was a risk of our conversation being overheard. As I thought about it, it struck me that it was possible that now that Ceresini knew that the Wasco team was on its way to inspect them, they might have someone keeping tabs on us, trying to pick up any scrap of information they could. A thoughtful, careful man was Billy Madden!

The train rumbled along through virtually constant rain – not fierce and heavy, like the storms I'd seen in Italy before, but like a typical English rain – constant, depressing and dull. Fortunately, it'd stopped by the time we reached Verona station. Even here, there was a minibus awaiting us, which took us to the Piazza Bra, with its huge Roman amphitheatre and large, but plain town hall. From there we walked a couple of hundred yards through pedestrianised streets to our hotel. From the outside, it looked like a converted palace, but inside was comfortable, unpretentious and reasonably priced – as I would've expected. It also boasted a small bar, where we gathered about an hour before dinner. Other than the five of us, the bar was empty.

"Ceresini operates in a small town a few miles from Verona, called Bussolengo. The grapes they receive from local vineyards are processed there, as well as grape juice and wine from local co-operatives. They blend their wine and store it. A small quantity of the best wine is stored in oak barrels for a year or more. The rest is kept in tanks and either bottled in the plant or put into tankers for export," explained Madden.

"Do they keep all their records there too?" asked Stephens.

"Yes. It's supposedly the heart of their operations.....What we are looking for are all documents relating to what wine comes in, from where, and where it goes. I want to get a clear picture of what happens to every drop of wine that ends up in tankers heading for Wasco and our bottling plant, where it comes from, how and where it is blended and when and where it goes into the

146

tankers.....and are the tankers that leave here the same ones that go on board ship in Genoa....? Much of this will need to be nailed down from their documentation. And we need to see their working documents, not what they feel like showing us. It's clear from what the EEC people have found that they are selling a lot more wine than they are producing or claiming to get from vineyards within their designated area. So we have to assume that additional wine is coming in from somewhere. We need to know how it's getting there, how it's accounted for in their records, where it goes.....Let's be honest with ourselves. If Wasco is buying this wine and you were Ceresini, with a much higher demand than you could cope with, where would you send the wine that wasn't Valdicocce, to Wasco and overseas companies like us? Or try to palm it off on the locals?"

"So you believe they've been diddling us?" suggested Whelan.

"It seems logical, don't you think? But we all have our jobs to do. I'm going to grill the management people and judge for myself how trustworthy I find them. I hope that'll also distract them a bit. Keith – I want you primarily to take samples of their wine, wherever you come across it. Get it bottled and labelled exactly where you located it. Sample some of it yourself and if anything tastes suspicious, make sure you indicate it as such with a dot at the end of the details you put on the bottle. But don't let anyone from Ceresini know what you've found. Harry – I want you to go through their logistics with a fine tooth comb – both the physical and documents. As I said, we need an accurate audit trail, as detailed and as complicated as they may have made it. Mrs Storey – I'd like you to go through their accounts, mainly to see whether they're giving us their real accounts or the version they use for public consumption. Since we know that they seem to be selling about double the quantity of wine what they appear to be receiving, their accounts have to be square that circle somehow. My guess is that their public accounts reflect the wine they are supposed to be receiving from their region and not their much larger sales. These must be disguised somehow in their accounts...or there must be some secret account which covers this additional cash-flow. I'd be grateful if you could see whether you can identify this...or at least get some reasonable evidence that it must exists somewhere."

"OK," replied Rosemary.

I knew already that this was what she was expecting to have to do. But, as she'd pointed out, if Ceresini's accountants were good, they wouldn't leave anything to pick away at. The only thing that would indicate that the public accounts were fraudulent would be if there was evidence that the costs and sales figures were much higher than those reflected in the accounts. So it was quite possible she'd be completely dependent on what Whelan and Stephens came up with. And, as she'd said to me, she wanted to make a positive contribution to the work, not rely on the people from Wasco.

We talked about other matters during dinner, which we ate in the hotel. Rosemary and I walked through the largely deserted streets to the Piazza Erbe and the splendid Torre dei Lamberti, then round by a different route to the Piazza Bra and back to the hotel. We said little. I knew Rosemary was feeling tense and anxious, but I'd also learnt that on such occasions it was better to let her speak about what was troubling her if she wanted to, rather than pushing her.

We were in bed by ten o'clock, which was early for us. Naturally, we continued our custom of christening the sheets and made good use of quite a sizeable bath. But I could tell that Rosemary was less relaxed than usual. Afterwards, as she lay on my shoulder in bed, she finally spoke.

"What will you be doing tomorrow?" she asked.

"I understand you'll be going to Bussolengo by car at 8 am," I replied. "I thought I'd see how I could get there by public transport. I'm sure there must be a bus or train there. Unless it's very unlike every other Italian town I've seen, there'll be a central square with a town hall and a church. I'll certainly be there at lunchtime. Before that, I plan to do a bit of exploring....I'm starting to think how I might go about that, but basically I want to find out about Ceresini from the locals....I feel just going to their plant, as Billy Madden calls it, is too easy. If you were running a big fraud like they seem to be doing, would you really keep all the evidence of it for anyone like Wasco carrying out an inspection to find? Surely you wouldn't be so overconfident that you'd assume no-one would ever suspect anything and want to check up?"

"So I might need to find the duplicate accounts somehow? Or be able to prove that the ones they'd shown me were fishy?"

"I'm not sure I'd want to rely on Whelan or Stephens coming up with anything....assuming I'm right and Ceresini are both clever and cautious."

"I was afraid you'd say something like that. You know as well as I do how little practical experience I've got of real accountancy. I've done bits to do with VAT in the City and then tracing the money of those Russian crooks, but that's pretty well all the real world experience I've got. And I've no knowledge of Italian accounting...I know I tried to learn more about it before we came away, but what I read in Brussels seems as lot less certain now I'm here....I'm just afraid I'll let everyone down..."

I knew there would be tears in her eyes. I kissed her head and gently pulled her on top of me, so we were facing each other. I kissed her lips.

"You won't let anyone down. I know you, Rosemary Storey. You'll do the best you possibly can...and then more. If you do that, you can't let anyone down. If you aren't certain about anything, speak to Stephens about it. He must've been an accountant for at least ten years longer than you...and if Madden really wanted the accounts taken apart, he would've brought along his own accountant to do it full time. He's a decent bloke, but I don't get the impression he rates the public sector much. In his business, accountants must be vital to their success. He knows as well as we do that neither the Civil Service nor the police place much reliance on accountants. You could count the number of qualified accountants in C&E on the fingers of one hand – and I'll bet it's not much different in the Met. I doubt whether his expectations of what you'll be able to achieve are particularly high.....You're here because he feels he owes us something for telling him about our suspicions about Ceresini and the other firms – not because he thinks we can do much. I get the very strong impression he believes that if something needs sorting out, Wasco will do it...and by themselves."

"I don't know how much of that you really believe...but..."

She kissed me and then lay with her head on my shoulder.

"I'm sorry I've been so stupid and cowardly over this....You know how I hate this leaping into the dark....But I will do the best I possibly can...."

"If you need to talk about anything...or just want to let off steam, I'll definitely be in the main square in Bussolengo tomorrow at one o'clock. I'll stay until about half past. I probably won't be too noticeable....after all, I don't want to draw attention to myself. But I'll look out for you.....Don't think you have to come. It's just I'll be there if you need me."

"I think ever since we first met, I've always felt you'd be there if I needed you....It's an odd thing...If you told me I might have to face a man with a gun tomorrow, I'd be a lot less bothered about it than having to go through pages of accounts...."

"As far as I'm concerned, I hope it's just the pages of accounts."

We slept, with her head on my shoulder as usual. We got up early and I watched her get into the car with the Wasco team, showing enough of her slim legs to distract any male Italian. I hoped that her day would go better than she feared.

The hotel reception directed me to the bus station and I caught a bus to Bussolengo shortly before 9 am. The countryside was pleasant and the morning was sunny, even fairly warm. The bus was heading for a town called Lazise on Lake Garda, so it didn't stop too often. It dropped me in the Piazza Vittorio Veneto and rumbled on its way westwards. I could see the tall tower of a church or possibly town hall, so I headed in that direction. But it turned out to be a church and definitely not in the town square. I spent the next twenty minutes or so walking up one street and down another, across another and along another before I finally found the town hall square. It was undistinguished – and what I at first thought was the town hall, turned out to be a bank. But it was called the Piazza Bussolengo and had a couple of cafes where I could keep an eye out for Rosemary at lunchtime. Meanwhile, I needed to explore the town and see what I might learn about Ceresini.

The town had a bookshop, which also sold newspapers, postcards and souvenirs – mostly of Verona or Lake Garda. There were lots of postcards of the view of Monte Baldo from Bussolengo, but only one card each for the two churches which I'd seen. It was too small to have local maps, but there was a little guide to the town, produced by a Paolo Murini on behalf of the "commune", which combined its history and locals of note – of whom there were few and none I'd ever heard of. But, as I read it, sipping a cappuccino in one of the cafes, I was able to learn about the rise and rise of the firm of Ceresini, started by a "partigiano" (hero of the resistance to Mussolini) from Bergamo, Luigi Ceresini in 1947. At that stage, he provided the opportunity for local Valdicocce wine-growers to sell some or all of their grapes or wine to him to sell to a wider market, so that both profited. He was behind moves to make Valdicocce recognised as a serious Italian wine, both at home and abroad. As more vineyards came into cultivation in the Fifties and Sixties, Ceresini became a large producer, with their own blending and maturation vessels and bottling plant established in Bussolengo. It was also noted that the plant had also been used to blend Camarolo wines, but when the DOC regime (Denominazione d'Origine Controllata) was introduced, Ceresini was compelled to produce those wines within the Camarolo region. At that time, a new plant was built, to cope with the increased volume of grapes and wine being produced, on a road going out of the town to the north west, not far from the River Adige. The old plant, on the Via Verona, on the opposite side of the town, was closed.

On the basis of what I'd said to Rosemary the previous evening, it seemed to me that a possible place where Ceresini might store the wine they were bringing in from outside would be this old plant. Though it'd been shut almost ten years previously, the vessels they'd used for storing wine might still be serviceable. If I could find where it was, I should be able to tell whether it was completely deserted or whether there were signs that it'd been in use recently.

And I had a story ready in case someone saw me snooping around.

I realised I didn't have a lot of time before I was due to wait in the main square in case Rosemary wanted to meet me at lunchtime. I set off, pleased that it was neither raining nor unpleasantly hot. I reckoned Bussolengo must be quite a pleasant place to live, close to the mountains, Lake Garda and the river. None of the buildings were particularly distinguished, but there was little that was ugly either. There weren't many people about, either pedestrians or vehicles. I found the Via Verona quite quickly, helped by knowing that it would be roughly in the direction from where I'd come earlier in the bus.

The former Ceresini plant was unmissable. There was a high wire fence round the outside of brick buildings that looked like a large warehouse, alongside a concrete structure that looked the worse for wear. Neither had any architectural merit. The brick warehouse looked like something hastily constructed in the aftermath of the war – an Italian version of King's Beam House! It had two doors at the front – one large enough to run a lorry into, the other for people. Along part of the front there were small square, metal-framed windows which, though dirty, remained unbroken. The concrete structure was a little higher, constructed from large concrete panels on a metal and concrete frame. Several of the panels had disintegrated completely, especially at the ground level....or perhaps they'd been smashed up and removed. Some of the higher ones had also gone, or were apparently rotting away, held in place only by the steel girders that ran horizontally between the main frame of the building. As a result, it was impossible to tell where the doors were....and only a few small windows survived, all having lost their glass.

Though the front gates were padlocked, there were several places where the wire fence had come away from the concrete posts to which they had been attached. There seemed to be no-one about, so I pushed my way through and went inside. There was no evidence of any vehicles on the concrete yard at the front of the buildings. But there'd been heavy rain the previous day, so unless someone had been there since then, any trace of visitors would've been obliterated.

The main door to the brick warehouse was locked, so I went round to the crumbling concrete structure. Still no-one appeared. I began to wonder if this place was being used for illicit purposes, it seemed to have been left surprisingly unguarded. So perhaps my guesswork was wrong. Inside, there was a metal structure, plainly rusty and unused for years, which looked like some sort of pulley and hoist system, possibly for moving barrels. All around was debris, pieces of metal and bricks and broken pieces of concrete. At first, I took no notice of it. But after I'd scoured the rest of the structure and seen nothing, except for what looked like the remnants of a door frame and metal doors leaning against the back wall, I began looking at it, purely because it seemed to be all there was left to examine.

Then it struck me, it looked a little odd. It looked unnatural, as though it'd been carefully arranged. The floor was concrete and, inevitably, quite dusty. But you'd expect debris to relate to something that had been there, either on the ground or fallen from higher up. The place showed no signs of vandalism. There were no graffiti – a noticeable, and suddenly suspicious, difference – from any other apparently deserted building or suitable wall I'd seen elsewhere. There were no abandoned bottles of beer or wine or coke cans or discarded cigarette packets or butts. If the local tearaways had been here, they might've kicked a few old walls down or destroyed remnants of the old machinery. Otherwise, you'd expect something like that to decay in its place. But the debris looked as though it'd been brought from somewhere else and carefully strewn about the floor.

But why? If I could get into the brick building, I might be able to work out what the concrete structure was used for. Presumably one was for storing the grapes as they came in and possibly the wine in barrels or perhaps large tanks and the other was used for bottling the wine. I wandered over to the brick building. At the back, there were several broken windows, at least two of which I reckoned I could get through. But I'd no idea whether someone might be watching the place. The fact that no-one had accosted me didn't mean there was no-one there. And if I climbed inside, I might find myself ensconced in the local police station when I was due to be meeting Rosemary.

I peered through the windows. Some rooms seemed to be offices. Others were larger. Indeed, these were next to a couple of very large doors – padlocked, of course – which looked suitable for bringing vehicles in. But was this where the wine or lorry-loads of grapes came in or where lorries carrying cases or bottled wine or tankers full of wine came out?

The brick building seemed older than the concrete structure. I needed to think about the chronology. If I assumed that Ceresini had started off here in 1947, what would he have been doing then? I guessed he'd've been bringing in barrels or even bottles and flagons of local wine as well as cart-loads of grapes. The wine would've been made here, bottled and taken out.

So why would he build the concrete structure later? Evidently, in view of its state of decomposition, it hadn't been built a lot later. What would he have needed to expand? Probably storage and his bottling capacity. But presumably the wine - whether as wine or in the form of grapes – would come in at roughly the same time, whereas he could carry out the bottling over a longer period. After all, Valdicocce wasn't like Beaujolais Nouveau that had to be rushed into the hands of gullible customers as fast as possible. So though he might need to extend his bottling capacity, the main pressure, as the business grew, would be on storage – both before the wine was made and for the finished product. So it was perhaps more likely that the concrete structure had contained some sort of racking system for the grapes and large barrels or tanks for the fermented wine. Would they have been removed to the new plant? Or sold?

If I was trying to conceal wine I shouldn't have, would I be storing it in barrels or tanks which could be spotted by even a casual trespasser? Instead, wouldn't I try to store it out of sight, somewhere which looked deserted, without "keep out" notices, without guards? That'd suggest underground tanks – and might well explain why the debris on the floor of the concrete structure gave me that peculiar sensation of not looking right.

There must be some way of getting into the tanks, of course. But that would mean grubbing around on the floor and possibly attracting attention. It would also be very hit and miss. I felt I needed a little more time to try and work out the best place to start. It seemed quite possible that once I started looking, if anyone was keeping surveillance on the place, I might not have much time to locate the tanks before I might have to leg it, smartish. In any case, it was getting close to lunch time and I needed to get back to the main square and get myself in position to see if Rosemary turned up. I returned the way I'd come, with no-one apparently watching or asking me what I was getting up to. It felt a bit odd....Indeed, the place as a whole seemed rather quiet. But then, I suppose most people would be working - presumably quite a few in the Ceresini plant. Perhaps others commuted into Verona to work?

It was twenty-to one when I reached the main square. Assuming Rosemary was coming from the direction of the "new" Ceresini plant, I went into the "Monte Baldo" restaurant and ordered minestrone and tagliatelle with pesto and pine nuts, accompanied by a glass of Moretti beer. I managed to get a small table by the window and kept an eye on the square, as I first waited for my meal and then ate it. About a dozen people came into the restaurant, mostly in small groups, who immediately started to converse in the loud and animated Italian style. Though I'd seen it irritate some of EEC auditors when we were in Rome, it didn't bother me – and today it felt as though it was enveloping me in a convenient anonymity.

I ate as slowly as I could. Kristen Pedersen, the forensic accountant in SEFF and reputedly Knud Henriksen's mistress, had once told me at a party about some Finnish dietician who recommended chewing every mouthful of food fifty times as a way of removing all digestive problems. I'd tried it briefly – with a plate of steak, chips and salad, if I remembered rightly. It turned every mouthful – whatever the original piece of food – into utterly tasteless cardboard....an effective slimming device, rather than improving one's digestion I'd felt. I thought about doing this now, purely as a way to pass the time. But after trying it twice, I stuck to taking a longer than usual gap between mouthfuls. But by the time the waitress asked me whether I wanted a dessert, I realised it was twenty to two. So I ordered an espresso and left about a quarter of an hour later.

I hoped that the fact that Rosemary hadn't appeared meant that her day was going well....or at least, not so badly that she felt she needed my support or advice. But I now needed to get back to the hotel in Verona in time for her return. But that should still leave me sufficient time to investigate the old Ceresini site further – and locate the underground tanks, always assuming they were there. I confirmed in a shop that sold newspapers and cigarettes what times the buses to Verona left and from where. Then I set off for the Via Verona.

There seemed to be nobody about as I reached the old plant and made my way inside as I'd done previously. As I'd been watching out for Rosemary and when I wasn't thinking about chewing my food, I'd worked out a plan for locating the tanks. If the debris had been placed there to disguise the existence of the tanks, it was unlikely to have been placed randomly. Indeed, there had to be some mechanism for lifting the lid of the tanks and moving it out of the way so that wine could be poured in. And it also struck me that as there'd been no obvious hollowness in the sound of my steps as I'd been walking around in the concrete building, either the lid was very thick concrete – and therefore hard to move aside – or the tanks were already mostly full.

I looked at the various pieces of debris. In four places there were what looked like the remnants of a column of brick. But if they'd been part of the same column, how come they were twenty feet apart? If the column had fallen, I'd expect all the pieces to be close and roughly in a line. When I stood next to one at the southern end of the building, I could see that they were pretty well in line, but twenty feet or more apart. I dragged the nearest to one side. It was heavy and quite hard work. But it was worth it. Underneath was a large iron ring, completely clean…Indeed, it looked as though someone was keeping it from rusting by wiping it with an oil rag, as some came off on my fingers. Just next to it I could also see the edge of the lid of the tank. The lid was evidently concrete and, I guessed, required a vehicle with a chain attached to the ring to move it. Certainly I wasn't going to be able to lift it on my own…not in a hundred years!

I wasn't going to learn any more from checking the other pieces of similar debris. It struck me that the most sensible thing I could do would be to get out of there, remaining unnoticed – with luck, and return to Verona. I was just at the edge of the building when I realised I hadn't replaced the piece of debris – or made it appear the same as it'd been before I disturbed it. So I went back and dragged it back into position and scuffed up some of the dirt by it, so that it looked undisturbed. Then I made my way out of the building.

I was just approaching the gap in the wire, when I heard a voice from behind me. It was quite a deep, guttural voice, speaking in Italian. I had no idea what the man had said to me.

"Are you speaking to me?" I asked in English. "I'm sorry. I didn't understand what you just said."

"Inglese?" he asked. He was a couple of inches taller than me and quite a lot bigger, but appeared quite fit. He was in his late twenties, with a beard and shaggy dark hair, with rather brutal features. Not the sort of bloke to tangle with in an alley on a dark evening!

"Si. Ma io parlo poco l'Italiano. » (*Yes. But I speak little Italian*)

"What you doing here? This private property. You should not be in here."

"I'm sorry. I didn't realise. I'm a historian of wine and wine-making. I'm writing a book about Italian wines. I'm studying Valdicocce wines and I believe this was the original site where Luigi Ceresini set up his business. I was hoping to see some interesting remnants of the winery, but it all seems to have gone."

"I don't understand. You come with me."

I decided there was no way the combination of his limited English and my limited Italian was going to persuade him to prevent me from continuing on my way, so I allowed him to lead me along the Via Verona to a small café/bar "Da Enzo", which reeked of cigarette smoke, coffee and red wine. Once my eyes were accustomed to the darkness, I saw a short man behind the bar. He was either completely bald or shaved his head. He must've been in his late fifties, with small, piggy eyes and a plump reddened face.

The big man was speaking to him, slowly, in Italian. Though I could understand a few words, the whole conversation meant nothing to me.

"Fausto says you were spying on the old Ceresini place," said the barman, in heavily accented, but intelligible English. "You don't speak Italian?"

"Only a little."

"Why were you there? It is forbidden to enter there."

"I'm sorry I didn't know. There didn't seem to be any signs. As I tried to explain to your friend…"

"Fausto is my son...."

"I was explaining to your son that I'm a historian of wine, currently employed by the Wine Standards Board in London. I write about the history of wine from when it was first discovered. But my current project is to write a history of Italian wine. I am working at present on the wines of this region, especially Valdicocce. Luigi Ceresini played an important role in the development of Valdicocce wine and I discovered from the local guide book that the place where he started his business was the ruins on the Via Verona. I hoped to see something that might make a good photograph for my book, but I found nothing that would be suitable. I was just leaving when your son spoke to me."

The barman said nothing to me but spoke at length to his son. I guessed he was probably explaining what I'd said and whether it fitted with what he'd seen of me. The big man called Fausto appeared to listen carefully. Then he peered at me and shrugged his shoulders. What I would've done if he'd indicated he thought I was lying, I wasn't sure. I reckoned I could get out of the café before either of them could lay a hand on me and I could probably run faster than either of them. But whether I could both keep out of their sight (and that of any other relatives, friends or neighbours they could drum up) and catch a bus back to Verona seemed problematical.

"You should seek permission next time if you wish to do this type of thing," said the barman, staring at me with his small, uncomfortable eyes.

"If I did wish to go back there, who should I ask permission?"

"You should go to the new Ceresini offices and ask there. You know where they are?"

"On the other side of Bussolengo, not far from the River Adige."

"You should also remember for the future that in Italy, people do not go on private land even if there is no notice telling them to stay out. It is illegal to enter private property without permission."

"I'll certainly remember that."

It appeared that I was allowed to go. I went out and headed back towards the town. I didn't look back, but I got the distinct feeling that Fausto was watching me from the door of the café/bar "Da Enzo" until I disappeared from sight.

I passed both the bar and the old Ceresini place while sitting in the bus going back to Verona. I deliberately sat on the other side of the bus, so I couldn't be seen. At least it didn't look as though Fausto had seen what I was up to – or I doubt whether they would've let me go so easily. That was the good news – and probably all of it. The bad news was that if anyone examined where I'd moved the debris which covered the iron ring, I reckoned they'd probably be able to tell that it'd been tampered with....and the only logical suspect would be me. Would someone check what I'd been up to? If I was Ceresini concealing a large quantity of illicit wine, I'd want to examine minutely what I might've been up to. But I wouldn't hand that task to a lummox like Fausto.

As we neared the suburbs of Verona, I also began to ask myself whether the barman, Fausto's father, had actually believed what I'd told him. As I'd done no damage and, presumably as far as Fausto was concerned, hadn't discovered anything, there'd be no reason to detain me against my will. There was no reason for them to know who I was. But I began to think that my cover story was perhaps a bit too clever. If they suspected someone of trying to find out where their illicit wine was being stored, a stranger who appeared to know quite a lot about wine put himself in the frame in a way that perhaps an industrial archaeologist might not have done. Not that there was anything I could do about it now, but I feared it might make it difficult for me to make another visit to Bussolengo.

But then there was scarcely enough there to warrant a further excursion without a rather stronger excuse.....Yet one thing was nagging at me.......There was evidently some sort of subterranean enclosure opened by using the recently-oiled metal ring and it was also being concealed. But did it contain anything? Did it contain illicit wine? Or something else? I didn't relish the idea of calling in the authorities – whoever they might be in this context – and finding either that the bird had flown or never been in the coop in the first place: in other words, when opened, the tanks were empty and looked as though they hadn't been in use for donkey's years.

Perhaps Rosemary and the Wasco team had discovered something that would enable my discovery to fit in better?

A PRIVATE SECTOR FACT-FINDING MISSION CHANGES UNEXPECTEDLY

I got back to the hotel not long after 4pm. It was unlikely that Rosemary and the Wasco team would get back much before 6pm. Certainly, Billy Madden didn't strike me as the sort of person who didn't do a full day's work. So I decided to spend an hour or so having a look at the sights of Verona. I felt a bit guilty doing it without Rosemary, but I told myself that if I found some really interesting things, we might be able to grab half an hour at some stage so I could show her.

I walked up to the Piazza d'Erbe and found behind it another square called the Piazza dei Signori, quieter and more formal, with some fine buildings, including one called the Palazzo della Ragione, the Palace of Reason. For a Renaissance building, it had an enlightened and rather cheering name. I wondered who had built it and for what purpose? Then I came across some wonderful tombs of knights in armour on great white marble pedestals, reaching up thirty feet into the air. These were the tombs of the Scaligeri rulers of Verona, who'd certainly intended to be as notable in their deaths as they evidently believed they'd been in their lives….even though I, and doubtless countless other tourists, had no idea who they were until we came to Verona. I continued on through the narrow streets, past several fine churches and more small palaces. Unlike what I'd seen of Rome, it'd seem that space was at a premium in Verona. Apart from the Piazza Bra on the edge of the old city, the squares were small and there seemed to be no vast palaces or other buildings. But there was also little evidence of the passion for pulling down old buildings that seemed to me to be in the process of ruining the individuality of many town centres in Britain. Though there were plenty of shops and cafes, I could almost feel myself going back two, three, four hundred years and believe that the city wouldn't look all that much different.

The Scaligeri tombs had whetted my appetite to see the Scaligeri castle which my guide book showed me was by the River Adige. But I'd eaten up too much of my time and decided just to meander back through the narrow streets to the hotel. The other place the guidebook tempted me to see, San Zeno Maggiore, was the best part of half an hour's walk, I reckoned.

No-one had returned by the time I got back, so I got a green tea in the hotel bar, feeling that I'd had enough coffee for one day. About twenty minutes later, I heard English voices coming into reception, which then dispersed. I went up to our room, to find Rosemary just unlocking the door. She turned and we kissed, as though we'd been apart for a month, rather than a few hours.

"Perhaps we should go inside, rather than shock the neighbours," she said.

"This is the city of Romeo and Juliet," I replied. "I'm sure the neighbours should be unshockable."

We kissed some more and then took a bath together, playing with the shower attachment and finished off making love on the bed, which creaked rather a lot.

"I'm sorry I didn't get to see you at lunch time," Rosemary said. "I assume you were there? We got lunch provided by Ceresini and there didn't seem to be any possibility of escaping."

"I was there. But I did a bit of exploring as well, so it wasn't a wasted day. How did you get on?"

"I'd probably better tell you after dinner. Billy Madden wants us all to meet up in the bar in…..about five minutes….So we'd better get dressed…"

"So – what have we learnt?" asked Madden, as we arrived. The Wasco team were seated in the hotel bar, each with a glass of beer. As we sat down, Whelan brought a couple of glasses over and handed them to us.

163

"They've definitely been selling more wine than they've been producing," said Whelan. "But the additional wine isn't being stored on those premises. There's no way they could ship wine through there any faster than they're doing now. The inputs and outputs just about balance. So the extra is being stored and shipped from somewhere else."

"May I ask whether the wine produced there is bottled or mainly shipped in bulk?" I asked.

"Most of it is bottled. The quantity that leaves there in bulk is just about sufficient to match what Wasco receives from them...."

"...Which is, of course, what they claim..." added Madden.

"But that's preposterous," Whelan continued. "They have half a dozen customers they supply in bulk. Where is that wine? And where is it being stored and shipped from?"

I decided to let them continue with their "wash-up session", as Madden called it, before adding my surmises.

"I'd say that the wine there was genuine Valdicocce," said Stephens. "There might be some stuff with grapes from just outside the region, but I doubt it'd be more than about 10% of the total. If we were genuinely getting our wine from that plant, I doubt we could really grumble about that....and proving it would be extremely tricky anyway."

"What about the accounts?" Madden asked Rosemary.

"The ones which they showed me are perfectly correct," she replied. "Everything balances and nothing sticks out at all. That's what makes them suspicious. I'm sure if you looked through Wasco accounts, you find things that were lumpy or needed some explanation. But these had nothing odd in them at all. And, of course, knowing that they're concealing a significant part of their sales and purchases means that the whole set of accounts are completely bogus. They've been created presumably for any external examination, but I doubt whether they bear more than a slight relationship to the real nature of their business."

"Do you reckon they have a more accurate set of books somewhere?"

"I expect so. But they aren't going to let us go anywhere near them. They're certainly not going to leave them anywhere we might come across them."

"So what we've got is some evidence that they're shipping a lot more than they're producing. So that additional wine has to come from somewhere. But we can't point to where it is. So we have suspicions, but nothing that'd really justify us breaking our contract with them?"

Madden sounded frustrated and irritated.

"I guess so," replied Stephens.

"We might have a bit more than that," I remarked. "I had a wander round Bussolengo today, just to see what I could find out about Ceresini. I got a locally-produced guidebook which told me a certain amount about Ceresini. When Luigi Ceresini set up the business in Bussolengo in 1947 he used different premises, on the other side of town from his present ones. I had a look at the place. It was dilapidated and looked as though no-one had been there for donkey's years. But some of that was deliberate. I came across what I think are a couple of large underground tanks. All I saw was a recently-oiled large iron ring, which I reckon is used to attach a chain to, so that it can be pulled sideways by a truck. It was carefully concealed by rubble, which I'm sure was deliberate."

"Are you sure it was a tank and not just the remnants from the old premises?"

"I'm not certain. But why would you conceal a metal ring like that under a piece of debris that didn't look as though it came from the building it was in at all? And why was the ring oiled, so that it didn't rust?"

"Were there any marks of anyone being there?"

"No. But it seemed to me they take care not to leave any evidence that the place is in use. I believe it's kept under surveillance – not all the time possibly. I was stopped when I was leaving the second time and asked questions by barman in a nearby bar...the bloke carrying out the surveillance was his rather dim-witted son......"

"But if they're bringing in wine from outside by the tanker load and moving it out also by tanker, I guess they wouldn't need to open the concealed tanks more than a couple of times," observed Stephens.

"But in that case, why bring the wine here at all?" demanded Madden. "Why don't they just keep it in the original tankers or even on the ship and just fiddle the paperwork?"

"I realise it's possible to bribe ship's officers and crew," I said. "But Lloyds List will generally tell you where a ship has been. So if the wine they're selling to the UK is Algerian, for instance, if the ship carrying it didn't put in at a suitable Italian port, it'd be very easy to check that the wine couldn't possibly be Valdicocce. In fact, it'd have to put in somewhere like Genoa. After all, would you really ship wine from this region through Bari or Naples?"

"I'd expect it to travel in unmarked tankers or ones with a name suggesting a completely different cargo," added Rosemary. "But it'd travel from here to Genoa in Ceresini tankers, with a load of paperwork we haven't been able to find yet."

I was pleased that she seemed to have regained her self-confidence....and her joie de vivre.

"Yes. I suppose using unmarked tankers would invite speculation," mused Madden. "But we can hardly demand that we see these concealed tanks. And if they haven't got any wine in them, it'd be a waste of time.....and I guess Ceresini would just claim they used the old tanks for temporary storage if the ones at their plant got too full.....And that's what they might do anyway......Marcello Ceresini and Giuseppe Montremoli, the two Directors I met today are extremely well-organised and seem to have an answer to everything."

"But if they do, why are they so furtive about it?" I asked. "Surely if these tanks are legit, you'd have official Ceresini signs and "keep off" notices posted and proper formal control over the premises and the tanks wouldn't be so carefully concealed?"

"Hmm...I suppose that figures....But I don't quite see what we can do about it."

"When I was stopped, I claimed I was a historian of wine, writing a book about Italian wines......and at present I was researching Valdicocce wine....and I'd learnt about the old Ceresini plant from the local guide book. Wouldn't it be plausible if I turned up at the new Ceresini place to seek an interview with someone there about their recent history, how the Valdicocce brand had developed in recent years, etc? And suppose I bumped into the Wasco team...It wouldn't be too unlikely that I might mention that I'd already been to the former plant. Wouldn't that give you enough of a lead to seek to have a look at the place?"

"I'm still not sure why we could plausibly do that?"

"I doubt whether even Ceresini believe that a team of this size with you in charge has just come over for a spot check. They must suspect you have suspicions about some of the wine you've been getting. Why don't you tell them straight out that you've heard via the British Wine Standards Board that the EEC have identified more wine being shipped or sold within Italy by Ceresini than they and their local partners produce? You are concerned that some of the wine which you've been shipped isn't Valdicocce. Assuming that the EEC are correct, the figures which you saw today suggest that every drop of Valdicocce which Ceresini export goes to Wasco. As you know that other firms in the UK also sell Valdicocce supplied by Ceresini, it isn't credible that they get wine that isn't Valdicocce, but Wasco gets all of it. Evidently they're getting wine from somewhere else and storing it outside their site....as their figures show, they couldn't handle more than they do now, but the EEC figures suggest that they do. That means they must either have a completely separate plant processing the wine from the original grapes or they're importing wine and storing it somewhere. You would feel more reassured about what was going on if you could inspect their old plant, which seems a logical place where additional wine might be being stored."

"That's quite ingenious....But I'll need to think about it.....Though I'm pretty certain Ceresini are conning us, I don't want to lose a supplier unnecessarily and on the basis of rather skimpy evidence."

"It's your decision, of course.....I think I'll go to Ceresini anyway tomorrow....in my guise as a wine historian. I'd like to get more details about what their former plant was like....If nothing else, it should give me a better idea as to whether those were tanks covered by concrete lids, as I suspect....And if they're difficult, I'll conclude that they've got something to hide."

I managed to persuade the Wasco team that we didn't need to eat in the hotel every night. We found a pleasant restaurant in the Piazza d'Erbe and Rosemary and I enjoyed sharing a large pizza "di quattro stagione", as well as various ice creams and sorbets enclosed in the skin or shell of the appropriate fruit or nut. And in view of the extreme moderation of Billy Madden and his team, I decided to forego an amaro after my espresso, something I'd got quite used to while on holiday in Bellagio.

"You seem a lot happier than yesterday," I remarked to Rosemary, when we got back to our room.

"The Ceresini accounts weren't as impenetrable as I'd feared," she replied. "I was worried that I wouldn't be able to understand them and that Madden would ask Stephens to help me out...But though I'm sure they're bogus, I didn't have any trouble with them. And though I didn't find anything fishy, neither did anyone else. Ceresini have concealed their tracks quite well....and Madden plainly had a frustrating day being smooth-talked by the bosses. They were extremely courteous and helpful....and we had a very nice buffet lunch, with as much Prosecco...or Valdicocce or Camarolo – Ceresini bottled, naturally – as you wished to drink."

"I bet Madden didn't have more than one glass."

"No. And neither did Stephens and Whelan...or me, for that matter. I stuck to the Prosecco, because I like it and because red wine - even a glass – at lunchtime makes me sleepy all afternoon."

"Probably what they were hoping for."

"In that case, they'd plainly forgotten the puritanical tendencies of many Anglo-Saxons."

"So what exactly are you all going to be doing tomorrow? Madden didn't mention anything this evening, so I assumed you must've talked about it earlier."

"I don't know either. There aren't any more accounts for me to look through. I don't know whether he's going to demand some more accurate records or whether he's planning some sort of confrontation...I haven't a clue."

I felt that there was possibly something Rosemary wasn't telling me. But she plainly wasn't unhappy and I knew well enough that there was no point pressing her.

The following morning, I left the hotel before Rosemary and the Wasco team did. Though I didn't have to wait long for a bus to take me to Bussolengo, I thought I spotted the Wasco hired car overtaking us as we drove past the outskirts of Bassone. While I was on the bus, I discovered there was a stop in Bussolengo about half a mile nearer the new Ceresini plant than where I'd got off the previous day, so I got to the plant rather sooner than I'd expected.

It was a modern-looking place, without much style, but no more than two storeys high, with that creamy concrete beloved of the Italians, which remained unstained by the weather.....something which I felt British architects who also favoured concrete tended to overlook, with a result that the original purity of line of many modern buildings in Britain was disfigured by ugly staining. Unlike the old plant, the place was festooned with banners in metal, plastic and linen with "Ceresini" in blue lettering on a yellow and white background. Several large adverts were set up on boards round the external fence. The main entrance had a small gatehouse, where a man with grey hair and matching moustache, in a blue jacket with a blue and yellow striped tie, controlled the entrance/exit barrier.

I thought I could make out the Wasco hired car in the car park in front of the building. I also noticed several huge urns with olive trees growing out of them placed at regular intervals between the car park and the main building.

"I am a historian of wine," I explained to the man in the gatehouse, speaking English slowly and loudly in the traditional manner. "I would like to speak to someone about the history of wine-making by Ceresini."

"Go to reception," he replied in a thick, but comprehensible English.

I headed through a largely full car park and through some glass doors into a wide, airy entrance hall, with a neatly coiffed, slightly forbidding-looking young woman behind a reception desk. She evidently had seen enough foreign visitors to know I wasn't Italian and addressed me in very competent English.

"Do you have business with someone here?"

I explained about my interest in Ceresini from the perspective of a historian of wine, but that I had no appointment. Indeed, I didn't even know who I might meet. She gave me a grave look, which may or may not have disguised the opinion that I was an idiot.

"I shall need to speak to Gaetano," she said, picked up her phone and spoke rapidly in Italian. I didn't understand a word, which in the circumstances, was probably a good thing.

"Gaetano says you will need to wait. He will see whether anything can be arranged," she explained. "There is a waiting room with coffee and tea facilities through that door."

I went into the waiting room. It was large, with the capacity to hold a hundred or more people. Perhaps it was used for parties or large meetings? There was a glass jug of filter coffee on a hot plate, with a flask of milk next to it. I poured myself out a cup and wandered round the room, wondering how I might contrive to "accidentally" bump into the Wasco team....working on the assumption that they would find it more difficult to discover me "accidentally".

On the walls were three pictures of Verona, a rather fine fortress by a lake, presumably Lake Garda, and a couple of what I recognised as Monte Baldo. Otherwise, there were several posters advertising Ceresini wine. I noticed it was only Valdicocce. Did they have another plant in the Camarolo region processing their Camarolo wine? Could they have been using that plant to conceal the additional Valdicocce wine? But....I recalled the EEC auditors had indicated that they were selling more Camarolo wine than they produced too. So that still suggested that the tanks at their old plant were being used.

I finished the coffee. I wasn't doing much good stuck in this room. I went back to the lady at the reception desk and asked where there was a toilet. She pointed one out, beyond the room I'd just been in. I used the facilities and was on my way back, when I saw Whelan coming down the stairs towards reception. I went over to him.

"Excuse me," I said, louder than I usually would. "Aren't you staying at the Accademia hotel in Verona? You don't work here do you?"

"I don't work here," replied Whelan. "I'm here on business. Are you here on business too?"

"Sort of. I'm a wine historian and I'm hoping to talk to someone about the role of Luigi Ceresini in developing Valdicocce wine. I don't suppose you could help me?"

"I'm only here for a couple of days. I've only met a couple of people here ...about business matters."

"Well, at least you're in this building. It's rather nice. I visited the old Ceresini plant yesterday on the other side of town. It's practically fallen down."

"There's another Ceresini plant? I thought this was the only one."

"It doesn't look as though it's being used any more. I suppose you could store stuff in part of it. But when I went there all the doors to the building were padlocked."

He continued on to the reception desk, apparently to see if the receptionist could get him a replacement battery for his calculator. I went back to the waiting room, thinking that it'd probably been a complete accident that we'd met. I hoped Whelan had the nous to make use of the information I'd told him so publicly.

I didn't have to wait more than another five minutes. Then another refined and well-coiffed secretary collected me from the waiting room and took me upstairs to meet Giacomo Sporagli, a man well into his sixties, with a fine head of long grey hair, a thin, tanned face and rimless glasses. He led me to a small meeting room, with stylish metal furniture and a view across the car park.

"You wanted to know about the history of Ceresini?" he began, in strongly-accented English. "My English is not so good, but I will try to answer your questions."

I explained my interest and then asked him to take me through what he knew about Luigi Ceresini and how he had brought Valdicocce wines forward in such a successful way. He told me that he knew Luigi Ceresini well. He had been one of his first wine-buyers, identifying suitable vineyards and cooperatives to buy wine from, to be blended into what we all recognised today as typical Valdicocce wine. I moved on to the setting up of the old plant, why that particular place was chosen, and so on.

"The land was going cheap," replied Sporagli. "Luigi Ceresini was never a man to spend more than he had to. Even today, though he is a very wealthy man, a millionaire many times over, he still lives in a small house on the shores of Lake Garda, when he could easily afford a large villa or even a palace....But he also wanted somewhere close to the roads and railways. He was always intending to sell his wine outside this region, to other parts of Italy and to other countries."

"And he moved to this location for the same reason?"

"Certainly, the land was cheap. But the old place was not big enough. The business had expanded so much that it was impossible to store the grapes, make the wine and then store the wine until it could be bottled and sold.....We did everything there. The grapes came in at one side and bottles of wine came out on the other side. We made the wine, blended it and bottled it....We even but some into tanks so it could be transported in bulk and bottled by some of our customers....Of course, they were required to include the name Ceresini on their labels prominently."

"I went to the old site yesterday. It looked rather sad. I always feel like that when I see somewhere that was once a hive of activity disused and in disrepair.....I'm surprised it hasn't been sold, so someone else could use the land."

"I would think that Marcello Ceresini, who runs the company since his father retired, has not received a sufficiently good offer for the land. Perhaps if we continue to expand, we might need to use the land for some purposes."

"I suppose you could park lorries there. Or even store empty wine bottles ready to go over to your bottling plant here."

"That kind of thing. Marcello must believe there is a use for it, for as far as I know, the land is not being offered to be sold."

I asked several more questions about the history of the company and wrote down detailed notes. If someone looked back through my notebook, it'd shown me up to be a fraud, but immediate impressions are often everything. By the time we'd finished, I'd managed to drag it out until a little after 11 am, but I really couldn't think of anything else I could do. Plainly I had no plausible excuse for remaining in the building, let alone trying to make contact with the Wasco team or Rosemary, for that matter. I put my notebook back into my bag.

"Would you mind if I drank a glass of water in the waiting room downstairs before I go?" I asked, thinking I could delay for perhaps another five minutes.

"Certainly," he replied. He led me out into the corridor and past a room where one or more secretaries worked and the lady who had brought me upstairs emerged and ushered me towards the staircase.

But then, just as I was about to head down the staircase, I spotted the man from the Guardia di Finanza I'd spoken to over dinner in a restaurant in Bellagio, but a few months ago. I recalled instantly that I'd told him what I did for a living and where I was working currently. He'd also seen Rosemary, so even if I might escape meeting him, he'd recognise her straight away. Of course, he could well be here on official business. But I was - perhaps unfairly, I accept – suspicious of all Italian officialdom, not least in relation to the protection of the reputation of their wine industry. So I didn't think that if he saw me, it'd be anything but inconvenient. So I muttered something about my pen and dashed off to the room I'd just left, hoping I wasn't doing it too conspicuously.

Once I got into the room – fortunately there was no-one there – I thought I'd better appear to look around on the chairs and floor for my "lost" pen. I intended to keep "searching" for a good five minutes. But as I was bending down behind the chair I'd been sitting at, I heard voices coming along the corridor, one of which sounded like the man from the Guardia di Finanza and another that of Billy Madden. It'd look really odd and require a lot of unwelcome and inconvenient explanations if I was to be seen by them, so I raced towards a door at the other side of the room. Fortunately, it opened, just as the door that I'd just come in by opened.

I glanced in front of me. The room was unoccupied, much to my relief. It was remarkably like the one I'd just left. I could hear several voices, doing what I guessed might be introductions, in the room next door. I decided I'd risk staying where I was and try to hear what was being said. I was intrigued by the presence of the man from the Guardia di Finanza and a meeting between Billy Madden and him.

174

I opened the door a fraction and peered through. I couldn't see more than three people from the front and the backs of a couple of heads. One of the latter was undoubtedly Billy Madden and the other looked as if it was probably Whelan. Two of the faces I could see were of people I didn't recognise. The other was the man from the Guardia di Finanza in Verona. But though those involved were largely unknown, I could hear what they were saying. My only concern was that the secretary I'd dashed away from in such a hurry, must surely have noticed that I hadn't returned and would already be scouring the building for me. I decided I'd take a risk and try to move a small side table – which they seemed to use for coffee jugs and cups and saucers – over in front of the door and put a chair behind it and then crouch under it. Though it might look a little odd from the other door, it might conceal me for a while.

Having done that as silently as I possibly could, I returned to listening to the conversation in the room next door.

"As you might imagine," one of the unknown men was saying, "we have been concerned as to why Wasco have felt it necessary to send such a high-powered team to examine our operations." He spoke English well, with a mid-Atlantic accent.

"I believe I've already explained that," replied Madden.

"You will understand that we wished to know as much about what you were doing as we could. We were already aware that allegations have been made in some quarters about this company and that the EEC have been conducting their own investigations of us. These allegations are unfounded and stem from the desire of certain EEC countries to damage the reputation of the Italian wine industry so that they can supplant it in overseas markets like Britain. So the Guardia di Finanza have been asked to check up on what is going on. We believe that you haven't been entirely straight with us, Mr Madden. One member of your team is a woman from the EEC Commission's fraud office, a policewoman from the Metropolitan Police in London, Mrs Rosemary Storey. And we know from passport control records that her husband, a fiscal fraud expert from Customs & Excise in London has also travelled with you, but does not seem to have been a member of your team. It is surmised that he has been snooping around, trying to discover or perhaps concoct evidence against this company. Perhaps you will enlighten us as to why these matters have been kept secret from us?" demanded Colonel Pedroni.

"I'm not at all clear that I've kept anything secret from you. When I first contacted you about this visit, I told you in writing that official sources in the EEC Commission had told me that there were concerns that the Valdicocce and Camarolo wine which had been shipped to Wasco by Ceresini might not be genuine," retorted Madden, sharply but coolly. "That was the reason for my visit. At no stage did I suggest that Mrs Storey was an employee of Wasco. I said she was a fiscal expert, which she is indeed – working in the EEC fiscal fraud service, as Colonel Pedroni has indicated. She is also a qualified accountant. She has been accompanied here by her husband, but he isn't part of my team. Wasco haven't paid either of their expenses. I suggest you ask Mrs Storey why the EEC fiscal fraud service wished to accompany us. But I think you could assume that they wished to check whether what they'd been told by their colleagues was accurate or not."

"There seems to be some possibility that Mr Storey has been posing as a historian of wine in order to snoop around the premises of Ceresini...." continued the man who'd been questioning Madden previously.

"That's a matter for him, not me."

"So you don't know where he is?

"At present, I haven't the faintest idea…"

"But I have," I added, coming into the room. "I happy to admit to a certain amount of subterfuge, but when people aren't being entirely open with me, sometimes that's the only way of getting to the truth."

"And you know what the truth is, young man?" demanded the man who'd been questioning Madden. I assumed that this was Marcello Ceresini.

"I know that Ceresini sold more wine – either here in Italy or shipped overseas – than it produced...by a large margin. It claimed EEC CAP export subsidies on wine that wasn't Valdicocce or Camarolo. The documents and records which you have shown Mr Madden and his team and my wife may appear to show that isn't the case, but the records of sales and exports which the EEC auditors examined show differently."

"There were evidently some errors in the paperwork which was shown to the EEC," replied Ceresini.

"You've apparently known about it for some time. Why haven't you done something to give the EEC the correct figures? Instead, you or someone in Rome has involved Colonel Pedroni in checking up on me – not just when Rosemary and I arrived in Italy the other day, but also when I was on holiday, over three months ago. That suggests to me that you've got something to hide."

"Our meeting in Bellagio was entirely by accident," declared Colonel Pedroni.

"I'm afraid I don't really believe in coincidences as convenient as that one," I retorted. It seemed important to keep them on the back foot.

"So that gave you the right to go snooping around, trespassing on private property?"

"For someone representing an entirely separate organisation, you seem to know a lot of things that could only have come from Ceresini," I replied. "In any case, there was no indication that anyone should stay out of the property to which I assume you're referring. No 'keep out, private property' notices. But a very careful concealment of two large underground tanks where bulk supplies of wine are stored."

"You couldn't possibly know this!" exclaimed Marcello Ceresini. "You're just making it up!"

"Then why are supposedly unused premises kept under surveillance? Why are the iron rings on either side of the lids of the tanks kept carefully oiled and then carefully covered with debris which plainly didn't come from the same building? If they aren't what I've suggested, why don't we go over there and you can show us that there are no tanks or that they haven't been used for years?"

"And why have you been showing us documents and records that plainly show an inaccurate picture of your business?" added Madden.

"You will remain here please," said Ceresini.

He, his companion – who I assumed was Giuseppe Montremoli – and Colonel Pedroni left the room.

"I can see that your reputation for skating on thin ice is well deserved," remarked Madden. "You are lucky that they evidently are using that place to store their wine."

"Do you know where Rosemary is?" I asked, suddenly worried.

"She said she was going to go over the accounts again, when I last spoke to her. But that was several hours ago. I haven't seen her since then.....You think she might also be skating on thin ice?"

"I wouldn't put it past her...But equally I wouldn't put it past this lot to take a hostage."

"They're not the Mafia, you know!"

"Not, as far as we know....But if another firm invited themselves into look at your books, would you get Customs or the police in to check them out? Or if you thought the EEC Commission thought you were up to something, would you do the sort of thing they've evidently been doing?"

"No...But we all know they do things differently here...."

"Precisely...."

"Well, I don't see there's much we can do about it. We'll just have to wait and see what they say when they come back."

ON THE RUN

After about half an hour, Ceresini, Montremoli and Colonel Pedroni returned.

"We see no point in continuing this conversation," said Ceresini. "We would now invite you to leave our premises. No doubt you may feel you have sufficient grounds for breaking your contract with us. We shall have to see what the courts say about that."

"If that's how you wish to play it, so be it," replied Madden. "I should warn you, however, that if you wish to preserve your reputation and that of Italian wines in general, bringing a court case is likely to be counter-productive."

"Then there is no more to be said."

"We shall do as you ask, but one member of our team is unaccounted for. Do you know where Mrs Storey is?"

"I do not. I have asked our security staff to locate her. If you will remain in the waiting room downstairs, we shall bring her down to you as soon as we have found her."

We trooped downstairs, followed by a security guard, past the reproachful eyes of the secretary who I'd given the slip to.

"You understand that Wasco cannot get involved in anything you've been doing on your own account," Madden told me, the moment there were no Italians in the waiting room.

"Of course," I replied. "But in view of what they said, I'd advise you to try and examine their former premises before you return to London. If they had nothing to hide, they would surely have taken us there and showed us."

Almost immediately, the door opened and the security guard beckoned us out. Rosemary was just coming down the stairs, escorted by another security guard and a different secretary. She was carrying her coat, with her bag slung diagonally across her shoulders. She rarely did that – and suggested to me that she had something concealed under her coat. She looked as though butter wouldn't melt in her mouth….and as pretty as a picture….Indeed, I noticed both security guards taking more than idle glances at her legs.

If she was trying to hide something, she was fortunate that we weren't searched on leaving the building. We headed over to the Wasco hired car.

"I'm afraid there isn't space for an extra passenger," explained Madden. "It's a bit of a squeeze in the back as it is."

"No problem," I replied. "I'll catch the next bus. There's a stop not far from here."

They were just about to get into the car, when there was a commotion at the doorway of the Ceresini building and a man who I hadn't seen before started shouting out in Italian "Stop! Stop that woman!"

"I've got their real accounts under my coat," Rosemary muttered to me. "We need to get away now!"

"Madden has just told me Wasco won't get involved in that sort of thing," I said. "We need another vehicle."

About twenty feet from where the Wasco car was parked were several motorbikes. My experience of riding motorbikes was limited and distant – I'd been taught and ridden one while doing my National Service some twenty years earlier. But there are certain things you don't forget – like the habit people have of sticking a spare key in the top of the petrol cap with chewing gum. The nearest bike was a 125cc Moto Guzzi – fast enough for my ability, if not our needs, but we'd be able to go where cars couldn't follow.

I climbed on to the bike, turned the key and kicked the throttle. It roared into life.

"Jump on and hold tight!" I cried to Rosemary, who did as she was bidden.

By this stage there were a couple of men, security guards and a secretary within ten feet of us. I assume deliberately, the Wasco hired car pulled out in front of them, giving us a vital few seconds to make our escape. Though there was a barrier at the gatehouse of the plant, it was evidently designed for cars, as it didn't go all the way across and we were able to dodge round it. The Wasco car drew up behind us, I noticed in my mirror. I hoped that they'd be doing their best to delay our pursuers...I could already hear the sound of a couple of cars being revved up loudly.

The first thing that entered my head was the need to get my hands on our passports. If the Guardia di Finanza were involved, they could certainly ensure that we could be kept in Italy and possibly charged with various offences – not least theft of Ceresini property, apparently by Rosemary and now by me. It was impossible to speak to Rosemary as we charged along. But my instinct was not to try to go directly back to the hotel. Cars would undoubtedly be a lot faster than us on an open road and we'd be caught well before we could get back to Verona.

So I turned right out of the Ceresini plant and then almost immediately right again, up a narrow road leading north towards the Adige. But after a low hill, the road veered to the right, meaning that we were heading right along the back of the Ceresini plant. However after a couple of hundred yards, it did a sharp turn and headed in the opposite direction down a tree-lined road. I was beginning to get a better feel for the bike, though going round the hairpin had made me wobble quite a bit and I could hear a sharp intake of breath behind me.

The trouble with every straight stretch of road was that any cars would be a lot faster than us. 50 kph seemed quite fast and when I revved up to 75, it felt rather too risky until I'd got used to riding again. But I was a lot happier when, after another hairpin turning us back in the direction of Verona, there was finally a road junction, which would force anyone following us to take a decision. The road we were on would have been a very pleasant, winding country road by the side of the River Adige in different circumstances. Every second I kept fearing that I'd see a pursuing car in my rear-view mirror. And the longer I didn't, the more I began to feel that our pursuers had come to the same conclusion as us – and had headed straight to our hotel at top speed to get possession of our passports. I had no illusions that they didn't know where we were staying.

Then we reached a bridge over the Adige. I decided to cross on to the northern bank and through the narrow streets of a small village and on to something more of a main road, where a sign on the edge of the village told us was leading "in all directions". As we hadn't been caught yet, I felt that the best thing was to get to Verona as fast as possible and get hold of our passports, hide somewhere and think what to do next. The road was flat and quite straight, passing through pleasant, if undistinguished countryside. We passed under the A22 motorway which led to the Brenner Pass. For a second I thought about taking it and trying to blag my way through the frontier controls on the Austrian border, but without passports, we weren't going to get far….and our experience in Vienna didn't suggest the Austrian authorities would be too accommodating in our present circumstances!

So I continued along the road, through a large village called Pescantina and onwards along the north bank of the Adige. A couple of times I got lost, but after a large village called Parona, we were on a straight road, which felt like the suburbs of Verona. The sight of the Verona road sign was both welcoming, but also made me realise that there would be police about, on the lookout for us and this stolen motorbike. The road we'd joined seemed rather too main for my liking, but if we were going to get over the other side of the Adige into the old city, I couldn't see how else we'd manage it. The first opportunity I could, I turned off on to some side streets, but soon realised the error of my ways, as I got completely lost and found myself heading back on to the main road we'd just left. So I stayed on it and was heartened by a sign off to the left for San Zeno Maggiore, which meant we were quite close to the centre of the city. I turned right past the cathedral and along past the Castelvecchio. Turning into the Vicolo San Silvestro, I spotted a dozen motorbikes parked in a line. I stopped, found a space in between them. Rosemary and I got off and I pushed the bike into the space, not forgetting to replace the key inside the petrol cap.

Rosemary and I and held each other in our arms and kissed almost fiercely.

"We need to get hold of our passports if we can," I said.

"Before anything else, I need a loo," she replied. "I didn't have time to go before we left and motorbike travel isn't good for my bladder!"

"There are public toilets in the Piazza Bra," I recalled. "I doubt whether the Italian police are staking them out."

We made our way - more by luck than judgement – along the narrow streets and found the toilets in the Piazza Bra.

"What are you going to do about the passports?" asked Rosemary. "Anyone travelling from the Ceresini place must've got here before us."

"My only hope is that they've been trying to catch us. Even though they may have the Guardia di Finanza in their pocket, I doubt they really want us in court making a whole load of inconvenient allegations – even though we have stolen one of their documents and a motorbike between us."

"So what? Are you just going to march in there and demand our passports?

"Yes. But you need to keep out of the way. While you've still got their accounts, we've got something to bargain with."

"OK. But where am I supposed to conceal myself? I've seen virtually nothing of this place."

"You know where we had dinner…in the Piazza d'Erbe?"

"Yes."

"Do you know how to get there?"

"Roughly."

"Well…Go up that narrow road there…the Via Mazzini….as far as you can go. At the end, turn left and you're almost in the Piazza d'Erbe. Go and get a drink and a pizza in the first café on the right there…and order something for me too, please. I don't expect to be more than five minutes behind you."

We kissed, more tenderly this time – and set off. I realised we were actually walking up parallel streets, but it seemed better that we shouldn't be seen together. When I got to the corner of the Via Scala, I peered into a shop window, while trying unobtrusively to see whether there was any police presence in the hotel. There appeared to be none. So I approached, expecting to be accosted by police at any moment. But nothing happened. I went into the hotel. I thought I could detect English voices in the bar, but I went straight to the reception desk. The usual receptionist appeared.

"We've decided to take the train to see Venice," I explained. "I'd be grateful for my passport and that of my wife please. I'll settle the bill at this stage."

"I shall need to prepare it for you….There will be an addition to cover the cost of the night which you don't spend with us."

"I understand. I will get our things from our room. My wife is ordering our lunch."

I went up to our room, fearing that when I came down the receptionist would've phoned the police and they'd be waiting for me. I chucked our stuff into the two small bags we'd brought with us and hastened downstairs. The bill was ready and I paid using one of my travellers' cheques. The receptionist handed over the passports and, breathing a huge – if wholly temporary – sigh of relief, I stepped outside.

It was, of course, possible that Ceresini and/or the Guardia de Finanza needed to catch both of us together. So when only one of us turned up at the hotel, they might've decided to stay their hand and follow me. As I made my way by a circuitous route to the Piazza d'Erbe, I didn't think I was being followed. But I could easily be fooling myself. I went into the restaurant. It was full with lunch time customers. Rosemary was sitting at a small table towards the rear.

"I ordered you a pizza and some water. I didn't know whether you planned to drive again....I see you got all the stuff."

"Including the passports. I guess they didn't think of it fast enough. Or they think we'll try to get out of the country the way we came in."

"I don't think we should be seen with these records. I wonder if we could post them somewhere safe?"

"They could be intercepted. Even if they aren't as quick-witted as we expected, I reckon they might well reckon we wouldn't try to get out of the country with stolen records in our possession. So they might well be checking the post from here."

"Then we should try to photocopy the most important bits. There must be somewhere out of the centre where we could do that."

"We also need to convert some travellers' cheques into cash. Then it'd be more difficult for anyone to trace where we've got to."

"So you've got a plan for getting us out of here?"

"I don't think we'll get out if we try to go back the way we came. I can only assume that they haven't gone straight for our passports because they believe they're bound to catch us when we try to leave. So I'd be watching the railway and bus stations, as well as Milan airport, naturally....but also any other international airport....After all, we could try to change our flights. So I conclude that we should leave the country by ship....But not Genoa. It's too close and Ceresini might well have good contacts there."

"So?"

"I need to look in a bookshop to see what ports have ferries going to Corsica – or possibly to Corsica via Sardinia or Elba."

"And how do we get there if we can't travel by train. Are you going to steal a car?"

"No. Another motorbike, I thought. If we avoid motorways, it'll be a bit slower, but we should still get to the coast by this evening."

"And our clothes and other things?"

"We should stuff them into one bag which we can tie on to a motorbike and get rid of the other one."

"How much cash have we got?"

"About fifty pounds in Lire. I reckon we need to change a hundred's worth of travellers' cheques....But I don't think the banks re-open until two."

"We've got plenty to be getting on with.....and we should get out of the centre of the city anyway."

We finished our lunch and found a bookshop nearby. I bought a Michelin guide to Italy, as it I knew it'd contain information about ferries, etc. Then we headed away from the centre and found a photocopying place, where Rosemary got photocopies of about half the pages in the hardback accounting book she'd continued to keep hidden under her coat. People at the photocopying place told us where the nearest post office was. So we walked there – four streets away – and bought a package to put the accounting book in and then sent it to Knud Henriksen's home address in Brussels. I should've known that Rosemary would keep things like that in her diary.

The banks were re-opening and we found a couple where we changed a hundred pounds' worth of travellers' cheques for Lire.

The next bit was more difficult. I'd had a look at the appropriate map in the Michelin guide and I'd identified Livorno as the nearest port which had sailings to Corsica, Sardinia and Elba. It'd be a long ride on a motorbike, but if we could go as far as Mantua or Parma, we might be able to get a train from there, as I doubted whether every station would be on alert for us. But stealing a motorbike is one thing when it's in a moment of panic, not so easy when you have time to contemplate it. Eventually we came to a multi-storey car park next to a supermarket, called "Ipercoop". There was even a corner filled with rubbish where we dumped my bag, having put everything else – apart from a few surplus shirts, etc – into Rosemary's rather newer bag. Then I picked out another Moto Guzzi – another 125cc, as I still didn't feel confident enough to ride a more powerful machine. I wasn't disappointed when I found the spare key in the usual place. We organised our stuff and set off.

We set off along side roads out of the city, just in case there were any roadblocks. But eventually we reached a huge roundabout by what looked like an old city gate on the south side of the city and just headed south along the main road. I kept looking in my rear-view mirror to see whether we were being followed. But there was so much traffic, it was impossible to say – though at the speed we were going, most cars sped past us. Soon we had to choose between what were evidently more minor roads and going either east or west along the motorway. We chose to remain on the minor roads, heading through rather uninteresting countryside. It meant that we didn't make particularly speedy progress. At least, we were unlikely to be followed – or so I hoped, and I kept peering into my rear-view mirror - and I wasn't sure I'd really want to get up to more than 80 kph anyway. Though I was feeling more confident in handling the machine, I was conscious that neither of us were wearing crash helmets – and the garage where we stopped to fill up on petrol didn't have any for sale, or I might've been tempted.

When we stopped, Rosemary also reminded me that we'd have to try and phone Knud Henriksen at some point. We were due to fly back to Brussels just after 2pm the following day. Our proposed route home was unlikely to get us back that day. In any case, he might start to get unwelcome and garbled messages about us…That was always assuming he didn't learn that we'd been arrested by some branch of the Italian authorities.

Mantua, which seemed a pleasant city, was a welcome sight. But an investigation of the station timetable suggested that there was no easy way to get to Livorno from there. So we had a bite to eat and a coffee and set off for Parma. At least it wasn't raining, but it was beginning to get quite chilly and Rosemary put her coat on.

"If I'd known we were going to ride all over the country on a motorbike," she remarked, "I'd've brought some trousers with me."

The road between Mantua and Parma was little different from that between Verona and Mantua, through largely flat countryside. The roads were perhaps rather straighter and I managed to keep up a rather higher average speed. All the way from Verona to Parma, there wasn't much traffic. What kept our average speed down was going through large villages and small towns, many of which had traffic lights, inconveniently parked cars and inattentive or reckless pedestrians. But by the time we reached Parma, I was beginning to feel quite tired. It was already getting close to dusk and if I was going to ride the bike in the dark, I was going to need at least half an hour's break.

We made for Parma station. However, just like Modena, there were no direct trains. Indeed, it looked as though we'd have to change twice and it'd take at least three and half hours. However, looking at the map, it was plain that we'd be having to ride across the Apennines in the dark. Though there were some main roads, the only one that looked remotely fast would add at least fifty miles to our journey.

"Going by motorbike is going to take at least as long," I said. "I think we might as well dump the bike here and go by train, even if it takes more than three hours."

There was a train going from Parma to La Spezia at 17.45, so we bought tickets for that and hopped on a couple of minutes before it departed. The compartment was full for a while, but after half an hour, it was pretty well empty. We hadn't had time to eat on the station and there seemed to be no dining car, buffet nor trolley service. It was now dark outside, so apart from a few lights amid the darkness and a glimpse of lit up buildings in the small towns we passed through, there was nothing to see outside. Rosemary dozed on my shoulder. I tried to sleep, but I felt I needed to keep awake in case there were police looking for us at any of the stations we stopped at. We hadn't had time to hide the motorbike I'd stolen in Verona, so once it was discovered, it shouldn't take the police long to find out which train we were on. I feared that there would be a search party for us getting on at one of the stops on our way or a welcoming party at La Spezia. Whatever we'd done at Ceresini, we'd plainly broken the law by stealing two motorbikes....But I still felt the Italian authorities wouldn't want us go before an open court....certainly not until they'd got hold of the incriminating book of accounts.

It felt an interminably long journey. Far longer than the two hours it actually took. As we arrived in La Spezia station, I peered out for any police, but couldn't see anyone. Perhaps they were concealing themselves, but we just had to take the risk. The train was going on to Genoa – the wrong direction as far as we were concerned. So we nipped smartly off the train and headed straight for the underpass on to another platform. But our precautions seemed to be unnecessary. So we bought tickets to Pisa Centrale, which seemed to be where we'd have to change for the first connection for Livorno. There was just enough time to nip out of the station and buy a plain pizza with a large bottle of water before the Pisa train departed.

This train was much more crowded, with people constantly getting in and out at the many stations it stopped at all the way to Pisa. Indeed, it felt like the exact opposite of what we wanted. It barely reached full speed before it slowed for yet another station. And we got merely the barest glimpse of the leaning Tower of Pisa spotlighted amid the surrounding foggy gloom of the city. I didn't expect to see police at Pisa station, where we had sufficient time to get a milky coffee and a very sweet piece of cake each. Then it appeared to be a Rome train which stopped next at Livorno. It was very full and we had to stand. Fortunately it took less than twenty minutes to get there.

We got out of the station and I asked at a newspaper and tobacco shop the way to the port, for boats for Corsica and Sardinia. Apparently there was a bus. It was just pulling away as we approached, but we ran after it waving frantically. I assume we must've been visible in the streetlights, as the driver stopped and let us in. As we travelled along fairly deserted streets, stopping infrequently, I thought we'd managed very effectively to draw attention to ourselves, should anyone be pursuing us. But on the other hand, I felt that the faster we got to the ship and to any frontier controls, the greater our chances of getting away before anyone could stop us.

The docks were largely deserted. There were three large ships moored almost in front of us. The bus driver had told us that the Corsica ferry was the furthest along to our right. It was now coming up to 10 pm. The ship sailed at 10.55. Rosemary spotted the sales office and we went in. Very quickly we discovered that there were no cabins or any accommodation whatsoever on the Corsican crossing. We could certainly buy tickets, but we'd have to make do with what we could find to sleep on. We bought the tickets and headed for the frontier controls.

Only there appeared to be no frontier controls. We walked up to the ship, showed our tickets and went on board, unhindered, our passports unchecked. It seemed too good to be true.

"Perhaps they'd actually prefer it if we were out of the country?" suggested Rosemary.

"I reckon they just don't work this late," I replied.

At any rate, we kept in the shadows looking over to the quay until the engines of the ship rumbled into life and we started to edge slowly away from the shore. As we did so a large black car roared on to the quay, but whether it had anything to do with us was anyone's guess.

Naturally, because we'd come on board so late, there was absolutely nowhere inside to lie down. Apart from the cabins and loungers, all the seats in the bar and café were occupied, as were any nook or cranny next to the gangways. So we decided to try and find somewhere out of the wind on deck, where at least we could stretch out....and it might also be sufficiently private for Rosemary to tell me finally what she'd been up to in the Ceresini plant twelve hours - which felt more like twelve days – earlier.

After a bit of scrabbling around in the dark, we found a place next to various nautical objects, under one bit of external staircase and behind another.

Apparently during the day the journey took four hours, but overnight took six, presumably because no-one wanted to arrive in Bastia at three o'clock in the morning. Not that it seemed to me that 5 am was a lot better. In theory, it meant we could snooze for a bit. But even though we were out of the direct force of the wind, it was chilly. Rosemary shivered. I put my arm round her shoulder. A short skirt was fine for diverting the attention of security guards and Ceresini's accountants, but was far from ideal on the deck of a ship at sea at night in early December. And, assuming the weather in Italy would be a lot warmer than at home, she'd brought a short summer mac, rather than a more suitable (and longer) winter coat.

"Don't you even think of taking your jacket off to keep me warm," warned Rosemary, as I started to undo a couple of buttons. "I can put up with this."

"OK. But I don't think we're going to get much sleep....So you can tell me what happened at Ceresini."

"I hope we can make some time during this journey to have some proper sleep. It's only the cold that's keeping me awake.....Ceresini?.......As Madden didn't give me any suggestions as to he wanted me to do, I decided to ask the accounting people for the documents which underpinned the accounts....records of purchases, sales, etc....even bank details...This seemed to get them rather agitated and they all disappeared. As I'd spoken, I noticed a couple of them look almost inadvertently in the direction of the door behind me, and a bit to my left. It seemed likely that the records were stored there...and possibly the real records of what they'd been up to. I was already thinking about nipping in there, but they came back quite smartly and said they'd have to check with Signor Montremoli.

"Unfortunately, one of them stayed with me, so there was no chance I could get into the room unobserved. But after I'd been sitting there for about twenty minutes, one of them came back, went into the room and brought out a sales ledger. It was one of those sales ledgers that'd make you deeply suspicious. Every item was entered in the same handwriting. Of course, it's possible that a single clerk fills in the ledger from different sales invoices, but it felt to me like a ledger compiled for official purposes, rather than being the real one. Nevertheless, I felt I had to appear to study it.

"I'd been boring myself silly going through what appeared more and more like a fake, when suddenly things started to happen. A phone rang and the two people who were keeping an eye on me both shot out of the room. It sounded as though someone had gone missing....you presumably.....and there was an unannounced visit from the head of the Guardia di Finanza. At any rate, it gave me my opportunity. I dashed into the room next door and started searching. It was a windowless storeroom containing mostly four-draw filing cabinets or cupboards. The filing cabinets all contained suspended filing systems with lots of documents – sales invoices, correspondence, and so on. The cupboards were stacked with box files. But I noticed that on one cupboard towards the back of the room, the box files seemed perilously close to tipping over the front edge of the cupboard. Sure enough, behind them was the real set of accounts, with a series of detailed notes and some calculations intended to ensure that the bogus set of accounts tallied properly.

"I knew there was no way I could ask to get them photocopied and just writing down in my notebook what was in them wasn't going to be much use either. So I decided I had to get away with the accounting book. Just as I was about to leave the storeroom and slip the accounting book under my coat, I heard people coming into the next door room. So I switched off the light, backed away from the door and crouched down behind the cupboard furthest from the door. Someone opened the door, switched on the light and peered in. Evidently they couldn't see me, as they almost immediately switched the light off and shut the door.

"To my horror, I heard a key turn in the lock. I waited until I couldn't hear any voices in the next room and went over and had a look at the door. Fortunately, it was an old-fashioned key with a bolt, not a yale lock – and they'd left it in the door, as I couldn't see through the hole. It took me a while to get the right implements, but eventually I was able to push the key out of the lock, catch it on some paper I'd pushed under the door beneath the lock and pull it back under the door. That was actually the hardest bit. The space between the floor and the bottom of the door was barely enough to get the key through....and I was worried all the time that someone might come back into the room and see what I was up to. But in fact by the time someone did come back, I was sitting at the desk looking at the bogus ledger, with the accounting book safely hidden under my coat.

"Of course, they weren't very pleased. I expected them to ask me where I'd been...I was going to say I felt sick and I was in the loo...But they just told me to pick up my stuff as the people from Wasco were about to leave."

"By the look of things, just in time," I remarked.

"I guess someone worked out where I might've been and checked the store-room. I doubt whether I was able to replace the box files exactly where they were before......Do you realise that in all this rush we've completely forgotten to phone Knud Henriksen?"

"We weren't expected back until late tomorrow afternoon. I've no idea how long it takes to get from Corsica to the French mainland, so I doubt we'll get home by tomorrow. But if we can phone by lunch time we should be OK...."

"Always providing the Italians don't ring him up and complain about us....Or more likely get Paolitti on his back!"

"Unfortunately there's nothing we can do about that."

I was about to say that the whole day was increasingly feeling as though it was completely unreal. But at that moment I could hear the noise of a helicopter quite close and within half a minute one appeared hovering over the stern of the ship, the direction we were facing. Then it switched on some floodlights and several seamen appeared on the deck about twenty feet away from us. Through the lights came a man attached to a cable, evidently being winched down on to the ship. Almost involuntarily, we shrunk back into our little hidey-hole. I could see no other reason for someone joining the ship in this way than to get hold of Rosemary and me. However, at this stage, the man who'd been winched down, disentangled himself and the cable disappeared up into the floodlights of the helicopter. Meanwhile, the man set off inside the ship, accompanied by the seamen. Within seconds, the helicopter had turned off its lights and wheeled away into the night sky, though we could hear the thump of its rotor-blades for several minutes afterwards until finally all we could hear was the rumbling of the ship's engines.

"Unless someone has been taken seriously ill and that was a doctor, I guess that bloke has come to look for us," observed Rosemary.

"Well, he'll have a job finding us."

"Perhaps he doesn't need to look. He just has to stop us getting off tomorrow morning."

"It might be a bit difficult. Even if this ship is Italian, once we're in Bastia, we're under French jurisdiction – and I'm not sure how he could stop us landing."

"I suppose someone hasn't gone to all the trouble of landing him by helicopter if they didn't think they could do something."

"Always assuming it has anything to do with us."

Though it was too cold to sleep, it didn't make the time pass any faster. Indeed, if anything I felt it slowed it down. A couple of times we got up and walked about, just to check our feet were still working. But once we got out from our sheltered nook under the staircase, the fresh wind blowing off the sea made us feel still colder and we moved back quickly. Poor Rosemary kept shivering, though she never complained. A couple of times I suggested we just went inside and walked about. At least she'd be warmer in there. But she felt we'd just be risking getting ourselves caught. I even gave her the photocopies of the accounting book which had been inside my shirt on my back ever since we got in the train at Parma. They were slightly warm and would help to keep the draught from getting up her back.

Eventually, we could see the ship changing direction and the engines slowing. Though it was still pitch black outside, lights appeared on the port side of the ship. We were evidently approaching Bastia harbour. I checked my watch. It was just before 5 am. The ship turned almost a hundred and eighty degrees and seemed to reverse into the harbour – or perhaps it was pulled by a tug. From where we were concealed, we couldn't see much. But it was apparent we'd be getting off on the starboard side.

We'd agreed that we'd leave the ship separately. Assuming there was someone looking for us, they'd be expecting to see two of us…and might be fooled, especially if one of us could slip past them off the ship. I reckoned that many of the passengers would be travelling with their vehicles, so there wouldn't be too many foot passengers, but Rosemary wasn't so tall that if she stooped and kept someone between her and anyone watching out, she might be able to slip past. And despite her feet feeling frozen, she'd taken off her shoes, which had fairly high heels, which, apart from making her seem shorter, also meant she could use her running ability if necessary.

I could hear the various ropes and chains being pulled as we tied up. We moved forward in the darkness, along the side of the ship – normally a place where passengers would sunbathe during the day. For an instant, the unpleasant thought occurred to me that it'd been some sort of hitman who'd been winched on to the ship from the helicopter, but for all my distrust of the Italian authorities, even I didn't think Ceresini could quite manage something like that. As we moved round, I could hear an announcement in French, for the "passagers du foot" to go to the forward starboard exit on deck D. We were on deck E, so we returned to the staircase by our hidey-hole and went down to the deck below, retracing our passage along the side of the ship. Ahead of us were several passengers with rucksacks or cases on wheels leaving the ship. By the edge of the gangplank were a man and a woman in the uniform of the ship's personnel and a man in a dark suit. I had no idea whether he was the man who'd been winched on to the ship. Unfortunately, he was between us and the way off.

"You go – as quickly as you can!" I told Rosemary. "He won't see you until you've got past him. Then just keep going as fast as you can. I'll meet you in that building where the passengers are heading."

"What about you?"

"Don't worry about me. If necessary, I'll barge him into the water!"

She set off, making no sound in her bare feet. From where I was lurking in the shadows, I could see her zip round the man in the suit and the ship's crew. By the time he'd realised who she was, she was half way down the gangplank.

"Hey!" he cried. But though I couldn't see her, I knew Rosemary would just keep going. Once on shore, we were a possible problem for the French authorities, but no longer within the grasp of the Italians.

The man in the suit looked round in my direction, plainly expecting me to come from where Rosemary had. But it was too dark for him to see me.

Despite what I'd said to Rosemary, I had no plan as to how to get off the ship. I thought about just trying to leg it fast as I could, but that would certainly give everyone - not least the French authorities - the impression that I was a criminal fleeing justice. That might well be true, but I still didn't want it being brought to the attention of the French frontier police if they didn't know already.

In the end, I decided I'd try the "Richard Hannay" approach. As several hippy types with large rucksacks approached the exit point, I walked up smartly and followed them off. I turned to both the ship's crew-members and thanked them for a pleasant journey. This seemed to put some doubt in the mind of the man in the suit. I was expecting him to grab at me, but he just peered at me suspiciously, but with an air of uncertainty.

"The documents are already off the ship and on French soil," I said, turned and walked off the ship on the heels of the heavily-laden hippies.

I could hear an exclamation behind me, but no footsteps, no police whistles - nor the sound of a weapon discharging.....which I realised would be actually be after I'd already felt the impact of any bullet. I didn't look back and headed straight into the waiting arms of my wife in the arrival hall. We kissed long and hard. Whatever else might happen, we were no longer on the run.

"SOME EXPLANATIONS ARE DUE"

Not wholly to my surprise, there appeared to be no French authorities on duty at that hour of the day. So we made our way through non-existent controls to French soil. However, unlike the authorities, other French establishments were already up and working at this hour – not least a café serving traditional French petit déjeuner - milky coffee, croissants and bread rolls, freshly baked - and the "services" desk of "Lignes Corses", whose ships travelled between Bastia and Marseilles. The reason for our early arrival soon became apparent. Moored next to the ship from Livorno was a similar ship which was due to depart for Marseilles at 7 am.

Though it wasn't cheap, we booked not just our passage but also a cabin. The only ones left were internal...But that was fine. It was a ten hour journey, which guaranteed we couldn't get back to Brussels that day, but we would get a chance to catch up on our sleep and try to work out how to make sense of what we'd been up to – both to ourselves and anyone else who was likely to ask. It seemed likely there'd be a fair number queuing up to demand to know what we thought we'd been up to. But as we showed our tickets and walked up the gangplank through the half-light of early dawn on to the ship, the events of the previous day seemed utterly and completely like something I'd dreamt. Verona. Modena, Parma, the train, Livorno, the chilly journey on the ship, even Bastia – all seemed unreal, almost as if I'd been watching some crazy film on TV.

"That was a very strange day," remarked Rosemary, slumping down on a bed. "Did we really do all that?"

"Yes. Whether we did the right things or not, I've no idea – and it's a bit too late to do much about it anyway."

"You know, I never even realised you could ride a motorbike."

"I learnt when I did my National Service. If it hadn't been for the feeling we might be being followed, I quite enjoyed riding through that Italian countryside with you holding on behind me."

"I guess it's more fun for the driver. I kept wondering whether we were going to fall off....and a short skirt may be OK on a motorbike in the summer, but it gets a bit chilly in the winter."

"Fortunately, after the first couple of miles when we got away from the Ceresini place, I felt I could control the bike OK. And it didn't go fast enough to change my mind about that. But I don't think I'd've fancied riding across the Apennines in the dark though."

"No. I wouldn't either. Especially if it'd started to rain. Those trains weren't very comfortable, but at least they were warmer and felt safer."

"So you won't be doing a 'girl on a motorcycle' thing then?"

"No. We did see that together didn't we? It was one of the silliest films, I've ever seen. Does anyone seriously think that wearing nothing under a leather suit and riding a motorbike for miles would be anything but extremely uncomfortable?"

"I was going to say – I don't know. I've never tried it. You have? But I agree – it was amazingly pretentious and sold itself entirely on the promise that Marianne Faithfull would be seen naked at some point. As I recall, wisely they put on late in the film, otherwise I guess people would've been walking out long before the end."

"Just so you're clear. Apart from having to try riding a motorbike when I was doing my police car training, I've never ridden one – and certainly not in leather.....I noticed you stayed until the end of the film, despite it being so pretentious!"

"I was interested in seeing passages showing Heidelberg. I remember thinking that films like that always choose somewhere picturesque. It wouldn't've been quite the same if her lover had been in Essen or Gelsenkirchen or Moenchengladbach."

"So you weren't waiting to ogle Marianne Faithfull?"

"I didn't think I needed to. I was already married to someone I loved. Besides, one of the effects of my father's views of the world was to make me draw a clear line between reality and fantasy."

"So you never had a crush on any actresses or singers?"

"No. It always seemed to me they were in a different world....different universe, really....I suppose if Audrey Hepburn had stopped by, I might've changed my mind.....But what someone is like on screen and in real life, who knows? Besides...more by luck than judgement I found someone who goes around stealing company documents and riding around the Italian countryside with me on stolen motorbikes."

"And gets frozen to the marrow on the deck of a ship in the middle of winter...well, in the winter anyway."

She smirked and we kissed, for quite a while.

Our cabin was small, consisting of two-berth bunk bed, a minuscule table with storage underneath, and a washroom containing toilet, tiny washbasin plus mirror and a shower. Before the ship had even got under way, we had thrown off our clothes and were making love in the shower and then again on the lower bunk bed. Afterwards, we slept for about six hours until pangs of hunger woke us and feeling refreshed and in clean underwear – our other clothes having got too screwed up in Rosemary's bag for us to wear – we found the ship's self-service restaurant and enjoyed a thick vegetable soup, steak and chips and a glass of red wine each. At one stage, I thought I saw a man in a leather jacket who seemed to be watching us, but he quickly vanished and was replaced by a noisy French family at the same table. Was he real or a figment of my imagination?

We went on deck, but didn't stay out there. It was grey, chilly and drizzling. I reckoned I could see the coast of France on our starboard side, but it was really too indistinct to be sure. So returned to our cabin.

"We've got to get some French Francs so we can phone Brussels when we land," said Rosemary. "You know what Emily and Sarah will be like when we don't get home at the time we expected....And it's a good job they don't know what we've been up to....And we'd better warn Knud Henriksen that we've complicated things a bit.....More than a bit, really!"

"At least we've got enough travellers' cheques left to get us home. I think the trains from Marseilles to Paris are supposed to be pretty fast."

"But even if we get one as soon as we get off the ship, I don't see how we'll be in Paris before midnight.....and I think it'd be better to get a proper night's sleep and arrive in Brussels fresh and ready to deal with whatever gets thrown at us."

In the event, but the time we'd got off the ship and walked to the railway station through pouring rain, under hastily purchased umbrellas, it was after 6 pm and faced with the choice of arriving at around midnight in Paris or waiting three hours and getting a sleeper, we chose the latter. We should arrive reasonably refreshed at 6.am at the Gare de Lyon and could transfer quickly by metro to the Gare du Nord for one of the frequent Brussels trains. We also reckoned that the sleeper would be cheaper and easier than trying to find a Paris hotel at that time of night.....and we weren't keen to spoil memories of the hotel in the rue St Roch where we'd spent a happy two days in 1967.

The evening was so wretched and we were too tired to do any exploring. Besides, I didn't think that we'd see Marseilles at its best on a chilly, wet winter's evening. So we stayed on the station and had a light meal. We found a public phone and explained to my mother that we'd been delayed and would be back the following morning. We also got Knud Henriksen at home...Rosemary having his number written in her diary, of course....He said that he'd had a rather oblique phone call from Billy Madden of Wasco not long before he left the office, to the effect that our return was likely to be delayed, but that doubtless we'd be in touch. But other than that, no-one had been in touch.

We promised to explain when we got back the following morning.

We returned to the station café for a coffee.

"Do you think we're being watched?" asked Rosemary.

"You know it's never worth asking me that. I thought we might be at one point on the ship coming here, but it seemed more like a figment of my imagination….Do you?"

"There are a couple of men who seem to be interchanging. They've both been with us in here….and I felt that one of them was watching us when we used the public phone. I accept it could be me imagining it. But I think we might keep an eye out."

But no-one seemed to be following us as we got on the Paris train. The sleeping car was a four berth, but as the train pulled out, no-one joined us. The attendant who checked our tickets, said that the other two berths had been booked by someone travelling from Marseilles, who'd evidently not got on the train. So we locked the door and enjoyed making love in leisurely fashion for the first time on a train. It felt rather adventurous going to bed naked, in case we wanted to do it again during the night.

"After doing it on a ship and now a train, there's only the mile high club left," I remarked, just before we kissed and went to sleep.

"Don't get any big ideas," replied Rosemary. "I don't think we've done it in a car either…and I'm not sure I fancy the gymnastics of that particularly."

In the middle of the night, we both woke when the train stopped at Dijon station. For a while we just enjoyed the sensation of sitting naked, with our arms round each other, listening to the noises on the station, just visible at the edges of the blinds of the compartment, and then the motion of the train starting off and then hearing the eerie screaming from the overhead electric cables. For a change, we felt adventurous and climbed up on to one of the top bunks and made love, almost pressed down by the low ceiling, always feeling that slight edge of excitement, as the train changed direction or trundled over points.

A couple of hours dozing and we were arriving in the Gare de Lyon. It was still dark and chilly. The clothes we'd brought with us for Italy were definitely not suitable for northern Europe. We plunged into the metro, grateful that we were a little ahead of the Parisian rush hour. Even so, that curious mixture of gaulloises and garlic pervaded the half-empty carriage. For a change, it seemed to take hardly any time at all to get to the Gare du Nord, where we were just in time to catch a train just before 7.30 to Brussels. While we sipped a coffee from the trolley service that came along the train, Rosemary told me that she didn't think we were being followed, but she still wasn't wholly certain.

Inevitably, by the time we reached Brussels, my mother would already be taking Emily and Sarah to school. In the normal course of events, Rosemary would pick them up at lunch time. In the hope that we might sort things out before then, we both headed straight for the SEFF offices.

Knud Henriksen was an early bird. So he – unlike many of our colleagues – was already at his desk when we arrived. We went straight in to see him.

"Apart from an unusual request from a General in the Italian Guardia di Finanza to meet me urgently, I've heard no more than I mentioned when we spoke on the phone yesterday evening," he began. "By the way, you both look as though you could do with a change of clothes. I don't know what you've been doing, but I hope you weren't planning to meet Commissioner Giulizzi in such a dishevelled state."

"We had to sit on deck on a ship overnight," I replied. "Are we expected to meet Commissioner Giulizzi?"

"If you've been poking a wasps' nest in Italy, almost certainly....But possibly not today. If you get a summons, I strongly suggest you shoot home and change...or go and buy some clean clothes in a store somewhere around here......So I take it you have been poking a wasps' nest?"

"You could well put it like that. The Wasco team were clever and diligent, but they seemed to be playing by a set of rules that wasn't going to get them anywhere. In any case, as I wasn't part of the official team, I was free to wander around a bit and I'm almost 100% certain I found the place where Ceresini stash their falsely-labelled wine….only a few miles from their main premises. But Rosemary got the most useful stuff."

"I was asked to examine Ceresini's accounts, which looked fine, but were completely bogus," added Rosemary. "But they unwittingly gave me an indication where the real accounts might be hidden. When I got a chance to search for them, I took it — and found them. They prove that Ceresini have been bringing in almost half their sales of wine from wine that shouldn't have the Valdicocce label. I only got a quick glance, but some seemed to come from southern Italy and quite a lot from Spain…..But I couldn't ask to get it photocopied and there was no point copying stuff from it into my notebook. They'd just deny what I written and say I'd made it up. So I decided to bring the accounting book back as evidence. I've got photocopies of the most important pages in my bag. The book itself should be on its way to your home by post, always assuming it hasn't been intercepted on its way."

"So you purloined Ceresini's accounts book. Presumably without informing them?" asked Henriksen.

"Yes," replied Rosemary. "I couldn't see what else to do. But they noticed it'd gone quite quickly. So we had to make a quick getaway – not in the company of the Wasco people."

"This involved borrowing a motorbike from Ceresini's car park to get us back to Verona and then borrowing another one to get us from Verona to Parma. We travelled by train from there to Livorno and then on to Marseilles via Corsica by ship and then train back from Marseilles here," I continued.

"Good God!" exclaimed Henriksen, almost laughing. "I fear you two are incorrigible…..And I reckon you can certainly expect a summons from Giulizzi or Paolitti. Of course, it's unlikely

Ceresini would want to press charges against you for purloining their motorbike…and I suppose there's no evidence you took the other bike…."

"Other than fingerprints, I guess," remarked Rosemary.

"So why does this General of the Guardia di Finanza want to meet with so urgently? It must have something to do with what you've been up to."

"A Colonel Pedroni from the Verona office of the Guardia di Finanza appeared in the Ceresini building yesterday morning. I was at a meeting which he and the Ceresini management had with the Wasco team. My impression was that he was hand in glove with the Ceresini people – mainly because we'd seen him before. He made my acquaintance briefly while we were on holiday in Bellagio in the summer. That seemed to be too much of a coincidence…."

"But, from what I could gather, he wasn't expected at the Ceresini premises that morning….Of course, he may have been there to blow the whistle on what Nick and I were up to," added Rosemary.

"If I meet this General Enrico Forlini, I believe you two should definitely accompany me. But I strongly suggest that you don't set down in writing what you've been up to. I assume that this book of accounts which you've sent me by post doesn't say who sent it?"

"No. We just stuck it in a package with your address."

"So if the package were to vanish, there'd be no evidence how it got here…..And the photocopies?"

Rosemary got them out of her bag.

"They're a little the worse for wear, I'm afraid," she explained. "They were used as an additional vest at certain stages of our journey…like going through frontier controls and on the ship between Livorno and Bastia…I don't think I've been as cold as that…ever."

"Have you any idea how Ceresini might react to this? They must know you've got away with records that show they're guilty of fraud – in both the commercial sense and in relation to CAP export subsidies, at least. Will they try to claim we can't use the records because they were stolen? Or would the publicity be so bad for them – and the Italian wine industry generally – that they'll be put under pressure to sort things out without making a fuss?

"I don't think we saw enough of them to be able to say. You'd have to say the second course of action would be more sensible, but people do illogical things when they're angry."

"In any case, on the commercial side, presumably it's up to companies like Wasco to decide what they want to do, if anything," I added.

"You need to get in touch with them...I guess there may be the odd fence which needs to be mended there," said Henriksen.

As we went back to our offices, I wondered whether the Italians might not try both approaches. Surely, with an Italian Commissioner as our boss, they'd want to give that route a go – on an informal basis. That would still leave room for a deal of some sort. But that depended on two crucial things – the book of accounts arriving at Henriksen's flat in Brussels and what Wasco decided to do.

I rang Billy Madden, but wasn't surprised to learn he wasn't available. For someone as driven as him, nearly four days out of his office would mean a lot of stuff to get on top of – quickly. Indeed, I was a little surprised that he got back to me later that afternoon – a couple of hours after Rosemary had left to pick up Emily and Sarah from school.

"You are back in Brussels?" Madden asked.

"Yes. We decided to travel by train and ship. I'm sorry….."

"I'm not sure what to make of you and your wife. I guess you've got some damning evidence about what Ceresini have been up to...?"

"Yes."

"But I doubt whether the circumstances in which it was obtained could make it evidence which could be used in a court."

"Probably not. But I doubt we were going to get anything any other way. I couldn't see the Italian authorities agreeing to us getting a search warrant for the Ceresini premises."

"You're probably right. Though I'm still not clear what that Colonel Pedroni was doing there on Wednesday. Do I take it that the accounts show that Wasco have been conned by Ceresini?"

"Yes. From what we can see, none of the Valdicocce wine you sold last year came from Valdicocce. It probably came from Spain, but it might've come from southern Italy."

"Presumably Ceresini will expect you to pass this information on to us?"

"I'd expect so. Rosemary was part of your inspection team, after all….and I should thank you for delaying them when we made our getaway."

"Knowing that they'd been conning us – not just with the wine but also throughout our visit – was motivation enough. I hoped that the five minute start you got was enough. It seems it was."

"We were very lucky. If they'd had any sense, they'd've headed straight for the hotel and nabbed our passports. As it was, thanks to your help, they evidently went chasing after us and didn't catch up with us."

"We were in the middle of lunch before they seem to have cottoned on to that. The police weren't at all pleased that your passports had gone and they were convinced we'd had something to do with it, until the receptionist said that you'd done it one your own more than an hour previously."

"I hope they found the motorbike eventually…We're not usually in the habit of walking off with evidence or nicking motorbikes…."

"But equally you don't like people you regard as crooks getting away with things…and at such times, you concentrate on getting the evidence safely away….I can quite understand it. It's fortunate that the evidence which you got seems to give me enough to cancel my relationship with Ceresini. No doubt they've got a load of fake Valdicocce and Camarolo ready to be dispatched to Wasco. They can probably find other mugs to take it – though I shall be warning my competitors here. We may be rivals – but if one of us gets found out selling dodgy wine, all of us suffer to some extent."

"Can you get replacement stock at this stage?"

"It seems to be unlikely. And our negotiations with all our Italian suppliers are going to be several levels more rigorous in future."

"Do you need any of the information which we picked up?"

"No thank you. I'd prefer not to. Ceresini know already what the position is."

That was pretty well all our conversation. Because of our "unorthodox" methods, he plainly couldn't quite get to the point of thanking us for the help we'd given Wasco in protecting their reputation. I also suspected that it'd be a long time, if ever, before I could seek their help in future. It was one of those conversations, which, if I'd said "see you", he would've said, "not if I see you first."

It was Friday evening. It was too late for a summons from Commissioner Giulizzi, who would have been on an aircraft for Rome at lunch time. No doubt he'd be getting his ear bent during the weekend. I made sure that the crumpled photocopies of Ceresini's real accounts were safely locked away and left.

I walked up the road to the usual tram stop and waited. It was bucketing down with rain and I was glad of the cheap umbrella which I'd bought in Marseilles. I noticed a man in a dark coat standing in a doorway about thirty yards away on the same side of the road. I don't know what attracted my attention to him, but the moment I looked in his direction, he turned away and appeared intent on watching the cars whizzing past him along the Rue de la Loi. It was an odd place to stop. Cars weren't supposed to halt at that point and the man didn't really look as though he was waiting to hail a taxi. He didn't appear to have an umbrella, yet the tram stop where I was standing had a shelter, which did a reasonably good job in keeping the rain off. And there was plenty of space in it. So I felt the uncomfortable sensation that he was following me.

This was increased, as when the tram for Woluwe arrived, and I got on, I could see him sprinting to get on the back. It was already quite full and I was standing towards the front. He kept himself almost hidden behind a couple of passengers close to the rear entrance. Was he following me? Who was he? Some branch of the Italian authorities? Or did the fact that Ceresini got some of their wine supplies from southern Italy mean they were in cahoots with the Mafia or a similar organisation?

He stayed on while people got on and off at Merode and Montgomery and all the time the tram continued along the rue de Broqueville, heading for Woluwe St Lambert. I usually got off at Slegers, the tram stop close to the old St Lambert church. But as he remained on, sitting down now, I stayed on until the junction with the Voluwedal, where I alighted, crossing the main road into the rue Voot, leading away from Voluwe St Lambert. I crossed the road into the Chaussee de Stockel and waited just round the corner. It seemed to me that if he was an innocent commuter, he'd be going up the rue Voot, the rue des Deportes or possibly the lane called the Montagne des Lapins. But he didn't appear at all. Even at a snail's pace, he should have showed up by now. The fact that he was waiting, suggested that he wasn't sure whether I'd spotted him and he needed to relieve my suspicions.

Risking bumping into him as he made a mad dash to the street corner to see where I'd got to, I turned back from where I'd just come – into the rue Voot. Within fifteen feet of the corner, there he was, looking suddenly away from me. There were no shops he could've gone into. He wasn't smoking a cigarette or pipe, so there was really no reason for his delay. I walked straight up to him, with a small and inconvenient thought suddenly zipping through my mind that he might have a gun and had been intending to kill me. But I told myself that the only people who could possibly wish me dead at this particular moment was

209

Ceresini – and they surely had enough sense to know that it'd just make things a whole lot worse for them.

As I reached him, I stared at his face. Conveniently, he'd parked himself just by a streetlight – which immediately suggested that he was something of an amateur at this. He looked down at the pavement and said nothing. He was a good four inches shorter than me, with short dark hair slicked back, clean-shaven, with the look of someone from a Mediterranean country who'd spent the last few years in the cold north. He was about my age, but could've passed for ten years younger. I stared at his face and then remarked,

"I've seen your face and I know you're following me. I'm assuming you don't know where I live. If you think I'm going to lead you there, I'm not. If you don't come with me and get on a tram going well away from here, the next steps I'll take will be to the nearest police station and I'll be making a complaint against you. Do you understand?"

He gave no sign of anything.

"Well?" I demanded.

He turned in the direction of the tram stop on the Voluwedal. His attitude indicated there was no point asking him any questions. I guessed his tactics were to remain mute in virtually all circumstances. So we waited in silence at the tram stop. A tram going south to Oudergem appeared after about ten minutes.

"Don't get off at the next stop and try and find me," I told him.

He got on to the tram. As it trundled away, I moved back into the shadows on the rue Voot side of the Voluwedal. The moment the tram disappeared from sight, I legged it between the cars coming along the Voluwedal and into the pleasant suburban streets of Voluwe St Lambert. Confident that I was no longer being followed, I continued home, by a more circuitous route than usual, to ensure I had opportunities to check that the man wasn't just a decoy and someone else was trailing me.

I decided not to mention it to Rosemary before Emily and Sarah had gone to bed. My mother had also retired to read a detective story – probably Agatha Christie. Such "bourgeois trivia" had been reviled so much by my father that she'd largely left off reading them. Now she could read them to her heart's content. Whether that felt like a satisfactory bargain, I rather doubted.

"That's our trouble," she observed. "We tend to rush in where angels fear to tread and without really thinking out the consequences. If you reckon this man was a bit of an amateur, perhaps it was just Ceresini trying to warn us off."

"It's a bit late for that. When I spoke to Billy Madden, it seemed pretty certain that Wasco were going to annul their contract with Ceresini."

"You'd think Ceresini must've been expecting that........But it's difficult to know what they might do. Whatever we might get up to in hotels, boats and even trains, we're discreet..."

"...and married."

"Other than that, we lived boring, routine lives....Would they threaten Emily and Sarah? Or perhaps kidnap them in exchange for the accounting book? I don't know what I'd...."

"I can't see that makes sense. They must surely know we've got back to Brussels and will've handed the incriminating evidence over. Even if we gave it back, they must know there'd be people who'd seen it, photocopied it, and so on. This isn't a genie that can be put back in the bottle by threatening us or our children...At least, I don't think so."

"Revenge or to deter anyone else from doing anything about what we've discovered?"

"If these were Sicilian wines, I might be worried about it. But Ceresini are a large company, selling their wines all over Europe and the world. They can do things to repair their reputation as far as the fishy wine is concerned, but if they start being linked to people being killed because they've crossed them, it seems to me they're heading for bankruptcy."

"So what was that man up to?"

"I can't really figure it out. He was far too obvious to do that sort of thing for a living. In any case, anyone with any sort of connections would be able to find out where we live without needing to follow me home......The only thing that seems to fit the bill is that the man wasn't linked to Ceresini, but to another Italian wine company or perhaps even to their equivalent of the Wine Standards Board and what it was intended to do was to remind us that life could be unpleasant for us if we go beyond dealing with Ceresini. Does that make sense to you?"

"Yes. But there are probably a dozen equally plausible explanations – and it could be none of them.....I fear yet again, we're going to have to be on our guard all the time..."

But nothing seemed out of the ordinary at the weekend. We took my mother Christmas shopping in the centre of Brussels and saw her off to her train early on the Sunday morning. Emily and Sarah took advantage of a brief lull in the weather to enjoy themselves at a local park and we took a bus to one of their favourites – the Royal Museum for Central Africa – making sure we bypassed the village of Tervuren, to avoid stirring up unwelcome memories of recent events. Apart from the fine building and park, neither of which looked their best in the rain, the exhibits, mostly from the former Belgian Congo, always fascinated our daughters.....and an ice cream and fizzy drink went down well too. I spared my mother this particular visit, because its colonialist nature would undoubtedly have drawn particular scorn and anger from my father and I wanted to spare her unwelcome memories too.

If we were being followed, someone was doing it with vastly greater professionalism than the man on Friday evening.

To no-one's great surprise, Rosemary and I were summoned, along with Knud Henriksen, to attend a meeting with Commissioner Giulizzi's chef de cabinet Paolitti as soon as we got into the office on Monday morning.

"Some explanations are due," he said, in his usual cold manner. The fact that he probably owed his career and possibly his freedom to me had long been forgotten.

We sat on – or perhaps "in" would be a better word – the plush sofas he had in his large, immaculately-furnished room.

"In regard to what, exactly?" demanded Henriksen. He had always disliked Paolitti – on more than one occasion describing him as a cockroach crawling around Giulizzi's nether regions – and, now he was leaving, had no need to butter him up.

"Events in Italy," replied Paolitti.

"The weekend calcio results? The latest political manoeuvrings? I believe you need to be more specific."

"I refer to two employees of SEFF involved in illegal activities in relation to an Italian wine-producer by the name of Ceresini SA."

"The only people from SEFF who've visited the premises of Ceresini SA are National Experts, technically not employees of SEFF. Perhaps you should tell us what you've been told?"

"As a result of some unproven allegations, quite possibly encouraged by overseas rivals of Ceresini SA, several men from the well-known British supermarket chain Wasco imposed themselves on Ceresini SA to check whether they had been shipping wines under the Valdicocce and Camarolo description, which were not, in fact, wines from those regions. Ceresini SA provided them with all the necessary documentation which showed that these allegations were false. However, somehow – possibly because they covertly apprised Wasco of the allegations – two members of SEFF staff accompanied the Wasco people….Mr and Mrs Storey. I'm informed that Mrs Storey took advantage of her position at the Ceresini SA offices to steal confidential records and when this was discovered, she and Mr Storey escaped by stealing a motorcycle belonging to one of the company's employees…..a Moto Guzzi Stornello, to be exact. It also appears likely that they then stole a similar motorcycle and took it from Verona to Parma, from where they left the country by train and boat, quite possibly illegally."

"I'm sure that Mr and Mrs Storey are capable of explaining their actions. But there are certain inaccuracies in your account which I should correct. First, the allegations that Ceresini SA had been shipping wine that wasn't Valdicocce or Camarolo under those labels was based on analysis by the EEC Court of Auditors from records provided by the Italian authorities. As part of our continuing attempts to improve the sources of information available to SEFF, Mr Storey accompanied the auditors on their visit to Rome to examine the Italian records. I'm sure you are aware of that. But I'll let Mr and Mrs Storey continue with this."

"The first thing I should say," I began, looking Paolitti in the eye, "is that the information which Ceresini SA showed to the Wasco team was bogus. The EEC auditors did a thorough analysis from various angles and concluded that Ceresini SA, among other firms, were declaring as sold or exported significantly more wine than was declared as produced in the Valdicocce and Camarolo regions. And since every bottle of wine produced there receives a CAP subsidy, there's no reason why anyone would want to conceal wine production there. Secondly..."

"I am informed that the EEC Court of Auditors officials were provided with information that has subsequently proved to be inaccurate."

"That's as may be. I assume officials in Rome will be able to produce the corrected information with all the underlying documentation...in the original copies?"

"I should expect so." He looked away. Like me, he suspected such original documentation didn't exist.

"Secondly," I continued. "I wasn't part of the Wasco team. I accompanied Rosemary to Verona, but I wasn't and never claimed to be part of the official Wasco team visiting Ceresini SA. But I did do a bit of looking around and discovered what I believed to be the place where Ceresini SA store the wine which they bring in from southern Italy and Spain to supplement the Valdicocce and Camarolo wines produced locally. Ceresini SA had several opportunities to show the Wasco team that my understanding was incorrect, but at no time did they do so. So I'm confident that a proper forensic search would reveal that the underground tanks in their former premises in Bussolengo have been used to store wine within the last year."

"That doesn't constitute proof."

"I agree. But in circumstances when a company is exporting as much wine under false labels as it produces, controls by the appropriate Italian authorities seem extraordinarily lax. Indeed, Ceresini SA appeared to be hand in glove with the local Guardia di Finanza, so the possibility of getting their help in obtaining detailed proof seemed unlikely."

"Which was why I took Ceresini's real book of accounts way with me," added Rosemary. "I'd examined the accounts and underlying documents previously. They were plainly bogus. Any accountant with any forensic skills could see that they were fabricated – with the so-called supporting documents plainly produced to complement the bogus accounts. The accounts which I found, which had been deliberately concealed from us, showed the true picture. I admit to taking them away. But in the circumstances, they were our one and only chance of getting evidence of what Ceresini had been up to. Like Nick, I couldn't see any evidence that the authorities were doing anything about these massive frauds, so I couldn't see what alternative we had, if we were going to nail them."

"The way you acquired the material certainly means that it would not be admissible in a court of law," observed Paolitti coldly...in between glancing at Rosemary's legs.

"I realise that. But we in SEFF have no powers to prosecute anyone anyway. The Italian authorities would have to do so and, as Nick said, they haven't seemed all that interested. It seemed to us that if we were able to produce plain evidence about what had been going on, they might feel they had to do something. And they'd know that SEFF had evidence which could be passed to the EEC Court of Auditors. The next time anyone looks at records of companies like Ceresini, they won't be fobbed off by the bogus stuff they palmed off on us.....Oh and by the way, I speak through my mouth, not my knees!"

Paolitti didn't turn a hair.

"Ceresini SA are demanding that their property is returned to them," he continued. "Will you hand it over."

"We no longer have it," I replied. "We sent it by post before we left Italy."

"I understand it was addressed to me," added Henriksen. "But it hasn't arrived yet. And if and when it does, I shall ensure that every page is photocopied and signed, so that whatever happens to the original, there can be no doubt about the information which we will continue to hold in SEFF. I'm sure you haven't been speaking directly to anyone in an organisation that has been committing serious fraud, not least in regard to CAP export subsidies, Signor Paolitti, but I would strongly advise you to consider where you wish to go with this. If the scandal involving adulterated Austrian wines blows up, the Austrians are very likely to name Ceresini SA among other Italian companies as being involved in fraudulent mislabelling of their wines. If it became known that Commissioner Giulizzi had been frustrating SEFF's attempts to deal with this fraud, it might make him popular in Italy, but it'd probably mean he'd have to resign as a Commissioner....You need to remember that your Commissioner has responsibility for the main EU organisation dealing with fiscal fraud. People and companies that commit frauds can be cunning and devious. In some instances they may bribe officials...though I'm not suggesting anything like that has occurred in this case, of course! But it means that on occasions we have to be alert to opportunities and sometimes unorthodox in our methods if we're going to have any chance of success."

"I believe there is a world of difference between what you call unorthodox methods and breaking the law of another country.."

"Indeed. So is condoning large scale fraud against the EEC budget as well as wider fraud by the mislabelling of wine. I suspect that in the circumstances, what Mr and Mrs Storey did - though possibly ill-advised – would be judged a good deal less harshly than an EEC Commissioner responsible for counter-fraud condoning exactly the sort of fraud he is supposed to be tackling."

"And getting someone from the Italian Representation to follow me in such an amateurish fashion only adds to the suspicion that the Italian Government wants these wine frauds covered up," I added, the knowledge of who the man who'd been following me suddenly hitting me in a flash. I'd seen him and spoken briefly in passing at one of Martin Finlay's many cocktail parties which I'd not been able to find a plausible excuse to duck out of.

"I know nothing about that," replied Paolitti, his eyes still flitting to Rosemary's legs.

"Then I suggest you speak to your compatriots," said Henriksen. "From where I sit, it seems that the Italian Government appears more interested in covering up a fraud by an Italian company than dealing with the fraud."

"I don't consider you've heard the last of this. You may expect a formal demand to return the document taken from Ceresini SA shortly."

"That's fine. But if I were you, I'd make sure that the chain that links Ceresini SA and Commissioner Giulizzi's office is beyond reproach."

With that, we left.

"I wish I could remember to wear trousers when I'm meeting Paolitti," said Rosemary, while we were having lunch later. "I really don't like being looked over like a piece of meat. But I like wearing short skirts. Once we're back in London, it'll be trousers or knee-length skirts – and I'd far rather wear short skirts or jeans."

"Perhaps you'll get a job in uniform when you get back?"

"I doubt it. Now I've got some of the accountancy qualifications….and the stuff I've been doing with that Russian money-laundering, I'm sure I'll be doing some finance job or analysing figures."

"It'd be a bit foolish of the Met to waste your qualifications."

"In any case, I'll need to start on the second half of my qualifications when we get back. So it'll mean a bit more of you ferrying Emily and Sarah around….but not on a motorbike, even with a sidecar!"

AN UNPLEASANT INCIDENT

Knud Herniksen informed us the following morning that "the package" had arrived. He was arranging to get it formally photocopied and witnessed. But he'd hang on to the original until such time as he received a formal request to hand it over. For a while I thought we might get a summons from Commissioner Giulizzi, but evidently between us, we'd given Paolitti enough to think about to deter him from bringing the big gun to bear on us.

We made several photocopies of the photocopies and I sent one to Van Zyl in the EEC Court of Auditors, after an explanatory conversation with Steve Bacon, about its limitations as a source of official evidence. Unsurprisingly, we heard nothing about what Wasco were doing in regard to Ceresini. But as Henriksen had said, we needed a little time to reflect on where we'd got to, what exactly we'd got and what we should do next. It'd only be a couple of days, as he was anxious to "put this to bed" before he left SEFF to return to Copenhagen at the end of December.

Brussels took the Christmas period less seriously than Customs & Excise. There were few office parties…and as far as SEFF was concerned, Gerry Fitzpatrick took us all out for an expensive and lengthy lunch. Otherwise, the early evening cocktail circuit revolved at a faster pace than usual. But Rosemary and I were less than four months away from returning to London and had no ambitions to join the EEC gravy train, so the excuse of young daughters at home was employed to good effect. It seems a bit "bah humbug!", but compared to two or three hours drinking someone else's choice of wine or beer and eating the inevitable canapes and assorted nibbles, an evening at home with Rosemary and my two daughters was vastly more enjoyable.

About a week after we'd got back to Brussels, we were summoned to a meeting with Gerry Fitzpatrick and Knud Henriksen, along with Henri Kervran.

"Have you been giving any further consideration to what we might do with the information which you gathered in Italy in this somewhat unorthodox fashion?" Fitzpatrick began, in his academic way.

"Since we in SEFF can't take action ourselves," I replied. "We were thinking of using the new information sharing arrangements to encourage EEC countries to take special precautions in examining table wines, especially those shipped in bulk. We thought we might indicate that wines labelled Valdicocce and Camarolo had been identified as coming from elsewhere. But more generally, we would suggest that importers need to look more carefully at the chain of supply and national wine standards boards and large importers might want to satisfy themselves that quantity of wines shipped from any region didn't appear to be significantly greater than the amount declared to have been produced."

"The Italians won't like that much," observed Kervran. "But from what I've been hearing, they can hardly take us to court.....It may just make these crooks a bit smarter, of course."

"That's always the way, it seems to me," I said. "It's a constant battle between those who want to get round the law and those who want to uphold it. There'll always be people thinking up new dodges and we just have to try to be smart enough to keep up with them."

"Of course, certain Italians won't like it at all," remarked Henriksen. "I'm sure you all know who I'm referring to. But I don't think they need to be consulted about this."

"I'd expect them to prefer very definitely not to be consulted," added Fitzpatrick. "It's a no-win scenario for those two...But I think we may well get some form of instruction to take a careful look at French, West German and Luxembourg wine fraud. Plainly, if there's fraud going in in Italian wine production, everyone must be at it as well.....Which reminds me, what, if anything, are we doing about the Austrian adulterated wine case?"

"Strictly speaking, it's a Danish case," replied Henriksen. "When Nick and Rosemary went to Vienna, they found that the Austrians were tackling the problem well....with one exception, control of the diethylene glycol which was added to the wine. I spoke to my opposite number in Vienna...or should I say my opposite number from next month....and followed it up with a letter, to point out that if they didn't deal with that aspect, they could expect SEFF to put out an information note to all EEC countries to check all consignments of Austrian wine for possible contamination. Naturally, he wasn't best pleased, but he agreed they'd put something in place and I have written assurances to that effect. So I think we let them get on with it."

"But we might check back sometime next year to see they actually done what they've promised. But what about the adulterated wine that's already been exported?"

"We reckon they've managed to retrieve about three quarters of it. I've asked the Danes to use the information sharing arrangements to inform other EEC countries. If they don't do it before the end of the year, they'll certainly do it in January."

"It's such a shame we can't do anything directly against Ceresini," commented Rosemary. "But I realise we don't have the evidence."

"I heard on the grapevine....a very appropriate word in the circumstances....that Wasco have cancelled their contract with them and other British supermarkets are queuing up behind them to do the same. So I think we can safely say that they'll have received some punishment....But I doubt whether anyone will chase them up over the CAP export subsidy fraud. The Commission usually delegate that to the appropriate EEC Member State," explained Henriksen.

"That's better than where we were....and the company will be getting their property back...and a couple of Moto Guzzi motorcycles are back in the hands of their rightful owners. So everything is in its right and proper place," added Fitzpatrick.

We'd learnt from Henriksen that Fitzpatrick had found the account of our flight from the Ceresini plant highly amusing. Doubtless the knowledge that he only had another three months or so to put up with our foibles was one reason why he took the matter so lightly.

As far as we were concerned, that appeared to be the end of our wine fraud work. Though we had the information from the Austrians about the Burgundy, Lastier-Couvrou, their information related to 1970 and it was difficult to see what SEFF could do about it. Henriksen had encouraged Henri Kervran to bring it to the attention of the appropriate people in the French administration. But other than that, we didn't have the right people or the right knowledge to be able to do anything – even supposing there was something that needed to be done.

I was looking forward to our second and final Christmas in Brussels. The family renting our house weren't due to leave until the beginning of March, so we had nowhere to stay in London. Staying with Rosemary's parents was out of the question, as their Christmas would be dominated by Rosemary's younger sister, Simone, and her family. There certainly wasn't space for us to stay with my mother and, though we'd invited her, she'd already had invitations from various old friends and, I suspect, reckoned (quite correctly) that Emily and Sarah would be rather too boisterous over the Christmas period. In any case, we didn't expect to spend another Christmas abroad, so we welcomed the prospect of a Brussels Christmas.

On the Wednesday after the meeting with Fitzpatrick and Henriksen, I was the one to collect Emily and Sarah from their school in mid-afternoon. Usually Rosemary did it, but she had to attend an after-work drinks affair with various police colleagues and contacts in Brussels and Interpol. Though she didn't enjoy such events, it wasn't something she could reasonably duck out of....and, as she said, you never quite knew when you mightn't need to make use of one of these contacts in future.

Emily and Sarah were their usual bouncy selves when I picked them up. Rosemary had evidently trained them well, as they were well-behaved on the tram and only started to let off steam when I gave them a half an hour in the local park before it got dark. Rosemary wouldn't be back until at least 7.30, so I got their dinner, helped them with the homework which the school had set them....mainly learning some French vocabulary....and then started to get them ready for bed. They were old enough to sort out their own baths and night attire, but needed some supervision over their teeth cleaning. Then I read to them....I was currently about half way through *"Lorna Doone".......*so that when Rosemary got in, they were ready for bed, but would have time to tell her about their day.

However, 7.30 came and went and then 8 o'clock. I wasn't particularly bothered. Sometimes it was difficult to make your escape from these parties without appearing discourteous. But by 8.30, I was beginning to get concerned. It was very unlike Rosemary to remain at a function of that sort as long as this. But just as I was beginning to think about putting Emily and Sarah to bed and see if I could find a helpful phone number, Rosemary came through the door.

She looked awful. Her clothes were dishevelled and torn and she looked frightened, upset and annoyed, all at the same time. She flung herself into my arms and cried quietly for a couple of minutes. Then she stopped – and doing her best to regain her composure, said to Emily and Sarah, who'd been standing about ten feet away, not knowing what to make of what was happening,

"It's all right, you two. I nearly got run over by a drunk driver and I was a bit shaken up. But I'm all right now. If you go to bed, I'll come in and tuck you up in a couple of minutes."

Whether they believed her or not, they both went dutifully to their bedrooms. I knew perfectly well she wasn't telling the truth. A narrow escape from being hit by a drunk driver would make

Rosemary annoyed, not frightened and tearful. While she said goodnight to Emily and Sarah, I made a large mug of tea. She came back into the lounge and sat next to me on the settee. Instinctively, I put my arm round her.

"It's all right, Nick. I'm not going to cry again….."

"What's happened to you?"

"I'm not quite sure……It was very sudden…and I don't really know why…."

"Why don't you start at the beginning and just go through all that happened to you?"

"I stayed a bit later at the Interpol party than I intended…There was a Chief Inspector from the Swiss police there who's been very helpful in getting the Russian drugs money traced, so I couldn't just dash off. He's very terse on the phone…Not so in person. But I suppose I got away some time after seven. I don't know exactly. I was hurrying to get a tram. But none came for a while and when it did come it wasn't very full and virtually everyone got out before Woluwe. I got off at the usual stop and was just about to cross the road when a car drew up with its brakes shrieking. Of course, I stopped as I thought if they were making that sort of noise they might be drunk and mightn't see me crossing the road.

"But two men got out. I didn't particularly think anything about it at first. But they marched up to me and tried to grab me.

'You're coming with us, Mrs Storey,' said one of them, a burly man with a black beard. 'You're going to get what's coming to you!' It was a foreign accent, probably Italian.

"He grabbed hold of my shoulder and the other tried to grab my other arm, but I struggled as hard as I could. I was twisting and turning and kicking and shouting. But unless there's anyone else at the tram stop, it's usually deserted round there and it isn't the sort of area where people in the flats look out of their windows during a winter's evening. I was fighting so hard, I heard my coat rip and I reckon I bit one of them on the hand, as he let go for a moment. But I knew they were too strong for me and

224

they were slowly dragging me towards the back of the car. I know I managed to butt one of them in the face, because he told me that after they'd finished with me, you'd want nothing to do with me.....that'd teach us to get on the wrong side of the wrong people...or something like that.

"But I wasn't going to get into that car without a fight. But it looked as though they weren't actually allowed to hit me. They had to force me into the car, but only by holding me, dragging me and pushing me. As we got close to the door, I put my legs up on the side of the car and tried to shove away from it....And it seemed to work for a second or two. They fell backwards....We all fell backwards in a heap. But it was a mistake. While I was on the ground, the second man, a lean man with a nasty face managed to get himself on top of me. The other one must've got up too as I could feel him holding my feet down.

'We were going to do this somewhere a bit more comfortable, but we can just as easily do it here, he said, sneering at me with breath that stank of cigarettes.

"He started grabbing at my clothes, while the other one started to pull my shoes off. It was at that moment, I finally caught on that they were planning to rape me. I struggled as hard as I could. But they'd got me down and I knew there was little I could do about it until one of them actually got his penis out. Then I might just get a chance to kick him where it'd really hurt. That was my only chance of getting away. But I was terrified and angry at the same time. How had I allowed myself to be caught like this?

"The man with the nasty thin face was just ripping my bra-strap when I heard an explosion close by...But it wasn't an explosion, I realised. It was a gun...but not a revolver...some sort of shotgun. The two men stood up and I tried to pull my clothes over myself and look round at the same time. But all I could make out were the headlights of a car. I couldn't see anyone. Evidently whoever had the shotgun was on the far side of the car, because he fired again, straight at the car belonging to the two men. There must've been a driver in there as well, because he started the engine and the two men bolted inside and the car sped away.

"I got to my feet. I wanted to thank the people who'd saved me. But the car just drove off after the other one. They didn't try to see how I was. I didn't even notice when they arrived. They could've been there most of the time….Anyway, I just sat on the pavement for a moment. I think I was in shock. I realised I felt frozen and I was shivering like mad. Then I was tearful and then angry…But I couldn't understand what was going on…..They plainly weren't just rapists who spotted me on my own at the tram stop….They must've been following the tram….Presumably they saw me get on it and this was all carefully planned……It must be that Ceresini stuff…We should've known they were connected to some nasty people…."

I thought she was going to cry again. But instead she picked up her tea and took several deep gulps.

"What do you…?" I began.

"I know you want to help, Nick," she said. "But all I want to do at this moment is to get out of these clothes and have a shower, so I can feel clean again. Just the hands of those horrible men on me…I feel so dirty…"

She went into the bedroom and emerged briefly in her dressing gown. I could hear the bath running.

I continued to sit on the settee, angry and confused. If I'd had that shotgun, I knew I wouldn't have shot at the men's car. I'd've done for both of them. Whatever we might've done to Ceresini or someone else, Rosemary didn't deserve to be treated like that. If I could find them, they'd wish they'd never even contemplated for a second raping my beloved Rosemary.

I got up and paced up and down, unable to contain my anger and frustration. Who had done this? How could I find out who it was? And who had saved Rosemary? Why hadn't they stopped and tried to help her? Had they been there all the time? What were they up to? Was it just some vicious charade put on especially to frighten Rosemary? Were the two cars in it together? Or what? There were too many questions and no answers. I couldn't even work out what we could do about it.

Of course, we could avoid either of us being caught in that way again...or at least we could do our best not to. But how could we find out who they were? Of course, Rosemary's impression that they were Italians, suggested a connection with Ceresini – not least because they'd be beginning to find out the extent of the damage that purloined accounting book was doing to their business. But it'd surely be too risky for a supposedly reputable company like that to get up to that sort of thing. But who actually owned the company? Where did they get their wine from. Supposing that wine which came from southern Italy came from vineyards or companies owned by the Mafia? And suppose they'd recently been told that Rosemary and I – Rosemary in particular – had just completely blown a lucrative business out of the water? These were certainly the sort of people who'd regard failure to take some sort of revenge as unpardonable weakness. But I couldn't see what Rosemary and I could do against the Mafia. And was what happened this evening sufficient? Or did they intend to be back for more?

Rosemary came out from the bathroom, wrapped in a dark blue towelling dressing gown-cum-bathrobe, which had originally been mine. It was much too big for her and she looked fragile, smaller than usual, with her short dark hair tousled from being dried on a towel. She sat down on the couch, curling her legs beneath her. I sat down next to her and put my arm round her should, kissing the top of her head. She leant forward and finished the rest of her tea – cold by now, of course.

"Shall I get you another one?" I asked.

She was silent for a couple of minutes.

"I feel so angry!" she cried out. "I was so feeble and stupid and cowardly! I'm a trained policewoman, yet I behaved like a frightened little girl!"

227

"Nonsense!" I replied. "You're the bravest person I know. However strong you might think you are, there are always going to be men who are bigger and strong than you, especially if there's two of them and they take you by surprise."

"I know….I know…But I hate how I felt…I don't think I've ever felt like that before…"

"And you won't ever again – not if I have anything to do with it."

We kissed and were silent for a while.

"I wish there was something we could do…" I began.

"What a fool!" exclaimed Rosemary. "I've just sat around feeling sorry for myself! The man in the second car shot at the car the two men were in. There must be a car around somewhere in Brussels with gunshot holes all over the back. I need to contact the Brussels police and report what happened. That's what any ordinary member of the public would do…..and in this case, I'm no different from any other member of the public who's been the subject of a rape attempt…and what those men did to me was assault, even if it wasn't anything worse."

She got up and went over to the phone and rang the police number. About forty minutes later a very young detective accompanied by an apparently even younger uniformed policewoman arrived. I'd persuaded Rosemary not to get dressed, but to put on her one and only nightdress under her dressing gown. I also put the clothes she'd been wearing when she was attacked on the table, retrieving them from the bin where Rosemary had flung them when she'd gone to have her shower.

The questions were predictable. Inevitably, the appearance of the second car and the shots aroused considerable interest. But as Rosemary was unable to account for why the car had appeared or why someone in it had fired the shots, there wasn't much to go on. The detective said they'd put out an "alert" to try and find the car that had been shot at. But all Rosemary could do was to say that her impression was that it was black and a fairly expensive saloon. However, as the detective remarked, either the car would have been stolen or it'd be concealed in a lock-up somewhere.

They left us, having asked Rosemary to go into the Woluwe police station and make a statement the following morning. I got no impression that they expected to find the men responsible...or their car, for that matter. Afterwards, as Rosemary didn't feel like eating anything, we sat on the settee listening to music on the radio for a while and then went to bed early.

"I'm sorry I was so feeble," she whispered, her head on my shoulder as usual.

"You weren't feeble at all," I replied. "If you hadn't fought so hard, they might well have got you into their car and driven off before the other one appeared."

"I suppose it's that feeling of being overpowered. It makes you feel feeble and pathetic."

We were silent for a while.

"I don't understand what was going on with the second car...the one that shot at the back of the first one," Rosemary said, echoing my own thoughts. "Why would you do that and not stop? Was it all some elaborate trick? But why? If someone wanted to hurt me, why didn't they just let those men get on with it? But if they wanted to gain my gratitude and trust for some reason, surely they should've stopped and let me know who they were? They might even have been there all the time....I didn't think I saw a second car when I was watching the road to cross, but then if it was parked, I probably wouldn't've taken any account of it."

"The only reason I can think of is that whoever was responsible for this deliberately chose you, as the men knew your name. But why didn't they hit you? If I was going to overpower someone, I wouldn't be grabbing them and trying to force a struggling woman into a car. I'd give them a good smack round the head — or better still - in the solar plexus, to knock the stuffing out of them. Then they'd be much easier to handle. It seems as though they wanted to rape and humiliate you, but not actually hurt you too much. Does that suggest that someone just wanted to make you extremely frightened, but not actually hurt you? And possibly because you struggled so hard and hurt the men, they got angry and were starting to hurt you, so the watching vehicle had to stop them, but without revealing who they were?"

"I suppose that fits what happened.....But I guess there are other explanations. But why just do that to frighten me?"

"Revenge? After all, it was you that took the accounting book from Ceresini's offices and led to their business being well and truly messed up. They might well not want to do anything that left any traces – like hitting you or raping you for that matter, because there'd be evidence afterwards....and they would have to have insulated themselves very effectively from whoever did it to you...because they'd be the obvious suspects.....Perhaps that's why there was the second car.....If you're hiring thugs to attack you, you probably need to make sure they're on a tight leash, if they really are supposed to terrify and humiliate you, but without leaving any traces."

"So....would that be enough, do you think? Or can I expect more of the same?"

"I can't really say, of course....The fact that someone in the second car fired those shots might suggest they think they've done enough. But they aren't going to get a second chance. Even if it means a row with Knud Henriksen or taking a pay cut, I'm going to go with you whenever you pick up Emily and Sarah. Nothing like this is ever going to happen to you again."

Rosemary said nothing. She leant up and kissed me. I could feel the silent tears running down her cheeks. Neither of us needed to say any more.

I knew there would be no possibility of encouraging Rosemary to take the next day off. It was probably better that she should immerse herself in work anyway. Though she had a couple of cuts and a few bruises, she was physically OK. We agreed that I would tell Knud Henriksen what'd happened. I didn't need to ask to be allowed to leave work early. Kind man that he was, he suggested it. But he'd always had a soft spot for Rosemary.

I spent a fair amount of the morning trying to work out how I could find out whether there was a connection between the attack on Rosemary and Ceresini SA. But even identifying the two men was well nigh impossible without fingerprints. Even if they were Italians, as Rosemary had thought, there were many ways they could've got to Brussels. And if they were any sort of professional thug, they'd probably got several passports, including ones from other countries. So though I thought of getting hold of passenger lists of flights from Italy – especially north Italy – since the Friday we'd arrived back in Brussels, I realised there was little point. As Ceresini must realise that any attack on Rosemary was likely to be linked to them, they wouldn't be despatching Italian thugs from Milan or Venice airports directly to Brussels. Assuming they'd come by air, they'd go via Paris or Amsterdam…And there'd be plenty of ways of arriving in Brussels by road in complete anonymity.

Besides, Ceresini might not even be directly involved. If my surmise that the suppliers of their wine from southern Italy were owned by or linked to one of the crime organisations who operated in that region, they probably had connections that could be activated in cities like Brussels without anyone having to travel more than a few miles. But would such an organisation have treated Rosemary in the way this lot had done. We'd seen *"The Godfather"* together – and even allowing for it being fiction, what had happened to Rosemary – whether planned like that or whether she was supposed to have been raped – didn't seem quite their style. It seemed unlikely that such people would've been concerned not to hit Rosemary or make it clearer why they were exacting this revenge.

And I still couldn't get my head round what the second car was up to. Though the explanation I'd given Rosemary was plausible, it was by no means the only one.

I'd taken Rosemary to the local police station after we'd dropped the children off at school. She'd promised to get a taxi from the police station all the way to the SEFF offices. Nevertheless, I was still relieved to see her when she arrived. We'd agreed not to mention what'd happened to anyone else in the office, other than Henriksen, so it wasn't until we had the office to ourselves while everyone else went out to lunch that she could tell me what happened.

"They were perfectly nice and took down my statement," Rosemary explained. "They said the vehicle that'd been shot at had been found....over towards Zaventem....It'd been set alight on waste ground, so there was no chance of getting any fingerprints or other evidence. Apparently it was stolen yesterday morning in the Schaerbeek area. But that was about it. Of course, because they just assumed it was passing rapists, they just told me to be careful....Not get off trams on my own or walk on my own along the quieter, less well-lit streets...Just what I would've said...They seemed to assume that the second car was someone who happened to be driving by, stopped and made sure I was safe, but didn't want to get involved....which was why they drove on......As plausible a theory as any."

"That bit might be....But do ordinary rapists go round stealing cars in the morning, arrive just after a tram has stopped in a quiet area, and then go on to set on fire the car they were in? You'd think the police might consider that a bit too calculated."

"I suppose a couple of ordinary rapists might steal a car and use it to follow a tram that they knew went through quiet areas and that mid-evening ones were likely to have quite few passengers. They could follow a tram once it'd left the centre and hang back and see who got off. And you'd probably want to make sure there was no evidence to link you to a rape, so setting light to the car afterwards mightn't be such a bad idea. But gangs of rapists don't usually strike just once. So if you were the local police, you'd expect to have seen this MO before...Of course, there's a first time for everything. But even without knowing anything about Ceresini, there were enough odd things about this which you'd think they'd want to follow up. But I guess it's going on file....and that's where it'll remain."

"Unfortunately, I don't see what we can do, either.....I've been thinking about whether we could trace a link to Ceresini, but I can't see how....And, of course, it might've been any possible partners from southern Italy who were responsible for this."

"And I doubt whether they'll try anything like that again. If they're as professional as they seem to be, they're bound to assume we'll be on our guard. The last thing they'd want to do would be to take the risk that something went wrong and we'd uncover a link to Ceresini or some other organisation.....Besides, the more I think about it, the more I'm beginning to feel that last night's unpleasant incident was intended to happen largely like that. It's possible they might've taken me somewhere more isolated and I guess they might've stripped me and raped me...But, as you said, they didn't hit me...which makes me feel this was more about frightening me in a very direct way, rather than anything more..."

"So that may be the end of it, you think?"

"We don't know anything like enough about who might've been behind it to say that.....and of course, if they know much about us, it might've been done to get us to travel together.....But we do enough of that in the mornings and at other times, so I can't see why they want to do that....especially as we'll now be on a tram in the middle of the afternoon, rather than after dark."

We worked through our lunch hour, just eating a sandwich and having some English tea together. There wasn't so much on that I needed to take anything back with me. So by mid-afternoon we'd left and were collecting Emily and Sarah from their school. We got off the tram, unfortunately being the place where Rosemary had been attacked. But her natural resilience meant that she seemed unmoved about being there. We walked home, up the Rue Vervloesem and along the Avenue des Vaillants.

Just as we reached our flat, a large, bright light bulb switched itself in my head. But I let it illuminate further thoughts in the back of my mind while we took Emily and Sarah to a nearby park and then supervised their half hour's homework, got their tea and eventually, put them to bed. I read some more of *"Lorna Doone"* while Rosemary cooked our dinner.... "Fromage sur pain grillé", an old favourite from home. Afterwards, we sat on the settee together.

"So what are you thinking about?" asked Rosemary. "I can always tell when there's something whirring around in your brain."

"It's that strange whining sound, like a soprano mosquito, I suppose?"

"It's very noticeable to anyone who knows you well, especially those with ultra-sensory hearing."

"Do you want me to tell you what's on my mind? Or do you want to tease me for a bit longer?"

"Please procede!"

"OK....If you're sure?"

"Get on with it!"

"You'll recall where you were attacked, of course. Why did they attack you there? It's a fairly busy spot, even in mid-evening in Winter? But as we were walking up Rue Vervloesem and the Avenue des Vaillants, I reckoned there were two much better places in the Rue Vervloesem and one in the Avenue des Vaillants. So why pick the Slegers tram stop?"

"Because they were following me and it was the first place they could grab me?"

"Exactly. But if they'd known where you live, they could've grabbed you at a more convenient and less risky place. They followed you and grabbed you there because they didn't know where we live."

"So?"

"Why didn't they know where you live?"

"Because they didn't need to. They'd just follow me and take their chance."

"That doesn't seem very professional to me. It strikes me that these weren't ordinary rapists. They knew who you were and they told you were going to get what was coming to you. The attack on you was planned. If you were going to plan an attack, surely you'd try and find out where we lived, so they could plan in advance the best place to attack you? Just following you in the hope of finding somewhere suitable doesn't seem to fit."

"OK. Suppose I buy that, where does it get us?"

"You remember I was followed by that bloke from the Italian Representation? Well, I got off at Tomberg deliberately, so he couldn't follow me to where we live. Assuming no-one was able to follow me more professionally, I'm left with the thought that he told the men who attacked you...or more likely the person who organised it....that we lived somewhere along the tram line up to and including Tomberg. So that's why the men who attacked you had to follow the tram you were on and wait 'til you got off. It's even possible that he was at the Interpol party you were at and told them you were likely to be travelling home alone on the tram?"

"The trouble is you know what he looks like and I don't.....But you're sure he works for the Italian Representation?"

"I'm quite sure about that. But I don't know what he's called or where he works there."

"Before we can do anything, we need to find out who he is. I suppose if he was at the Interpol party, he'd've been on a guest list...But sometimes people just turn up to these things and no-one really notices."

"I need to think back to that cocktail party of Martin Finlay's where I met that bloke briefly. I guess he was just introduced as Leonardo Da Vinci from Italrep. People don't usually tell you what other guests do, they expect you to find that out for yourself if you feel you need to."

"Would Martin Finlay remember? I realise he's moved on...But he's got a job in the Commission hasn't he?"

"Council Secretariat actually...Or at least, that's what I think he told me. It was higher grade and quite a lot more money, so he chose that rather than what he'd been offered in the Commission. Whether he'd remember this bloke, or whether he'd even be prepared to try, who can tell. But I can certainly have a go."

SNOOPING IN SCHAERBEEK AND ELSEWHERE

Martin Finlay wasn't the easiest person to track down. Indeed, I suspected it was one of the secrets of his success in life. By and large, he found you rather than you finding him. However, this was one of those occasions when nothing and no-one was going to put me off. So I got hold of him shortly before lunch the following day. He didn't sound as though he was particularly pleased to be tracked down by someone with Customs connections. His new job was in the part of the Council Secretariat dealing with foreign and trade relations, which would give him access to a certain amount of foreign travel and the diplomatic circuit in Brussels, which would undoubtedly prove valuable in due course for him to pursue the next step in his career. Being identified too strongly as a former denizen of HM Customs & Excise wasn't part of this scenario. (I also realised that whenever I dealt too closely with Martin I risked being infected by his version of bureaucratese, christened "eurocratese" by Rosemary and me).

I caught him coming out of an EEC Council working party on trade negotiations with Japan, on his way to lunch. Given that the lunch would almost certainly last the best part of two hours, I reckoned he could spare me ten minutes or so.

"You realise I don't have anything to do with SEFF in my present post," he began. "And I've been busily forgetting as much as I could of my previous post. It creates more room for all the nouveautés....So please don't make the assumption that there's anything in particular I can recall from my former life."

"Let me try....Perhaps I should tell you the reason why I'm asking is that two men attacked Rosemary on Wednesday evening, deliberately. If another car hadn't come along and

237

frightened them off, she might well have been raped. From what they said, it seems pretty well certain that it was revenge for something we've been involved in tackling an Italian wine fraud."

"It has been said that if you play with fire you're likely to get burnt....However, though I've less passion than you two about not letting crooks get away with it, I don't like crooks who pick on women either. But I'm not clear in what capacity I can help."

"I was followed by a bloke from Italrep a few days before the attack on Rosemary. For reasons I needn't go into, it seems quite possible that he has a connection to the two men who attacked Rosemary. The only time I've ever met him before was at one of your parties at the UKREP offices about eight or nine months ago. I've been racking my brains to remember why you wanted me there.....I think it may have been something about VAT."

"That narrows the field down rather less than you might imagine. But there'd be no reason why I'd been keen for you to attend anything involving VAT structure, rates or policy..... So,,,,hmmm....it can only have been VAT information sharing or mutual assistance....Does that ring a bell?"

"Not really.....But I haven't got a better suggestion."

"Someone from Italrep, you say?"

"Yes. My recollection is that you or possibly someone else I was talking to introduced him to me as Marco Polo from Italrep, but he moved on almost immediately, so other than saying hello, that was about all the contact we had. All I can tell you about him is that he's about your height, with short dark hair, slicked back and a Mediterranean complexion.....Not much to go on, I'm afraid."

"The trouble with Italrep is that few of them specialise much. So Giovanni Gotti, who was my oppo on the VAT Sixth Directive didn't do any other VAT. And he's as tall as you and prematurely grey. Lorenzo Spacchioni broadly fits your description, but I don't recall him ever covering any VAT. You understand that in Italrep, they rarely understand much of what they're negotiating about – especially in working parties and that sort of arrangement. They're just mouthpieces for the written briefing emanating from the relevant ministries in Rome. Did you get any feel for this chap's age?"

"At the time I felt he was about my age, but could pass for ten years younger."

"That sounds like Silvio Vascone. I'm not sure why he would've had any interest in VAT. He was actually a rare specialist among the serried ranks of Italrep.....from their agriculture ministry, an expert on the CAP. A timorous, devious pipsqueak. From Calabria originally, I believe. A fellow of infinite variety, but no jest, to misquote Hamlet.....I don't ever recall him doing anything on VAT or anything else you've been involved in. But you know what events like that are like — someone you haven't invited turns up because they want to have a quiet word with someone you have.....It'd certainly explain why he didn't see the need to converse with you."

"I assume he's still here in Brussels? He won't've been posted back to Rome?"

"Highly unlikely, dear boy. Unlike the Brits, the Italians believe in the value of experience and contacts. So their chaps get posted to Italrep from anything up to ten years. Any time one of them gets posted back to Rome, a plume of white smoke is seen billowing out above the Italrep offices."

"Thank you for that. You've been extremely helpful. I'm sorry I've delayed you for your lunch."

"I fear it's just put off the evil hour. Guy Dupont and I are lunching with two Japanese diplomats, who insist on eating Japanese food. Brussels is excellent at very many cuisines, but I fear Japanese isn't one of them....The things I do for Europe!.....I trust my help won't lead to Silvio Vascone being found in the same state as Yorick."

"If I'd seen him and known he'd set it up on the evening Rosemary was attacked, there would've been a distinct possibility of that...But now I'll stick to the rule of law."

"As Elvis Presley sang, 'That'll be the day'."

As he'd been helpful, I refrained from mentioning that it was actually Buddy Holly. In any case, it was rarely possible to be absolutely certain when he was being serious and when he was having "a bit of a jest". At any rate, I left him to his Japanese meal and headed back to the SEFF offices.

"I have a name – Silvio Vascone – a CAP expert in Italrep," I told Rosemary. "But we both need to think how we can go from there to getting him to tell us what we want to know."

"I doubt we'll be able to get much information about him officially. Once we start poking about, he's bound to be alerted and I reckon our only chance would be to catch him unawares, like Counsellor Khrestinsky."

"In that case, all I can come up with is that I need to follow his example, and follow him from Italrep to his home and see whether there's any possibility of getting him on his own then."

"Let's just think about that for a moment.....We didn't really want any information out of Khrestinsky. But if it was the sort of information that'd get him killed by someone else if he revealed it, he would've risked us killing him and not told us anything. Is this man Vascone going to be more scared of us or the people who got him to spy on us? If we're going to get anything out of him, you're either going to have to convince him you're more likely to do him serious harm than his Italian contacts or we're going to have to think of something else."

"If I'd been able to get hold of him yesterday, when I was still bitterly angry about what'd happened to you, I might've convinced myself that I could really hurt him. But I doubt even then he'd believe I'd do worse to him than blokes whose business is hurting people."

"But I think following him home is important – especially if you make sure he doesn't see you. Some background is always likely to be useful. If he's a CAP expert, Henri Kervran must've come across him. Perhaps we can get a bit about him from Henri."

"I suggest I leave that to you. He's another one who has a high opinion of your legs."

"That's an incredibly sexist remark.......which is absolutely true, of course......When we first came here and I was able to wear the sort of clothes I like, I thought continental men were very different from Englishmen, never looking me in the eye. But it didn't take long for the penny to drop....."

"So – which would you prefer, being able to wear the short skirts you like wearing and have your legs ogled or wear knee-length skirts or trousers and have them look you in the eye?"

"That's not a question I intend to answer.....Not least because I'm not sure which."

Rosemary was able to have a chat with Henri Kervran before we left together to pick up Emily and Sarah.

"You know I'm not really sure we need to keep doing this," Rosemary remarked, as we made our way to the school. "After we reported the attack to the police, they'd have to be extremely stupid to try and do something similar again. It's possible that they think I've had my lesson. And if they're professionals, I'd expect them to be long gone by now."

"So what did Henri Kervran tell you about Silvio Vascone?"

"His first comment was quite enlightening, in view of what we were up to with Ceresini. He said that the French regard the CAP as giving German money to Gaullist small farmers. But the Italians regard it as a form of reparations for what the Germans did to Italy during the last war. In other words, it's a virtually fool-proof way of making money without worrying greatly whether it's legal or not. So how the Italian Government views the CAP differs markedly from how the French, Germans and British regard it. Their officials are of necessity defensive, obstructive, devious....but also knowledgeable...Which is, unusually for the Italians, why they have a couple of attaches who know the CAP inside and out. Silvio Vascone is one of these. His grade is Counsellor or Deputy Director, though he isn't called a Counsellor in Italrep, for whatever reason. He's considered

241

determined to the point of obduracy, but extremely knowledgeable. By and large, he doesn't negotiate. He tends to repeat the same point over and over again and if under immense pressure, refer the matter back to Rome. But he's also a past master at obfuscation. He's reputed to have kept his wife and children back in Italy and has a flat somewhere over to the south of Brussels in the Uccle area, where he's believed to take the Italrep secretaries no-one else desires. Henri said he got most of his knowledge about him from others. Vascone isn't really the sort of man anyone ever gets to know, but from personal acquaintance, he's difficult to talk to. A man of sang-froid. You might wonder, Henri commented, why such an unsociable man works for Italrep, where you'd expect an ability to work with others and considerable sociability would be a requirement of the job? He assumes it's down to what he knows – and just as likely, who he knows back home."

"That should make him easier to pin down in the Brussels phone book."

"I'm ahead of you. He has a flat in the Rue du Ham. It must be very close to St Job's church. And there's a tram stop quite nearby. I had a look on the large scale map of Brussels in the office. He can get a tram from close to the Italrep offices which takes him almost to his doorstep."

"Nowhere to intercept him for a private chat?"

"Not that I could see. It didn't even look much of an area to do any surveillance either. There's a square – St Job's Square – close by. But there's no reason to suppose we could conceal ourselves there without it being pretty obvious."

"I'm not sure what we could observe that would be of any use to us. I can't imagine he invites Don Corleone and other Mafia dons into his flat. Beside, setting up the attack on you is presumably done and dusted. So he's no reason, as far as we know, for stepping out of line. And I'll bet his financial affairs are as pure as driven snow."

"From what Henri said, I agree. He also sounds like the sort of person who can't be caught off his guard and is unlikely to break down under pressure. Besides, we're not likely to be nearly as frightening as whoever got him to set up me being attacked....I'm not sure we're getting anywhere fast...."

"Let's try to think a bit more about how he might've got involved. You took the accounting book and we escaped from Ceresini on the Wednesday. We arrived back in Brussels early on Friday. Evidently Paolitti had been briefed by someone from the Italian side over the weekend. But Knud Henriksen had got this urgent request to meet General Enrico Forlini of the Guardia di Finanza by the time we met him on the Friday....Did you ever heard what happened at that meeting?"

"No. I'm pretty sure it was cancelled."

"Forlini or Henriksen?"

"Forlini, I think. I can check."

"While you're checking, you might want to find out whether Forlini contacted Henriksen on the Thursday or the Friday....And Vascone followed me on the Friday evening. Someone could hardly have contacted him on the Wednesday could they? At that stage they surely wouldn't've known whether we'd managed to get out of the country or not. Though assuming that helicopter landing on the ship had something to do with us and was presumably official, I suppose people would've thought it was likely we'd get away - by late evening on the Wednesday. I guess they would've checked you out before, if not once you'd turned up at the Ceresini plant. So they'd know where we both worked. But who would contact Vascone and how? Would an official like Vascone, who presumably needs to avoid having anything fishy linked to him, take a direct phone call from Ceresini, a company which has just been caught out in a large scale fraud? And even less Don Corleone, Ceresini's supplier of southern Italian wines...and possibly the Spanish ones too. So, do they go through the Italian Agriculture Ministry in Rome? Or some sort of Italian wine producers' federation? Or is this where

General Enrico Forlini of the Guardia di Finanza comes in? Who knows how all these organisations actually work together behind closed doors?"

"If Vascone wishes to avoid what you might call unorthodox contacts, anything that might cause people to ask questions later, it seems to me the safest route would be by way of the Italian Agriculture Ministry. Presumably Ceresini and the southern Italian wine-producers you keep calling Don Corleone have stooges within the Ministry? But it seems to me, you'd need a good reason why someone from the Guardia di Finanza would contact someone in his position, especially if they both know it's linked to some fishy business and people here might start tracking back after something unpleasant had happened to me."

"So what was General Enrico Forlini up to then, I wonder?"

"What was Colonel Pedroni doing at the Ceresini plant on the Wednesday morning, I wonder? Perhaps it was him that'd been doing the checking up on you and me and went there to inform Ceresini that they had a nosey British policewoman poking around in their affairs?"

"I'm still puzzling over meeting him in Bellagio. Could it really been completely coincidental? It just doesn't feel right."

"Leaving them aside for a moment, it means that even if we could do so, there's no way we could tell from phone calls to Vascone from the Italian Agriculture Ministry whether one involved setting him up with a contact, who then told him to follow you to find out where we live......I can't see an official from the Ministry setting that sort of thing up directly, can you?"

"No. I'm sure you're right there....So he either meets his contact here...or more likely contacts him by phone...."

"Why doesn't he meet his contact here?"

"Unless the Italians have some sort of permanent hit squad here in Brussels, I don't see how they could possibly have got a contact here by Friday morning at the earliest, especially if he needs to kept well clear of all of this. I'd imagine that the person who organised the attack on you arrived during the weekend, separately from the men who actually carried out the attack, who might have easily come a day or two later....."

"But how do they know where to steal the car they used? Is there any particular reason why you'd steal a car in Schaerbeek and dump it at Zaventem? Other than the fact that Schaerbeek is the other side of town from where Vascone lives?"

"Schaerbeek is a stop on the train from Zaventem airport. If they flew into Zaventem, they might've stayed at some doss house in Schaerbeek. And, of course, if they were on their way back to the airport, dumping the car in Zaventem would be well on their route. I guess they could even walk to the airport from there....Though I'd guess they probably took a bus."

"So Vascone could've suggested staying in Schaerbeek. Would the organiser have stayed nearby, I wonder? And might dumping the car in Zaventem have been a trick to make the police believe they'd flown out of Zaventem, when in fact they drove somewhere else and returned to Italy from a completely different airport?"

"Would Vascone meet his contact at all? Or would it just be a couple of phone conversations? And where would they have met? Would Vascone stick out like a sore thumb in Schaerbeek? Or the contact in central Brussels?"

"I guess Vascone wouldn't want to run the risk of being seen with someone who he couldn't explain satisfactorily. That might just mean a phone call....But I guess he'd want to make such a phone call outside the office...and not from home either. Would there be any reason for him to use a public call box?....That's assuming he doesn't want to give anything away about being in touch with these people....."

"The trouble is, we can keep going round and round asking questions and not get anywhere fast. So let's try and go for what we think is most probable and see where it takes us," I suggested. "I'll go first, if you like?"

"OK. You do your Sherlock Holmes act – and we'll worry about the assumptions later!"

245

"Very well.....I don't think Vascone met his contact before he tried to follow me home on the Friday evening. I don't think there was time to set it up safely....I doubt whether the contact had arrived in Brussels by then anyway. But I think he reported what happened directly to the contact when they met, probably during the weekend. It'd be much easier for Vascone to have a plausible reason for being in Schaerbeek over the weekend than during the week...or quite possibly being in the centre of town then. I think they met in Schaerbeek and Vascone reported all he'd been able to find out about us. The contact thought it was pretty pathetic and probably took a tram ride just to see the area for himself. The men who attacked you probably arrived separately over the period Sunday to Tuesday morning, but probably all stayed in the same cheap hotel in Schaerbeek. The organiser stayed somewhere else....Probably somewhere like the cheap hotels in Boulevard Emile Jacquemin. No-one asks questions of single men staying in the hotels round there, so I'm told."

"The red light district, I take it?"

"Yes. An area where no-one sees anything and hears nothing....Not somewhere where Vascone would wish to be seen. But I reckon it's the sort of place where the organiser feels most at home......At any rate, that's my suggestion....and I reckon there's a cheap hotel not far from Schaerbeek station that had three Italians staying there in between last weekend and Wednesday morning."

"Tomorrow is Saturday. Why don't we take Emily and Sarah on an excursion? They can see the Atomium. They've always said they wanted to go back. Then we might have a snoop around Schaerbeek, just in case we spot any likely hotels. It'll be a bit of a trek — but perhaps if we do Schaerbeek on our way, so to speak, we can keep them going with lunch and then the Atomium in the afternoon......I assume you aren't just interested in finding out whether three Italians stayed somewhere in Brussels and , if so, where?"

246

"No. If we locate them, in Schaerbeek, I hope, we'll need to try and work out where they might've met Vascone. The only way to nail him down will be by having evidence that he met the people who attacked you. If we can get their passport numbers, we'll be starting to have something that will make him uncomfortable."

The next day, we took the tram to the Gare Centrale and a train from there to Schaerbeek. The moment we approached the station, I knew why it rang a bell. For a suburb of a relatively small European capital city, it boasted an unforgettable railway station – large and ostentatious – once described to me as "a mixture of Keble College, Oxford, and a chateau on the Loire".

"We could've got here quicker by tram," observed Rosemary, who'd noticed the tram lines outside the station.

"I'm trying to follow their thought process. They'd arrive by train from Zaventem. I doubt whether Vascone would want them wandering around and getting lost. So I guess he would've suggested a hotel as close to the station as possible."

"Would he have come here to have a look? I suppose there might not have been enough time? So if you're Vascone, which road do you choose on the map to pick your hotel?"

"You want to give these Italians nice, simple instructions. So you come out of the station and turn – right or left? Straight on across the square means dodging trams, so that's a complication. Also there may be passengers waiting for trams you have to push past, who might remember you. So - I'm right handed, I suggest going right. But not a hotel that overlooks the railway, I suggest."

We made our way round the station square. The first road we came to ran along by the side of the railway. The next one – Avenue Princesse Elizabeth - seemed ideal. Indeed, if anything it was too ideal. In the first couple of hundred yards, there were a dozen or more nondescript hotels, exactly the sort we were looking for.

"I'm cautious. So I don't suggest the first or the second hotel on the right. I go for number three. 'Hotel Exelsior'," I said.

"Not very aptly named, I should say. I suggest that you try those hotels you fancy for the next quarter of an hour or so while Emily, Sarah and I have a drink – and possibly an ice cream," replied Rosemary.

"Could we have waffles?" asked Sarah. "I love waffles and ice cream!"

"As long as you don't ruin your appetite for lunch."

As it happened, they scarcely had time to order their snack. The Hotel Excelsior turned up trumps. It was, as I expected, dingy and down-at-heel, but spotlessly clean and efficient. The receptionist was a Walloon woman well into her middle age. A combination of my SEFF pass and C&E Commission convinced her to summon her boss, the manager, a sandy-haired Flemish man in his early forties.

"I work for the Service Européenne contre la Fraude Fiscale," I explained in English, always the safest way of conversing with a Flemish speaker, if you didn't know Flemish or Dutch. "We're investigating cross-border frauds committed by an Italian organisation. We believe that in relation to this, three Italians stayed in this area very recently. They would've checked out last Wednesday morning and arrived the previous weekend or possibly last Monday. I'd be grateful if you could tell me whether you had three Italians staying here, please?"

"Would they have arrived together?"

"Not necessarily. But on Monday and Tuesday nights, there would've been three of them here. One was burly, with a black beard. Another was lean, with a narrow face…."

"Yes. I recall them to mind. Signor Bruni and his two colleagues…..Let's have a look in the register….Signor Marco Bruni arrived on Sunday. Signor Piero Fabbri and Signor Giovanni Collina came on Monday. They all paid up and left on Wednesday morning, as you suggested. Paid cash. Kept themselves to themselves. Ate out….including breakfast."

"Do you still have the immigration forms? It'd be helpful if I could take down the passport numbers, though I suspect the passports are fake or stolen."

"Just give me a second......I can't say I liked the look of them much. The man with the thin face, Fabbri – I think that was him – looked like the sort of man who'd torture his grandmother for ten centimes......Here they are...."

"Thank you."

I wrote down the passport numbers and the, undoubtedly false, names, thanked the manager and left. Rosemary, Emily and Sarah were in a café in the station square, Sarah enjoying her usual struggle with waffles and ice-cream, which usually resulted in a quarter of the waffle on her clothes and a similar proportion of the ice cream on her face or clothes.

"That was quick," said Rosemary. "You struck lucky!"

"Not luck, deduction," I replied. "And they certainly chose the right sort of place. The manager of the Hotel Excelsior is Flemish and plainly doesn't know any Italian. Otherwise he might've cottoned on to the fact that his Italian guests were called the Italian equivalent of Mr Brown, Mr Smith and Mr Hill!"

"So now you're going to use your great powers of deduction to work out where they met Vascone?"

"Yes. If all of you are prepared to put up with that? Apparently, the two men who attacked you – probably Fabbri and Collina – stayed in their rooms a fair amount of the time. Bruni, who was smaller and presumably the driver, went out rather more of the time. I guess he was scouting cars to pinch and finding out a bit about the road network in these parts."

"Of course, it's possible he was the organiser and the only one who met Vascone?"

"They all went out for lunch and dinner. But Fabbri and Collina didn't get here until round about midday on Monday. It's certainly possible that Vascone met Bruni on Sunday, but I reckon he met all of them on Monday evening."

"So where do your powers of deduction tell you they ate?"

"Italian? Not Italian? They're probably rather conservative eaters... like these two....But they'd undoubtedly be speaking in Italian and wouldn't want to be overheard. So not Italian, I think. But nothing fancy...or a curry place, for instance."

"So what – a 'steak-frites'?"

"Yes. That sounds about right. They might be 'moules-frites' fans, but a bog-standard Belgian restaurant – which'll probably do burgers, sausages and stoemp as well - strikes me as the right sort of place. Nothing too fancy, but ideally sufficiently private for Vascone not to feel he sticks out like a sore thumb.....and probably not too far away. If these three blokes don't really know Brussels...and certainly don't know Schaerbeek.....I doubt they'd be wanting to wander too far from their hotel."

"So we start in the Avenue Princesse Elisabeth?"

"I reckon so."

So far my powers of deduction had worked a treat...or perhaps I just found it easy to slip into the mind of an Italian thug. At any rate, the first Belgian restaurant we came to, the "Wit Vlees", adorned with Maes Pils signs, looked the part. The manager, a typically dour example of Flemish manhood, replete with spiky blond hair and moustache and manner to match, wasn't unduly impressed by the documents I'd showed him. But when I mentioned we were seeking to track down some Italians, his manner changed. Evidently he didn't like Italians. He was able to confirm that five Italians had dined there on the Monday evening – three of them meeting the descriptions of Vascone, Fabbri and Collina. He also gave me a decent description of Bruni and the unknown fifth man....The one of Bruni tallying well with what the manager of the Excelsior Hotel had told me.

"Now what?" asked Rosemary, who'd be lingering outside.

"It depends whether you want to eat here in Schaerbeek or whether you need some time to let the waffles and ice cream settle down and we could have lunch by the Atomium."

"Can we have lunch in the top sphere?" asked Emily.

"I don't think there's room there for too many people. So it may be booked up or we might have to queue for a long time," replied Rosemary. "But we could certainly see whether we can. You've had a rather dull morning, so it's right you should have a reward."

"Are you going to be able to catch those men who tried to hurt you?"

(Of course, our daughters were bright enough to have picked up what'd really happened to Rosemary within a day or so. Fortunately, as she'd suffered no lasting damage, their worries could be relieved...or mostly relieved, I suppose).

"Probably not," replied Rosemary. "Fortunately they only frightened me. But I think we now know who they were and why they wanted to frighten me. But they'll be out of the country by now. But we hope we may be able to find out who got them to do it."

The journey to the Atomium involved a change of trams and took a while, trundling through not very interesting suburbs of north Brussels, until we glimpsed the large, shiny and frankly weird and wonderful Atomium. During the journey my brain was ticking over, thinking about what we'd learnt that morning. Some inconvenient and uncomfortable thoughts emerged.

I suppose that as it was so close to Christmas and cold day which a leaden sky threatened to make worse, there were no queues to go into the Atomium and we got a table for lunch on the top sphere. The prices were, appropriately sky-high and the quality average...but at least they did a children's menu. And we were rewarded for our journey by the sight of a heavy snowstorm, the first of the winter, blowing fiercely across the whole of the city, gradually turning everything in front of us white. We watched for the best part of an hour – even the usually mercurial Sarah struck spellbound by the transformation wrought by the snow.

By the time we got back to our flat, there were several inches of snow on the ground and we all felt frozen. But cups of hot soup and the remainder of the morning's baguette....with slices of chocolate hidden in the middle in the case of some of us.....soon warmed us up.

"Well, at least we've got some answers," said Rosemary, as we sat together on the settee, after the children had been tucked up for the night, and we'd chosen classical music on the radio rather than French, German or Belgian pop music.

"But several questions remain," I replied. "I suppose we have to do this sort of thing in order, but I realised this afternoon, there were a whole series of questions I should have been thinking about. First, how did Vascone know what you looked like? How did these men recognise you? And even more important, how did they know you'd be on that particular tram, on your own, on that particular evening? After all, you did something unusual. Usually you collect Emily and Sarah. And it's rare that you travel home on your own in mid-evening. Is it really credible to think that they were just hanging around places where we might be and struck lucky and spotted you on your own leaving that Interpol do? They had to know you were at that Interpol do – and that you were on your own. And if they were sending out Bruni on Sunday, with the other two the next day, did they already know you were attending that Interpol do? Who found out – Vascone or the anonymous fifth man?"

"I told the Interpol secretariat I'd be going to their party about a week before we went to Verona. So my name would've been on a list somewhere in Interpol. Would they tell anyone who asked who was going and who wasn't.....I suppose Vascone in Italrep probably has access to some sort of diary of parties. I guess these diplomats have to do a lot of them and they may have to parcel them out. So they might have to have a schedule. I guess if you knew a bit about me, you might reckon that'd be a party I might attend."

"I wonder if I rang up and said I was from Italrep or whatever and asked whether Mrs Storey was attending their Christmas bash, because I wanted to have a chat to you about some work you were doing where there were matters of mutual interest, whether a secretary would just tell me without thinking about it?"

"Probably...But I don't recall seeing anyone like your description of Vascone there. I've been racking my brains to remember who was there, as it seems to me it quite possible that someone there was the one who tipped these men off when I left."

"Whoever it was had to know the person was you. I know I don't think there's anyone like you, but if you look around Brussels there are plenty of attractive women in their thirties, with short dark hair, wearing short skirts to show off their legs. You'd hardly want Bruni and his thugs to go attacking the wrong woman. So there had to be someone at that Interpol bash who was able to confirm who you were."

"I suppose if you were Vascone, you might keep well out of my sight. But if you asked someone whether Mrs Storey was there and to point me out because you wanted to have a word with me, there would've been a fair number there who could've done that."

"And then, when you leave, he uses a walkie-talkie to tell the blokes outside that you're on your way.....But anyone checking back seriously ought to follow the path we've just taken. Would someone cautious like Vascone go along to a party which he hadn't been invited to and had no obvious business interest? The Brussels diplomatic circuit isn't so large that he could bank on remaining anonymous."

"So who was it? This mysterious fifth man?"

"Possibly. I wonder who would either be invited or, if he turned up, it wouldn't appear odd? Even if no-one knew who he was, if his credentials were OK, no-one would turn a hair."

"I'm not sure I see where you're going."

"Well...If Vascone turns up, he's going to need a plausible excuse to attend the Interpol bash, because he's got no other reason to be there. On the other hand, I could turn up and because I was your husband, no-one would bat an eyelid...So it was either someone with a plausible excuse or someone who fitted in...."

"Like General Enrico Forlini, who was so keen to meet Knud Henriksen, but then never finalised the meeting. They may not be the most respected police force on the continent, but the Guardia di Finanza do have a fair credibility in Interpol......Now where did that come from?"

"It sounds plausible though....And it might explain his cancelled meeting with Henriksen. It'd be quite reasonable for someone from the Guardia di Finanza to complain to Henriksen about what we'd been up to on their patch....and it'd certainly be a good reason for him to come to Brussels. But then he couldn't be sure Henriksen might not bring one or both of us along to their meeting....And of course, if you were there, you might well recognise him if he was at the Interpol bash and there'd be an inconvenient link between him and the attack made by those Italians on you."

"So he could be the fifth man?"

"It'd certainly explain why he'd want to meet up with the others in an out-of-the-way place like Schaerbeek, rather than some posh restaurant in the Petite Rue des Bouchers."

"And we can probably find out a bit about him...including whether he was in Brussels last Wednesday.....and whether he was at the Interpol do."

There was nothing we could do on the Sunday, but on Monday morning, Rosemary was busy making phone calls to various contacts. We caught up over our sandwich lunch in my office.

"I rang the secretary who arranged the Interpol party," Rosemary explained. "I said that I'd met an Italian man from the Guardia di Finanza, I thought, but I couldn't remember his name, but I needed to get in touch with him. She confirmed that Italrep had asked to get General Enrico Forlini into the party on the Monday and that he was ticked off as having attended. So I rang a contact in Interpol and said I'd had a brief chat with General

254

Enrico Forlini at the Interpol party, but I'd had to leave before I was able to get any details from him. A couple of phone calls later, I learnt that he's commander of the Veneto region, which includes Verona. I mentioned that he seemed to know a lot about southern Italy and I was told that his previous post was in Campania in the south. Apparently he's a Christian Democrat nominee....In the Italian system most appointments are parcelled out between the main political parties. Forlini is a Christian Democrat and the commander of the Guardia di Finanza in the Veneto region is a Christian Democrat post."

"The Italian Communist party is a lot bigger and more successful than in Britain. I wonder if there's a Communist head of police somewhere? That would've amused my father!"

Now it was my turn to bend the truth a little and impersonate various people in tracking down General Forlini's recent whereabouts. Using Rosemary's Interpol directory, I found the phone number for the headquarters of the Guardia di Finanza Veneto Region, located in Venice, naturally enough.

"Good afternoon," I said, speaking in German-accented English. "My name is Dietrich Goetz. I work for Hans-Georg Adler, Counsellor at the West German Representation to the EEC in Brussels. Herr Adler's interests include financial and fiscal fraud. He had been hoping to speak to General Forlini when he was in Brussels recently, but he has been unable to locate him. Is he now back in Venice, please?"

"Yes. He returned last Thursday. Do you......?"

"Oh what a pity! Herr Adler was particularly keen to meet face to face on a delicate matter. I expect it was what the English call a flying visit to Brussels?"

"He was in Brussels from Monday until Thursday. I am sorry your Herr Adler was unable to meet him. At the present time, he has no plans to go to Brussels."

"I shall inform Herr Adler. He will have to consider whether the matter is sufficiently urgent to meet General Forlini in Venice. I am most grateful for your courtesy and your help."

I rang off.

General Forlini would have flown in and out of Zaventem. I had a Customs contact there who was able to confirm that he had actually arrived in the early afternoon of Sunday.

Had he been in contact with the Italian Embassy to the Kingdom of Belgium or Italrep? As his office had contacted Knud Henriksen and he'd managed to wangle an invitation to the Interpol party, it seemed to me he must've been in touch – probably with Italrep, as the Brussels office of Interpol would have far more dealings with the EEC than with the Belgian Government. However, getting information out of them was going to be trickier. There was a Counsellor in the West German Representation called Herr Adler and an attaché called Goetz. But the chances of a secretary in the Guardia di Finanza office in Venice having come across them struck me as zero and I wouldn't't've rated General Forlini's much higher. But people who worked in related areas in the different Representations were an incestuous circle, constantly meeting, negotiating, drinking, dining, trying to outsmart each other.

I decided on a bold, but risky approach.

"Hi," I spoke to the telephone receptionist at Italrep, in as good an American accent as I could muster. "I'm Jim O'Hare from NATO. SEMNA secretariat. We cover the South Europe, Mediterranean and North African sectors. I understand there was a General Forloni from Italy in town last week. I believe we needed to speak to him. Is he still here, do you know?"

"I'm afraid I don't. I'll have to check. Please hold the line."

I waited while the line crackled, hoping that she was checking up on General Forlini, rather than the existence of Jim O'Hare from the SEMNA secretariat of NATO, which I'd just invented. After about five minutes, I could hear the receiver being picked up.

"There was a General Forlini…not Forloni…here in Brussels at the beginning of last week. But I don't believe he has anything to do with NATO. He's a General in the Guardia di Finanza, the

Italian financial police." There was a faint note of contempt in her voice, the contempt of the knowledgeable European for the brash and stupid Americans. (The fact that it was but thirty years from when they'd lost many lives to liberate Western Europe seemed to have been long forgotten). But it was the response I was hoping for.

"Is that so? I was informed that he was a man I or General Carver, my commander, should meet. Someone here seems to have made an almighty snafu. Is there someone I could contact here, just in case it was this General Forloni who my General wished to meet?"

"You would need to contact Signor Silvio Vascone. It appears that he was General Forlini's contact while he was here."

"You've been very helpful. Thank you. I'll give General Carver my sitrep and see what his plan of action is now the scene has been clarified."

I hung up. It seemed to me that the circle had been squared. The question now was how could we use this information?

"QUASIMODO'S" HUNCHES PAY OFF

"Do you think I'm still at risk?" asked Rosemary, as we made our way to pick up Emily and Sarah from school. "As far as we can tell, all the Italians who came here to carry out the attack on me have left."

"I think you probably are safe now," I replied. "But until we've nailed Vascone down, I reckon we should still be cautious. Who knows – he may be involved in planning something quite different as we speak?"

"Have you thought about how we might get Vascone nailed down?"

"No.....I'd still like to think a bit about how General Forlini was involved in this. It seems an odd thing to do, to come over here and get involved with some thugs attacking you. I know I've had misgivings about what Colonel Pedroni was up to at Ceresini...and the reports you hear about the Guardia di Finanza aren't particularly flattering. But why would he deliberately come here and risk being associated with an attack on a policewoman? I can see that Ceresini and possibly some rather less reputable suppliers might want to get some revenge on you, whoever you were. But it seems incredibly risky for someone who's supposed to be on the side of law and order."

"Perhaps he's been bought and paid for by the Mafia? If they tell him to jump, he just asks how high."

"It's possible, I suppose. But would even the Mafia want someone who might be quite valuable to them for years risk his career in a revenge attack on you? I realised they may have made losses that they don't like, but it must be a drop in the ocean to anyone other than perhaps Ceresini. It doesn't quite seem to balance right."

"But he does seem to have been here at the right time. Why else did he come here? I realise there might've been some point to a meeting with Knud Henriksen to complain about what we'd been up to, especially if the Guardia di Finanza were actually investigating Ceresini and we trampled all over it. But he never went ahead with the meeting. If he wasn't involved with Vascone and these other men, what was he up to? And if it wasn't him who pointed me out at the Interpol party, who was it?"

"He's the only person we've identified at that party who had possible links with what we were up to in Italy. But presumably there were other Italians from Italrep there too? We've no idea who may owe who what sort of favours there. Before we corner Vascone, we need to be sure of our facts. If General Forlini wasn't involved or perhaps even being used as a decoy, Vascone is going to laugh in our faces."

"So we really need to know the names of everyone from Italrep who attended the Interpol party. I don't think I'd better ring again. She's likely to recognise me."

"I'll do it in the morning. You'll need to give me a plausible name so that I can ask about an Italian I met at the party."

I rang the Interpol office in Brussels the following morning, in the guise of Commander Cedric Partridge of New Scotland Yard, who had a very plummy accent.

"I'm terribly sorry to bother you, but one of my colleagues from the Metropolitan Police, WPS Rosemary Storey, who is on secondment to the Service Européenne contre la Fraude Fiscale, attended a Christmas party at your offices last week. She mentioned to me that she'd had an interesting conversation with some chap from the Italian Embassy or perhaps their Representation to the EEC there in Brussels. Unfortunately, she didn't get the chap's name. I wonder if you'd be so good as to oblige me by telling me who from the Italian Embassy or Representation attended the party. I should be extremely gratified."

"I'll have to dig out the list. Do you wish to hold or shall I ring you back?"

"I have to attend a meeting shortly, so it's perhaps better that I hold on...I am most infernally grateful...."

I was beginning to wonder whether I was perhaps overdoing the Bertie Wooster impression, but the telephone-receptionist would probably have had to have lived in England to have spotted it...and her English accent seemed very French. I waited for nearly ten minutes, beginning to worry that she'd had to get the list from someone who was being difficult, or just asking the sort of questions I would've preferred not to answer.

"Attending from the Italian Embassy was Signor Angelo Rondino. From the Italian Representation to the EEC, Signor Giancarlo Ugolini, Captain Fabio Borinello and Signor Silvio Vascone. There were two other Italians also attending – General Enrico Forlini from the Guardia di Finanza in Venice and Captain Gaetano Ruggieri from the Service Européenne contre la Fraude Fiscale. I guess your colleague must have known who he was."

"I am eternally in your debt. That was enormously helpful of you."

I was glad Rosemary wasn't listening. I still had fond memories of her "Penelope" impression when we first visited the "Whittingtons" squash club in the Houndsditch ten years or so ago. I would've had to endure several weeks of teasing for my Cedric Partridge impression.

But on the other hand, it just added to the last of possible suspects. I got hold of the office copy of the latest diplomatic list and was able to rule out Rondino straight away. He was plainly a spook, as his duties were vaguely commercial – and he had no obvious link to Interpol if he wasn't in the security business. On the other hand, Ugolini and Borinello would need further checking. Ugolini was supposedly responsible for transport matters at Counsellor level. Borinello was an attaché, supposedly specialising in the Customs area. It'd be interesting to see whether

Henri Kervran or Conor O'Leary had come across him. I certainly hadn't. Neither were obvious invitees, it seemed to me. Ruggieri was, however. But I was surprised Rosemary hadn't mentioned seeing him there.

I bumped into O'Leary first. His impression was that Borinello was a naval officer, whose main interest was the CFP (Common Fisheries Policy) and covered mainly Customs preventive issues. He felt that Borinello was on a relatively short-term secondment from the Italian Navy based in La Spezia and looked as though he couldn't wait to get back there. I decided to move him into my "possibles" list, rather than "probables".

I went into Rosemary's room, but Marc Dierich was there, so I went back to my room to wait for her. Fortunately Hans-Georg Meyer, who shared my office, had returned to Stuttgart for a lengthy Christmas break. Within ten minutes, Rosemary came in. I explained what I'd found out.

"I assume you wanted me to do something?"

"I was wondering if any of your Interpol contacts might be able to tell you anything about Ugolini, in particular. But obviously, anything they might be able to tell you about Captain Borinello or Rondino might be useful. I confess, I believe Rondino is a spook – mainly because his duties have nothing to do with Interpol...."

"That's equally true of the other two."

"But when I had dealings with the man calling himself David Watson from the British Security Service about the Russian drugs stuff, one of the things he mentioned in passing – probably to show off – was that there were no spooks in the EEC Representation offices. Because of the way they worked, it'd be too obvious......On the other hand, if I can pick Rondino from his attendance at an Interpol bash, I guess the Soviets probably could too."

"It's still worth me asking about him, I think."

"I agree....There was another thing. Your Capitano Ruggieri was on the guest list too. You never mentioned seeing him."

"He told us loudly as he was leaving at about five-thirty that he was scheduled to attend three parties that evening and he was going to have a problem standing up straight at the Interpol one. From that I gathered he'd be going there last. He hadn't arrived by the time I left. I have to say if he was involved I'd been amazed....He's just about the laziest person I've ever come across. I'm absolutely certain he got this job because of who he knows, because he hasn't actually lifted a finger to do anything in all the time we've been here."

"But he does doing nothing very well."

"I'll see what my Interpol contacts are prepared to tell me."

She returned about forty minutes later.

"Ugolino is a liaison point for a big Interpol operation involving lorries moving between Italy, Austria, Switzerland and Germany. Quite rightly, my contact wouldn't say more than that. But I think that means we can rule him out. Captain Borinello has been working with the Italian Customs and Coastguard services and Interpol about illegal immigration from North Africa into the EEC, notably Italy and France. He seems squeaky clean too....So we come back to General Forlini, do we not?"

"Hmm.....I just think he made himself too conspicuous....let me try something...."

I picked up the phone and rang Forlini's office in Venice again.

"I'm sorry to trouble you," I began in my best Italian-accented English. "But I am extremely disappointed. When General Forlini visited Brussels recently, he did not make time to meet me, even though we are of the same service and I represent the interests of the Guardia di Finanza here in Brussels."

"I'm sorry," said the female voice at the other end of the line. "But who are you?"

"I am Ruggieri, Capitano Gaetano Ruggieri. Was it not I who spoke to General Forlini about the problem in Bussolengo and suggested he contacted the manager of the people involved here?"

"General Forlini is not available. He is on a tour of inspection. You may speak to his staff officer, if you wish."

"I do so wish."

She put the phone down and as it hummed and crackled away, I motioned Rosemary to leave the room, as her laughter might easily be audible at the other end of the line.

"Giuseppe Sordi here," said a deep voice. "Capitano Ruggieri?"

"Si."

"Perche parliamo in inglese?"

"Because I share a room with a Frenchman who understands Italian but not English."

"OK. You wanted to speak with General Forlini?"

"I have just learnt that General Forlini visited Brussels in the first half of last week, but did not do me the courtesy of meeting me. I did not know he had been here until earlier today. Did I not alert him to the problem which was occurring in Bussolengo and suggest that he contacted the manager of this office, who could deal with the two people from here that had caused the problem?"

"You telephoned him on the Thursday, as I recall?"

"That is correct. I understand he spoke to the manager here – Signor Henriksen – the following day. But when he came to Brussels he did not meet Signor Henriksen. Nor did he pay me the courtesy of meeting me, even though I represent our service here in Brussels. I merely wish to register my disappointment."

"But there must have been some mistake. My understanding was that you advised General Forlini not to contact you or to be seen with you at any cost. You also advised him, if what he told me is correct, not to meet this Signor Henriksen because he would probably insist on bringing to any meeting the people who had caused the problem in Bussolengo, which would make the meeting counter-productive. He will have made a note of this conversation on file. I can check if you wish?"

263

"That will not be necessary. We must have got our wires crossed somewhere along the line. But it would be helpful if we could meet the next time General Forlini visited Brussels."

I rang off.

"Eh! Signor Nick! 'Ow well you speaka da Italiano!"

Rosemary had evidently been listening from the corridor. It was surprising with a smirk that wide she was able to get it through the door to my room. I explained what I'd just been told.

"But seriously, why did you think it was Ruggieri? I'd completely ruled him out."

"A mixture of our old friend Ockham's Razor and Sherlock Holmes's comment that if you've exhausted all the other possibilities, the one you're left with must be the right one, however improbable. General Forlini just seemed too obvious. I think he was encouraged to come here as window dressing. First he was going to meet Knud Henriksen, but Ruggieri subsequently advised against it – once he was here, of course. And then between him and Vascone, they got him an invitation to the Interpol bash, which is probably quite a big thing for a regional commander in the Guardia di Finanza, even if you're a General. They probably also arranged a couple of meetings in between, just to keep him busy – and well away from the SEFF offices."

"So if he didn't tell those men who attacked me that I was leaving, who did?"

"Ruggieri. The one name in all of these who knows you well by sight. All he had to do was wait outside until you came out and point you out to the men. He was probably waiting in their car. Then all he had to do was gargle a glass of whisky and appear at the Interpol party acting a little the worse for wear and no-one would be the wiser. I guess Ruggieri's function is to provide intelligence to whoever pays him – with Giulizzi and Paolitti at the top of the list, naturally. I reckon he keeps his ear close to the ground, especially when there's anything going on relating to Italy. So he'd be aware of our investigations in broad terms rather than detail. It wouldn't surprise me at all if he hadn't encouraged

Colonel Pedroni to make our acquaintance in Bellagio….and, when I come to think of it, got him to go to Ceresini that morning, knowing we were there and were likely to be employing our usual unorthodox methods to get at the truth. He'd certainly know we'd gone to Verona with the Wasco people and we were visiting Ceresini. There's no great leap of imagination from there."

"That all makes perfect sense to me. But then who was it who stopped those men from raping me by shooting at their car? There was Bruni driving, with Fabbri and Collina attacking me. Ruggieri would have to stay at the Interpol do. And General Forlini knew nothing about any of it. Was it Vascone? Surely, he would've wanted to maintain an alibi by staying at the Interpol party or at some event where he had plenty of witnesses? But if not him, who?"

"Let's check something with the switchboard and then I may be able to check out a hunch."

"Your hunches have been working quite well today, Quasimodo – so lead on!"

We made our way to the switchboard room, where a couple of bored Belgian woman handled SEFF's calls. As we were a counter-fraud organisation, Gerry Fitzpatrick had insisted on a system that logged outward and inward calls, which had already proved useful. I was banking on Ruggieri being too idle to go outside and cover his tracks effectively. Sure enough, on the Thursday morning, there was a call to the Venice number which I knew to be that of General Forlini's office, as well as several to Vascone, who it seemed was the direct contact with Bruni, Fabbri and Collina. Then – to my pleasure and relief – was a phone call to another Italian number at around 9 am on the fateful Wednesday when Rosemary and I were at the Ceresini plant.

We returned to my office and rang the number.

"Guardia di Finanza. Prego?" replied a woman's voice.

"Vorrei parlare con Colonnello Pedroni, per favore," I replied. (*I wish to speak with Colonel Pedroni, please*)

"Colonnello Pedroni non e qui. Chiama domani, per cortesia." *(Colonel Pedroni isn't here. Call tomorrow, please)*

"Lui e ancora a Bruxelles?" *(Is he still in Brussels?)*

"No. E tornato giovedi scorso. Oggi e a Padova." *(No. He returned last Thursday. Today he is in Padua)*

"Grazie mille. Chiamo domani." *(Thanks a lot. I'll ring tomorrow)*

I rang off.

"You sounded almost Italian," observed Rosemary. "Did you find out what you wanted? Are your hunches twitching?"

"Fortunately the lady at the other end was quite terse. The problem with knowing a bit of a language is asking a question and being completely unable to understand the reply. But she told me what I wanted to know. He confirmed what I'd begun to suspect – that Colonel Pedroni was in Brussels at the time you were attacked – and I'm willing to lay a Pound to a Lira that it was him who shot at the car when those men were attacking you."

"Uh? Was that another deduction or a shot in the dark?"

"A bit of both – though a shot in the dark would be more appropriate.....It was something you said on the boat about that morning at the Ceresini place. You said that the Ceresini people told you that the visit from Colonel Pedroni was unannounced – and it threw them into a bit of a panic. I'd taken the view that Pedroni was a Ceresini stooge and that he was helping them to nail us down. But once I started to realise that General Forlini was probably clean, I needed to consider the possibility that Pedroni was also clean."

"If he was so clean, why did he spy on us in Bellagio and seem so chummy with the Ceresini people?"

"I suspect that Ruggieri gave him a line. If I was him, I'd say that we were snooping around, treading with our big feet on his turf and at the end of it, we'd probably be trying to make out that the Guardia di Finanza were certainly incompetent, if not actually in cahoots with crooks like Ceresini."

"So, knowing we'd be in Bellagio – presumably because Ruggieri told him – he did what we'd probably do and checked us out as unobtrusively as he could. Then Ruggieri tells him we're up to no good at the Ceresini plant – removing evidence or perhaps planting evidence to make it look as though the Guardia di Finanza are involved in their crooked dealings – and he shoots along there to sort it out. How does that get him to Brussels?"

"We may well need to ask him. But my guess is that he's the one who sends the bloke on to the ship to Corsica to try and get back from us whatever we're supposed to have taken. That fails. But next day he gets a call from General Forlini along the lines of 'what the hell has been going on in your patch? I'm being encouraged to go to Brussels to complain about some EEC officials messing us about. What's been going on?' Pedroni naturally asks what Forlini has been told. I reckon he was told something close to the truth, that you'd taken the real book of accounts. At this point Pedroni sees a flash of light. Ruggieri has been playing him like a fish. Ruggieri is being paid by Ceresini or one of their partners to keep them out of trouble. So what is Ruggieri up to? Why has he got General Forlini to go to Brussels? Is he the piece of misdirection intended to hide what's really going on? Perhaps Forlini and he have a chat. Perhaps he just thinks he'll follow Forlini's footsteps and see what Ruggieri is up to. And assuming Ruggieri is up to something, what could it be? When it comes down to it, there's not much – get the accounting book back and get revenge on you or me, possibly both of us. And if you think about it, what's the point in getting the accounting book back? Ceresini can almost certainly insist on it. But once we've got it, we've almost certainly photocopied enough of it to be able to use it against Ceresini....and in any case, the damage is already done. Wasco are pulling the plug on their contract with Ceresini."

"So revenge is most likely. But why would that bother Pedroni? We've hardly done anything to endear ourselves to him."

"I'm guessing that he's a decent bloke. He doesn't like crooks like Ruggieri and Ceresini taking revenge on fellow law enforcement officers. He particularly doesn't like being manipulated by Ruggieri...a junior officer, after all.... and I think he'd want to frustrate whatever he'd got planned. So he kept in General Forlini's shadow....I guess at some stage he managed to find out what Ruggieri looks like, assuming he hadn't met him before....And presumably he was aware that Forlini was flying back to Venice on the Thursday morning, so if he was window dressing, the Interpol bash was the last opportunity for Ruggieri to act. So he waited outside – carefully concealed, of course – and spotted Ruggieri waiting until you left and get followed. He had to get a taxi and catch up. When he saw what was happening to you, he fired his gun and frightened the men away....But there's no way any Brussels taxi driver is going to hang around after an incident like that, so he had to leave his help unexplained. And without evidence, there wasn't much he could do about Ruggieri at that stage...and as no permanent harm was done to anyone, he may well feel that sleeping dogs are best left undisturbed."

"Well, it's certainly a theory. But it's going to need a bit more substance before I'm convinced. You're going to ring Pedroni in the morning?"

"Yes. And I'd like to encourage him to help us nail Ruggieri."

"Unofficially I assume."

"I guess so. It's possible he intends to do something when Ruggieri is back in the Guardia di Finanza. But I reckon if he got this job in SEFF to do the sort of things he's been doing, he's got enough powerful friends to protect him against allegations made by local commanders, based a long way from Rome."

"So we might even be able to help him."

There was little else to do in the office, as it was so close to Christmas and with Knud Henriksen leaving as well. There was going to be a Christmas party in the office on the Friday evening and a special lunch given by Henriksen the following Tuesday, with quite a restricted guest list. He was giving drinks to everyone in the office on his final day, but it seemed that only Gerry Fitzpatrick, Henri Kervran, Kristin Pedersen, Conor O'Leary,

Marc Dierich, Ruggieri, Rosemary and me were invited to lunch. Apparently we constituted "the Originals". Rosemary commented that we sounded like a cheap ITV detective series.

The following morning, I phoned back to the Verona office of the Guardia di Finanza – as myself this time.

"I am somewhat surprised you wished to be in contact with me," remarked Colonel Pedroni, speaking English, fortunately for me. "The last time we met, you did not appear to trust me very much."

"Circumstances can be deceptive. And I now believe I owe you a debt of gratitude for saving my wife from being raped and possibly worse."

"How in heaven's name did you work that out?"

"Through following my thoughts and hunches from various pieces of evidence, backed up with a number of phone calls, which you'd probably regard as unorthodox. But the conclusion which I reached was based on a strong belief that various events were manipulated by Capitano Gaetano Ruggieri, one of my colleagues. It was he who I believe encouraged you to check Rosemary and me out when we were on holiday in Bellagio and to go to the Ceresini offices when Rosemary and I were there."

"I assume you have a certain amount of evidence to support this?"

"Some phone logs in this office. I haven't checked them all out, but there was a phone call made from here to your office in the morning Rosemary and I were at the Ceresini offices with the Wasco people. That was actually how I found out your office phone number and that you'd been in Brussels at the time Rosemary was attacked."

"So that was you yesterday. Giulia thought the caller had a rather peculiar accent. And you have also been phoning General Forlini's office in Venice?"

"Yes. His visit to Brussels looked extremely odd. At first I thought he might've been involved, but it seemed more likely that he was being manipulated by Ruggieri and his accomplice in the

Italian Representation, Silvio Vascone....You understand that I wasn't seeking revenge, but to understand who had been involved, so that I might be certain no-one would attack Rosemary again. We think what happened has been considered to be sufficient retaliation for what she did in Bussolengo, but we couldn't be sure until we'd discovered who was responsible and how they did it."

"So you are aware of who is telling Ruggieri to do this?"

"No. We assumed it might be Ceresini or perhaps one of their partners, the people who were sending the wine that was exported under Valdicocce and Camarolo labels. But we couldn't see how we could identify them....and certainly not bring them to justice."

"I think you could safely say that they are untouchable. But do you propose to bring Capitano Ruggieri and his accomplice Vascone to justice?"

"Not justice in the ordinary sense of the word. More like natural justice. I'd like to get Ruggieri removed from his present post and returned to Italy and the same for Vascone, if I can manage it. I'm sure neither of them will name any of the people they owe favours to or who pay and protect them, but there's no reason why they should be in a position to keep on doing it, don't you agree?"

"I take it you have a plan?"

"Yes. But it'd require General Forlini and you to make a brief visit to Brussels."

"I think when I explain to General Forlini what has been going on, he will be only too delighted to accompany me. When would you like us to come?"

"As soon as you can."

A DIFFERENT SORT OF
CHRISTMAS PARTY

I got a phone call a couple of hours later, telling me that General Forlini and Colonel Pedroni would arrive in Brussels mid-morning on Friday. It was time to bring Knud Henriksen and Gerry Fitzpatrick up to speed. Rosemary and I met them first thing on the Thursday morning, well before Ruggieri would arrive in the office.

"You said this was concerned with your work on the Italian wine fraud," Knud began. "You realise that we've done all we could."

"Yes," I replied. "But what we haven't told you, Gerry, is that Rosemary was attacked when she travelled back alone from the Interpol party last Wednesday. They were Italians and they were threatening to rape her when someone from another car fired shots at their car and they escaped. We reported this to the local police, but after they found the car that'd been shot at abandoned, we doubted whether they'd get very far...or that they'd try particularly hard, as Rosemary was unharmed apart from some scratches and bruises..."

"You're all right now?" Fitzpatrick asked Rosemary.

"I didn't feel too good on Wednesday evening, but trying to find out who did it and why has helped me get over it. You see, as they were attacking me the two men said I had it coming to me....And as they were Italians, I felt it must be some sort of revenge for what happened in Italy."

"But you didn't think of mentioning it to us, of course."

"It was a supposition," I replied, realising that Knud evidently hadn't informed Gerry for whatever reason. "There were some things about the attack which we wanted to check out. Like how did someone know Rosemary would be on her own that evening, but apparently didn't know where she lived? Why were the shots fired at the men's car and who by? And various names and odd coincidences started to appear as we began to dig around a bit."

"So you dug around some more – and probably did things we don't need to know about."

"Nothing illegal, I assure you."

"What did you uncover?"

"Excuse me for answering this way – but the thing we didn't uncover was who was ultimately responsible for the attack on Rosemary. We can speculate, but there's no way we'll ever know. It was possibly Ceresini, the firm we annoyed in Verona, or their associates or partners. But we do know who was involved and how it was arranged. The men who attacked Rosemary gave their names as Fabbri and Collina. The driver was called Bruni. They stayed in Schaerbeek while they were in Brussels....."

"Smith, Hill and Brown.....aliases, of course," remarked the multilingual Henriksen.

"Fortunately those organising it didn't use aliases," I replied. "Before any of this happened – actually on the Friday after we got back from Italy, I was followed by a bloke called Silvio Vascone from Italrep. Initially, we thought he'd organised it. But we began to concentrate on how anyone knew Rosemary was at the Interpol party last Wednesday evening and how the Italians were tipped off when she was leaving the party. We managed to get hold of the guest list. Vascone was on it and so was General Forlini, the man who sought an urgent meeting with Knud after our escapade in Verona, but then never followed it up. He seemed rather unlikely and we didn't know how Vascone knew who Rosemary was. But presumably someone could've pointed her out to him at the Interpol party."

"But nothing we'd found out explained how someone had come along after I'd been attacked and fired shots at the men's car and then driven away. Nick had one of his hunches, which he likes to call deductions – or even the application of Ockham's Razor – and after a few phone calls, he identified both who had fired the shots and who'd organised the whole thing.....Capitano Gaetano Ruggieri. We don't know who's paying him or who he owes favours to, but we have evidence that he was manipulating colleagues in the Guardia di Finanza from the summer, because of our examinations into the Italian wine frauds."

"Good evidence?" asked Fitzgerald.

"Two linked pieces. First, the telephone logs from here to certain Guardia di Finanza offices and also to Italrep at relevant times. Second, the word of General Forlini and Colonel Pedroni, the Guardia di Finanza commander of the Verona region. Pedroni was the one warned that we were trying to set up Ceresini and indicate that the local Guardia di Finanza were in their pockets by planting evidence in the Ceresini offices. Forlini was encouraged to complain to you and come to Brussels for several days, but then advised not to meet you, but various meetings and an invitation to the Interpol party were arranged to keep him occupied."

"Why on earth did he go to such lengths?"

"Window dressing. With him in town, Ruggieri had an excuse to get out and about a bit – mainly to liaise with Vascone. But also, if anyone subsequently started to look carefully at the sequence of events that led to Rosemary's attack, his presence muddied the waters," I explained.

"So he was the one who fired the shots that saved Rosemary?" asked Henriksen.

"No. He seems to have been in complete ignorance of what was going on all the time he was here. But Colonel Pedroni had begun to smell a rat. When Ruggieri phoned General Forlini on the Thursday when we were travelling back here through France to arrange a meeting with you to complain about what we'd been up to, naturally Forlini phoned Pedroni to find out what the hell had been going on, what was this about some stolen book of accounts. At that stage, Pedroni twigged that Rosemary and I were after Ceresini and weren't doing anything to blacken the reputation of the local Guardia di Finanza. And he also started to wonder why Ruggieri wanted Forlini to go to Brussels. Why would he do that? To get the accounting book back? That seemed unnecessary as we'd give it back, having photocopied it. So what other motive was there than some form of revenge? And was Ruggieri trying to inculpate General Forlini? So Pedroni also travelled here and shadowed Forlini. He was outside the Interpol offices when Ruggieri identified Rosemary leaving and it was him who fired the shots at the car when the men were attacking Rosemary."

"And he has said all this?"

"Not wholly. We didn't speak on the phone for all that long. But he and General Forlini are coming here on Friday to formally identify Ruggieri. Neither of them like being played like dummies by a junior officer, even if he does appear to be well-connected. And I thought they might come in handy if Commissioner Giulizzi seemed to be cutting up rough."

"By that, I assume you're expecting him to be removed from SEFF?" said Fitzgerald.

"It's entirely your decision, of course. But we doubted whether you'd want someone here who plainly is working for someone else, probably quite a lot of other people, and directly contrary to what he should be doing," replied Rosemary.

"And we thought you wouldn't want to hand over the problem to Knud's successor when he or she arrives," I added.

"I admit that quite a lot of the time I wish you two were going to join me back in Copenhagen," remarked Henriksen. "You'd certainly liven things up, but I reckon it might feel it a bit wearing....and the surprises might become a bit unwelcome....I realise that you have good reasons for operating the way you do, but you also need to remember that your superior officers need to be kept informed rather more regularly than you seem to believe."

"I'm sorry about that....." began Rosemary.

"But I'm afraid I was thinking mainly about finding out who'd arranged for men to rape and beat Rosemary. If it hadn't been for

Colonel Pedroni, I can't bear to think what might've happened," I added.

(I admit I always had less regard for my seniors' amour-propre than Rosemary did.)

"We also got on to Ruggieri quite late on," continued Rosemary. "If it had got around that we were looking into who'd attacked me before we identified him, he might've been able to cover his tracks more effectively."

"But I'm sure you can also see that inviting these two Italians over without consulting us looks as though you're putting a pistol to our heads," said Henriksen.

"I can certainly see how it could look. That wasn't our intention," I replied. "We wanted to make sure you had sufficient evidence on hand when you confronted Ruggieri. I confess we assumed that when we told you what we've just told you – about one member of your staff deliberately arranging to have another member of your staff beaten and raped – that you'd want to deal with them appropriately."

"OK. OK," said Fitzpatrick. "I don't think we need to lock horns about this. The only person who's actually been hurt in all this is Rosemary and I can entirely understand why Nick and she would want to bring those responsible to book....We'll meet them by all means and hear what they have to say and deal with Ruggieri subsequently.....And I'm sure Rosemary and Nick will want to advise us on how best to choreograph this."

"All we need, I believe, is that you should see the phone logs and then speak privately with General Forlini and Colonel Pedroni," said Rosemary. "What we need to avoid is Ruggieri knowing in advance what's going on. I wouldn't put it past his connections to try and prevent Forlini and Pedroni coming here. Once you've spoken with them, you can decide what to do."

"But I think we know what needs to be done. If it wasn't because we need to dot the "i"s and cross the "t"s, so Ruggierei has no way of escape, I'd tell the idle fellow to be gone now," said Fitzpatrick.

"In any event, we can expect him to try to use Giulizzi and Paolitti to keep him on....Always assuming that's what he wants," added Henriksen. "Knowing what they're like, I think you two should expect to join us when we get summoned......I can't say I don't relish the prospect of making life a bit difficult for those two as my parting gesture."

He had recovered his usual good humour. I could perfectly understand why he didn't like Rosemary and me organising things behind his back and then leaving him with virtually no room for manoeuvre. My former boss, Doug Nash, had complained about my "Lone Ranger" behaviour and I understood how it would irritate my superiors, even though I knew I was doing it for a good reason. And whereas I regarded Doug Nash as a hierarchical twerp, I respected Knud Henriksen a lot. So I was sorry to have annoyed him, even if I couldn't see quite how I could've avoided it.

I decided to meet General Forlini and Colonel Pedroni at the Zaventem airport on the Friday morning. And for the first time ever, I rode into Brussels in a taxi. Naturally, I thanked Pedroni again for saving Rosemary and also thanked both of them for coming to Brussels.

"I do not find pleasure in being messed around by a junior member of my own organisation," observed Forlini.

"Nor being lied to and played for a fool," added Pedroni. "Though I should add that it is fair to say that we are not too enamoured of the methods employed by yourself and your wife."

"I'm afraid that when we saw you apparently hand-in-glove with the people we knew to be committing large scale fraud at Ceresini SA, after you'd spoken to me when we were in Bellagio on holiday, we were reluctant to pass evidence to you that we feared might never see the light of day again. I'm sorry for that. It was one of Captain Ruggieri's bits of manipulation that worked too well."

"Unfortunately people like Ruggieri tarnish the reputation of the whole organisation."

We said little more as the taxi made its way to the main Commission building where Fitzpatrick and Henriksen were waiting. Forlini and Pedroni confirmed the phone calls they had received from Ruggieri. They felt that as they'd travelled all this way, they wished to be involved in unmasking Ruggieri. Though Rosemary and I would've liked to have been present, six would have been too much of a crowd.

I hoped that afterwards he might have put his head round my door to give me a parting shot or two, but apparently he gathered up a few personal possession as left the building immediately. Shortly afterwards, Rosemary had the chance to thank Colonel Pedroni in person, before he and General Forlini departed, for what looked like a couple of hours of Christmas shopping.

To no-one's great surprise, before the SEFF Christmas party got under way, Fitzpatrick and Henriksen were summoned to see Commissioner Giulizzi. As expected, we accompanied them. We arrived at the palatial accommodation. The door to Giulizzi's room opened and Paolitti emerged.

"Not those two," he said, pointing at Rosemary and me.

"It's all of us or none," replied Fitzgerald firmly.

Paolitti disappeared back inside, emerging a couple of minutes later to usher us all inside.

"Do you have some animosity towards my fellow countrymen?" demanded Giulizzi fiercely, regarding us all as a group.

"No," replied Fitzgerald. "But Gozzoli was indiscreet and allowed himself to be a pawn in the hands of a Soviet agent. Captain Ruggieri arranged an attack on a colleague in SEFF and, because he was in the pay of commercial interests, lied to colleagues in the Guardia di Finanza in an attempt to prevent a large fraud being uncovered. I treat people for what they are, not because of their nationality."

"And should I refuse to allow Capitano Ruggieri to be dismissed from his position in SEFF?"

"You'll have my formal letter of resignation immediately afterwards. I imagine the press would wish to know why. As I don't believe in lying to the press, I should feel compelled to explain the reasons why."

Paolitti was whispering in Giulizzi's ear.

"That is what I regard as blackmail," snarled Giulizzi.

"It is a statement of fact. I feel sure that my Commissioner would not wish to interfere in my management of SEFF, to demand that I retain someone who has behaved in this manner."

Paolitti continued whispering.

"I understand that the reason for Capitano Ruggieri's actions were connected with illegal activities by certain of his colleagues in SEFF – notably Mr and Mrs Storey there."

"Mr and Mrs Storey were examining illegal activities committed by an Italian company, Ceresini SA, based on information obtained lawfully from various sources, including an official audit by the EEC Court of Auditors."

"Moreover," I felt obliged to add, "as early as last August, Capitano Ruggieri lied to Colonel Pedroni, Commander of the Verona office of the Guardia di Finanza about our work. At that stage, neither of us had ever been to Verona or Bussolengo, for that matter. The reason why he did that was to attempt to prevent the fraudulent activities of Ceresini SA and their partners from being uncovered."

"But you cannot deny that Mrs Storey removed a document from the Ceresini SA offices illegally," cried out Paolitti.

"I removed a document which Ceresini SA had kept concealed, which provided evidence that they had been engaging in systematic fraud. At the time, I had no doubt that if I had attempted to seize it formally, it would've been taken from me. At that time, thanks in large part to Capitano Ruggieri's manipulations of people like Colonel Pedroni, I had reason to believe that if I handed the document over to him, it'd be the same as handing it back to the employees of Ceresini SA," replied

Rosemary, looking Paolitti straight in the eye. (As was his custom, he'd taken to examining her legs).

"And a correct response to what Rosemary did would be appropriate legal action – not arranging to have her beaten and raped," I added.

"I'm informed that was never intended. The action was merely intended to frighten her."

"That's a highly illuminating statement," remarked Henriksen acidly. "How do you know that?"

"When he spoke to me after you dismissed him, Capitano Ruggieri…."

"Capitano Ruggieri admitted his part in this matter then? Why was a member of SEFF involved in such a matter at all? How could you expect anyone in SEFF to work with a colleague who'd been involved in planning an attack on a colleague – even if it was 'only' intended to frighten her? It's the behaviour of a despicable creep and I suspect if you insisted on him remaining in SEFF, you'd find precious few of his colleagues prepared to remain with him…not just the Director."

Paolitti was whispering in Giulizzi's ear again. It was the critical moment. Would Giulizzi demand Ruggieri was reinstated? Or had Paolitti's ill-judged intervention sealed Ruggieri's fate?

"Very well," said Giulizzi, looking at all of us with yellow poison in his eyes. "Ruggieri goes. He will, however, be replaced by another Italian."

"No surprise there," retorted Henriksen, who, of course, had nothing to lose. "We all realise that you need a spy in the camp. But can you possibly make sure that the next one is actually prepared to do some work….for SEFF, not on his own account!"

Judging by his face, there were several things Giulizzi would've liked to have said in response, but a full-blooded clash between a plain-speaking Northerner and a devious Southerner was averted.

"I believe that's all we need to discuss," said Fitzpatrick, with more than a hint of a smirk hovering round his lips. "We have the SEFF Christmas party to attend. You are both welcome to join us of course."

He almost snorted with laughter as we left the room.

"You realise after that, that they could delay appointing my successor until you've moved on," said Henriksen, between guffaws, which must've been audible in Giulizzi's room.

"Unfortunately, there isn't time for Nick and Rosemary to get up to any more mischief with our Italian friends in the next three months," added Fitzpatrick.

"But I believe I need to have a private word with Paolitti about Vascone. I don't why he should come out of this as fresh as a daisy," I remarked.

"OK. We'll see you back at the office," replied Henriksen. "Make sure you nail both of those creeps down properly!"

I'd already agreed with Rosemary that Paolitti was unlikely to bend to my proposals if she was there – the male ego getting in the way.

I waited until Paolitti emerged – about ten minutes later. He did not look a happy bunny.

"Why are you still here?" he demanded. "I thought you'd had your moment of triumph!"

"You know perfectly well why I'm here. There's unfinished business from the attack on Rosemary. As you well know, five men were involved. We have descriptions of them and logs of several incriminating phone calls, including ones by Capitano Ruggieri. I cannot imagine that he didn't make sure that the blame was shared between him and his colleague."

"I don't know what you mean."

"In that case, I'll follow the correct procedures. Rosemary reported her attack to the local Brussels police. So they'll have a file on it. She and I will go along to the local police station and bring our evidence along with us. We have descriptions and passport numbers for Signori Bruni, Fabbri and Collina, including where they stayed and where they met Ruggieri and his colleague Silvio Vascone, from Italrep. We also have statements from

General Forlini of the Veneto region of the Guardia di Finanza and phone logs from the SEFF building. Of course, that might not be enough to get Ruggieri and Vascone convicted, but knowing what the police are like here, once they know these are EEC bureaucrats and Italians, we can reasonably assume that it'll be all over the local papers – and who knows where it might go from there. Indeed, weren't you the person who recruited Ruggieri? And Gozzoli, for that matter? Any investigative journalist worth his salt might well start asking inconvenient questions about you....and by extension, Commissioner Giulizzi, whose trusted assistant you are."

"This is blackmail....A favourite tactic of yours, I'm beginning to see!"

"If that was my game, what would there be to stop me bringing into the light of day certain telexes that indicate you are a tool of the Soviets? Because I'm not blackmailing you. I'm proposing to follow the rules. I have information about the attack on Rosemary which I could and probably should draw to the attention of the Brussels police. Simply, what I want is some sort of justice for the people who aided and abetted the attack on Rosemary. We both know we can't get at the people who planned it – though I wouldn't put it past you to know who they are. But we can mete out some justice to those involved here. Or do you think that making arrangements for Rosemary to be attacked is perfectly excusable?"

"Of course I don't. But there are wider considerations."

"I'm narrowing them. Either you carry out what I ask or I'll be going to the Brussels police directly from here, along with my dossier of evidence."

"I realise you believe I'm a despicable creep – that was what Henriksen called Ruggieri wasn't it? But I'm not devoid of a sense of honour. But you must understand that Italy isn't like England. Politics and government are complicated and much of what goes on is unseen. If we bend, it may well be because the alternative is being broken....."

"I believe I understand what you are getting at...But you should also realise that both Ruggieri and Vascone are now of no use to whoever really employs them. The moment I go to the local Brussels police, they will be known and their connections to these shadowy people you allude to will come into the daylight. Besides, I guess that the people who employ them expect them to operate competently. In this case, neither of them did. How was it that Rosemary and I were able to track down not just Vascone....who, incidentally, tried to follow me in the most amateurish manner imaginable..... and Ruggieri, but also Bruni, Fabbri and Collina? Ruggieri was too lazy not to use the SEFF switchboard for his phone calls, all of which were logged. Do these shadowy people really want to use men who are so incompetent?"

"There may be connections you and I know nothing about...."

"To be honest, I don't really care about that. I intend to get justice for the attack on Rosemary. You know what I'm proposing to do. But I'm willing to listen to a suitable alternative, if you can come up with something suitable."

"OK. OK. I can get Vascone sent back to Rome. But that's about all. Once he's back in Italy, if he's protected, he'll be protected. If you want him horsewhipped or prosecuted, you'd better go ahead with what you propose."

"I think you can do a little better than that. Though I'm sure you don't know any of these shadowy people yourself, I reckon you know those that do. Through them you can make sure that the incompetence that Vascone and Ruggieri showed in this gets back to those who employed them. I realise I won't be able to tell directly whether you have such a conversation. But I do have ways of finding out what happens to those two...and if their lives remain plain sailing – as Gozzoli's seems to have done – you might expect me to break the habits of a lifetime and leak certain telexes to the right people...And that definitely is blackmail!"

"You don't trust people very far, do you, Mr Storey!"

"I trust you not at all Signor Paolitti....And if Vascone isn't on his way by the new year, I'll follow my alternative course of action....And please don't suggest to someone that if they recover the evidence Vascone will be in the clear. There are several copies of the dossier, many in secure places and held by a number of different people. Because I don't trust you, I'm making sure I have watertight precautions."

"I will therefore do as you wish. You will have to hope that no-one ever gets anything to hold over you."

"Indeed. I doubt you are the first person to say something similar. Nor do I expect you to be the last."

I returned to the SEFF offices, where people were already engaged in getting the Christmas party organised.

"Did it go OK with Paolitti?" asked Rosemary, as I arrived, giving her rather more than a peck on the cheek.

"Yes. As well as could be expected. Vascone will follow Ruggieri out of Brussels and their employers will get to hear of their incompetence. But I couldn't see we could get any more...And whether their incompetence causes them any inconvenience, who knows? But I think I got Paolitti bothered enough to make sure the word goes in the right ears."

"Thinking of what Ruggieri got up to, I always find it interesting – even faintly alarming – how if you can get someone who is loathed against you, how people rally to your side."

"A tactic worth remembering, I suspect," I replied.

"But, of course....Once you identified Ruggieri, you knew he'd go sneaking to Paolitti...and so you also knew we could keep Gerry and Knud in the dark a bit longer....You can be quite a cunning rogue in your own way, Nick Storey."

"All in a good cause....The trouble with Knud is that he doesn't disguise his feelings very well. I felt if he knew too soon, he'd start giving Ruggieri the sort of look that'd tell him something was going on....and he might well have been able to erase some traces of what he'd been up to – or get some powerful friends to pre-empt what we were up to.....part of the unseen element of the Italian government, according to Paolitti."

"It'll certainly seem very strange here without Knud. Not the same place at all."

"All of the original group will've gone by the spring, apart from Gerry. Think how strange it'll feel for him!"

For once, we had a baby-sitter for Emily and Sarah, so we could stay at the Christmas party for a fair time. Gerry Fitzpatrick made an announcement that Capitano Ruggieri had been summoned back to Rome urgently and wouldn't be joining us. I doubt whether anyone believed that was the truth, the whole truth and nothing but the truth. But I doubt whether anyone – other than perhaps his fellow-countryman, Andrea di Pietro, missed his presence at all. Apart from that announcement, Fitzpatrick made a short speech thanking all of us for our efforts and notably Knud Henriksen who was about to depart for bigger and better things.

It felt rather like the end of an era, something cemented by the farewell lunch which Knud Henriksen gave for "the originals" the following week.

But then it was Christmas – our last in Brussels - and a New Year which would see us back in London and doing who knows what?

Richard Hernaman Allen   March 2014

Glossary

AP	Assistant Principal (fast stream training grade)
C&E	Customs & Excise
CAP	Common Agricultural Policy
CCC	Customs Co-operation Council
CFP	Common Fisheries Policy
Coreper	Meeting of heads of Member states' ambassadors to the EEC
DG	Commission Directorate General (followed by Roman numerals)
DOC	Denominazione d'Origine Controllata
EEC	European Economic Community
FAO	Food & Agriculture Organisation (UN agency)
FEOGA	Fonds Europeen d'Orientation et de Garantie Agricole
GUD	Gestion de l'Union Douaniere (Customs Union department of the Commission)
IB	Investigation Branch (C&E)
Italrep	Italian Representation to the EEC
MAFF	Ministry of Agriculture, Food & Fisheries
MO	Modus operandi
OCX	Officer of Customs & Excise (obsolete grade since 1972)
OECD	Organisation for Economic Cooperation & Development
OGD	other government department
On the QT	on the quiet
RDA	Revenue Duties Division A (C&E)
SEFF	Service Européenne contre la Fraude Fiscale

Stat	C&E Statistical Office
UKREP	UK Representation to the EEC
VM	VAT Machinery Directorate (C&E)

Printed in Great Britain
by Amazon

16951725R00167